Helsing
DEMON SLAYER

The Dragon's Paladins

LIANE ZANE

ZEPHON ROMANCE
Boston, Massachusetts

This is a work of fiction. Names, characters, places, and incidents are products of the author's imagination or are used fictitiously and are not to be construed as real. Any resemblance to actual events, locales, organizations, or persons, living or dead, is entirely coincidental.

HELSING: DEMON SLAYER. Copyright © 2025 LeAnn Neal Reilly. All rights reserved under International and Pan-American Copyright Conventions. No part of this text may be reproduced, transmitted, downloaded, decompiled, reverse-engineered, or stored into any information storage and retrieval system, in any form or by any means, whether electronic or mechanical, now known or hereafter invented, without the express written permission of the author. For information, email zephonbooks@gmail.com.

Digital Edition AUGUST 2025 ISBN: 978-1-963515-11-4

Paperback Edition AUGUST 2025 ISBN: 978-1-963515-12-1

Paperback and Digital Edition Cover design by LeAnn Neal Reilly

Contents

One

Dianne Markham halted as familiar raucous laughter bounced off the wide windows along the corridor around her. *Jasmyn and Tessa.* For a moment she froze, her grip on the plastic cup filled with frozen rosé wine slipping a little. What were they doing walking this way? The quickest path to their cabin was behind the bar area to the elevators next to the cafeteria. Did they know she'd lied about going to the bathroom?

Dianne took a steadying breath. No. They hadn't seen her circle around behind the bar and sneak among the rows of tables burgeoning with swimsuit-clad people eating deep-fried buffet food and drinking cocktails with lots of ice and cheap liquor. She was sure of it. Not that it was hard to slip past the periphery of the crowded pool deck. The cruise was almost over. Today was a sailing day, and the pool the most popular spot on the ship.

A shriek of merriment pierced her eardrum. Jasmyn's hot-pink reflection swam across the window in front of her. The woman's clothing was as loud as she was.

Dianne looked around frantically. What should she do? She'd never make it to the mid-ship elevators in time. Could she make it to the stairs?

Her gaze passed over the word *library* embossed on a plaque that she must have passed dozens of times over the past eight days.

Almost without thinking, she tugged the door next to the plaque open and slipped inside. None of the handful of people scattered around the quiet room, reading or playing board games, looked her way. Not even the massively muscular male sitting in the sunny corner wedged between the window and bookcase. The paperback he held looked tiny in his paws.

Paws.

Yikes. What the hell was wrong with her?

He was just a guy. A guy that she kept noticing, over and over, on this cruise from the underworld. A cruise with almost four thousand other passengers and crew members. And yet he kept inserting himself into her line of sight. He'd even brushed against her at check-in. Then again, he towered over almost everyone with a vague sense of menace and an intensity that would have drawn her gaze regardless.

Dianne shook herself. She didn't have to imagine that he had some demonic hold over her awareness. What she did or didn't think of this beast of a man was on her, not him. It wasn't his fault that she'd dashed into the library looking for sanctuary.

A muffled peal of laughter filtered through the glass door behind her, sending Dianne's heart racing and her feet scurrying to the farthest corner. Where The Beast squeezed in at the too-small table like a linebacker trying to attend tea with dolls.

Pulling out a chair, she dropped into it and bent over her tote bag to tug out the large silky wrap that she'd just bought at the souvenir table set up on the pool deck. None of her friends had seen it. It looked like something her mom would wear, with its large red-and-white hibiscus petals nestled against a royal-blue background.

Across from her, the clean scent of the sea mixed with something warmer seemed to cocoon the hulking male figure, who now stared at her.

Even though her heart raced at being so close to The Beast, she ignored it and his smell to wrap the fabric around her shoulders, the frosé still held in one hand.

A moment later, Jasmyn's voice sliced through the serene air. "I could have sworn I saw her come in here."

"Isn't that her in the corner?" asked Tessa, whose quieter voice nevertheless carried in the small room bordered by a floor-to-ceiling window.

Dianne's eyes widened before her gaze caught The Beast's. Holy damn, he was attractive. She didn't really take in individual features, simply fell into his hazel eyes under dark, straight brows. Her breath caught in her throat as inspiration hit her.

The Beast's eyes narrowed a second before Dianne placed her free hand over his holding the book and leaned forward to kiss him.

He stiffened.

"Just go with it," she murmured against his lips, although now her heart beat double time.

Was she scared of him—or of how he'd respond? No man had ever reacted like that when she made the first move. The Beast's scent embraced Dianne, making her thoughts swoon and sending them into dizzying disarray.

And then he kissed her back, one hand skillfully threading its way through her hair to palm the back of her head as he deepened the kiss.

"Are you kidding?" scoffed Jasmyn's voice across the room. "She swore off men, remember? Especially gym bros. Besides, she wouldn't be caught dead in that wrap."

Forgive me flashed Dianne silently to the other patrons. She sensed movement and heard a few annoyed murmurs.

Jasmyn, oblivious to the growing ill will at her disruption, continued. "C'mon. Let's go back to the cabin. I've been saving some really potent shit. Gummies. You'll love them. No Dianne means more for us."

The library grew quiet moments later. Dianne continued to kiss The Beast, his soft beard brushing against her cheek.

He disengaged from her, however. She felt the disconnection from him as a loss even as his gaze mesmerized her. Flecks of gold danced against a green background rimmed in dark brown.

Dianne expelled a soft breath. Damn. That was the best kiss she'd had in years. Maybe ever ....

His hand holding her head slipped to the table between them. He pulled back. "They're gone, you know. You don't need to kiss this 'gym bro' any longer."

"Thank you for playing along," she said. A pang passed through her at her words. She ruthlessly squashed it.

He shrugged. "You expected me to, didn't you? Wouldn't want to disappoint." Sarcasm sharpened the edge of his words. "Now, if you'll excuse me, I'd like to read in peace. Don't spill your drink as you leave. They frown on that in libraries."

Shocked and strangely hurt, Dianne nodded. "Of course." Gripping the handle of her tote, she stood before glancing at his book. She smiled, her sweetest, brightest smile. "But you might want to turn it around first. Then again, maybe you're used to reading your spy thrillers upside down."

With that, she spun on her heel and walked as gracefully as she could toward the door where she exited without a backward glance.

She felt The Beast's frowning gaze on her the entire time.

Ryan Helsing watched the breathtakingly beautiful blonde glide away from him. Damn! She caught him pretending to read. What would she make of it? And why, oh why, had he kissed her? She didn't need him to participate to sell her little act, no matter how his weasel-self wanted to justify it. He hadn't needed to devour her like a beast, though Lord knew that Dianne Markham qualified as the Beauty.

Ryan compartmentalized his interaction with Dianne Markham. He knew that he needed to get his head in the game. Olivia Kastrioti had entrusted him with this mission. And he had never failed before. He had no intention of doing so now, no matter how her sister affected him.

He looked down at the book he held. It was the first thing he'd grabbed after ducking into the library to keep from being spotted. He'd never imagined that Dianne would have the same idea.

Ryan ran a hand down his face and slid the book back on the shelf next to him. Clearly, he hadn't been out among ordinary people in too long if the laughter, swimsuit-clad women, and freely flowing liquor lured him. He'd willingly left that life behind when he accepted the Kastriotis' job offer as head of their security team. He hadn't regretted it until now on this mission. With this particular package.

Sighing, he shoved back from his seat and stood. He'd taken the seat in the farthest corner facing the door as his training had ingrained in him. As if there was a real threat from the grannies playing poker at the next table or the drunken middle-aged couples lounging by the pool. No wonder he wasn't taking this assignment seriously. Whatever had prompted Olivia to send him to shadow Dianne, it couldn't merit the time of a former Army Ranger who now battled *daemons* and possessed humans called *bogomili*. The kind of threat that never showed up on recon—until it already had its claws in someone.

Ryan left the library and headed for his cabin. As much as he needed to relocate Dianne Markham and keep eyes on her, he also needed to keep his distance from her for a few hours. She'd made him, even if she didn't know it yet. He had a slim hope that she'd chalk it up to the size of the ship, which after all, was smaller than her alma mater, the University of Massachusetts. But if Markham had inherited even half the instincts and smarts that her older sister Olivia had, he knew she'd suspect him of something.

That was a big if in his book.

Olivia had become a badass covert operative. Her little sister? She didn't look like someone who'd ever faced down real danger. But that kiss? That was another story.

As the elevator to his deck slid to a stop, Ryan called up details from the file on Markham that Miles Baxter, the operations chief for Kastrioti Security, had provided him. Twenty-nine. Never married. Social-media-marketing consultant. Entrepreneur. Inveterate party girl at night, girl boss by day. Large, boisterous group of college friends, with whom she often spent weekends, whether at clubs or dining out. String of boyfriends and casual hookups, though she'd recently gotten rid of her dating apps and scrubbed her social-media profile in a vain attempt to cleanse her image. Nothing really disappears on the Internet.

Ryan opened the door to his cabin, one of the interior ones with none of the amenities. In fact, it was little more than a metal-walled cave. He didn't mind. As a Ranger, he'd spent years using his pack as a pillow. And then there was SERE school. Survival, Evasion, Resistance, and Escape. He'd once spent three days barefoot in the woods with a combat knife, a length of twine, and a candy bar. So, no, he didn't mind a cheap cruise fare.

Likely the only times that someone like Markham had to use a pale imitation of SERE skills was when slipping the advances of an unwanted male or surviving a day-long marketing seminar with bad coffee and stale croissants.

Ryan might not mind the claustrophobic cabin dominated by a double bed, but he did mind the lack of options for camouflage onboard a cruise ship. He wasn't a spy for God's sake. He was a warrior. Urban warfare still involved military gear, weapons, and tactical clothing. Not flip flops and swim trunks. And if he wanted to contact operations control where cell service didn't exist, he'd use a sat phone.

He felt as restless as a wild horse trapped inside a catch pen, stripped of every instinct but the need to bolt.

Slipping off his sneakers, he doffed his clothes, folding each item neatly and stacking it in the small closet at the side of the cabin. Then he pulled on the swim trunks that Olivia had packed for him. She'd found a ridiculous blue-and-green swim camo pattern. When she'd handed them to him—in front of Beta Nagy, no less—she'd commented dryly that she wanted him to feel at home in a pool.

Olivia Kastrioti. She was like a den mother, quartermaster, and master sergeant all rolled into one. When he'd signed on to work for Kastrioti Security Services, he'd assumed that her husband, Mihàil, would give him his marching orders even though Olivia had recruited him. He'd assumed wrong.

Oh, Ryan had no doubt that the imposing Albanian general called the strategic shots when it came to their interminable battle against Dark *Irim*—Fallen Watchers who'd traded purpose for power and made Earth their playground. But the demi-angel worshipped the ground that his beautiful wife walked upon. And he was too intelligent not to see how exceptionally capable she was tactically. Or how she never forgot their central mission: to protect innocents.

It was almost as if the CIA had trained her to be a *zoti*'s lady—a title of respect in Albania for a leader's wife. A lord who was also a *drangùe*—half man, half dragon. Mihàil had once told him the old Albanian myths got the shape right, if not the source. Storm warriors, they were called. Born to fight monsters like the kulshedra. The truth? They weren't born to save anyone. The *Elioud* were fallout from a war Heaven never finished. But St. Michael hadn't abandoned them. Redemption came with a mission—to protect the world from what their forefathers had unleashed.

A mission Olivia's younger sister knew nothing about.

After Ryan had donned the absurd camo swim trunks, a T-shirt, and flip flops, he grabbed the lanyard with his cabin keycard and slung it around his neck. Then he pressed the tiny waterproof earwig into his ear. Its specialized long-range harmonic technology would permit him to communicate with Olivia back at the Kastrioti estate in Fushë-Arrëz, Albania. Unfortunately, it wouldn't work inside the ship's hull. He had to go out on deck.

And somehow manage to speak without anyone catching sight of him talking to himself. As always on this job, a cocktail in a plastic cup and a slightly unsteady gait would have to suffice as cover. Not exactly what the Rangers had trained *him* for.

As he shut the cabin door, laughter echoed down the passageway. He stiffened. Being caught belowdecks with little room to maneuver gave him the creeping willies. He hadn't joined the Navy for precisely this reason. Jumping out of an airplane was much preferable to living inside a tin can.

Turning, he saw a young couple in their late twenties strolling toward him holding hands.

A memory of walking hand-in-hand with Arly on a beach in the Bahamas took him by surprise, squeezing his chest like an invisible harmonic vise. It had been more than a year since his fiancée had dumped him and the pain still caught him unaware at times.

Damn, dude, get ahold of yourself he lectured silently as he nodded at the couple.

Ryan returned to the pool deck, alert to the cruise goers and crew members who crowded the passageways and public spaces. He saw nothing to raise any red flags. Which made perfect sense. Olivia had shared no intel on any human terrorist activity related to this sailing, just said she wanted eyes on Markham, who wouldn't understand or appreciate having a former Army Ranger bodyguard. If Olivia had specific worries, likely they related to the shadowy world of the *Elioud*, a race of demi-angels tasked with defending humanity against Dark angelic forces.

As he made his way across the pool deck, Ryan scanned the rows of chairs and tables. No one paid him any attention.

Scratch that. There were several women in one of the hot tubs who seemed to watch him as he made his way to the stairs to the upper deck. Despite the wet hair and swimsuits, he recognized the rest of Markham's friends: Caroline Hartley, Mercedes Lopez, Alexis Hammond, Ivone DeSousa, and Germaine Grimes. He'd memorized the names and all the salient details from the mission brief. Along with Tessa George and Jasmyn White, Dianne Markham's friends could be best summed up in a few words: entitled brats.

Not individually, no. Some were downright admirable. Mercedes Lopez, for example, was a critical care nurse at Mass General Hospital in Boston. And Germaine Grimes worked in research on infectious-disease panels at a small startup in the suburbs. In fact, most of the women had something to do with healthcare. It was the one thing beyond drinking too much and dating like sailors on shore leave that they shared. Even Markham did social-media marketing for local hospital systems and doctors' offices.

Ryan ignored the titters from the five women in the hot tub as he mounted the deck stairs. He could feel their lascivious gazes on his ass. Obviously, they didn't see a lot of men who followed the Ranger physical-fitness regimen. Then again, they'd have to go to the gym more often to increase their odds of doing so.

At the top of the stairs, he headed straight toward the front of the ship. It was crowded even on this upper deck as people soaked up the sun on this sailing day. Tomorrow it would be deserted as the passengers hit the penultimate port of call, Split, Croatia.

Dammit. He'd forgotten his cover cocktail in the onslaught of focused female gazes.

He looked down at his cellphone, which displayed a tracking program. He'd dropped a nanotracker on Markham on the first night of the cruise. Miró Kos, the Kastriotis' head of development, had assured him that it was virtually impossible for Olivia's younger sister to find it, let alone remove it. It was also impervious to scans, temperature fluctuations, and water exposure. The tracker was so tiny that he'd had to use a specialized delivery device in the form of a dissolvable sticker to attach it to her purse—a sneaky act he hadn't learned in the Rangers. After that, the nanobots in the tracker, keyed to Markham's personal harmonics, activated and migrated to her skin. A little creepy, true, but effective.

The tracker showed that the package was in her cabin.

Ryan checked his phone. He'd missed check-in by almost half an hour. Olivia wouldn't say anything, but he'd worked for the Kastriotis long enough and gone through enough action to be able to hear what wasn't said.

He tapped his earlobe where his own nanocomm array clung to his skin. "Aerie Actual, this is Demon Slayer."

His call sign had seemed appropriate last year when he'd witnessed his first actual *daemons* and possessed humans, but right now with the smell of the Adriatic fresh in his nostrils, it just seemed overwrought. Ryan shifted both forearms onto the railing and pretended to gaze into the distance. Maybe he'd look like he had a momentous decision weighing on him.

"Demon Slayer, this is Harlequin. You're thirty minutes' late checking in." Olivia's calm voice betrayed nothing. "According to the cruise itinerary, you're sailing today. You haven't gotten distracted from your mission, have you?"

"No, ma'am," said Ryan, irritation hardening his tone. So much for thinking that his commander wouldn't call him on being late.

"Then I'll have your sitrep."

"Package appears to be trying to evade her friends, Harlequin. She nearly made me this morning in the ship's library when she ducked inside." He left out the gut-punching kiss from the daily summary.

"Why?" Now a sharp note broke his commander's normally smooth tone.

Ryan's irritation made him blunter than was wise. "Probably because they've been trying to get her laid ever since she went cold turkey from dating apps and going to clubs."

"That's your take?" she asked. "Based on what? That Dianne's traveling with her girlfriends instead of a boyfriend? That you got into her phone and didn't find the Flrty app with dozens of swipe-rights on it?"

"Based on the fact that she doesn't drink as much as they do. Or wear skimpy clothes. Or send come-hither glances at all the men around her." Ryan shifted his weight as he looked east. He could see the Albanian coastline as a slate blue along the horizon. "At least three of the other women have hooked up on this trip. And the rest cheer them on. Except your sister."

"But you think she used to be like them."

"Hard to imagine spending so much time with friends you're nothing like," said Ryan. "Plus, she didn't scrub *their* social media accounts. Her friends Jasmyn and Tessa have also said a few things when she's not around." He didn't add that they'd complained that Olivia's sister thought she was better than them now.

"Maybe they're the sort who like drama. They're stirring up trouble. I know the type."

"Except none of the other women disagrees or sticks up for your sister. Not even the two with steady boyfriends."

Olivia sighed. Even though she was hundreds of kilometers away in the Albanian mountains, it sounded like she stood at his shoulder.

"Dianne always did have poor taste in friends. Okay, listen, just keep a safe distance for now. If she really does suspect you shadowing her, it's going to make your mission harder."

His mission? Somehow, he was supposed to get close enough to Dianne Markham to convince her to go with him to Fushë-Arrëz when she disembarked. And if that kiss was anything to go by, she wouldn't forget him or go anywhere with him, not if she really wanted nothing to do with men.

He didn't share his doubts. "Copy that, Harlequin," he said instead, filing the emotional IED under *not my problem*.

Two

Dianne spent the rest of the afternoon in the cafeteria on the top deck where her friends never wandered. Even so, she sat in a corner away from the main walkway to the outside, watching. It wasn't ideal. Although her back was to the wall, she couldn't really escape if Tessa or Jasmyn spotted her. But given Jasmyn's promise of some 'potent shit' in the form of cannabis gummies, Dianne was fairly confident that those two had disappeared to their cabin before heading midship to the pub for wings, fries, and cocktails.

No, it was Germaine, her own cabinmate, that would find her. The woman was a research scientist in infectious diseases. That's what she did, after all—find elusive hidden things, like pathogens in degraded blood samples.

Dianne sighed. What was she going to do about her friends? It wouldn't be so tricky avoiding Jasmyn and Tessa, who'd long been the dedicated party girls of the group and lived in Boston where they worked rather generic jobs at large employers and spent many nights at clubs.

But she and Germaine, who worked near many of Dianne's clients, often grabbed lunch on less-busy workdays and sometimes had dinner and a girls' night hanging out in one of their apartments. They actually did more than drink alcohol and engage in shallow talk about guys, fashion, social trends, and the immediate gratification of their desires.

If Germaine found her, she'd want to have a real conversation about what bothered Dianne, which she fully knew.

Dianne didn't want to play the game anymore. The game where she still had time to find the right man and settle down. Start a family. Germaine understood Dianne's growing restlessness with their group's lifestyle but didn't agree. She said they were both young and needed to focus on their careers—a sentiment Dianne had stopped echoing, though she hadn't yet dared to contradict it aloud.

But Dianne's older sister Olivia had left a career to get married and start a family.

Which meant that she must have fallen hard. And Dianne's brother-in-law must be out of this world in more dimensions than just the physical.

Dianne had met Mihàil Kastrioti only a handful of times in the past four years. That's what happens when people pursue international-business careers, like her sister Olivia. They tend not to return home very often. Even before Olivia got married after a whirlwind courtship in a small ceremony on

Mihàil's Albanian estate with only their parents and aunt and uncle able to attend on such short notice, she'd rarely been home. Not since the summer she'd survived a terrorist attack on Ibiza. She'd dropped out of Brown and moved to Bethesda before eventually going to Vienna for a master's degree where she'd met her husband.

Mihàil Kastrioti was exceptionally handsome, tall and muscular, with piercing blue eyes that seemed to read Dianne's soul from across the distance of time and space. The way he looked at her—like he could see through her carefully constructed defenses—left her heart racing and her skin prickling, a mix of fascination and the urge to flee.

Where in the world was she going to meet a man like that, one able to knock her out of her current trajectory and rock her whole world?

An image of The Beast rose in front of her mind's eye, his presence in that sunlit library as vivid as a scene caught in amber. Their impromptu kiss surged to the surface of her memory, heat blooming through her chest as if it had just happened.

Even hours later, it still had the power to make her feel as if she'd had an entire bottle of wine at dinner.

"Hiding?" Germaine's voice dissolved the pleasant fantasy. "The ship's not that big, Di. Here." She sat down across from Dianne, sliding a frozen concoction across the table toward her. "I know you're not trying to see how many drinks you can consume with the included open bar, but these frosés really are more like slushies than cocktails. Trust me, I'm a scientist. I know you can't suffer impaired judgment from one."

Dianne hid her sigh and accepted the drink as it was meant: a peace offering. "Thanks." She took a sip. The icy, sweet liquid tasted like spring break. "Did you know that Jasmyn brought marijuana gummies on the cruise?"

Germaine tilted her head. "No, but I'm not surprised. She's become quite addicted to them. She's high most of the time these days. Or haven't you noticed? It's part of why she's so obnoxious and has no filter."

Dianne felt a little sheepish. Only a little. "No. She just seemed to be, well, *more* of herself these days. She's never had a filter."

Germaine nodded. "Her job has turned into a real drag. One of her friends at work has been accused of sexual harassment. She knows he's innocent because she knows the female employee involved as well as the details of the claim, but what with 'MeToo,' her company wants to be seen as taking a tough stance. Jasmyn's been put in charge of handling the case for HR. She's been trying to keep both employees from suing. If that's not enough to tie her into knots, her friend also blames her for his forced leave of absence during the internal investigation."

"I didn't know that."

"Well, you've missed a few girls' nights in Boston. Plus, I noticed her efforts to self-medicate and took her for a big breakfast of chocolate-chip pancakes at The Toast."

Dianne rolled the melting frosé between her palms, changing the subject. She set the cup down so she'd be less likely to finish it quickly. "Did I tell you that Olivia had a baby? A daughter named Luljeta Emily."

"Named after your cousin Emily?" asked her friend, a thread of understanding running through her voice. After Dianne's answering nod, she asked, "Is 'Lewl-yeta' an Albanian name?"

Dianne nodded. She twisted the silver ring on her middle finger. She'd had the key to her cousin Emily's diary embedded into it. "Apparently my mysterious brother-in-law was married when he was younger and his first wife died. That was her name. When they sent out the birth announcements, they said it means 'Flower of Life.'"

"Still, it's a little weird, don't you think, that Olivia agreed to name her baby after her husband's first wife?"

Dianne shrugged. "I seriously doubt that Olivia stands in the shadow of a dead woman. She's always been clear about who she is and what she wants. She's big enough to honor someone that her husband loved before she was even in the picture." As she said this, Dianne knew it was true.

Germaine sipped her own drink as she studied Dianne before dropping what their friend group had dubbed a 'truth bomb.' "It's the baby, isn't it? That's why you're fixated on finding someone." She tilted her head. "Wait. When was she born? It must've been around Christmas. I thought it was just a New Year's resolution that hadn't yet lost steam, but now I think you're trying to be like Olivia. But you're not Olivia, not by a long shot. You're much more fun, and you don't take yourself too seriously."

That stung a little, despite what her best friend highlighted as her good qualities. Germaine had an unerring sense of others' sore spots.

Dianne shifted in her seat to cover her discomfort before saying, "Well, maybe I can be. I've spent my life thinking

'WWOD. What would Olivia do?' And then doing the opposite. Maybe it's time to take a different approach."

Now Germaine let another truth bomb fly.

"Our friend group won't survive losing you. You're the one we all watch, you know. If you're pulling away ... the rest of us won't pretend it doesn't change things. Jasmyn and Tessa already have enough trouble keeping their eyes on the career prize, but I know that you inspire them to keep trying. The rest of us ... well, let's just say it won't be long before Caroline and Mercedes settle down."

Both of their friends had steady dates who seemed serious about them. It was one of the things that Dianne admired about the other women. She'd never been able to find any guy compelling after half-a-dozen dates. Lately, it took only two.

She shook her head as she dipped a fingertip into her drink. "It's not only my new niece. I'm just not having fun anymore, Germaine. Work's good, but ... I don't know. Something's missing. It's getting harder and harder to motivate myself."

Germaine smiled. "You just need to expand the dating pool. Your sample size is too small. You've missed a lot of opportunities. Take that guy over there, for instance." She nodded to a nearby table where a single man sat. A napkin lay crumpled on the used plate in front of him.

He caught Dianne's gaze and smiled. He had dirty-blond hair that was a little shaggy and unkempt in a deliberate manner. Likely he used any number of products for that look.

An image of The Beast assaulted her. His neat brown hair and beard did *not* look like he used products beyond all-in-one shampoo-and-body cleanser. Or, more likely, a bar of something basic like Dial or Irish Spring.

Mmm. She could imagine dipping her nose to the back of his neck and inhaling the fresh, green scent as her fingers raked his scalp.

Dianne shoved the image into the back of her mind. She picked up her adult slushie and drank half of it. "Maybe you're right," she said to Germaine, forcing a smile. "But I don't need a wing woman on this mission."

Germaine shrugged. "Suit yourself. I've got my own prospect waiting by the pool. He hasn't caught a glimpse of me in this new swimsuit yet." She stood. "But don't take too long, Di. There's only two more days on this cruise. You'll be back in the burbs soon enough where the prospects are a lot less appetizing. As your resident research scientist, I can tell you an orgasm or three does wonders for your motivation."

Dianne nodded. Germaine shot a grin over her shoulder as she passed by Dianne's 'prospect.'

Dianne sighed as she watched her friend walk away. It didn't escape her attention that the guy with the surfer locks watched Germaine as well, his gaze glued to her friend's shapely backside visible through the clinging coverup she wore. Then he turned in his seat. Seeing Dianne looking at him, he pushed from the table and stood before coming over to her. His Hawaiian-style shirt slipped open as he strolled to reveal his chest. At least he was fit.

"Want some company?" he asked. "I'm about to go to the bar. I can get you another of whatever it is that you're drinking or something else. The sky's the limit. It's on me." He lifted his guest card and grinned, aware that they both had unlimited bar packages.

"I'm sure you draw the line at top-shelf liquor," she said, feigning friendliness. She lifted her half-melted strawberry-infused wine and jiggled the cup. "I don't think the bar here has this one. You choose. Just make it fruity and cold."

"I've got just the thing for you," he said and headed to the bar at end of the deck.

While she waited for her new friend to return with their drinks, Dianne's thoughts drifted again to the mysterious Beast. Did he have his own Beauty? Or was he like her, traveling as a single on a Mediterranean cruise? She hadn't seen him with anyone, male, female or group of any size. He appeared to be alone. Every time she'd glimpsed him in the crowded public spaces of the ship, he'd either been on his phone or watching others from the closest bar as they participated in various activities, a ubiquitous—and untouched—drink at hand.

The Beast hadn't looked relaxed and happy. No, not at all. If anything, he'd given off the vibes of someone who didn't want anyone to approach him. She recognized the tactics because she'd been using them herself.

What was he doing right now? Maybe she could draw him out ... the idea gripped her with a force that caught her off guard.

Stop it, Dianne, she lectured herself. *You're just being willful. You want to pick your own prospects, not have your friends do it for you. A challenge is just a bonus. You're not really interested in him.*

The faux-surfer dude appeared carrying two plastic cups with a drink layered in red, white, and blue like a bomb pop, the frozen confection she'd enjoyed from the ice-cream truck during her childhood.

"What's that?" she asked, interested despite herself.

He grinned as he handed it to her. "A Miami Vice. Well, the cruise version. It's strawberry daiquiri on the bottom, piña colada in the middle, and blue curaçao on top."

"Sounds yummy." Dianne sipped the grownup popsicle, getting a mouthful of sugary strawberry and rum.

"Swirl your straw to mix the flavors," the stranger advised, "like this." He demonstrated, muddling the colors.

Dianne bristled inside. She preferred having the flavors mix and meld as she drank rather than forcefully compelling them together. And like that, she realized that she really couldn't do this, couldn't continue down the path towards a meaningless sexual encounter with someone she likely had nothing in common with and wouldn't see after the cruise.

She held the drink in front of her like a shield, one hand on the cup and one hand on the straw, and studied the man across from her. The more she saw of him, the less attractive he seemed. It appeared she no longer needed even two dates before identifying a nonstarter.

"What's your name?" she asked, certain that she'd get only his first name. Or a fake name.

"Taylor. Nice to meet you." He held out his hand.

Dianne ignored the proffered hand. Instead, she set the nearly untouched cocktail on the table, pushed her chair back, and stood. "Thanks for the drink, Taylor, but I've changed my mind. I don't want company right now."

He dropped his hand, his face darkening. "Suit yourself." He pulled her drink towards him, lowering his gaze in dismissal.

That was fine by Dianne. She pivoted and headed toward the elevators, feeling 'Taylor's' hostile gaze on her back the entire distance.

Instead of returning to her cabin, Dianne spent the next two hours fruitlessly combing the ship for the intriguing stranger she'd come to refer to as The Beast. For someone who'd seemed to always be in the periphery of her vision for the past eight days, the inability to find him now that she wanted to unnerved—and annoyed—her.

"Someone's out of sorts," said Germaine in the cabin later as they got ready for dinner. "Taylor a clumsy lover?"

Dianne whirled and looked at her friend, who stood in her bra and panties while searching through their overflowing closet. She was speechless for a moment. Germaine had planted the 'prospect.'

Her best friend pulled a stretch-knit sleeveless dress out and took it off the hanger. "I swear the best lovers are the guys who look like they work with their hands for a living. You know, plumbers. Carpenters. Electricians. Not guys who use product in their hair." She laughed as she tugged the dress over her head.

Dianne, who'd already pulled on a pair of white stretch jeans and a sleeveless, V-neck blouse with a smattering of sequins, decided that she had to get out of the cabin. She didn't even think that she could go to dinner with her friends.

"I wouldn't know," she said, grabbing her purse and her key card. "I'm not going to dinner with everyone. I need to get a drink instead."

Germaine looked at her. "That bad?" she asked, apparently unaware that she'd caused Dianne's ill humor.

Dianne opened the cabin door before saying over her shoulder, "Tell the others I'll see them at the theater at 8." She didn't wait for Germaine's nod.

She took the elevator to the main deck, not sure where she wanted to be. Home. Alone. Thank God tomorrow was their last port. They'd be back in Ravenna on Monday, and then she'd start the long flight home.

She started walking toward the main lobby bar, wending her way through the retail space where the ship's photographers displayed the numerous photos they cajoled passengers to let them take. That's when she saw him.

The Beast stood inside the fine-art gallery, absorbed in studying an oil painting of the Mediterranean coast, its Cypress trees reminiscent of Provence and Tuscany.

Her breath caught. The memory of his palm pressed against the back of her head as he took charge of their kiss swept away all thought.

Before she could reconsider or even question why she wanted to talk to the silent, intimidating man, Dianne headed toward him, stopping at his side. Sweet Lord, but he really was as massive and intense as she remembered. She hadn't just built The Beast up in her memory.

He looked at her. In his eyes, she saw recognition.

He remembered her. Thank God. That kiss had rocked her world—surely she'd made some kind of impression.

But had it hit him the same way?

Dianne bit her lip, uncertain how to proceed.

"Hiding from your friends again?" he asked, the sympathy in his voice nearly undoing her.

"Yes," she said before blurting a little breathlessly, "will you go to dinner with me?"

He blinked several times, obviously surprised at the invitation.

"Or not," she said, starting to turn away. To run away, if she were honest.

The Beast caught her arm. His large fingers and palm were warm and the skin a little rough. He must work with his hands then. "Aren't you going to wait for my answer?" Amusement colored his deep, slightly raspy voice.

Dianne felt herself blushing like a teenager. She opened her mouth and nothing came out. Then she swallowed, cleared her throat, and swallowed again. The Beast waited patiently, watching her. She couldn't tell if he judged her and found her wanting.

"Yes, of course," she said, her voice almost a whisper.

He tilted his head. He raised his other hand and brushed a thumb over her cheek. "You don't need any makeup," he said. "Blushing suits you." He dropped his hand. "Do you like steak? I have a reservation at the Brazilian restaurant for seven."

"I love Brazilian food," she said. "It's pretty common where I'm from."

He smiled, the first genuine smile that Dianne had seen on the man's face. She couldn't believe what it did to her insides. "Excellent." He raised his wrist to consult a heavy-duty analog watch with bronze fittings and a graphite-colored cloth band. "That leaves us with an hour to kill. How about a drink in the Mainsail Lounge?"

"That sounds good," said Dianne, aware that accepting meant that she'd miss attending the Cabaret show with her friends. "I'm Dianne, by the way."

"Ryan," he said, holding out his hand.

She set her own hand in his, marveling at how his fingers engulfed hers. Despite their size, they were elegant and long. Something about the way he held her hand made her feel protected. She found herself disappointed when he dropped it and gestured for her to lead the way.

They took the elevator to the Mainsail, which was on the highest deck near the prow with amazing views. It was normally quiet at this time of day with only a handful of passengers having cocktails before dinner, but it would pick up later with an event. A couples gameshow, Dianne thought.

Ryan guided her to an empty sofa near one wall of windows. He didn't sit next to her, however, choosing to take a seat in an upholstered chair on her left. There was something about the way his gaze took in the rest of the lounge that made her look around, too. But she saw no reason for his obvious vigilance.

While they waited for their cocktails, Dianne finally asked what she'd wanted to know ever since their kiss. "Are you traveling alone? You're not hiding from friends somewhere are you? You keep looking around like you expect your girlfriend to catch you cheating." She laughed a little nervously.

Ryan's piercing gaze settled on her. He shook his head. "I'm not here with my girlfriend. I'm working actually."

Working? What did that mean?

Dianne frowned and waited while the server set their drinks on the low coffee table in front of them before saying, "How can you be working on a cruise? I've seen you on all the same excursions and at the same shows. You don't seem to be having much fun, but you also don't appear to be doing anything different from me."

Ryan's eyes narrowed a fraction as he leaned closer. His heat and scent enveloped her, drugging her senses.

Until his next words threw cold water on her.

"That's because you're my job." He paused, gaze sweeping over her like a battlefield assessment. "Your sister sent me to protect you."

Three

Ryan watched as shock displaced confusion on Dianne Markham's irritatingly beautiful face, followed rapidly by disbelief and then anger. He wondered if she'd get up and leave as she'd done earlier with the guy her friend Germaine had recruited.

Remembering the insolent bastard's sulky expression after Dianne walked away made Ryan's fingers tighten on the glass of his drink. When the bottom-feeder tried to tail Dianne, Ryan made sure he rethought that move. That was when he knew that he had to engage Dianne more directly. She'd just made the approach unnecessary.

Dianne didn't get up to leave now. That was good. Ryan didn't feel like going after her.

"What do you mean Olivia sent you to protect me? Protect me from what?" Before Ryan could respond, however, she continued. "Why you? How do you know Olivia? I thought she ran an Albanian company that makes and exports herbal spa products." She glared at him as if he'd told her that Olivia was really a black-market gunrunner, and he one of her lowlife enforcers.

Ryan waited for Dianne's barrage of questions to stop. "Are you done?" he asked when nothing else came out of her, not hiding his impatience. "I'm not here to explain your sister's business, and I sure as hell can't explain what she wants to protect you from. As for why Olivia sent me?" Ryan shrugged. "I don't know. I'm the Kastriotis' chief of security. It would have been more appropriate to send someone under my command, but I don't think Olivia trusted anyone else with your safety. You can ask her when we get to Fushë-Arrëz."

Dianne's jaw dropped as Ryan spoke. "What?" she asked. Her voice rose to a squeak. Her cheeks pinkened, but this time Ryan knew that the beautiful young blonde's heightened color conveyed anger, not budding passion.

He shoved his disappointment down deep. Only the mission mattered.

"Olivia sent me to escort you at the end of the cruise to the Kastrioti estate."

Dianne's eyes widened. Then she blinked, her blue-gray gaze snapping. She sat up, her spine infused with steel he didn't know she had. For the first time, Ryan got a hint of her older sister, the formidable former CIA operative, in the woman across from him.

When she spoke, her voice had hardened. "I'm not going anywhere with you, even if my sister were the Queen of England handing out tiaras."

Ryan sighed. So much for being honest and direct. All the women in his life now—well, except perhaps Stasia Kos, whose sparkling eyes seemed to find Ryan infinitely amusing—appreciated that approach. He'd forgotten how much finesse civilian women, especially Americans, required in conversation. He hadn't worked on that verbal skill since Arly.

"Look, I know I'm not handling this well, but my lady has a sixth sense for bad things on the horizon. If she thinks you're in some kind of danger, you are." He paused, frustration mounting at the incredulous look on Dianne's face. "You can call her tomorrow when we're in port."

"'My lady'?" asked Dianne. "What does that mean? It sounds positively medieval."

Ryan felt his own cheeks grow warm. He'd slipped and referred to Olivia by her honorific.

Damn, but this was getting harder by the second. If he continued to screw up, he'd have to kidnap Olivia's little sister in order to get her back to the Kastrioti estate.

Ignoring Dianne's comment, he leaned forward. "Olivia warned me about approaching you. She said you do everything the opposite of her."

Dianne, who'd started to interrupt, sat back, blinking. What was that about?

Just then Dianne's friends, including her cabinmate Germaine, appeared in the Mainsail Lounge from the far entrance and began scanning the patrons scattered around the space. Ryan sat back, preparing for an incoming invasion.

A moment later, Jasmyn shrieked, "Girlfriend! There you are! We've been looking all over the ship for you!"

The other four women turned to look where Jasmyn pointed, and then they all headed toward Ryan and Dianne like a buzzing swarm of bees.

Jasmyn plopped down next to Dianne on the long sofa while Tessa sat on the other side of Jasmyn. Mercedes and Caroline hung back, both wearing unhappy expressions. Germaine stood on the other side of Dianne with a small smirk playing about her mouth.

"Damn, girl! We thought you were sulking alone in a bar," said Tessa, who then shot a sidelong glance at Ryan. "Instead, you're sipping some extra hot tea."

Jasmyn leaned around Dianne to get a better look at him. "Hey! I recognize you from the library. You're the gym bro who kissed our girl like she was the last woman on earth."

Mercedes and Caroline hovered just behind the others, their expressions tight—less disapproving of Dianne, Ryan thought, than of the whole public display.

Germaine's smirk curled at one corner, but her gaze lingered on Ryan a half second too long. Measuring. Cold. Then she looked at Dianne. "Well. Looks like Di's not quite as off-the-market as she claimed."

Finesse? Had he used that descriptor only moments ago for dealing with civilian women from the U.S.? What he should have remembered was that a group of them required U.N.-level diplomacy.

Ryan kept still, letting them swarm, curious to see how Dianne would hold the line.

She laid a hand on his thigh, the warmth of her touch burning through the thin fabric of his pants and stealing his breath. Then she leaned in and said, "Not gonna lie. I *am* a bit salty right now. But I'm not in preschool. I don't need anyone to help me drink my tea."

"No offense, Queen," said Tessa, raising her hands in mock surrender, gummy-pink nails catching the coppery light of the setting sun as her eyes flicked toward Jasmyn.

"Keep it sweet," added Jasmyn with a laugh, bumping Dianne with her shoulder.

Germaine folded her arms. "Let's go. Di's clearly in capable hands." She gave Dianne a wink—but when her gaze flicked back to Ryan, something behind it curdled. Not malice exactly, but ... something. He couldn't name it, but his instincts filed it away.

The group migrated to the bar where Alexis and Ivone waited, cocktails in hand and chatting with a couple of men they'd met earlier in the cruise. Tessa and Jasmyn chattered and laughed. Mercedes glanced back once, lips pursed, and Caroline followed with a sigh.

Ryan checked his watch. "We've got forty minutes before dinner. That is, if you want to maintain your cover."

Dianne's fingers slipped from his thigh. He tried not to miss them. Discipline kept him still, but every nerve was awake now, keyed to the memory of her touch through the thin fabric of his chinos.

She sat straighter, then gave a small sigh. "I'm sorry I snapped earlier. I'm just ... in a weird place. None of this is normal. But for now"—she glanced toward the bar where her friends lingered—"you're the devil I don't know."

Ryan took a sip of his beer, watching her. Flippant words, maybe. But she had no idea how close they were to the truth.

"No offense taken," he said.

By the time they reached the Brazilian restaurant, the sharpness of her earlier nerves—the strange thrill of asking The Beast to dinner—had worn off. Dianne had expected something like a date. This wasn't that. And now that she was certain of it, she could almost enjoy herself.

Ryan didn't turn out to be much of a conversationalist, so Dianne drank more wine than she should have and plunged into asking him questions about Olivia, Mihàil, and Luljeta, who was now six months old.

"Have you never visited your sister in Albania?" asked Ryan after Dianne had peppered him with numerous questions about the mountains and the culture.

She shook her head. "No."

He'd finished his meal already, having methodically devoured the meats—*picanha*, *linguiça*, and *cordeiro*—barely pausing to inhale the warm, crusty *pão de queijo* and piles of vegetables.

He tilted his head and studied her but thankfully didn't press her about not traveling to Albania, either in the last five years that Olivia had made it her home or with him at the end of the cruise.

Instead, he nodded at her nearly untouched *brigadeiros*. "Aren't those truffles good? I thought chocolate was irresistible to women."

Dianne shrugged. "The ones I get back home are better. Plus, I'm not very hungry."

"How long does this date have to last to keep your friends at bay?" Dianne thought she saw a mischievous glint in his eyes as he spoke.

"How much time do you have?" she asked, toying with the stem of her wineglass.

"That long?" Now Ryan really did smile, that incredible smile that turned the corners of his eyes up and transformed his rugged features. "How about a walk on the deck? Clear your head from the bottle of wine you drank?"

Ah. So he'd noticed.

Dianne nodded. They headed outside the steakhouse to the nearby sliding glass doors to the deck where the deep-blue Adriatic beckoned on the horizon.

Instead of walking along the perimeter of the deck, however, Ryan guided Dianne to the railing with a hand on her lower back. Lord, was she tipsy! That large, warm palm against the thin fabric of her blouse felt divine.

After a few moments in companionable silence looking at the moon glinting on the waves, she shivered in the cool breeze off the water.

"Cold?" asked Ryan as he leaned both elbows on the rail.

"Mm, maybe a little." She shifted towards his heat, a sudden intense desire for him to pull her into his side and wrap his big arm around her waist taking her off guard.

He didn't.

Instead, he turned against the rail and lifted his chin toward the pool. "They're starting a dance party in a few minutes. It'll be warmer among everyone else, especially if you dance."

"Sure," said Dianne, hoping that her disappointment didn't sound obvious.

"After you then," he said, gesturing. He didn't replace his hand on her back.

As they walked, Dianne's awareness of the large male next to her bordered on the extreme. She didn't have to look at him to sense how much space he took up. Or feel the heat he generated. Or smell his musky, woody cologne. On some primal level, she recognized an apex predator. Dangerous, perhaps deadly even, but still she felt safe.

Maybe it was her hypersensitivity that alerted her to a subtle shift in Ryan's demeanor as they came out onto the pool deck where dozens of people—men, women, and children—already gathered around a crewmember handing out glow sticks.

"Is anything wrong?" she asked.

He looked down at her. She saw his expression change as he did, his narrowed eyes widening and the tightness around his mouth easing. She didn't think it was because he liked what he saw in her face. Rather, her gut told her that he didn't want to alarm her.

"Sorry, I get a little antsy around groups of strangers. Hazard of the job."

"You run into a lot of trouble working for an Albanian businessman? What is he? A mobster?" Dianne laughed at her question. As if Olivia would ever have anything to do with a criminal, let alone marry him and have his baby.

Ryan's hand came back to Dianne's waist, stopping her laughter. "You'd be surprised what kind of trouble the Kastriotis attract" was all he said as he encouraged her to the side of the deck.

He stopped in front of a pillar, turning his back and leaning against it. This time, he pulled her into his side as she'd wanted him to do earlier, but it only served to emphasize the tension in his body. His gaze continuously scanned the growing crowd and the crew setting up as a band in the center of the deck between the two pools.

Either something was definitely wrong or he was a delusional paranoid.

Dianne needed to distract herself from her growing uneasiness. "How'd you come to work for my sister and her husband?"

Ryan spoke without looking at her. "I met your sister in the hospital in Prague last summer. She offered me a job after I stepped in to defend her friend Beta from a Russian thug. Got shot for my efforts."

"Shot?" Dianne's voice squeaked, her eyes widening.

Ryan looked down at her. "Don't worry," he said, smiling a little now. "It's not the first time. It comes with the territory when you've seen combat."

"You're ex-military?" Dianne couldn't keep a slight hint of scorn from her voice. She'd never met anyone who'd taken a career in the military seriously. It seemed like a less-than-optimal career choice.

"Yes, ma'am. Army Ranger. Don't worry," he said again as Dianne pulled away from him. "It won't rub off on you." He sounded amused, but Dianne also thought she heard a bit of sarcasm, too. "We're not actually on a date. My mission is to get you safely to Albania, and for that my military training comes in very handy."

There it was again. Of course, he hadn't moved on after she'd told him that she wasn't going anywhere with him. Boy, did it rankle that she was simply a *mission* for him. She took a decided couple of steps from the imposing male, who watched her with hooded eyes as she did.

Or maybe what bothers you, girlfriend, said a tiny inner voice, *is that this gorgeous male specimen clearly doesn't think much of you or your friends.*

Ryan hadn't said so in so many words, but Dianne had sensed it when the others showed up in the lounge earlier. His posture. His demeanor. His brooding silence. He thought that they were frivolous, silly women. It didn't matter that she'd started to view them—and herself most of all—that way too.

Crossing her arms, Dianne turned from The Beast and watched the antics of a group of preteen boys and girls chasing each other with glowing neon wands, their necks ringed with matching electric magenta, luminescent sky blue, and acid yellow. For a brief instant, she wished she could go back in time and have nothing more to hold her attention than whether she could touch her friends with a glowing, flexible plastic stick before they could tag her.

"Would you like some?" Ryan's question interrupted Dianne's wallowing reverie.

"What?"

He nodded at the children. "Those chemlights?"

"Oh, I don't care." Dianne shrugged and turned back as the trio of crew members in the band began a sound check while the group's singers stood in front of mic stands watching the drummer and bassist.

Across from where she and Olivia's guard dog stood, Dianne saw Germaine, Tessa, and Jasmyn enter the pool deck. On Germaine's right, a black-haired man in a loose, white island shirt and blue island-style pants seemed fixated on her cabinmate's every word. Tessa and Jasmyn, not far behind, giggled and stumbled among a small group of people that Dianne had seen them with at various events throughout the week. She suspected that they all were imbibing in more than alcohol, though they were certainly doing plenty of drinking.

"Here."

Dianne had forgotten Ryan as she'd observed the others. She looked down as she felt a tap on her right hand. He'd slipped past her and claimed a few glow sticks from a nearby crew member.

Dianne glanced at the cluster of plastic rods, some thinner than others. "Thanks."

She started to take them from him, but Ryan snapped several of the thinner ones at one time in a massive fist before handing them to her.

"Cool trick."

"I try." Even though he said this lightly, Ryan's gaze wasn't on Dianne. He was surveying the deck again.

Dianne's uneasiness returned. She looked around as she linked several luminous bands around her wrists. She saw nothing unusual. The band had started playing 80s music, and people now danced, joy suffusing their faces as they waved their glow sticks and sang along to familiar lyrics. Everyone wearing white and light-colored clothing practically glowed under the dance party's numerous black lights.

"What's wrong?" she asked Ryan. "Your constant vigilance is starting to freak me out." She laughed a little, trying to downplay her jitters.

His response only added fuel to them. "Good. It'll make you pay attention."

Dianne sucked in a startled breath. His jaw had hardened under its short beard, and even in the dim ambient lighting, his gaze had a sharp edge. Then she realized that despite being dressed casually, his black chinos and graphite-gray button-down shirt meant that he didn't glow. He'd essentially turned into an indistinct silhouette while her white jeans and the sequins in her blouse made her a target.

He'd prepared for the party. To watch her? Or to guard her? Or something else?

Crew members wove through the gathering twilight dancers, their trays carrying shot glasses of phosphorescent-green liqueur and clear cellophane packages of gummy candies. Dianne's gaze caught the candy's shape. It reminded her of Jasmyn's contraband 'treats.'

Over the next half an hour, more cruise guests swelled the ranks of the party until the entire pool deck writhed with swaying, jumping, and undulating bodies of all sizes and ages. Although there was a final night tomorrow before the cruise ended, only the young and diehard partiers would stay up drinking while everyone else packed for disembarking. Tonight was the night for everyone to let loose.

Dianne wanted to enjoy herself, so she pretended that Ryan's proximity signaled interest in her rather than a job requirement. It was a pleasant fantasy, aided by a few shots of the melon liqueur she grabbed when Ryan's gaze traveled elsewhere. Although he didn't dance, she danced next to him, shrieking and singing as her tipsiness increased and the crowd grew more rowdy from the free-flowing alcohol. Every now and then Ryan stepped in to glare at anyone who got too close to Dianne, and once he even grabbed a guy and shoved another who'd stepped in to sandwich her between them in a common club-dance bump-and-grind.

She had no idea how long she'd been dancing when the music transitioned into a ballad. As people trailed off to refresh their drinks and plop, red faced, into chairs at the tables lining the sides of the deck, Dianne turned to Ryan and grabbed his hand.

"Dance with me," she said, an overwhelming desire to push the fantasy as far as it could go rising, heady and reckless, in her inebriated brain.

His face went blank, and he let her drag him farther onto the middle of the deck among a knot of devoted dancers.

Dianne turned as Ryan came to a stop behind her, pressing herself against his chest and going onto her toes to wrap her arms around his neck. For a moment she didn't think that he was going to react, and then his warm, woody musk enveloped her as his arms came around her waist.

Sweet Lord, but he felt *so* good.

Sighing, Dianne closed her eyes and nuzzled the base of his neck. In response, he pulled her against him until she could feel every delineation of his pectoral muscles and the ridges of his abdomen through two layers of clothing. They fit together perfectly. She wriggled herself against his heat, her breasts tightening in reaction to the stimulation as her core tingled. She wanted this man, and she didn't care what happened afterwards.

Almost as soon as she had that thought, the band segued into *Highway to Hell*, the hard-rock anthem's guitar chords and growling vocals calling the assembled partygoers to dance to the final song of the party. Everyone still on deck—which seemed to be everyone on the cruise not already in bed—surged back into the open area between the two pools.

And then all hell broke loose.

Dianne's eyes snapped open, but the world had already tilted into chaos. She blinked. All around her, fluorescent whites glowed ghostly under the black lights, their skin tinted with unnatural pulses of violet and green, as if their bodies no longer belonged entirely to them. Shadows pooled under cheekbones and jaws. Open mouths seemed too dark—grotesque, yawning things—as if something inside the dancers wanted out.

A chill twisted up her spine. Not from the breeze.

Then Jasmyn and Tessa crashed into her, pulling her from Ryan with clawed hands and manic laughter. The crowd surged behind them, jostling her off balance. Their eyes were wild. Grins stretched too wide. Fingernails bit into her arms as they dragged her away.

Staggering, barely able to keep her balance, Dianne caught the band's lead singer tearing into the chorus as the crowd exploded—popping and jumping like kernels in a scorching skillet, waving glowing batons, their voices rising in manic unison.

Somewhere in her mind, something tried to swim free of the haze. This wasn't right. None of this was right.

She looked back—just in time to see Ryan standing perfectly still, a dark monolith against the writhing sea of dancers.

His eyes locked on hers.

And then the crowd swallowed her.

Four

Dianne tripped on someone's foot and went down, hard, on her right knee. The sharp pain cleared some of her fuzzy thoughts, but now she struggled to stand. People jostled around her, and several of them stepped on her bent leg or pushed against her back.

"Jaz! Tess!" she said, raising her voice almost to a shout as she looked for her friends, who seemed to have disappeared.

As she came to her feet, someone's elbow connected with her cheek. That pain wiped her head clear, brought water to her eyes, and nausea to her throat. Retching, Dianne threw out an arm to keep her balance, hit a meaty body part, and heard a grunt. She couldn't see because her eyelids refused to stay open after the inadvertent punch. Terror rolled through her as she felt herself pinned in, nearly blind, and being pummeled by endless elbows while bodies rolled her farther away from Ryan like rollers in a car wash.

Almost as soon as she thought of him, The Beast appeared next to her. Her eye above her injured cheekbone had started to swell, but the uninjured eye widened enough to see his massive form blocking the demented dancers behind him while he grappled with the others surrounding her. He pulled Dianne into his side, holding her easily with one arm as he pushed people out of his way. He looked like the god of thunder and felt like heaven.

She'd never been so glad to see someone in her life.

Unfortunately, there was no way off the pool deck from this side. They would have to either fight their way through the mass of people in front of the band or head along the side where fewer people watched the end of the party, mostly sitting at the tables. The Beast turned to head that way, but her injured knee crumpled, and she staggered, kept upright only by his firm grip. And people began streaming from the pool deck as the song ended, clogging their path forward.

Without warning, The Beast lifted Dianne, one handed, up and over his shoulder, his forearm pinning her thighs against his rock-hard abdomen. Giving a little shriek, Dianne clutched at his neck to keep from sliding sideways.

"I've got you," he growled. *He growled.* The words rumbled through his chest and the soft bristles of his beard rubbed against her forearm.

The people on the side of the deck, who'd remained more subdued than those dancing, moved out of their way like the Red Sea parting. Dianne saw the slack look on some of their faces, but on several she thought she saw something sly, malicious even. A tremor rolled through her at this vision.

Behind them, shrieks filled the air. Dianne looked up to see other men carrying other women, some struggling. Worse, she thought she saw some of the preteen children also being roughly handled, while in the dim light and confusion, she imagined that there were knots of people on the deck boards in sexual positions. Most seemed enthusiastic, but to Dianne's horror, she saw a teenaged boy grabbed from behind and held by a middle-aged man while another man shoved his own shorts down. She looked away.

What was happening here?

Germaine appeared out of nowhere to block her view as they entered the hallway into the ship's interior. She looked disheveled. Her light-brown hair frothed around her face, wild and tangled. Her clothing sported rips and tears. Only one foot still wore a sandal, whose strap was broken. She clutched at The Beast's arm holding Dianne, hardly slowing his stride.

"Dianne! Thank God you're okay!"

"Keep moving," said The Beast without looking at Germaine, who tripped along at his side. "We've got to get clear of this deck before they seal the exits."

"What do you mean?" asked Germaine as they rounded the corner toward the elevators.

"Put me down. I can walk," said Dianne at the same time.

Ryan ignored both of them. To Dianne's surprise, he passed the elevators and headed toward the stairs in the middle of the deck. She saw a small group of passengers waiting in front of the elevators watching them with their mouths hanging open. Then Ryan plunged downward, the relentless rhythm of his jogging causing Dianne's stomach to clench as her blurry monocular vision sought to make sense of their surroundings.

Germaine paused at the top of the stairs, looking over her shoulder toward the hall that they'd just left. Violence and noise rumbled their way. She shook the broken sandal from her foot and then plunged after Dianne and Ryan, practically running to keep up.

They went down three decks. At the landing to Deck Eight, Dianne gasped out in time with his steps, "I'm going to throw up if you don't let me walk."

Instead of putting her on her feet, The Beast switched his hold so that he cradled her in his arms. Then he turned toward the stairs again.

"Where are you taking me?" asked Dianne, realizing that it wasn't her cabin on Deck Eight.

"To my cabin," he said. "On Deck Four."

"Di, you don't know this guy. Don't let him take you anywhere." Germaine sounded breathless. She halted on the landing in front of the elevators. She looked up the stairs where tumultuous, discordant voices rushed towards them. "We should wait this out in our cabin."

The Beast looked at Dianne, his eyes serious and direct. "It's not going to get better. You need to trust me. This is why Olivia sent me."

Dianne went with her gut. Looking at her friend, she said, "Come with us."

Germaine shook her head, panic clear on her face and in her voice. "I can't."

Behind Germaine, the elevator dinged, and the doors started to slide open. Hands began pulling at the edges, trying to force them wider. The deranged babble on the stairs sounded like it was only one deck above them.

Ryan didn't wait for more discussion. "Hold tight," he said, his jaw set.

Dianne's hands came around his neck of their own volition just before he headed down the stairs. The last view she had of Germaine was her friend's back as she sprinted barefoot toward the hallway leading to their cabin.

Ryan made it to Deck Six before a handful of teenagers appeared on the stairs behind them. Dianne's heart nearly stopped when she saw them. It was like something out of a horror movie. A zombie movie. Only these kids weren't dead, nor did they have bloody mouths, slack jaws, and unfocused gazes. No, they'd been transformed in some way that Dianne couldn't process. They looked like nightmare creatures from a medieval painter's fevered dream. Eerie glowing energy leapt and sparked around them in a visible cloud.

They locked their malevolent gazes on Ryan and her.

A moment later, the tallest male teen landed in a crouch next to Ryan just as he reached the landing. A wave of energy rolled over Dianne, blacking her out for an instant. When awareness returned, she saw the teen crumpled on the stairs above them in the midst of the other adolescents, who writhed and struggled to get free of him.

Ryan threw Dianne over his shoulder again before she could protest, holding her with one arm. The world around her moved again. One stride. Two strides. And then he grabbed the banister and jumped to Deck Five just as the elevator doors opened, regurgitating adults who surrounded them in a hissing, screeching, seething mass.

Rough hands pulled Dianne from Ryan. Painful electric jolts stung her all over her body. She came violently alert, but her vision had come unmoored from her brain. Nothing that she saw fit together in any meaningful way. Vivid flashes of vermillion, lime, and dirty eggplant pierced her good eye like glass shards. Worse were the sounds. Like hundreds of snakes, insects, and wounded animals.

She felt herself being carried and struggled to get free. But the stench of rotten eggs smothered her. Coughing and flailing, she struck bone and flesh, a scream clawing at her throat but her lungs too clogged to give it breath.

Ryan appeared, distinct and clear in the sensory morass. Dianne's gaze locked on him. A visible blue-white aura surrounded him, and his gaze flashed with lightning under thunderous brows. He looked like an avenging angel.

Ryan grabbed one of the creatures clutching Dianne. She heard bone snap, followed by a sickening howl and its weight lifted from her. A thud coincided with Ryan engaging the second creature still gripping her.

After an interminable period of grunting and snarling, the creature's grasp slackened. As it exhaled, the scrabbling of thousands of claws crawled up Dianne's spine and then faded away. Her vision cleared at the same time, leaving her cold-stone sober and shaking.

Ryan pulled the man from Dianne. She didn't know if he was alive or dead, which terrified her. Other bodies lay slumped along the corridor where the creatures had sought to escape with her. Some of them lay in unnatural positions.

Dianne snatched her gaze away and sat up, pushing herself against the wall between two cabin doors.

Ryan leaned over, his hands on his thighs, panting. Dianne focused on his face, which had dozens of razor-thin cuts that bled into the sweat streaming from his brow. His clothing, soaked in blood and sweat, hung in tatters.

He turned his head towards her. Their gazes met and held for a moment.

"Are you hurt?" he asked as he knelt and began running his palms over Dianne's body. Something about his efficient, but gentle, strokes almost undid her.

But she couldn't allow herself to cry now, not when this stranger had just put himself into harm's way for her sake.

"I don't think so." Her voice croaked from her. "At least, not as badly as you." She raised a finger to touch his cheek as he bent over her, probing her bruised knee with sure, careful fingers.

"I'm fine," he said gruffly. He sat up, dropping his hands from her. "Do you think you can walk? We need to get to my cabin before more of them find us."

Dianne bent her right leg. The knee protested, but she didn't think anything was broken or torn. "Can you help me stand?" she asked.

He nodded and reached for her hand, pulling her to her feet without effort. Dianne wobbled and braced herself against the wall until she got her balance. As long as she didn't have to outrun a horde of crazy people, she thought she could make it down one deck to Ryan's cabin.

"Ready?" he asked. At her nod, he said, "Take this corridor to the center of the ship. I'll guard our rear. Stop at the end and stay out of sight until I confirm the stairs are clear."

Dianne nodded again and began picking her way around the men on the floor, using the corridor wall to keep her balance. She did her best to ignore the ordinariness of their features, the Hawaiian shirts, the polos, the shorts, sandals, and flipflops. The blank stares on several of them. The blood and broken bones.

Up ahead, a cabin door opened, and a woman peered around the frame at them. Her eyes widened. Dianne ignored her. As they passed, the woman's gaze traveled to the corridor behind them. She screamed and slammed her door shut.

Dianne fixed her view on the end of the long, claustrophobic passage and refused to think about anything other than reaching it. She felt Ryan's reassuring bulk behind her. Her knee throbbed as she walked, and her right eye had swollen completely shut. The whole side of her face ached.

After an interminable effort—which likely only took a few minutes—she reached the opening to the next set of elevators and stairs near the center of the cruise ship. The whole time they'd encountered no other passengers or crew in the strangely silent vessel. Just as she stopped and before Ryan could move around her to verify that it was safe to head down the stairs to Deck Four, the ship's PA carillon sounded, which was unheard of at this time of night.

"Attention, this is James, your assistant cruise director. We're experiencing a technical issue with our onboard electrical system that requires us to have everyone return to their cabins until further notice. Safety lighting will now switch on, and all elevators will be offline."

The overhead lights dimmed, and lights along the base of the walls glowed to life.

James continued. "Crew members are stationed on every deck and will assist anyone having difficulty reaching their cabins. Please refrain from calling the service desk with questions for the next two hours. I'll provide you with updates while our technicians assess the issue. Please be assured that our backup generators have engaged and that this is simply a precaution. The ship remains on course to dock in Split, Croatia, at seven a.m., and all passengers will be able to disembark at eight."

Ryan, who'd moved to Dianne's side while the assistant cruise director spoke, glanced behind them and then down at Dianne. "Wait here." He spoke in a low voice and didn't stay for her response.

She peered around the edge of the opening while Ryan ran through the empty space in front of the elevators to the stairs, where he jumped to the landing leading to the deck below. He waited a moment, his head tilted as he assessed what he could see of the next deck. Then he waved her forward.

Dianne pushed off the wall, only to be yanked by her hair. A hissing female voice burrowed into her ear and crawled down her spine. "Ah, ah, my pretty. Going somewhere? Come back and party with me."

Then the woman, whoever she was, began to drag Dianne backwards as if she weighed nothing, even when her knee caused her to stumble and nearly fall. In fact, they seemed to fly down the passageway that Dianne had only moments before struggled to travel. The stranger pulled Dianne through an open cabin door not far from where the bodies of the drugged partygoers had fallen.

Not a single body remained.

The cabin door slammed shut on its own. Almost instantly her captor swung Dianne back and forth between the closed wood door of the closet and the metal hull like a dog shaking a prey held in its jaws. She hit her head against the closet door and then her left shoulder.

A moment later a massive *boom* rocked the cabin door as if under assault by a battering ram.

The stranger began to laugh, an unnatural, high-pitched sound that broke unevenly and ended in a gurgle. "Someone wants to take you back, little girl. Wonder if he's willing to play tug-of-war?"

The door opened abruptly, and Ryan fell into the cabin and into Dianne, who crumpled to the floor with the force of his impact. She managed to get her left hand out to break her fall, but her face still kissed the industrial-weave carpet.

It took her a moment to realize that Ryan stood above her, straddling her shoulders as he faced the stranger.

"Not today, *daemon*," he said. The authority in his voice sent shivers down Dianne's back.

She started to push herself up to see to whom Ryan spoke, but her left wrist screamed at her, and she collapsed on the floor again. When she whimpered involuntarily, Ryan shifted. An instant later, Dianne slid across the floor and smashed into the foot of the bed, hitting the top of her head. She sagged into the floor, struggling to remain conscious. She turned her face where it rested on the scratchy fibers and lifted her gaze.

In front of her stood the woman who'd watched them walking through the passageway earlier. Instead of a fearful expression, she now wore a sly smile. She took a step.

"Stop! I command you in the name of *Elohim*, the Creator of Heaven and Earth," said Ryan as he advanced again to stand over Dianne.

"Please," said the woman, her oddly modulated voice wheedling. She eased another foot in front of her. "I meant no harm, paladin." The last word grated like a fork caught in a running garbage disposal.

The temperature in the cabin dropped. Dianne quaked. When she breathed out, she saw a frosty cloud.

"Stay back." The Beast had returned in a growl. He lifted Dianne in his arms. She shrank against him, trying to burrow into his warmth and away from their sinister antagonist.

"Or what?" asked the woman. "You won't harm a woman, will you?" She opened her mouth and exhaled. A miasma of decay enveloped Dianne, who began gagging.

The low light in the cabin extinguished.

Bodiless voices laughed around them in an icy whirlwind, tearing at Dianne's hair and pulling her scalp. She shrieked, but the foul breeze swallowed the sound and grew in strength.

Ryan clutched Dianne to him, straightened his shoulders, and lifted his chin. Then he began chanting, his rich, husky baritone vibrating his chest and instantly allaying Dianne's terror. "*Crux sacra sit mihi lux. Non draco sit mihi dux. Vade retro Satana.*"

As he sang, light emanated from a pendant on his chest that Dianne hadn't noticed before.

The *daemon* hissed and sprang ten feet into the farthest corner of the cabin, its black hair wild and limbs splayed. Ryan continued singing in unfamiliar, yet somehow soothing, Latin. The blue light expanded, glowing softly until it created an ethereal cocoon around Dianne and him. Shadows played on the possessed woman's face as if a legion of dark spirits tormented her.

The cabin shook violently as if the ship was being tossed in a hurricane. A thousand tormented voices rose in mind-numbing babble.

But Ryan's gaze held Dianne's. It promised safety. It promised victory.

Without warning, the window in the cabin exploded outward, and the mineral scent of the sea rushed in. The unholy cataclysm quieted.

After Ryan's chant ended, the only sound to be heard in the strangely quiet room was the woman's sobbing. The celestial glow remained around them, if dimmer.

In the otherworldly light, Ryan's gaze had turned inscrutable. "Let's go. We won't have any more trouble before we dock in Split."

He slipped his hand into hers and turned to leave. Dianne looked back toward the woman, who sat in the far corner of the cabin with her arms around her knees, rocking back and forth and muttering between sobs.

"What about her?" she asked.

Ryan glanced at the woman. His gaze, already inscrutable, shuttered. "There's nothing I can do for her. If I had a harmonics modulator keyed for humans ...." He squared his shoulders. "But I don't."

He tugged Dianne toward the door, leading her back along the corridor toward the stairs. In the dim emergency lighting, the faint glow surrounding them threw odd shadows on the walls and closed doors. Many doors had been thrown open, the contents inside the cabins tossed around. But they appeared empty. Shivering, Dianne leaned closer to Ryan, whose stride matched her hobbling one.

They made it to the stairs without being accosted. They'd gone halfway down to Deck Four when a crew member wearing a sidearm appeared on the deck below. He stopped when he saw them, his hand coming to rest on the weapon at his waist. Even in the gloom, she saw that his gaze took them in.

"Where is your cabin?" he asked. "I will escort you."

Ryan lifted his chin toward the far side of the deck landing. "4458."

The security officer waited for them to exit the stairs before walking alongside Dianne. Tension rolled from him. When they reached the cabin, Ryan turned back to him.

Touching something that glinted on the security officer's chest, he held the man's gaze. "Do you believe?"

The fear in the man's eyes shifted to confidence. His shoulders pulled back. "I do."

To Dianne's amazement a new radiance revealed a crucifix on his chest, expanding to meld with the faint glow that still emanated from Ryan's own pendant.

"Good." Ryan nodded. "Because it will keep you safe."

The man nodded back. He waited until Ryan had swiped his keycard before pivoting and walking away. A pale aura limned his figure as he disappeared in the murky light.

Ryan drew Dianne inside his cabin where emergency lighting illuminated the gloomy space.

She waited until he'd shut the door behind them before asking, "What in the hell is going on? What happened to those people? And why did you call that woman a demon?"

Ryan ignored her. By the sounds and his shadowy movements, he seemed to be searching for something. A moment later, artificial light sprang from an object in his hands as he turned to Dianne.

"That's because a *daemon* possessed her," he said, his voice grim. "The *daemon* sent for you."

Five

Dianne swayed on her feet after he said that, and Ryan cursed himself silently for not taking care of her injuries and physical needs first. There was time enough to bring her up to speed on the reality of the immaterial world of angelic beings and the hidden war being fought between the Heavenly Host under the Archangel Michael and the Fallen Watcher Angels, or Dark *Irim*, and their vast legions of evil minions, human *and* spirits.

Like the *daemons* who'd possessed the dance party on the pool deck of their cruise.

"We can discuss this later," he said, setting the emergency lantern he'd activated down on the small desk. "It's time to take a better look at you."

"I'm fine," she said, but the sharpness she intended ended in a slight groan that ruined it.

Turning to her, Ryan said, "I'll be the judge of that" as he placed both hands on her upper arms and eased her toward the bed.

She didn't resist and let him guide her to a sitting position. The gorgeous blonde who'd knocked his socks off earlier at dinner and nearly distracted him from his one job—namely protecting her—looked worse for the wear. Her right eye had swollen shut. The silky blond hair that his fingers had itched to run through had become a tangled mess with an obvious bald spot low and on the right side. Angry scratches crisscrossed her cheeks and the skin of her bare arms, even the skin of her upper chest, showcased by the formerly dramatic V-neck of her blouse.

"First, some water," he said, stuffing his fury at her injuries into the mental compartment that he'd built for such distractions. If he hadn't, he might have been dead in combat a long time ago.

He opened the small refrigerator wedged next to the closet. He'd stockpiled several bottles of water even though he'd brough a large refillable metal bottle in his luggage. In his experience, he could manage a survival scenario without a lot of things, but drinking water wasn't one of them.

"Here," he said, handing her the bottle. Thankfully, she accepted it. "You'll need to flush out whatever toxin they spiked the shots and gummies with, so keep sipping that."

"It felt like ecstasy, only worse," she said. When Ryan looked at her, she shrugged, winced, and went on, "I tried it in college at a club." She didn't elaborate, but Ryan sensed regret in the curt statement.

Kneeling, he searched in his backpack, which he'd slid under the desk. He had several chocolate bars there. He swiveled on his knees and handed Dianne one of them. "We all make mistakes. Mine just involved a fast car and alcohol. Make sure you eat some of that chocolate." He nodded toward the candy bar she held. "Dementors are real, and sugar helps when your adrenaline crashes."

He paused a moment as she took that in. "But this wasn't just a party drug gone bad. The *daemons* manipulated the reactions of those who'd taken it. Anything nasty, cruel, selfish, ravenous—all of humanity's basest inclinations—the *daemons* fed on and amplified. Then they possessed anyone who opened the door of their will to them."

"It seemed like damn near everyone except you," said Dianne before sipping water. She looked at the chocolate in her hand. "WiseHerb. I don't recognize this brand. It must be European." She raised it to her nose and inhaled. "Rosemary? That's an interesting choice."

Ryan returned to his pack to search again. "Take it up with your sister." He turned with his med kit in hand. "That's her company. It mostly makes herbal products, but she recently negotiated a deal with Ghanian and Sierra Leone cocoa farmers to import cocoa beans as long as they don't use child labor. I brought some of the first product lines."

"Sounds like Olivia. Out to save the world." Ryan heard a note of bitterness leavened with wistfulness in her voice.

He opened the kit on the bed next to Dianne and pulled out a penlight. Snapping it on, he turned to her. "Look at me. I'm going to check your pupil, see if you got a concussion from being tossed around like a bag of potatoes."

She sat patiently while he used his thumb to raise her eyelid and told her to look in different directions. The uninjured eye reacted normally, but it didn't rule out a concussion. He'd know more when the swelling on the other eye subsided.

"What was that you sang back there?" she asked as he turned the light off and dropped it into the med kit. "It sure didn't sound like something you learned in the Army."

He grabbed the cotton swabs and hydrogen peroxide to clean the cuts on her face, upper chest, and arms.

"Saint Benedict's Prayer for Exorcism," he said as he doused a cotton swab.

"Seriously?" she asked.

He heard the skepticism in her voice. Ignoring it, he continued to dab the cuts on her face.

She persisted. "That seems a little superstitious for a badass ex-soldier."

Dianne appeared more focused on their conversation than what he was doing, which was good. He was sure the lacerations stung, especially as the *daemons* would have used harmonic spurs to disrupt the cells they sliced through.

"You'd be surprised. Many of us wear medals into battle, even if we're only battlefield believers. But since I've worked for your sister and her husband, I've learned that there are more things in heaven and earth than are dreamt of in your modern philosophy."

Dianne pulled back at that. Her single eye, its blue iris flecked with slate, fixed on him. "Hamlet? You're seriously quoting Hamlet to me?"

Now Ryan tossed the used swab onto the desk next to him with a bit more force than necessary. "What? Dumb gym bro can't read Shakespeare?"

Dianne flinched, and Ryan regretted his fit of pique. As he turned to run his fingers through her hair, checking her scalp for unseen cuts and bruises, she said, "I'm sorry that my friends called you that. I should have said so before."

Ryan looked at her. She looked upset even through the wild bramble of bloody cuts on her face. "Eat that chocolate," he said gruffly, "your blood sugar is crashing."

She blinked and reached for the chocolate bar where she'd left it on the bed next to her hip. As she moved, her breasts brushed Ryan's chest where he leaned over her. A zing of electricity shot through him, making him want to growl. He ignored it. It had just been a long time since he'd been this close to a woman's body. But he had a mission to do, and he'd vowed never to pursue pure, selfish pleasure again.

Dianne unwrapped the candy bar and broke off a square. "Would you like some?" she asked, holding it out to Ryan.

It would be so easy to lean in and let her feed the chocolate to him, her fingertips caressing his lips until he captured them with his teeth ....

Ryan shook his head. "I can wait until I'm done checking you. This patch on your scalp looks pretty tender. You'll need to shower and wash it thoroughly so it doesn't get infected. I'll get you some antibiotic cream for afterwards."

Dianne had popped the chocolate into her mouth. "Mmh-mm," she said.

Ryan began running his hands over her as he'd done in the corridor after the rabble of *daemoniacs* had ripped her from his hold. His heart thudded at the memory. He'd thought he'd lost her in the powerful harmonic eddies swirling around them. Their malevolent joy at gaining the object of their pursuit had damn near destroyed the structural integrity of that part of the cruise ship. Even now he could recall the spongy feeling of the steel beneath his feet.

But the *daemons'* distraction had been their undoing. As usual with the dumb mothers, driven and pulled this way and that by their irrational lusts.

That, and Ryan had nearly flared. He wasn't even an *Elioud*, just a former soldier wearing specially designed harmonic tactical gear. But, damn, he was glad that Miró worked for the good guys. It was his harmonic chainmail that protected Ryan. Was that the reason the *daemon* had referred to him as a 'paladin'?

He shoved that thought to the side. He'd ask the *Elioud* warriors when he returned to the Kastrioti Estate. Over the past year, he'd learned to live with all the gaps in his knowledge of the angelic realm and its intersection with the human world. Beta, who'd married András in a battlefield ceremony last December, had told him not to pout about it in her typical straightforward way.

"Do you think that you are alone in a scary new world?" she'd asked. "What exactly about being in military intelligence prepared me to transform into a dragon, hm?"

"Good point," he'd said. He didn't have the *cajónes* to tell Beta she didn't need the military or anything else to teach her how to be a dragon.

"I'll shower when I return to my cabin," said Dianne, bringing Ryan back to the present.

"Negative," he said, his hand coming to her left shoulder. She winced and pulled away. He slipped his fingers inside her sleeveless blouse to feel along the top of her shoulder and around to her back. "That hurts?"

Dianne nodded. "Yes. That demented woman somehow managed to throw me against the wall. I banged my shoulder pretty hard."

Ryan eased onto the bed and moved Dianne so that he could raise her shirt. He shone the penlight on her upper back where a massive bruise had already turned an ugly purple on her shoulder blade.

"I've got a cold pack and a sling. I can tape the pack to your back while you keep your arm elevated. I think it's just bruised, but we'll know more when we can get it x-rayed." He pulled her blouse down and knelt on the floor again to manipulate her right knee. "This too. It's pretty swollen, but I think it'll be okay after I wrap it and put a cold pack on it. You're not going anywhere for a few hours, so you might as well lie down and get some rest."

He stood, ignoring the twinge in his upper back and the aches in his knuckles. He'd taken quite a few blows himself, but it wasn't anything he hadn't experienced before, sometimes on a daily basis. None of the *daemon*-possessed dancers had the strength or training of any of the *Elioud* warriors with whom Ryan trained regularly. The pain certainly didn't come anywhere near the gunshot wound he'd earned last June for stepping in to aid Beta against some Russian black-ops goons.

Ryan looked down at Dianne, who sipped the water he'd given her. "As for returning to your cabin, that's not happening. As soon as we dock in Split, and they let us disembark, we're getting off this cruise ship from hell."

Dianne stared at Ryan's back as he unbuttoned his tattered shirt and slipped it from his arms. Despite the blood and torn clothing, his skin remained perfect and unblemished by bruises and scratches, though she saw old scars reflected in the indirect light of the portable lamp on the desk. And when she thought *perfect*, she meant perfect. Or as close to perfection that a mortal male could achieve that it didn't matter. There wasn't an ounce of fat on him. The definition of his muscles, furthermore, seemed more due to actual physical labor than hours in a gym—despite what her friends had said. There were indecipherable letters scrawled on his upper back over a pair of wings. And on his left upper arm, a tattoo read "Helsing" in a gothic script over a wooden stake wrapped in a string of heads of garlic and dripping blood.

Somewhere in the back of her mind, Dianne recognized that he'd been right about needing the chocolate. She was starting to feel better and now disbelieved his lurid explanation for the drugged behavior of a bunch of cruise-ship passengers, including herself. Ecstasy made you highly suggestible. It's why she'd imagined that woman levitating.

Instead of balking, however, Dianne's curiosity about Ryan's tattoo won out over her growing irritation at his highhanded manner.

"Big Bram Stoker fan, are you?" she asked as he pulled a fresh T-shirt over his head to her disappointment.

When Ryan looked over his shoulder towards her, a question on his face, she tilted her head to signify his arm where the tip of the stake and drops of blood showed beneath his shirt sleeve.

He turned towards the refrigerator. Grabbing a bottle of water from it, he said as he shrugged. "Guess so. It's not every day you read a novel whose protagonist has the same last name as you." He twisted the cap from the bottle and raised it to his mouth.

"'Helsing'? That's your last name?" Dianne's annoyance eased a notch. "That's kinda cool."

He drank half the bottle in one long, powerful gulp. Dianne watched the play of his throat muscles in fascination. Now attraction as well as curiosity warred with her annoyance, perversely making her more annoyed.

"It certainly didn't hurt to have it as an English major."

Dianne blinked a few times. She didn't know what to say to that revelation. "You're just one surprise after another. Why did you go into the Army?"

She bit into another square of chocolate, finding the lavender strangely compelling. In fact, her headache dissolved as she chewed. She exhaled and shoved the whole square into her mouth. Olivia was a genius. Was there anything she didn't do well?

Ryan began rummaging around inside his closet as he answered. "The usual. I wanted to see the world. Eat kebabs. Kill people." When she scoffed at his answer, he glanced over at her. "What? Isn't that what you think soldiers do? You East-Coast types don't seem to recognize the call of duty or feelings of patriotism."

"What does 'East-Coast types' mean?" she asked, a little stung that he'd profiled her and found her wanting. Worse, she knew he was right about her.

He looked at her and shrugged. "Most of the guys I served with came from the Midwest or the South. I assumed that military service isn't a big thing where you're from. Admittedly, an induction on my part. I guess we're both guilty of a little pride and prejudice."

He turned back to the closet just as Dianne realized that he'd referenced the classic English romance novel by Jane Austen. "Finish that chocolate. Your sister and her friends have imbued it with special properties to heal and protect you against *daemonic* attack." He lifted his own bar and waggled it. "I prefer the ones with Hungarian paprika."

Then he toed the chair out from under the small table and sat down before tearing the wrapper open and putting half of the candy into his mouth at once. "I'll take the chair," he said after chewing and swallowing, "You take the bed." It was a clear command.

He shoved the last of the chocolate into his mouth, followed by the last of his water. He pitched the empty bottle in the trashcan under the desk, before whistling. The light, which resembled a portable camp lantern, winked out, throwing the cabin into penetrating blackness relieved only by the emergency lighting.

Dianne watched Ryan's silhouette as it relaxed, her jaw dropping a little.

Well, she wasn't staying here all night, giving into his delusions. Maybe he had PTSD or whatever it was that combat veterans came home with that made them think they heard gunshots in the middle of the night. She narrowed her eyes as she studied him. He'd also probably never been to a club dancing. Not that he would have any trouble dominating the dancefloor. He moved with the grace of a panther. He'd be divine to slow dance with, all that muscle surrounding and protecting his partner.

That thought made Dianne wonder what kind of woman he liked. After all, their dinner together hadn't exactly been the romantic date she'd envisioned when she asked him. She'd just saved him the effort of approaching her as Olivia's head of security. She was just his mission.

Despite her rational brain reminding her of this, her irrational brain continued wondering about his romantic life. Maybe he had a girlfriend. Or wife. Somewhere she'd gotten the distinct impression that guys who went into the military often married young.

She shook her head. *Never mind that, girlfriend*, she admonished herself.

Still, she looked at his hands resting on his waist. Faint light kissed his form, making him look like a being from another world—likely an artifact of the ecstasy on her vision—but no ring gleamed on his left hand.

Dianne finished the unusually tasty chocolate her sister had created and chased it with the bottled water. She should have felt exhausted, but instead, she felt exhilarated. Alive, as she hadn't felt in years, actually. A fight for her life with a sexy man at her back apparently gave her a thrill that going out to nightclubs or meeting guys on Flrty couldn't match. Was it anything like what Olivia felt when she'd met Mihàil?

Dianne glanced at Ryan's shadowy form again.

What would Olivia do? Insist on leaving? Then incapacitate the much-larger male when he refused? Even with her black belt in karate, Olivia wouldn't be able to overpower Ryan, who was half a foot taller and much heavier. Dianne might believe that women could compete with men in many arenas, but women kicking men's butts belonged in superhero movies, not real life. She'd just have to wait until he fell asleep ....

"Might as well lie down," said Ryan with his eyes closed. "It's a long time until sunrise."

Crossing her arms and huffing, Dianne flopped back onto the bed.

Stop acting like a petulant teen, she told herself. *You got yourself into this mess. He might be delusional, but he's got a chivalry complex. There are worse things in life.*

At that thought, an image of the teenaged boy caught by the two men at the dance party rose in Dianne's memory. She shuddered. Why had she imagined that? Was there something perverse in her that wanted to see such acts?

The next thing Dianne knew, voices on the deck outside the cabin woke her. For a moment, she forgot where she was and stretched. She couldn't remember a time when she'd felt better.

"We're docked," said a voice, startling Dianne. "That means we can disembark soon."

Dianne rolled over and sat up. Ryan, dressed in a form-fitting black T-shirt and black cargo pants, stood not far from the end of the bed in his cabin. He wore a massive backpack and a serious expression. In his right hand he clutched wadded fabric.

Dianne frowned. The events of the previous night had faded into a vague, slightly ridiculous dream. She raised both hands to her face, gingerly touching her right eye, which had been swollen shut last night. Then she ran her fingers through her tangled hair along her scalp. No tenderness or stinging resulted, but she did feel a bald spot behind her left ear. Her right knee still hurt, though she was more certain it was only a bad sprain. Even her shoulder felt okay, though she'd know more when she took off the sling.

"Your injuries are largely healed," said Ryan, watching her. "As I said last night, the chocolate that the *zonjë* and her companions developed is restorative. They've actually been engineered with bio nanoparticles that fix damage at a cellular level. But we should still have your shoulder and your knee x-rayed to be sure."

Dianne's jaw fell open. She let her hands drop to her lap. "Since when has Olivia studied bio-nano-whatsit?"

Ryan shrugged. "Dunno. You can ask her when we get to Fushë-Arrëz. Here, put this on." He tossed the fabric he'd been holding at her. "It's been woven with harmonically tuned nanothreads to defend against *daemon* attack. Once you put it on, the nanothreads will be keyed to your personal harmonics."

Dianne, who'd caught the item while Ryan spoke, held it up now. It was a diaphanous, white, long-sleeved tunic long-enough to reach her ankles. It didn't look like it could stop a hangnail let alone a drugged harpy with the strength of three men.

"I'm going back to my cabin," she said, dropping the translucent garment on the bed and standing. She squared her shoulders. "Now."

Something changed in Ryan's features at her declaration, something indefinable. He simply looked even more chiseled from granite, and his eyes turned frosty.

"No. You can put that tunic on by yourself or I'll put it on you." He took a step toward the bed and her. "You can either come with me on your own or I'll carry you. Your choice. Either way, we're getting off this ship now."

The coldness in his tone sent a shiver of premonition down Dianne's spine. Despite this, she lifted her chin and held her ground. "You can't carry me off the gangplank. The security officers will stop you."

Ryan tilted his head. "Are you sure about that?" he asked in a soft, menacing voice.

Six

Ryan saw when Dianne understood the truth of his threat. She sucked in an audible breath, and her face turned pale beneath the fading bruises.

He absolutely hated doing it. But he'd run out of time, and he couldn't risk another *daemon* attack, not now when his harmonically charged chainmail had already absorbed so much discordant energy. It would, of course, recharge given enough time, but for now, he was vulnerable—and the *daemons* on the ship would sense that soon enough once they came looking for Dianne again.

At least she hadn't crumpled into a sniveling ball. Beneath the fear, he read her fury. She needed to find that backbone of hers for what he suspected was going to be an arduous, dangerous journey down the Dalmatian coast and into the mountains of Albania.

He checked his watch. It was almost 0800. The ship had docked in Split an hour ago. What would have happened if he hadn't been on board when the *daemons* attacked? Would they have overcome the crew, burning through them like a raging wildfire through dry timber?

Don't go there, Helsing, he warned himself.

Instead, he said to Dianne, "I charged your phone." He tossed it to her. "You can call Olivia once we're in port and somewhere safe."

If the *Elioud* didn't contact Ryan first. The harmonic activity from last night wouldn't have reached the operations center during the attack once they left the pool deck, but they would be desperate to know what had happened, especially once Ryan's nano system reconnected and transmitted a record of the reverberations.

Defiance sparked in Dianne's gaze. Color returned to her cheeks. "You bet I will." Grabbing up the protective tunic that Miró had designed for her, she stormed past him and yanked the bathroom door open before catching his gaze. "I *can* go to the bathroom first, can't I?"

Well, that had worked as well as he'd hoped.

"Of course," he said, stifling the urge to pull her out of the cabin anyway.

Five minutes later—just as he was considering banging on the door—Dianne opened it. She'd pulled the tunic on over her blouse from the previous evening. Her hair had also been neatened and pulled into a low ponytail while her face looked damp as though she'd washed it. Out of nowhere, the image of her waking in his bed a short while before, her hair tousled and her face blurry with sleep, struck him.

"What?" asked Dianne, touching her hair.

"Nothing," he muttered and turned on his heel to open the cabin door. "Have your guest ID? We're not coming back once we leave this cabin."

Dianne, her eyes narrowed, pulled the lanyard with her ship's ID out from where it had been tucked inside her blouse.

"Great," said Ryan, gesturing for her to exit.

Dianne moved past him. Even after the evening she'd had, he still caught the faint scent of her perfume, something exotic like jasmine and rain. His nostrils flared as he inhaled. It twisted around his insides, reminding him of a different time, a different world, a different Ryan who thought that someday he'd find the girl of his dreams and build a life with her.

A world before he knew that malevolent spirits lurked, plotting the destruction of humanity.

Ryan fell in behind Dianne as she headed toward the midship where two separate exits to the dock allowed passengers to disembark. His muscles tightened as he spied passengers coming toward them from the other side of the corridor. They seemed innocent in their white cotton blouses, cutoff shorts, and flipflops, but he'd been with the Kastriotis long enough to know that *daemons* delighted in taking over the defenseless.

The young women passed without morphing into monsters with claws and fangs.

When they approached the nearest disembarkation point, Ryan saw passengers waiting in a line that extended into the landing in front of the elevators. As he and Dianne turned from the corridor, he scanned them, his total focus on potential threats. Almost all of the passengers appeared to be retired and midlife couples beating the rush to get off the ship and into port. They'd likely gone to bed early and missed the *daemonic* fun. His chainmail remained quiescent. No *daemon* activity disturbed its sensitive harmonics.

Dianne moved to stand at the end of the line. Ryan stopped behind her. Even without the *Elioud* ability to read personal harmonics, he could see her tension.

"What's the plan after we get off?" she asked, faking a casualness that her stiff neck belied.

"We head to a safehouse where I can pick up some gear and the keys to a vehicle. Then we drive down the coast. All goes well, we'll be at your sister's by nightfall."

"I see." She didn't sound like she saw at all.

They'd reached the security checkpoint where an alert officer sat next to an elevated stand watching a monitor as passengers scanned their cruise IDs when someone called out behind them.

It was Dianne's cabinmate, Germaine.

Ryan exhaled, clenching his jaw to keep from swearing. How had she found them?

The security officer's gaze traveled toward Germaine. He dipped his chin toward the scanner. "Next," he said to Dianne, who held up the line.

Dianne glanced at him. "Sure. Sorry." She swiped her ID card, still in its protective plastic sleeve, over the scanner.

Ryan stepped forward, forcing Dianne to move ahead, and pressed his own card against the scanner's glass.

"Hey!" she said, her gaze flashing. "You don't have to be such a dick."

Ryan ignored her to put a hand on her lower back. "We don't have time to waste with her," he said as he moved closer to her side.

Dianne glared as she let him guide her down the metal gangplank. "She's my best friend. I can't just blow her off. And she's not going to just let you take me without asking a few questions, no matter how hot you are."

Ryan nearly lost a step at that comment. She thought he was hot. It took him a moment to understand the implication of the rest of her words.

As they stepped onto the asphalt of the landing, he said, "You texted her."

Dianne's gaze flashed again as she looked over her shoulder at him. "Damn right I did! She's got my back, just like I've got hers. Something a Ranger should understand."

She stopped next to the gangplank and crossed her arms, clearly waiting for Germaine, now descending the angled metal treads, to join them.

"Call Olivia."

"What?" asked Dianne, who'd been focused on the impending showdown with Germaine.

"Call your sister," said Ryan, his teeth clenched.

Germaine halted across from Ryan. She glanced at him and then back to Dianne. "Are you okay?" She placed her hands on Dianne's forearms, appeared to think better of it, and stepped back, dropping her hands at her sides. "I've been worried sick about you since last night."

Ryan tilted his head, studying Dianne's best friend through narrowed eyes. Something sounded odd about Germaine's voice. Insincerity maybe? But that made no sense, unless she'd only shown up to placate Dianne .... He wished he could read harmonics to know more. "You can see that she's fine."

"She *looks* fine," said the other woman, shifting so that she stood between Ryan and Dianne, "but she sent an SOS. Why are you taking her off the ship? Just because she spent the night with you doesn't mean that you own her now."

Now Germaine sounded downright hostile.

Ryan had no idea how to handle this. Despite his earlier threat about carrying Dianne off the ship, he couldn't just grab her and carry her off. Germaine gave off vibes of being someone who'd taken a self-defense course and would do something stupid like try to knee him in the groin. Once she got involved, so would the handful of crew on the dock and the other passengers streaming by. He didn't worry that he'd be able to evade capture, but he didn't need the local authorities notified. It would only slow them down.

Cruise passengers streamed past, some looking at the three of them in open curiosity.

Olivia's familiar voice sounded in his ear, ending his dilemma. "Demon Slayer, we've registered intense *daemonic* activity on your personal grid. Sitrep ASAP."

Ryan, his eyes narrowed as he watched Germaine, started to answer his superior regardless of how odd it would seem to the two women. Before he could speak, Dianne stepped around her friend. She looked embarrassed.

She cleared her throat. "You've got it wrong," she said to her friend. "Nothing happened between us. He just took care of me after that insane dance party."

"Then what's the problem?" asked Germaine, her eyes narrowed. "Is he taking you off the ship against your will or not?"

"Helsing?" said Olivia in his ear. "How copy?"

"The sitrep can wait. Your sister can't," said Ryan to Olivia. "We're in port. She needs confirmation of your orders or she's making a big scene."

Germaine and Dianne swiveled to look at him. Germaine's gaze gleamed in odd avarice. Dianne's brows had bunched in confusion, distrust visible beneath her puzzled expression.

Then her cellphone rang.

She looked at the screen, amazement now lifting her features. She glanced between Germaine and Ryan. "It's Olivia!"

Ryan sucked in a sharp breath through his nose, his jaws again clenched.

Dianne swiped the answer button and lifted the phone to her ear. "Hello?"

Olivia heard the wonder in her younger sister's voice. And the thread of anger. Clearly revealed over the enhanced cellphone technology that the *Elioud* and their retainers used.

"I guess you've met Ryan Helsing, my head of security," she said, feeling her way into the conversation. She needed more intel about the situation. If Ryan's harmonic grid had absorbed as much *daemonic* energy as it had recorded ... well, she needed to get them out of there *now*.

"You can say that," said Dianne, her words clipped. "What the hell, Livia? You sent this, this *beast* to grab me? How did you even know I was on a cruise?"

Olivia sighed and pinched the bridge of her nose. She really didn't have time for this. Her feet ached. So did her upper back. Mihàil, who'd read the tension in her sore muscles, had offered to rub her shoulders for her, but he'd looked half dead himself, though that shouldn't have been possible given how much angel blood flowed through his veins. But their daughter, only seven months old, had been up teething all night. It was the reason Olivia hadn't checked the system logs until the cruise ship had docked in Split.

She hadn't wanted to drag Miles into the ops center to monitor this side job. He was already covering for Ryan's absence. And Miró needed to stay close to Stasia, who expected their first child in a matter of weeks, not lose sleep because Olivia had a foreboding about her wayward little sister partying on a Mediterranean cruise.

Olivia injected patience into her voice when she answered her sister. "Mom told me about the cruise. I'll explain what's going on when you get here, but Di, you know I wouldn't have sent someone to 'grab' you."

Dianne sighed. When she spoke next, she sounded a little less irate. "No, I know that. Ryan told me you sent him to protect me. Now he wants to take me to Fushë-Arrëz. Like right now. We just got off the ship, and he's planning to pick up a car and drive me into Albania *today*."

"That's right. " Closing her eyes, Olivia paused and gripped her courage. It was always hard to convince civilians about imminent threats, but coming from an older sister, it was almost impossible. "And if he's telling you that you need to leave now, you need to trust him. It's literally his job, and he's one of the best at what he does."

Olivia watched the nanotracker that Ryan had slipped onto her sister. She'd moved about ten meters away from him. Olivia imagined her chief of security glowering, his keen gaze searching, searching for the next threat.

Dianne continued arguing.

"But it's over the top, don't you think? Maybe he's been out of civilian life too long. He's a little uptight. I mean, yeah, the dance party looked more like a rave. I won't lie. It got a little scary there." Dianne laughed. Olivia heard the nerves her sister didn't intend to show. "But in the bright light of morning, everything seems fine. *I'm* fine."

"Dianne." Olivia let her authority as the *zonjë*, the wife of a *zoti*, swell her voice. It was just short of compulsion, which none of Archangel Michael's warriors would ever use, not that she wasn't tempted.

Only Dark *Irim* compelled humans against their will.

Olivia heard her sister gulp.

"What?" asked Dianne in a low voice.

"You have to trust me. Trust Ryan."

"Actually, I do trust Ryan." Olivia heard reluctance before Dianne hurried on. "But I don't know why we have to leave the ship right now. All my stuff's still in my cabin, including my passport." She paused. "I can't just leave everyone before the end of the cruise, Livia."

Olivia exhaled and stood, pacing around the TOC, where the two young staff members that Miles had recruited to monitor their security systems had just started the day shift. They glanced at her, but being well trained, returned to their tasks. It was a good thing that Olivia had sandboxed Ryan's personal harmonic system. She didn't need Mihàil to see the danger. He had enough on his plate right now.

The sense of foreboding filled her again, sharper and more urgent. She tamped it down.

Now she exuded casualness. "Don't worry about your stuff or your passport. They can be recovered later." She paused. "Mom and Dad are here. And Michael's flying in tomorrow."

"Really? Wow." Dianne sounded stunned. "How did you get him to leave his burgeoning career as a tech-finance bro? He keeps insisting AI's going to change the world in five years." Her tone sharpened. "This from the guy who once tried to mine crypto from a Nest thermostat."

Olivia mentally rolled her eyes but only said, "I offered to fly him in for an extensive look at our business analytics. Maybe we're not a high-profile client like he normally handles at Fortress Financial, but there he's a low-level data analyst. I'll get him on some higher-level financial strategy." She paused. "Plus, Mihàil has a chef who makes *pašticada* with gnocchi and a well-stocked wine cellar."

Dianne huffed.

And then Ryan's voice broke in over the harmonic communication network.

"Incoming," he said, urgency sharpening his voice as a monstrous *daemonic* presence spiked his proximity sensors.

"Stay with me," said Olivia, going back to the workstation that she'd been using and sitting in front of it, her body aches forgotten. "I'll give you tactical support. "

"Copy that," said Ryan, his voice in battle mode now. His tracker moved closer to Dianne's.

"Hey! What the hell, Ryan!" shouted Dianne. Then she yelled, "Holy shit! What's wrong with those people?"

Olivia winced. Her baby sister was caught in an oncoming rush of *daemoniacs* ....

She acknowledged that and then checked it. She couldn't be a big sister right now. She had to be operations control for her security chief, alone and facing a horde of the possessed in a city where they had few assets.

With a defense system already drained from an overnight Dark attack of unheralded proportions.

"Go with Helsing," she said, slipping into her command voice again.

"Copy that!" said Dianne, echoing Ryan. She sounded breathless already. And scared.

Olivia noted that both Ryan and Dianne moved away from the ship at a clip that meant they ran. Almost at the same time, she opened a desktop window using a program that Miró had developed specifically for the *Elioud* to access their assets.

"Head north toward the Old Town," said Olivia as she connected to their safehouse in Split. She'd be able to mobilize a local team to aid Ryan but not before he engaged the *daemoniacs*. "Almost a klick to Diocletian's Palace. You should have a visual of it." She paused, then added, "Weapons hot on your judgment."

Please, St. Michael, Commander of all that's holy, let Miró's harmonic rounds be effective.

She hated to think what would happen if the possessed couldn't be stopped. But they'd never deployed this particular ammo outside of live testing at their development site. There might be permanent harmonic disruption of the individuals the *daemons* had coopted.

They might even die.

"Roger wilco."

Olivia fitted an earbud into her ear and tapped it. Speaking into the mic, she ordered the voice system to call the Split housekeeper.

For the next few tense moments—probably no more than thirty seconds but it felt like hours—Olivia had no idea what was happening on the ground in Split.

"Germaine!" screamed Dianne, breaking the suspense.

Olivia narrowed her eyes at the harmonics-tracking application running in an open window on her workstation monitor. There was an odd clump in the dissonance closing on Ryan and Dianne. "Demon Slayer, do you have eyes on Germaine Grimes?"

"She followed us off the ship, Harlequin." Ryan sounded grim. "She's being swarmed by three large males."

"Help her!" cried her sister, her panic setting Olivia's nerves into overdrive. "They're going to tear her apart!"

Olivia watched the screen, her eyes wide with horror. Every instinct screamed at her to order Ryan to bug out with her sister and leave the other woman behind.

Instead, she leaned forward and said, "Engage enemy, Demon Slayer."

Dianne thought she'd lost her mind.

One moment she'd been standing on the dock whining like a teenager about leaving all of her friends behind and the next Ryan had grabbed her by the arm and pulled her away from the ship.

"What the hell, Ryan!" she said.

And then her gaze snagged on passengers flooding through the security checkpoint and rushing down the gangplank, their expressions rabid and fixated on them.

Actually, it felt like they'd fixed on *her*.

She said something in her panic, to which Olivia responded again using that implacable tone of command that Dianne had never heard from her older sister before. It focused Dianne like nothing else could.

"Go with Helsing."

Dianne found herself saying "copy that" as if she'd become a soldier. And then she let her hand slip into Ryan's.

They sprinted toward the end of the pier, rushing through thick groups of unwary cruise passengers and local citizens offering walking tours of Split's historic city center. Distantly, Dianne heard complaints that turned into shocked babble. People began to scatter.

Ryan's gaze had trained ahead of them. Dianne heard him say, "Roger wilco."

She scarcely had time to wonder how he communicated with Olivia. She'd glanced back toward the ship when she caught sight of Germaine, surrounded by three large men.

"Germaine!" she yelled without thinking, coming to a halt.

Ryan said something, but Dianne couldn't understand anything. Her best friend stood, terror twisting her features, as rough hands tugged on her arms, her clothing, her hair.

"Help her!" screamed Dianne, trying to tug her hand from Ryan's iron grip and move toward Germaine. "They're going to tear her apart!"

An instant later, The Beast emerged. He pulled her on the other side of a black van waiting for a group of tourists.

"Don't move," ordered The Beast, glaring at her long enough to catch her gaze.

Dianne nodded, struck dumb now by the surreal tableau under the clear morning sky.

Then he pivoted and ran back toward the group, which had collected more stark-raving-mad passengers like moths drawn to a flame.

Dianne's jaw fell as Ryan plowed into the tallest male, who'd gripped the neck of Germaine's blouse and ripped it open to her waist. The male exploded away from Germaine as if hit by a massive shockwave. He landed on his back, motionless.

The second male didn't go as easily.

Snarling, he turned and grabbed Ryan by the neck while the third male began dragging Germaine by the hair as she flailed, trying to hit and kick him. Dianne's hand flew to her throat and her breath whooshed out of her lungs, but then she sucked in a lungful of air before taking a step toward the mob.

"Stay put," said Olivia.

Dianne looked down. Her phone was still in her hand, the line to Olivia still open.

When Dianne brought her gaze back to the unreal melee, it had only gone from terrifying to hopeless. Ryan now battled two frothing lunatics, one hanging from Ryan's back where he appeared to be gnawing on Ryan's neck, while the second grappled with Olivia's chief of security in a fury of arms and clawed fingers. More lunatics swarmed toward him.

He'd be overwhelmed at any moment.

Germaine had managed to trip the large male dragging her, sending him to his knees. As Germaine kicked at his head, trying to dislodge his hold on her, he pivoted toward Dianne, who'd ignored Olivia's last command to run toward her friend. At the same time, the man clinching Ryan in a bear hug halted, raised his head, and fixed his doleful gaze on her.

Then he howled and headbutted Ryan, who staggered backwards under the weight of the male clinging to his back. An instant later, the head-butter and Germaine's attacker together broke into a run toward Dianne.

Seven

Pain exploded in Ryan's head as the *daemoniac*'s skull crashed into his, sending him reeling. The creature on his back had sunk talonlike fingers into his shoulders and gnawed on his neck with the singular focus of a wild animal. Even though the weakened harmonic chainmail prevented his attacker from piercing Ryan's skin, it still hurt like hell.

For an instant, he lost awareness of everything except the sheer need to survive as he went down on one knee, his hand on the pavement catching him out of simple instinct.

Dianne's bloodcurdling scream cleared Ryan's mind.

His gaze came up, the scene around him crystal clear and its action slowed to a fraction of its normal human speed. He didn't question this uncanny focus.

He simply recognized Dianne's imminent bodily harm. And his duty to stop it, without regard for himself.

Roaring, Ryan came to his feet, throwing the possessed man off his back. He barely registered when this attacker crashed to the ground, rolling and coming to its haunches.

He ignored the swarming *daemoniacs* from the ship.

He ignored the panicked people who clogged the pier in a desperate rush to escape.

Instead, he sprinted faster than he'd ever run to reach his principle, who'd just screamed his name.

The male who'd pivoted from Germaine tugged on Dianne's protective tunic while the male who'd smashed his head into Ryan's sat on her thighs, giggling. Germaine swatted both men about the head, crying and screaming, and about as effectual as a gnat.

Ryan wrenched the first attacker from Dianne's legs. He felt the power leave his replenished chainmail and heard an unnatural grunt from the *daemoniac*. The man landed, hard, on the asphalt.

Ryan kicked him in the head before turning back to the second attacker, who gleefully twisted Dianne's tunic around her neck, choking the life from her.

A bolt of fury raced through Ryan. He grabbed the *daemoniac*, whose high-pitched scream stopped all activity on the crowded pier.

The *daemoniac* stiffened, its eyes going wide, and then slumped in Ryan's grip.

Ryan shoved the limp body to the side and away from Dianne as Germaine, sobbing, untwisted the tunic and began to pull it over her friend's head.

"No," said Ryan, putting a hand on Germaine's wrist. When she looked at him, wide eyed and panting, he shook his head. "That stays on her."

He glanced over his shoulder at the renewed tumult around them. For now, no *daemoniacs* targeted them. For the moment, the malicious creatures had switched their sights to the easier prey around them.

"Is she able to stand?" He nodded to Dianne, who sat up with Germaine's help and sucked in broken breaths. He didn't have time to check her over.

"Demon Slayer, I registered several harmonic discharges," said Olivia in his ear. She paused. "At higher output than designed." Concern threaded her voice.

"I don't know my own power, Harlequin," he said, reaching down to pull Dianne to her feet. He glanced at the motionless *daemoniac* lying next to her. "I think I lost one."

"Copy that," she said. "Transpo is still fifteen minutes out. You need to get to the Old Town and find someplace secure to wait for the exfil team."

"Roger that," he said.

Dianne looked around. She didn't seem to register the tumult. "I-I"—the hoarse words stuck in her injured throat. She coughed. "—lost my phone."

Ryan ignored her to address Germaine. "I'll get you as far as the palace over there"—he lifted his chin toward the obvious Roman ruins overlooking the harbor—"but then you're on your own. My advice? Stay off that ship."

Germaine blanched, looking over her shoulder. "What about the others?"

Just then, a piercing scream rent the air before cutting off abruptly. Visceral sounds of grunting and snarling thickened as possessed people streamed toward a growing clump of bodies. Ryan saw blood and gore on the jaws of several. It looked like a scene out of a zombie movie.

His stomach twisted. He looked away for a moment, leaving his answer to Germaine's question unsaid. Instead, he asked Dianne, "Can you walk?"

She bit her lip and nodded, her fingers drifting to her neck, now swollen and red. Ryan clenched his jaw and flexed his useless fingers.

So much for the protective tunic. It didn't defend against actual physical attack.

He gestured to Germaine. "You take point. Dianne, you follow. I'll take the rear."

The women nodded and turned to head toward the palm-lined Riva Promenade along the waterfront. It was deserted. Even the street next to the pier had emptied of all traffic. In the distance, strident sirens competed with the disturbing discord around them.

He grabbed Germaine's arm before she took a step. "Be ready to run on my order."

Germaine's gaze darted behind him. Ryan saw something slither across it, something that he doubted he'd seen correctly in the early morning glare. He could have sworn that avarice mixed with the regret ...

Germaine looked at him, and he saw that she realized he'd been watching her.

"Don't worry about me, soldier boy," she said, dismissing the frenzy of violence on the pier behind them and heading toward the waterfront boulevard.

Ryan narrowed his eyes as he followed behind the women. Was it just a snarky throwaway comment based on his supercilious manner? Or did she know more than she ought about his military service?

Up ahead, Diocletian's Palace loomed over the harbor. The seventeen-hundred-year-old imperial sea fortress built by the Roman emperor after whom it was named, now a UNESCO site, spanned more than thirty-thousand square meters and housed shops, cafés, restaurants, and apartments.

Ryan strode behind Dianne, swiveling every ten meters to survey the action behind them. His chainmail would alert him if any *daemoniacs* approached, but old habits die hard. He wanted to see the enemy coming.

That's how he caught sight of the mob that formed just after they'd passed the second of three piers on the route to the city center. There appeared to be a leader in the midst of the ragtag group. He pointed at their trio. The *daemonic* playthings swiveled and burst across the asphalt as one, humming and clicking like a swarm of yellow jackets. The air around them wavered.

"Run!" shouted Ryan, grabbing Dianne's hand to lead her toward a bus station on their right. "Go, go, go! We've gotta find shelter."

Mercifully, Dianne responded to his urging and began running. Despite this, Ryan had to modulate his stride so that he didn't cause her to fall. He couldn't afford to carry her.

Germaine trailed behind, terror twisting her features. She kept throwing glances over her shoulder at the speeding horde, which was unnaturally advancing on them.

Daemons did that. They rode their possessions hard.

"Harlequin, this is Demon Slayer," said Ryan into his comm as he ran, aware in the back of his mind of the irony of that call sign. "I'm gonna need a little help. We're about to be overrun by these zombie bastards. They're literally out for blood."

"I see them, Demon Slayer," said Olivia, her cool tone suggesting that everything was copacetic. It was one of the things Ryan liked most about his boss. "On the other side of the bus station is a parking lot. Acquire a vehicle. Exfil team is still five minutes out."

"Copy that," he said. He tugged Dianne toward one of the coach buses, which idled. He briefly considered stealing it.

"Germaine!" said Dianne, managing to push her friend's name out through her damaged vocal cords.

"I got her."

Ryan burst into the open around the end of the bus in time to see Germaine trip and tumble to the pavement. She looked back, her hands propping her upright. The *daemoniacs* were only a few hundred feet away, rushing like a human river along the unobstructed street. He realized that his dash to recover Germaine had meant ceding the approach to the parking lot from this end of the bus station. They would have to go through it, a choice he didn't want to have to make.

Ryan didn't bother yelling at Dianne's friend to get up. That only worked with soldiers.

Germaine surprised him by rising to her feet as he reached her. She took his hand. Ryan ran, not holding back. Somehow Germaine kept pace.

They made it around the bus where Dianne waited. Ryan grabbed her hand as they passed, tugging her along. His urgency must have communicated itself to his harmonic tactical system because he felt a tingle as his fingers wrapped around hers. A responding zing from her tunic skimmed his skin like a lover's touch.

Germaine and Dianne had maneuvered between the bus and the station when Ryan spotted the leading *daemoniacs* streaming into the spaces between buses from the street. Several broke off and headed around the end of their bus, clearly intending to cut them off on the other side.

They needed to *move* or they'd be trapped.

"Pick up the pace!" he yelled at Germaine, whose long strides carried her to the lead.

She looked over her shoulder at the onrush of the possessed, flinching and missing a step before catching herself. Then she raced across the gap toward a glass door into the station. Dianne followed, but by the time Ryan cleared the end of the bus the first attackers arrived. Ahead, he saw what had been a middle-aged woman—probably a wife and mother—reach for Dianne even as fingers clawed at his shoulder, his side, his upper back.

Fury ignited inside Ryan. He was *not* going to fail this mission. He was going to bring his principal, safe and sound, to Fushë-Arrëz.

Energy rolled up his arms as he blocked the nearest creature. As soon as he plowed into one, a tremendous harmonic wave exploded from him. It was like nothing that Ryan had experienced so far with the weapon that Miró had been developing for non-*Elioud*.

It launched the man he grabbed as well as half a dozen *daemoniacs* behind him into the next bus and scattered others approaching that way.

Ryan kept running until he got close enough to pull Dianne's attacker away and fling her into the bus behind them. Germaine had been blocked by several *daemoniacs* from entering the station but managed to break free and run ahead to the next entrance, trailing several of the creatures.

Ryan couldn't take the time to make sure Dianne hadn't been hurt again.

Scowling, he placed his palm on her upper back and said, "Get your ass moving, Markham."

As he spoke to her, he felt harmonic energy transfer from him to her, crackling the air between them. An ethereal blue light flared along the fine woven mesh of the tunic.

Picking up her pace, Dianne hunched her shoulders and hustled past the bus. Ryan engaged several smaller possessed people, faster than their compatriots but less able to stop a trained fighter used to sparring formidable *Elioud* warriors.

Up ahead, Germaine tugged on a door, but it had been locked. Whirling, she began fighting off a group of women and feral children, their eyes glittering and teeth snapping.

Ryan couldn't worry about whether any of the possessed would overwhelm her. His sole focus had to be on Dianne.

Somehow Germaine broke free of the creatures and raced down the sidewalk in front of the station. Dianne followed in her wake, Ryan a few meters behind. They passed the next three buses with *daemoniacs* of all ages chasing them. Most ended up turning on one another, snapping and growling like a pack of wild dogs, but a dozen with a little more innate intelligence still driving their actions kept pace with them, looking for any opening to swoop in.

It came at the last bus in the line. Germaine halted as a team of three large males cut off her escape on the other side of the bus. Dianne, caught unaware, ran into her friend. Ryan stopped five meters back from the women, his gaze scanning the area as the remaining males, their *daemon* hosts clearly restrained, took care of the wilder ones blocking their approach. They twisted necks in a trained, disciplined manner.

A medium-height male with fathomless brown eyes gestured to the others using quick, crisp movements. The rest of the men fanned out around him in a two-tier perimeter, blocking access to the street, their hard gazes fixed on Ryan.

Ryan recognized fellow soldiers.

His palms grew slick with sweat. His harmonic system had been seriously depleted after the numerous high-energy discharges. The unexpected transfer of power to Dianne's protective tunic moments before would have left him only minimal juice for critical functions like autonomous vitals tracking or beacon pings.

Police sirens blared as multiple cars passed them on the nearby D410, heading south toward the pier with their cruise ship and the scene of the first attacks.

"Harlequin, can you send a little law enforcement help our way?" he asked.

"Copy, Demon Slayer." She paused. "Don't make me assign you a new call sign, Helsing."

"No, ma'am," he said, bracing as the *daemoniac* in charge flicked two fingers, and two of his men moved forward as a coordinated unit.

A moment later, one of the *daemoniacs* on the other side of the bus grabbed Germaine, who shrieked as he pulled her toward him, struggling.

Ryan flicked his wrist, opening the custom carbon-steel knife that he'd secreted in a pants pocket. Miró had encased the folding knife inside a harmonic damper that kept the ship's metal detectors from recognizing it. He'd rather have a combat rifle, but in close quarters, it would do.

And Ryan had mastered the art of knife fighting as a Ranger, then taken that skill to another level with tips from Beta Nagy.

One of the approaching pair nodded at the other, who abruptly rushed Ryan.

Followed half a second later by the other man.

Ryan held steady until the last second, swiveling to shove the attacker's head into the bus next to him with his free hand before pivoting toward the second man with the knife.

He plunged the blade into this attacker's thigh before the first attacker, shaking his head and blinking his eyes, rushed back at him. Ryan took multiple blows to his ribs and back as both *daemoniacs* pummeled him despite his repeated vicious strikes with the knife.

Sweat sheeted into his eyes, and his fist gripping the combat knife grew slippery with blood.

Behind him, he heard Germaine fight with one of the three males, who seemed to be playing with her as a cat plays with mice.

He broke free of his attackers long enough to see that Dianne stood, motionless and alone, her eyes wide in her bloodless face as she watched her friend's torment.

Please, St. Michael, let me get to Dianne, thought Ryan.

Almost as soon as he thought this, two squad cars screeched to a halt in the street beyond. Officers jumped out a moment later, shouting and pulling handguns. One officer, who'd remained on the driver's side of his vehicle, aimed his weapon over its hood.

The men attacking Ryan paid no attention. They just kept coming, trading blows for wounds.

As he shoved one of the attackers from the embedded blade of his knife, Ryan caught sight of the *daemoniac* leader glancing over his shoulder before nodding to his men, who peeled off in hunting teams of two.

One team for each of the three police officers facing them.

The officers began yelling, and then one after another began firing their guns as the *daemoniacs* ignored their commands to halt.

The next moment, Dianne screamed, a ragged sound that drew Ryan's gaze like a lodestone.

To his shock, she rushed toward the tall male who'd grabbed Germaine and dragged her backwards with an arm across her throat. Ryan glimpsed the male's head snapping back, followed by his aiming a cruel grin at Dianne, now struggling against the grip of another male.

Then the *daemoniac* Ryan had stabbed in the chest grappled him in a bear hug while the other began jabbing him in the lower back with sharp knuckle punches. Ryan's knees began to sag under the relentless onslaught.

Until the air vibrated around him, supporting his weight. Ryan's flagging spirit rebounded.

Harmonics.

It took several seconds before the *daemoniac* squad attacking them registered the new presence. They paused, grimaces twisting their features.

The humming increased in pitch and intensity, calling forth a response in Ryan's personal harmonic system and swelling in volume around the combatants. The male punching Ryan gasped and clutched his head while the one gripping him broke off with a shriek. The acrid scent of smoldering flesh assailed Ryan's nostrils an instant before both creatures combusted.

The other *daemoniacs* threw their heads back, their hands over their ears, and howled.

Around Ryan and Dianne, the *daemoniacs* likewise exploded in a spontaneous eruption of ash and blue-white flame, suspended in the air before cascading to the pavement in a rush. The acrid scent of charred flesh hung heavy in the abrupt silence.

All except the leader, that is. Instead, his eyes narrowed to slits as he clenched his fists and grimaced, straining against the disruptive force of the nanodrones that Olivia had sent as Ryan's backup. Ryan's personal harmonics system has acted as a tuner and amplifier, recalibrating the harmonics of the human vessels to an angelic key.

After a long struggle, one of the leader's eyes popped with a hiss. Vitreous gel oozed down his drooping cheek. The hum of the nanodrones dissipated.

Ryan shook his head, exhaled a sharp breath, and then squared his shoulders.

Then he stepped forward, the knife held in a backhanded grip, ready to engage this final enemy. An enemy no longer strengthened by the horde.

Without a word, the *daemoniac* spun and loped away, its lopsided gait testament to the energetic battle it had just fought on a cellular level—fought and barely won.

Ryan let it go. He sensed that this wave of the battle had ended. They needed to get out of here before the evil spirits had time to regroup and possess more human vessels, willing or unwilling, for their foot soldiers.

As he turned to leave, an object laying on the pavement next to where the leader had stood caught his attention.

Ryan stepped forward and picked it up. It was a small, ornate metal charm that resembled a hand with two short outer fingers and three extended fingers. A blue-white-and-black crystal that reminded him of the ubiquitous Eye of Athena found at tourist shops around the Adriatic dominated the tiny metallic palm.

What an irony. The ancient design purported to protect the holder against the malign influence of the Evil Eye.

He pocketed the peculiar charm as he strode back toward Dianne, refusing to contemplate what he'd find. Behind him, three of the police officers remained lying on the pavement where the *daemoniac* hunters had brought them down, one still and two moaning. Ryan ignored the rapid, urgent speech the officer shouted at him. It was obvious the man ordered him to stop, but that just wasn't in Ryan's game plan, not even when the cop started shooting.

Ryan made it unharmed to where Dianne knelt over Germaine, sobbing.

Thank God she was alive.

"We must go before more of them find us," he said, peering over his shoulder toward the street. His neck itched. It wouldn't be long.

Dianne turned a red, wet face to him. It hit him like an unexpected gut punch.

"She's hurt," she said in a broken, raspy voice.

Ryan clamped his jaw and said only, "Let me see."

He moved beside Dianne, kneeling on one knee next to her best friend to assess her injuries. Germaine's ravaged face and torso resembled raw meat. Her right leg had been fractured, and her femur poked through the skin of her thigh. He touched her neck and found her pulse surprisingly strong. She'd need immediate medical care.

All the more reason to get a move on.

He looked at Dianne. "Are you hurt?"

She shook her head. "No. Every time one of those—those—" She floundered for something to call the human shells inhabited by some of the nastiest *daemons* Ryan had ever encountered "—tried to grab me, they acted like they'd gotten shocked by a downed powerline."

"That's a pretty apt description, though I don't know how that tunic got so supercharged." He glanced at her, relief washing over him that she was unhurt. "We have to go. Now. I'll carry her."

Unfortunately, it meant stowing the knife ...

Dianne nodded. Again, Ryan's relief caught him by surprise. He put it away along with the knife. There was no time for anything but the mission, even if that had grown to include Dianne's friend.

"Harlequin, this is Demon Slayer," he said as he lifted Germaine in his arms. "Thanks for the assist. Package is safe, but her friend needs medical attention yesterday. How far out is that transpo?"

"Well, Demon Slayer, given that you're taking your sweet time, transpo will meet you in the bus parking lot in ninety seconds. Do you think you can manage that?" His boss's dry tone reassured him.

"Wilco," he said.

Then, nodding at Dianne to lead, he stepped away from the bus station and headed for the parking lot behind the building.

Olivia let out a deep breath and leaned into her hands. The calm hum of the TOC contrasted with the tension she'd felt as she'd watched the discordant energy swarming after Ryan and Dianne. For a brief instance, she'd even imagined that she'd connected to Dianne using angelic sonar as she'd done when the Dark *Irim* Asmodeus had held Mihàil in frozen storage in a meat-processing plant years ago, before they'd been married.

Her sister's terror had been Olivia's terror ...

"What exactly is going on here, *zonja ime*?" asked her husband, the *zoti*. The lord.

It was never a good sign when he addressed her as 'my lady' in the tone of voice he reserved for command operations.

Olivia dropped her hands to her lap and swiveled the desk chair around to face Mihàil's thunderous blue gaze.

"Or do you intend to keep me in the dark about the legions of *daemons* rampaging in Split? The ones you sent Helsing—a mortal human—to face alone?"

Eight

Pressure encased Dianne's head in a blinding cocoon. She'd barely heard anything since the moment when that immense humming swelled around them. It had seemed to come straight from her heart. She'd watched in horror as Germaine had been set upon by three brutal men, who'd laughed—*laughed*—at Germaine's terror and pain. Dianne had reacted on instinct, rushing forward to thrust the heel of one hand under the jaw of the man dragging Germaine from safety.

He'd given Dianne a fiendish grin as if enjoying her weak attempt at defending her friend, then deliberately broken Germaine's leg, all while holding Dianne's gaze.

She'd turned in frantic need to Ryan, only to see him grappled by a massive man covered in multiple bleeding wounds while another punched him, over and over, in his lower back. He'd started to crumple under the assault.

Ryan, The Beast. Had she really thought that?

Dianne had opened her mouth to yell again, but the scream caught in her throat, strangled by panic.

They were going to die, and she knew it.

That's when the pressure had started. The unbearable pressure to do something, anything, to change the outcome no part of her could accept.

She'd fixated on the inhuman combatants battering Ryan, feeling the surreal humming rise in pitch until the one hugging him had clutched his head. Then the other had shrieked, an unholy sound that made the hair on Dianne's head and neck stand until her scalp tightened.

Then it got truly bizarre.

An awful stench of burnt meat assaulted Dianne's nose only to culminate in a shocking event. Ryan's two antagonists disintegrated in a *whoosh* of fiery smoke and ash followed by howling from the other attackers, who proceeded to combust in fountains of ash and flame.

Their leader had remained standing, however, and Dianne's heart rose to her damaged throat, nearly choking her as she saw him stand upright after the humming had ceased. One eye had burst from its socket, the clear jelly dribbling down his cheek, which slumped as if it would melt from his face. The ghoulish sight seized her in a full-body spasm, raw and involuntary.

Unbelievably, Ryan had straightened his shoulders, gripped that wicked-looking black knife he'd brandished out of nowhere, and stepped forward, motioning to the other man with one hand. That bastard had only stared in defiant malevolence at Ryan before spinning on his heel and limping away past the sole terrified police officer still brandishing a weapon in shaking hands.

The pressure in her head had abated, at least until the police officer began shooting at Ryan, who, cool customer that he was, turned his back on this new danger and strode toward Dianne. The large plate-glass windows of the station behind him shattered, sending shards over him in a jagged mist to tinkle on the pavement. Dozens of bleeding cuts, of which he seemed singularly unaware, opened on his face.

The pressure returned, clogging Dianne's ears so that it sounded like everything was deep underwater. Everything except Ryan's voice, whose gruff, clear baritone caressed her as if he whispered into her ears.

Now he walked at a brisk pace with Germaine cradled in his arms toward the parking lot behind the bus station, where passengers and drivers gathered at the windows, staring at them. Dianne had to jog to stay ahead of him. Overhead, thickening gray clouds moved across the previously clear sky, adding to the tension gripping her. Around them, bodies lay scattered among dropped backpacks, purses, random shoes, and a smattering of cars with smashed windshields and idling engines. In the distance, sirens continued to wail.

It was a nightmare scene from an apocalyptic big-budget American movie.

Ryan's gaze swept the four lanes of roads that bordered the bus station and then the harbor, as if he expected an attack at any moment from any direction, including the Adriatic.

"Shouldn't we try to take one of these cars?" she asked, shivering as she looked toward the nearest traffic lane. She didn't know if her tremors were from nerves or the dropping temperature. Or both.

Ryan shook his head. "Negative. Olivia's sent help for us. They'll be here any time."

Germaine, who'd passed out when the evil brute had broken her leg, moaned.

"They'll be able to give her some emergency medical care faster than we can get her to the local hospital."

Dianne nodded, though she really had no comprehension of the gravity of Germaine's injury. But Ryan didn't seem fazed at it. Likely he'd seen worse on a real battlefield ... then it hit her all at once that this *was* a real battlefield.

"You knew this could happen, didn't you?" she asked, halting on the sidewalk, carefully avoiding a man and woman whose death throes had tangled their limbs together.

He stopped next to her. For the first time since they'd left the ship, he held her gaze. His was grim. "Yes." He paused, his gaze searching hers now as if he wondered how much to say. How much she could handle. "But I had no idea it would go from zero to one-eighty this fast."

Something changed in the air around them. Dianne wasn't sure what. It felt like the sudden drop in pressure before a major thunderstorm.

Ryan's gaze came up, like a gazelle scenting a lion. "They're coming again." He lifted his chin toward a nearby café. "Let's get inside there. At least I can defend against them until our ride arrives."

He left unsaid that they might be trapped inside.

Dianne hurried forward to open the door, her own gaze scanning the area. An invisible warning slid over her skin, raising goosebumps in its wake.

The door to the café turned out to be unlocked, thank all that was good and holy.

Dianne had pulled it wide for Ryan and a moaning Germaine when she observed a mass of people marching toward them from the pier, their faces without expression and their eyes flat. They clogged the road next to the station and the lanes beyond the divider, filling all the pavement to the edge of the water.

She darted a glance over her shoulder north toward the city center where the Roman ruins stood watch over the harbor.

It was worse.

Way worse.

The mob moving toward them at an ungodly speed stretched as far as she could see. It was a veritable army, loudly discordant even at this distance. But not as disciplined as the mass from the south. Pockets of brutality broke out like bubbles in lava: snarling and violent clashes disrupted the army's progress only to disappear in the inexorable flow. The air shimmered above them, as if indeed the bodies below radiated magma-levels of heat.

It would be only a matter of minutes before the two groups of *daemon*-warped humans met. She, Germaine, and Ryan would be caught between them.

A massive headache hammered at her.

"Close the door," said Ryan behind her.

Dianne didn't move, caught in the grip of tension from within and without.

"Markham!" Ryan's voice pierced the invisible veil holding her hostage.

Blinking, Dianne slammed the café door shut, locking it for all the good it would do. She whirled around to find Ryan laying a now-writhing Germaine on the floor.

"What are we going to do?" she asked, hearing the stark fear in her voice.

Ryan stood upright and caught her gaze with his astonishingly clear one. "*We* aren't going to do anything," he said. "You'll be fine as long as you don't take off that tunic. And Markham?" He paused. "Stay out of my way."

Then he spoke into thin air as he'd been doing all morning. "Harlequin, this is Demon Slayer. Where's that transport you promised me?" His voice sounded as implacable and rough as unpolished granite.

To Dianne's shock, Olivia's voice slid into her ear—tight, breathless, and underlaid with an intensity that made her skin prickle. She couldn't explain how she knew it, but the *sound* whispered things the words didn't say.

"Understood, Demon Slayer," said her sister. "Transport vehicle has gotten caught in a traffic jam on the D410. Can you hold that location until they clear a path to you?"

"Do I have a choice, Harlequin?" Now Ryan sounded grim. As he talked, his eyes scanned the shelves behind the counter in the café where bottles of alcohol stood. Then his gaze snagged Dianne's. "Looks like it's time for some good old-fashioned Molotov cocktails."

Miles Baxter, who'd spent the previous day running NAV teams on defensive maneuvers around the perimeter of the Kastrioti estate, yawned as he filled his coffee cup in the breakroom for the tactical operations center. The Nano Aerial Vehicle technology had become more reliable since they'd first deployed it last fall, especially with the addition of fixed physical anchors that also acted as tuners and amplifiers around the sprawling, mountainous grounds. Now it was just a matter of training the human operators in using the *Elioud* tech, especially the riflemen who'd benefit from the invisible spotters and targeting systems.

Once they'd completed incursion testing and hardened the mesh network that the riflemen relied upon, they'd deploy more of the anchors farther afield, eventually along the borders of Albania itself. Provided that they could recruit enough local operators for the additional NAV teams necessary to operate the expanded mesh network, nothing short of a nuclear warhead would penetrate the Balkan country, even if Mihàil Kastrioti, who defended the border as *drangùe*, died.

Miles had also spent the better part of another shift in the TOC itself, working with his new second-in-command, who'd been a team leader for those same nano drone operators until a week ago. It had been two years since Miles had pulled long shifts in the field as a CIA recovery expert, and he was growing soft if his fatigue was anything to go by.

Or old.

He laughed to himself as he poured a dollop of cream into his coffee and shook his head. He was way younger than that great Hungarian lug András, who'd been born just after World War I, making him nearly a hundred years old. As for Mihàil and Miró, well, those two seasoned *Elioud* warriors were so old they might as well be immortal.

Sweet *Elohim*, Miles was practically a baby at 36. Human or not, he should be able to cover for Ryan Helsing, the Kastriotis' chief of security, whose second-in-command didn't need Miles looking over his shoulder. The silent, capable man listened to Miles's commands and then executed them, often more quickly and effectively than Miles had ordered. Only access to the ops center required Miles's authority.

Miles grabbed some nuts and cheese with which Olivia had stocked the breakroom along with one of the addictive chocolate bars her company made. He liked them all, but this morning he sought out the dark chocolate with purple peppercorns from Vietnam. Despite their name, these tiny berries added a complex, fruity sweetness that reminded him of the three years he'd spent in southeast Asia as a young field operative with the CIA. If he were honest, the flavor of the exotic peppercorns reminded him more of the energy and drive he'd had back then.

He could use a little of both right now, at least until Helsing returned from whatever mission the *zonjë* had tasked him while her husband was distracted strengthening alliances with other *Elioud* warriors along with building up his own network of assets. Although Miles suspected that Olivia had purposefully kept her husband out of the loop, he would never give her game away, not even to the fearsome *zoti*.

But when Miles walked into the TOC a few minutes later, he saw that his discretion no longer mattered. Mihàil knew. And by the looks of it, the *Elioud* commander was pissed. Miles had never seen Olivia so white or trembling. She'd always been a cool customer, even when he'd been chasing her through Disneyland Paris for the Company.

Of course, Miles had to sally into that scenario and deflect some of the ire aimed at her. Olivia was tough and didn't need his help, but he'd give it, even if he didn't owe her for rescuing him from the soul-destroying job he'd had at the American intelligence agency.

"Hey, Boss One and Boss Two," he said, lifting his mug to each of them in turn, Olivia first. "You both look tired. Luljeta keeping you awake?"

He walked to the command desk for the operations center, which belonged to whomever operated as Aerie Actual, and nodded at the junior staff member who'd held operational authority during the graveyard shift. She got up so that he could relieve her as commander.

As operations director, Miles had a small, but swanky, office in the Aerie, the new, uncompleted operations building that Mihàil had ordered built after Asmodeus's *bogomili* had attacked them last December. Miles hoped he'd get to spend more time there than currently, but for now he did all his office work in the ops center.

He set his mug down on the desk and turned to face the power couple. Olivia sat at a corner workstation with Mihàil standing an arms' length away, his expression thunderous. Electricity swirled in the air between them.

Crossing his arms over his chest, Miles looked at each and said, "Okay, out with it. I'm pretty sure you aren't hiding in the ops center from your teething baby. Something must be going on."

Olivia jerked upright a moment later, her eyes widening. She spun in her chair, dismissing them. "Understood, Demon Slayer," she said, an edge in her voice Miles had never heard before. "Transport vehicle has gotten caught in traffic on the D410. Can you hold that location until they clear a path to you?"

That's when Miles caught sight of the monitor behind Olivia, which showed a street-level view of a seething mass of people along a coastal promenade. A dynamic black-and-white graphic overlay showed the distorted harmonics around this mob in stark relief.

"Holy crap! Where's that?" he asked, as if the answer might come with a body count.

He came to stand next to Mihàil, his gaze scanning the various text blocks running along the bottom and right side of the livestreaming video. The GPS coordinates had a text label: Split, Croatia.

The next moment, Helsing's voice came through the TOC's speakers. All of the staff, including the two from the night shift who'd remained working on non-urgent tasks, sat up. Without being told, they knew that their jobs had just moved from routine to battle mode.

"I'm gonna go old school on this one, Harlequin," said Helsing. "Better hope your team reaches me before I run out of Aperol and kitchen towels."

"Get my helo ready," said Mihàil, growling into the pointed silence. "I want Alpha team along for the ride, standard gear and weapons. Wheels up ASAP."

One of the staff said, "Yes, sir," before spinning in her seat while murmuring via the comm system to the flight crew, who'd moved onto Alert status as soon as the *zoti* had walked into the TOC. ASAP was code for five minutes.

Mihàil glanced at Miles, who couldn't suppress the instinctive shiver that raced down his spine at the supernatural glow lighting the *Elioud*'s angelic blue eyes.

"What assets do we have between here and Split?" his commander asked, already heading toward the door.

Behind him, Olivia stood, her gaze riveted to Mihàil's back.

Miles narrowed his eyes in thought. "We've got a couple of teams installing network bollards with day bases in Kastrat and Belaj. There's also Shkodër, which has the prototype truck, but it's up on a lift while diagnostics are being run."

"Miró has a Daemon Buster ready to test," said Olivia aloud, shifting her feet apart and folding her arms across her chest.

Miles knew that they'd already been discussing the *Elioud* tech architect's latest design telepathically. He wasn't surprised when the *zoti* stiffened and halted without turning.

"I can guide it," said Olivia in a stubborn tone that suggested they'd already *disagreed* about using the prototype harmonic missile. "It cleared diagnostics days ago."

"Do as you will," said her husband. "You have already made it clear that my judgment on this matter means little to you."

And saying this, he disappeared. Literally. Miles would never grow used to the supernatural powers his *Elioud* bosses wielded, especially the *zoti*, whose mother was an angel.

Olivia, shooting a cryptic, narrowed glance at Miles, sat back in her chair.

"You've got your orders, Farm Boy," she said, her voice ringing with her authority as the *zoti*'s lady as she alerted him that she'd taken command of the TOC by using his personal call sign. "Get those teams on the road, and work up a plan to extract Helsing. He's the only one standing between my sister and an army of the damned."

"What do you want me to do?" asked Dianne behind Ryan, clearly ignoring his answer about her not doing anything. The panic in her voice had died. "I can help. I tended bar a few summers on the Cape during college."

Ryan refrained from saying that knowing how to mix Cosmopolitans and open beer bottles had little to do with making poor-man's grenades. Instead, he pulled bottles from the shelves and lined them on the counter behind him.

"You're gonna need a larger supply," she said when he didn't answer. "And someone to hand them to you."

"Okay," he said without looking at her as he began ripping towels into strips for wicks. "Grab all of the alcohol there is, the higher the proof the better. After that, check and see if there's a supply in a stockroom or pantry or we'll only have a few bottle bombs."

Not nearly enough to keep the meat puppets at bay. But he didn't say that thought aloud.

"Right," she said. She turned and left his side.

Behind him on the café floor, he heard Germaine panting and muttering. He didn't have the time to focus on her. Through the windows and door, he could hear the multitude of *daemoniacs* outside on the promenade and street from the pier. Despite the glass buffer muting the clamor, he estimated that the most determined individuals would be upon them in ninety seconds.

A familiar icy calm descended. The *Elioud* described it as their battle senses engaging. Even though he didn't have the ability to read harmonics or heat signatures, Ryan had gotten to the point where he could almost envision them.

Today his senses had heightened to an acute edge, slowing his sense of time and lending a clarity to his vision that he'd never before experienced. He knew that he would have time to prep all of the bottles. St. Benedict's Exorcism Prayer chanted through his thoughts as he doused all of the makeshift wicks with vodka before stuffing them into open bottle necks.

Dianne dropped a crate of bottles on the counter next to Ryan's elbow. She began twisting caps from each and sliding them in front of him. They worked in silence, quickly and efficiently assembling a stockpile of simple incendiary devices in the crate.

And then time ran out.

Ryan looked up as the first wave of the doomed swelled on the sidewalk in front of the café.

"Here," said Dianne, handing him a couple of flaming "cocktails," her hands steady, her eyes fierce with purpose.

He hadn't even seen her procure a book of matches or lighter, but he didn't question it. Grabbing each burning bundle, he strode to the door, Dianne at his heels. She unlocked the door, shot him a glance filled with confidence and terror and something else, and then pulled it wide.

Ryan yelled and lobbed the bottles at the feet of the forward attackers, one to the north and the other to the south. They crashed against the pavement, flaring up onto the clothing of the targets. Ryan didn't stay to see any more results. He pivoted and ran back to the counter, where Dianne handed him two more bottles before restocking the crate with half a dozen more and running after him.

For the next thirty seconds, they kept up a steady bombardment. But although individuals caught fire, shrieking and stumbling into their comrades, sometimes even pulling several down as they flailed, the implacable horde kept coming.

Ryan threw the final Molotov cocktail, which hit a tall male in the head. As the target's hair burst into flames, his murderous glare remained locked onto Ryan. He shoved his companions out of the way and rushed toward the café.

Ryan managed to slam the door in his face.

Then the *daemoniac* roared and smashed the top of his head into the glass, sending a web of cracks racing from where his forehead connected.

The creature kept bashing his skull into the reinforced material, blood streaking it as flames engulfed him. Dozens of more *daemoniacs* launched themselves at the windows, their violent battering sending rivulets of breaks and blood along its once pristine surface.

It would be only moments before the glass gave way, and they exploded into the formerly cheerful café with a rank deluge of gore and *daemonic* lust.

The roar of an engine and automatic gunfire cut through the bestial noise. A moment later, a Range Rover plowed through the attackers, pinning some under tires and against the glass. It screeched to a halt with the rear passenger door aligned to the café door.

An armed Kastrioti asset opened the vehicle's door and brandished a combat shotgun, aiming it at them. Ryan pulled Dianne away, and the man blasted the weakened glass door.

"With me," said Ryan, pulling Dianne after him before she could say anything.

She let him guide her to the other man, who pulled her into the SUV. Ryan waited until she'd been seated before pivoting to run back to get Germaine, who'd managed to sit upright, leaning on her elbows. He scooped her up and carried her back to the Range Rover as the driver and the other man shot their weapons from both sides at the undeterred *daemoniacs*, who climbed over each other like rats or insects trying to get into the armor-plated vehicle.

Ryan lunged into the SUV's rear seat, pulling the injured woman onto his lap while yelling, "Go, go, go!" even before he swung the door closed.

A moment later, a massive detonation shook the waterfront promenade thirty meters away. Its blast wave rocked the Range Rover, sending the SUV's rear tires sliding across the pavement. All around them, the possessed citizens and tourists fell abruptly to the ground as if they were marionettes whose strings had been sliced at the same time.

The driver recovered from the fishtail and floored the gas, speeding east on the D410 highway and freedom.

Behind them in the bell tower of the Cathedral of St. Domnius, a one-eyed *daemoniac* stood watching impassively as the reinforced luxury SUV gunned its engines and raced away. The vitreous gel had dried on his cheek, but he'd already forgotten the initial spurt of pain as his eye burst. The human to which the eye belonged had long succumbed to its master's will—a master in the form of a *daemon* who'd withstood the painful harmonics that had overcome his fellow *daemons*.

The same *daemon* who'd engaged the paladin inside a weak female vessel, now broken and discarded like the worthless plaything she'd been.

The *daemon* waited until the Range Rover had traveled beyond the limits of the current male vessel's remaining eye. Then he lifted the cellphone the woman had dropped on the pier, its line still open to someone named Olivia.

Someone powerful enough to wield harmonic weapons the *daemon* had never encountered before. True harmonic weapons, measured, precise, and deadly across distance. Weapons no being with human blood had ever wielded.

Weapons no being short of an angel should *ever* be allowed to possess, let alone wield.

Worse, the *daemon* had sensed the harmonic bond, slender and weak as it was, already formed between the paladin and the woman. The vulnerable woman who had a blood relationship with this supernaturally powerful Olivia. The bond between the paladin and this unshielded woman must not be allowed to become permanent.

Thoughtfully he pressed the call-end button and slipped the device into his vessel's pocket. He had his own powerful weapon that would enable him to infiltrate and poison the fragile human relationship.

And destroy the *Elioud* stronghold from the inside.

Nine

Except for Germaine's soft moaning, silence gripped the interior of the Range Rover, whose acoustics shut out sounds from the engine and road. Or rather, her friend's moaning and Dianne's pounding heartbeat, but she was pretty sure that only she could hear *that*. It amplified Germaine's pain against a rushing background of white noise.

Dianne glanced down at Germaine's thigh on the seat next to her, unable to keep her gaze from the glistening white bone protruding through the flesh of her best friend's bare thigh. Hot acid burned the back of her throat at the sight. She swallowed hard, trying not to get sick. They didn't need the contents of Dianne's stomach spewed onto the SUV's luxury leather while they raced for their lives from the hellish scene behind them.

She dragged her gaze back up and caught Ryan watching her. The myriad cuts on his face had stopped bleeding, except for one high on his cheekbone. Dianne had the insane urge to rise up onto her knees and swipe her thumb across it.

"We'll stop as soon as we're clear of the harbor," he said in a calm, matter-of-fact voice. "Markos has extensive battlefield medical training."

The dark-haired man in the front passenger seat shifted and looked over his shoulder, but Dianne only saw the side of his face. "Don't worry. It looks worse than it is." Despite his reassuring tone, Dianne saw a look pass between him and Ryan. "I'll give her some morphine. She won't feel anything for the rest of the trip."

The driver threw a glance over his shoulder. "How'd it happen?" he asked in a gritty voice, his eyes meeting Dianne's in the rearview mirror.

"One of those—those—" Dianne couldn't bring herself to say *daemon* regardless of the evidence. "He broke it with his hands." She heard the disbelief in her voice.

The driver whistled. "Damn! Know how strong you'd have to be to do that? Her leg's not that big, but the femur is the strongest, densest bone in the body."

Despite his words, he didn't sound all that rattled.

Dianne wanted to scream. Instead, she struggled to push her rising anxiety down. For a moment, it strangled her until she managed to shove it into a hidden well inside her chest she didn't even know existed. Something, a lid, a door, slipped into place and contained it.

She inhaled and looked out the window next to her at the glistening Adriatic. How was it that the sun still shone? Shouldn't it be covered with black swarms of locusts? Shouldn't the cerulean water be transformed into blood red?

Then she looked back at Ryan, who was still watching her. "I suppose this is all just another day on the job for you? You've probably seen worse injuries on the battlefield."

He didn't sugarcoat his answer. "A *lot* worse."

"Are they—those people back there—are they dead?" she asked, her trembling voice barely above a whisper. "The people on the cruise ship, too?"

Ryan lifted a shoulder, careful not to jostle Germaine, whom he cradled within the protective cage of his arms. For a painful moment, acute envy twisted in Dianne, but she squashed it ruthlessly.

"I don't know," he said, a shadow across his gaze that had nothing to do with the glare as they drove east.

"Does that mean you've never seen this—this behavior—before?" asked Dianne, icy terror shooting to the pit of her stomach. In that instant, she realized that she'd unconsciously believed that this massive warrior, who'd saved her life several times in the past twelve hours, knew what they faced and how to overcome it.

"Not in the civilian population, not to this extent, no."

"What happened to those men? The ones in front of the bus station. You know ...." Her voice trailed off. Another thing she couldn't bring herself to say: *the ones who'd been cremated before our eyes.*

"We deployed some gnats," said the driver. "Once those babies lock onto your frequency, you can't shake 'em. But *that's* never happened before. Only time I've seen anyone go up in a ball of fire, one of the *Elioud* laid hands on him. It must be a glitch."

"Or an upgrade," said Markos.

"Whatever," said the driver grinning at the medic. "Would've liked to have some in the Teams. Bin Laden would never've known what hit 'im before he went up in a humongous ball of fire."

"One of them survived," said Ryan in a grim voice. As he said this, Germaine uttered a sharp gasp and moved restlessly, muttering, almost as if she relived her leg being broken in her unconscious state.

Dianne shivered, remembering the cold malice radiating from the ruined visage of the man who'd clearly been the leader. Unlike the others, he'd been completely rational.

And he wanted to kill them.

They stopped fifteen minutes later at a large mall off the highway. It was still early on a Saturday morning in July, so the parking lot was largely empty. Their driver parked the Range Rover in a spot on the far side before he and Markos got out and ran to the rear.

By that time, Germaine had come around and grown vocal. Babbling hysterically, she slapped at Ryan as he opened the door behind him. When he moved to get out, she grabbed onto the SUV's window frame with both hands, her voice rising in a near shriek.

Ryan shot a look at Dianne. "A little help, please. It will go better for her—and us—if she calms down so Markos can take a look at her leg. We can't stay here long."

Dianne nodded. Wordlessly, she opened her own door and stepped down, her knees buckling as her feet touched asphalt. If Markos hadn't returned to take her hand, she would have fallen. As it was, she swayed into him.

"Easy there," he said, smiling down as he steadied her, before leading her to the rear where Ryan had carried the still-writhing Germaine.

Dianne forgot her own unsteadiness as her heart went out to her best friend, who must be in unimaginable agony.

Letting Markos's hand go, she stepped forward and reached for Germaine, who managed to strike Dianne in the face with one of her fists. Her head snapped back, starbursts of light filling her vision. At this assault, Ryan, who'd done nothing to protect himself until now, set Germaine into the back of the SUV before grabbing both of her wrists.

"Enough!" he barked. "We can leave you here in this parking lot with a call to the locals. Or you can get control of yourself and let my medic take care of you."

Germaine responded to the clear note of authority in Ryan's tone. Blinking rapidly, she held her eyes wide and looked around them as if realizing where she was.

Dianne took the opening to step closer and put her hand on her friend's upper back. "Germaine, I'm right here with you. You're safe." She looked at Ryan. "Can you give her some of that chocolate? It'll help, won't it? If nothing else, it'll distract her while Markos does something for her leg."

Ryan shook his head. "Negative. She's in shock. Markos will start an IV to get her fluids. You can have some chocolate and water, however."

Dianne felt a spurt of disappointment. He'd said the chocolate had healing properties. When she'd awakened this morning, all of her injuries were gone, and thick hair had already sprouted on the bald batch.

Ryan directed a pointed glance at the driver. "Barts, get her both." Then he spoke to the waiting medic. "Markos, give the injured woman a morphine shot *now*."

Both men moved with alacrity to follow Ryan's orders. It was clear who was in charge.

Dianne accepted a chocolate bar and a bottle of water before crossing her arms. She watched as Markos pulled out an epidermic needle and administered the powerful narcotic. Almost immediately, Germaine relaxed into Ryan's arms. He and Markos eased her onto her back on the flat area created when the driver folded down one of the third-row seats.

Ryan turned to Dianne. "You need to eat and drink that."

"I will," she said, not taking her gaze from her friend while Markos bandaged Germaine's thigh and the driver started an IV bag.

She felt Ryan shift closer to her.

"I mean it," he said.

"I'm fine."

"Regardless, eat the damn chocolate, Markham." Saying this, he began running his large hands over her shoulders and down her arms.

Sharp irritation shot through Dianne, taking her by surprise. She whirled, forcing Ryan to take a step back.

"I said I'm fine. You're the one who's bleeding." She gestured wildly toward the oozing cut on his cheekbone. "I bet you're black and blue from the way those monsters were beating you."

Her voice broke on *monsters* and began to waver with unshed tears, making her even more irritated. Why couldn't she be as cool and collected as he was?

Ryan dropped his hands and narrowed his eyes. "That's irrelevant, Markham. It's my job to protect you."

"Is it your job to die for me?"

"Yes."

Dianne's jaw dropped. She'd dated men who weren't even willing to compromise on where to sit in a movie theater, let alone risk bodily harm for her. She had no idea what to do with this blunt acknowledgment.

Ryan's gaze traveled to a point over her head. "Go for Demon Slayer," he said.

Dianne sidled closer. For the second time since they'd left the ship, she heard her sister's voice, taut, sharp-edged, and vibrating with the strain of command, in her ear. "Sitrep, Demon Slayer."

She was attempting to parse that foreign word when Ryan said, "Your sister is fine, Aerie Actual. Grimes, however, sustained a full fracture to her left femur. Unless you've got angels on standby, I need a medevac yesterday."

He appeared to listen before responding, "Copy that." Then he looked down at Dianne. "You're in luck. Your brother-in-law will extract us by helicopter. We'll rendezvous somewhere along the highway."

Before Dianne could ask any questions about this astounding bit of news, Ryan gazed over to their local rescuers. Markos had positioned Germaine's injured leg next to her good leg and now wrapped medical tape around both, creating an effective temporary splint from the uninjured leg. Next to him, Barts searched through a large black bag stuffed with dangerous-looking guns. The man felt his commander's gaze and looked up.

"Boss, what's the plan?" he asked.

"We leave in two mikes. The *zoti* brings a team to extract us, LZ forty klicks south. Make sure you secure the cargo. And get me a weapon and plenty of ammo."

"Copy that."

Ryan nodded at the chocolate and water still clutched in Dianne's hands. "Looks like you can take that to go."

Two minutes later they were back in the Range Rover and speeding northeast toward E65, the scenic two-lane highway known as the Adriatic Highway, which followed the mountainous coastline. Dianne had pleaded to ride in the third-row seat next to Germaine's head. Ryan didn't look happy about it, but he nodded and took the second-row seat opposite hers so that she remained in his line of sight. At least he'd let Markos apply some sort of battlefield stitches to his split cheek. It was slightly swollen but blood no longer ran into his beard.

Dianne scarcely noted how quickly they moved among the traffic, but somewhere in the back of her mind she wondered how the world outside could look so normal. Did any of the other vehicles' passengers know what had happened at the port this morning?

It was as if she'd stepped into an alternate dimension where nothing made sense.

After they'd been driving in silence long enough that Dianne's head began to pound, she remembered the water and chocolate still lying in her lap. Although Ryan hadn't yet reminded her to consume them, she'd seen the looks he'd directed at her. They didn't feel overbearing. She didn't know why she thought so, but he radiated concern. It anchored her.

Uncapping the bottle, she drained half of it in one long pull. Her headache eased. She realized that her stomach had also started to ache, from stress and hunger. She opened the chocolate bar, this time a white chocolate scented with lavender. As soon as she smelled the sweet chocolate and delicate floral confection, her headache lifted. She broke off a piece and let it melt on her tongue, closing her eyes with a sigh.

"About time, Markham," said Ryan.

When she opened her eyes, she saw that he watched her, a small smile playing around his beautiful mouth. Why did she want to nestle into his warmth like a cat rubbing against its owner?

At that thought, she said, "Why do you keep calling me Markham? My name's Dianne."

He blinked a few times before responding. Something changed in his posture and expression. The smile disappeared. "Finish the chocolate. We'll be at the extraction point in half an hour."

He leaned forward to talk to Markos and the other guy.

Well, damn. That was pretty clear.

Scowling, Dianne broke another piece of the candy off and slid it into her mouth.

"He's not that into you, girlfriend," said a weak voice next to her.

Startled, Dianne almost choked on the chocolate. Taking a quick sip of water, she wiped her lips and swiveled in her seat to see Germaine watching her. Her friend's pale blue eyes were large in her wan face.

"You're awake!"

"Morphine's good, but I'm sure he underdosed me," said her friend, the scientist. "He doesn't want to overestimate my weight and cause me to stop breathing."

Wincing, Dianne leaned forward and put her hand on Germaine's shoulder. Markos had covered her friend with an emergency thermal blanket and only her head remained visible. "I'm sure he'll give you more once we meet up with Olivia's husband, Mihàil."

A strange light brightened Germaine's face. "He's coming?"

Dianne nodded. "He's apparently got a helicopter and more guys like Ryan." Her gaze slid to the man she'd thought of as The Beast. He still conferred with the other two men. "I have a feeling my brother-in-law isn't just an Albanian businessman."

"That's obvious," said Germaine. She coughed and then grimaced. "Which is why it's a good thing his paid bodyguard doesn't want to hook up with you."

Ryan glanced at them. He wore a frown, but his gaze seemed to look past them. Dianne wondered where his mind was. She looked back through the rear window, uneasiness filling her. Whatever had possessed those people had been directed at *her*. And Olivia had sent Ryan before it had happened, almost as if she'd known.

Suddenly Dianne knew that it was only a matter of time before they were attacked again. She couldn't worry Germaine about that.

"That's fine. I don't want to 'hook up' with him, either," she said, breaking off another piece of the lavender-infused white chocolate. She glanced forward at the others. Would it really hurt to let Germaine suck on a small square? "I'm done hooking up. Nothing like staring death in the face a few times to clarify my priorities."

"Oh, I don't know," said Germaine, her gaze drifting toward the rear window. "It kinda makes me want to live my life to the fullest. That is, if I make it out of this alive."

This jolted Dianne. She leaned even closer to her friend. "You listen to me. You *are* going to make it out of this alive."

As she said this, Dianne didn't know if she wanted to convince Germaine or herself.

Germaine brought her gaze back to Dianne's face. She studied Dianne for several long moments. "Are you sure you can trust Ryan? I mean, if you wouldn't hook up with him ..."

"I trust Olivia. She sent him. That's good enough for me."

"Well, in that case, can I have some of that chocolate?"

Dianne shook her head. "They said you're in shock and can't have food or water."

"Please? Just a square? It smells so good. Plus, my mom always said if you want food, you're not that sick. I promise to let it melt on my tongue."

Dianne sighed.

"I'll trade you," said Germaine, her eyes suddenly bright. "Remember that charm bracelet I got in Dubrovnik? The one that the guy said would bring me good luck? I bought one for you, too. I was going to give it to you for your birthday, but I don't want to wait."

"What? You have it on you?" asked Dianne surprised.

Germaine nodded. "After last night, I thought I should give it to you this morning. It's on my right wrist, next to mine. I'm feeling a little weak. Can you take it from me?"

"Sure."

Now Dianne felt doubly guilty about the chocolate, which she knew was restorative. Reluctantly, she broke off a piece, looking over her shoulder at Ryan.

She sure hoped she wasn't making a mistake.

Ryan braced himself against turning around and interjecting comments into the quiet conversation between Dianne and Germaine in the Range Rover behind him, He didn't want to give Dianne any more information about how well he could hear her. It was almost like she was in his ear, like the *Elioud* or anyone acting as Aerie Actual. It was part of his personal harmonic system design, this built-in frequency that kept him in contact with the ops center.

But only the ops center and his demi-angel bosses.

He shouldn't be able to hear Dianne's voice so clearly. It'd been one of Olivia's stipulations, to which he'd agreed. Tracking her onboard the ship had been one thing; listening in on Dianne's conversations another. They'd agreed that it was an unnecessary invasion of Dianne's privacy. Under the circumstances, he wasn't surprised that Olivia would have enabled it somehow, either via the nanotracker or the enhanced tunic. He just wished she'd warned him.

Whatever Olivia had done, the system was buggy. Germaine's voice had an odd buzzing to it that blurred her words so that they were almost unintelligible. It didn't matter. Ryan still heard her pushing again at Dianne about not trusting him.

Frankly, Ryan didn't know why Markos hadn't knocked the tiresome woman out.

A headache began to push at him. He raised a thumb and rubbed at his temple. He hadn't followed his own order to eat chocolate and rehydrate. He'd been too busy coordinating the exfil with Mihàil and the helo pilot as well as getting a sitrep from Markos and Barts about the *daemonic* activity in the region. He'd eat and drink now. No telling when or where the next attack came from. Whatever *daemon* had launched such a massive assault on them in Split would be rallying his forces. They were literally endless and didn't have to possess human vessels, though by this point in his career with the Kastriotis, Ryan understood that human vessels had tradeoffs. More controllable but less powerful.

He prayed that it would be *daemoniacs* and not *daemons* that he faced. He didn't know if he could take the powerful spiritual beings head on.

He stole a glance at Dianne as he accepted a chocolate bar from Markos.

Despite her hair being a mess and her jeans torn and dirtied, Dianne was unscathed and still heartbreakingly beautiful. Thank God for that tunic. His hand strayed to the St. Benedict medal he wore under his shirt, the pad of his thumb rubbing the engraved image. He'd been one of those battlefield believers he'd told her about. Now he just believed.

If only he believed he was up to the mission.

"That is your first mistake," said Beta in his mind. He didn't know if it was a memory, wishful thinking, or her actually casting the thought into his head. All the *Elioud* communicated telepathically with each other. He'd never heard that they did it with mere mortals, but if any of them could, Beta Nagy would be the one.

Okay, he'd converse, if only in make believe, with the demi-angel whose knife-fighting skills left him in awe. It was a decent distraction from the creeping feeling of imminent attack. But even his harmonic system had gone on the fritz. He saw nothing outside the Range Rover's windows to disturb the serenity of the Adriatic sky.

"What mistake?"

"Doubting" came the acerbic answer, as if the tall Czech *Elioud* spoke into his ear. "*Daemons* use your feelings against you. You don't have time for feelings, not for yourself and definitely not for her. Stick to the mission, soldier."

Ryan almost laughed. Despite his imagination, or maybe because of its lack, Beta sounded like every CO he'd ever had.

Dianne gasped behind him. Retching came a moment later followed by sounds of thrashing.

And an unholy growling and hissing signifying the presence of a *daemon*.

Ten

Miles knew as soon as Beta Nagy walked into the ops center behind him. An invisible shock wave propagated outward from her into the space, which was large enough for twenty personnel. Turning in his chair, he watched her walk to Olivia in the far corner of the room. Where Olivia exuded the confident command of a born leader, the black-haired Czech radiated a tightly leashed menace that always put Miles on edge. It didn't help that he'd seen her transform into a mythical dragon and rip another dragon to shreds. But he'd also witnessed as she vowed love for and fidelity to András, the giant Hungarian *Elioud*, on the battlefield beforehand. Beta was a threat, but she was *their* threat.

The two women conversed for a moment before Olivia looked over at Miles. Taking his cue, he got up from his desk and came over.

"Ma'am," he said, nodding at Beta before giving his attention to his commander, whose tense posture suggested that whatever her friend had told her was anything but good news.

"Beta just spoke with Helsing." Olivia paused, glancing at Beta as if seeking confirmation. The Czech said nothing. Olivia looked back at Miles. "Via harmonics."

She waited while that sank in.

Crossing his arms, Miles studied both women. "I take it you don't mean he used his comms."

Olivia shook her head. "They weren't activated. He spoke to her telepathically."

"What does that mean?" asked Miles, looking back and forth between the two *Elioud*. "Ordinary people can't use harmonics unaided."

"Well, he did," said Beta. She narrowed her eyes. The air vibrated around him, and he caught a hint of heat and ash. "Do you doubt me?"

Olivia ignored her. "We don't know what it means. I sent a message to Miró to see if he can explain it. Regardless, before Ryan's transmission ended, Beta read significant discord in his harmonics."

"A *daemon* manifested nearby," said Beta. "Within three meters." She didn't have to say inside the vehicle.

"One who bypassed the defenses on the transport vehicle. And Ryan's system confirms Beta's assessment. Now we can't raise anyone in the transport vehicle on comms."

Miles looked between the two grim *Elioud*. "The *zoti* is still thirty minutes from Trnbusi." Trnbusi, a small Croat village on the team's route, had been designated as the extraction point.

"Do we have any assets in the area? Any at all?" asked Olivia, a hint of desperation in her voice. "How about the truck? Is it really up on a lift right now?"

She was asking about the Eagle, a prototype truck that had a detachable, two-person harmonically powered helicopter that launched from its bed. It was being built and tested in Kastrioti facilities in Shkodër, a process overseen by Miró's second-in-command, Willem DeVries. In theory, the cutting-edge aerial vehicle could transport its occupants several hundred kilometers within seconds.

In theory.

So far, the test pilots had only flown the little bird fifty kilometers outside of Shkodër in sixty seconds. Still faster than Mihàil's AW139—and that was one of the fastest private helicopters on the market—but Helsing's vehicle was more than 350 kilometers north of the Eagle. The fact that Olivia asked about it underscored the direness of the situation.

Miles considered his answer. "It's on the schedule for test flights today," he said, carefully choosing his words as he considered how to answer her real question. "They planned to extend the range another hundred kilometers."

"So, it's ready to go then?" asked Olivia, her gaze searching his face. He knew her well enough by now to read tentative hope in it.

He nodded.

"Then send it to Helsing ASAP," she said. "Loaded for bear."

"Copy that," he said, pivoting to return to the ops director's desk. It sounded like it was time to say a Hail Mary and hope the Eaglet was ready to fly far from the nest.

Thirty seconds after Germaine slid the square of white chocolate onto her tongue, she started gagging and retching. A foul-smelling foam bubbled from her open mouth. She began thrashing, ripping the IV from her arm in the process and loosening the stretch bandage wrapping her thighs together. In an instant, Dianne understood that if not stopped, Germaine would make her injury worse, maybe far worse.

Then Germaine began hissing and growling like a cornered wild animal.

Dianne unclipped her seatbelt and swiveled in her seat even as Ryan yelled something. The Range Rover leapt forward, throwing her into the rear with Germaine, whose hands had become claws. One managed to scratch Dianne's cheek. It was all she could do to duck her head under both arms as the injured woman struck her with unimaginable force. Somewhere in the back of her mind, she noted that the gossamer jacket she wore radiated an ethereal blue light.

Ryan somehow maneuvered his large body into the rear, shielding Dianne from her crazed friend. She couldn't see well through her hair and watering eyes, but she had an impression that he pinned Germaine under him before struggling to capture the other woman's hands.

The speeding SUV abruptly swerved across the other lane before Barts yanked it back, throwing Dianne against the rear window. She shoved her hair from her eyes in time to see Germaine's head strike Ryan's forearm like a cobra. The other woman bit down, hard.

Before crying out and pulling away as she choked on foam and virulent curses.

Ryan, whose arm bled from the bite, grunted before grabbing both of Germaine's hands. She moaned, whipping her face from side to side, but she was otherwise trapped under his weight and could no longer move anything else. He gripped her slender wrists in one massive hand while his other scrabbled for the med kit next to Dianne.

"What do you need?" she asked, her heart beating so tight and fast it felt like a vibrating golf ball lodged at the base of her throat.

"There's a syringe with droperidol in the kit. You'll have to inject her."

Dianne nodded and turned to lean over the large black utility box that their rescuers had brought filled with medicines, bandages, and emergency medical devices. It took her several tries with shaking hands to open the kit's latches, her heartbeat now a rapid pinprick against her shallow panting. She scanned the contents of the kit, landing on the compartment with prefilled syringes, but as she opened its separate lid, the SUV lurched sideways again, knocking the heavy box on its side and sending its contents across the rear of the vehicle.

A car passed in the other lane, its horn blaring.

"Shit!" she yelled as black started to edge her vision. *Oh, Lord, please let me find it.*

"You got this, Markham!" Ryan's no-nonsense tone snapped Dianne back from the precipice.

Dianne's eyesight clarified and landed on a syringe marked *droperidol.* She snatched it up and removed the protective cap from the rather evil-looking tip.

Twisting, she said, "Where?"

"Her thigh." He shifted backwards to reveal Germaine's legs, his free hand now pressing into one of the other woman's shoulders. "Here. Before she does any more harm."

As Dianne leaned over, her friend began speaking in a deep, guttural voice that crawled over Dianne's flesh. She ignored it and gripped Germaine's uninjured thigh.

"That's nice," hissed Germaine. "You like touching me too, don't you? Yes, you want to stroke me. *Yessss.*"

In shock, Dianne realized that her fingers had started to caress Germaine's smooth skin.

"Markham," said Ryan, again focusing her. "Do it now! It needs time to take effect."

Dianne jerked and plunged the needle into Germaine, who screamed hoarsely before laughing. The sound made the hair stand up on Dianne's whole body.

She looked up at Germaine's face and froze. The other woman's blue eyes had dilated and turned an eerie frosty color. Her lips were an ugly shade of purple, and her fine hair stood away from her head in a static halo.

This new Germaine clamped a hand on Dianne's wrists and lifted her face within inches of Dianne's despite Ryan's effort at restraint. "Wanna party?"

"Dianne!" yelled Ryan, pushing at the levitating woman at the same instant the driver jerked the wheel, sending the Range Rover careening into the vehicle next to them.

Germaine laughed again and continued laughing while their driver struggled to keep the SUV under control and from rearending a truck. Pressure built inside the vehicle's cabin, making Dianne's head pound and her ears ring.

Ryan pulled her from Germaine, who clung to Dianne with a viselike grip totally unnatural to her physical size. When he tugged one of Dianne's hands free, Germaine followed and struck at his side with stiffened fingers. Ryan grunted but only shoved the deranged woman away from them and pulled Dianne into his other side.

Dianne saw blood glistening on Germaine's fingers, from the base to manicured fingertips.

The driver slammed on the brakes, sending all three of them tumbling around the back. The med kit hit Dianne in the head, while Germaine continued to grasp her wrist so hard, she thought her bone would bruise.

"That tunic won't save you, Little One," said Germaine through a sly grin.

The SUV lurched forward.

Ryan hit Germaine in the face. Releasing Dianne, she rolled to the side and vomited. Their vehicle shuddered to a halt once again.

"Helsing!" yelled Markos. "We've got company."

Dianne strained to look outside the Range Rover's cracked front window. What she saw did little to relieve her terror.

An alien machine that resembled nothing more than a stainless-steel dragonfly perched on the highway in front of them, blocking both lanes. As she watched, one of its bubble-like glass eyes lifted upward to reveal a well-built blond man with a chiseled jaw who looked like he should walk a fashion runway instead of an airport one. He stepped out and was joined by a severe-looking woman wearing sunglasses and black clothing from the other side of the weird vehicle. She carried a large black weapon across her body and scanned the highway and mountains around them.

"The calvary is here!" said the driver. "I don't know how they got here so fast."

The medic looked at him, relief easing the tight muscles in his jaw. "Never look a gift horse in the mouth."

"Never, dude."

Dianne felt Ryan relax a fraction, though his visage still showed him on high alert.

"Who is that?" she asked.

He looked at her. She saw a hint of wonder in his gaze. "Willem. He works for the Kastriotis. Looks like he can get you out of here to safety."

A violent mix of emotions cascaded through Dianne, so tangled she had no idea what they included beyond relief and disappointment.

"What about you?" she asked, emotion clogging her throat. "What about Germaine? Whatever that is, it doesn't look big enough to take all of us."

Ryan looked at Dianne, his hazel eyes as hard as granite. Something flickered there that she didn't catch. Instead of answering her, his gaze lasered over her face.

He lifted his chin to indicate her cheek, which burned as if etched by acid. "Did she hurt you anywhere else?"

Dianne shook her head. "No." Germaine's bloody fingers invaded her memory. "What about your side? There's so much blood on her hand from when she attacked you."

"Just a scratch," he said. "Nothing a bar or three of Wise-Herb's finest artisanal chocolate won't fix. Don't worry. I only need half a miracle."

Before Dianne could push against that characterization, the one named Willem engaged the liftgate on the Range Rover and arrowed a no-nonsense look at them. His survey took in the three of them, including Germaine, who'd slumped against the sidewall, unconscious finally.

He locked gazes with Ryan. "The *daemon* won't be subdued long. More are coming."

"I know," said Ryan as Dianne said, "Wait! What does that mean? More *daemons?* Here?"

The black-haired woman, who'd taken up a position not far from the SUV's rear, tensed as she looked back toward the little whirlybird. "Boss," she said, "They're here."

The air around them seemed to electrify, and the sky darkened as if a massive storm approached. A mighty wind buffeted the corridor of the highway caught between low mountains and the coastal plain. The armed woman's long black hair swirled around her head, but nothing else moved. Ethereal blue light sprang around her and her companion in an awe-inspiring halo. A faint answering gleam rose along Ryan's skin, matching Dianne's tunic, which still glowed.

Against the palpable dread threatening to smother them a cavernous voice echoed inside Dianne's head. *You're mine. You've been mine for a long time, Little Girl.*

Darting a terrified look at Germaine, she saw her friend's unnatural gaze fixed on her, malevolence burning the air between them.

Ryan had no intention of meeting his fate crouched inside the rear storage area of an armored luxury SUV. He'd been a Ranger precisely because he needed to face whatever enemy came his way in the open and standing, if possible, not skulking in a tin can.

He wriggled his way to the edge of the vehicle and set his feet on the ground, ignoring the excruciating pain in his side that made it hard to breathe.

"I will take her," said Willem, reaching for Dianne.

Ryan narrowed his eyes and stared at the much shorter—and lighter—*Elioud*, an architect by training and now Miró's right hand in R&D. He might have the advantage of angel blood, but Ryan had a few tricks up his sleeve that would more than compensate in a matchup.

"I misspoke. I defer to you," said Willem, a gleam of amusement flashing in his gaze. He turned back to his companion. "Marta, now."

Ryan glanced at Dianne, whose pale face belied her brave silence. "Put your hands around my neck."

She obeyed without comment.

Cradling her, he braced his thighs against the Range Rover, clenched his jaw, and stood. As he did, Marta activated a harmonic shield that drew on the energies of their modified SUV as well as the prototype helo, turning them into nodes in a larger defensive system.

And not a moment too soon.

A maelstrom of discordant energy slammed into the shield, disgorging a mass of *daemons*, whose gleaming eyes and sharp incisors were the stuff of nightmares and hallucinations. They immediately threw themselves against the shield, completely surrounding the Kastrioti crew and blocking out what little sunlight had remained.

Dianne started and gave a little scream, which she muffled against Ryan.

Tremors raced through the shield's finely woven frequencies and visible gaps began to appear. Ethereal light sprang from Willem's fingertips as he began weaving a complex pattern in the air while chanting something unfamiliar to Ryan. Ryan's harmonics responded, vibrating the drum of his chest.

All around them, sweet music began to swell, pushing against the discordant energy, repairing the fraying harmonic fabric. The other Kastrioti warfighters took up defensive positions around the shield's base, adding energy from their personal systems to its complex harmonics.

The soft blue glow of Dianne's tunic brightened to a phosphorescent white. Ryan glanced down and saw that she now stared at the vile Dark spirits, her mouth open, but her eyes narrowed. She no longer trembled like a rose in a hailstorm. Instead, she sat forward, her spine firm and her chin lifted. Something swelled in his chest as he looked at her.

It was the oddest, yet most comforting, sensation he'd ever felt in his life.

For a long interval, the team's integrated defense expelled the *daemons* and harmonized the shield with the celestial plane. But the *daemons* howled and scrabbled at the glowing barrier in furious hatred so visceral it threatened to choke

Ryan, whose harmonic chainmail had needed retuning and charging after Split. It had failed to protect him already.

He was in danger of failing.

The mission, soldier echoed Beta's voice in his memory.

Ryan lifted his chin and began chanting St. Benedict's Exorcism Prayer. Dianne shifted in his arms, her breasts rubbing his chest, and electricity swarmed through him like a beehive, unexpectedly juicing his harmonics and making his voice husky.

Without being ordered, Markos and the two other Kastrioti warfighters joined him. Their human chant blended in a pleasing counterpoint to Willem's *Elioud* one.

If they hadn't had access to the *Elioud* ability to read and respond to angelic harmonics, which operated outside of created time and space, they would have been caught off guard and sent mad long before they tore each other to shreds. Or worse, possessed by a legion of *daemons* and used in whatever way the Dark spirits wanted.

As they'd used Germaine Grimes.

As they'd do once the shield vanished.

Already Willem's wet face shone, and sweat soaked the underarms of his shirt. He swayed, buffeted by a powerful current, as he maintained the shield's fundamental frequency. He'd likely used a great deal of his *Elioud* power getting the prototype copter to them, and even he couldn't sustain a defense against so much bitter chaos and discord.

It wouldn't be long now. Disordered harmonics had seeped into the space under the shield, which had lightened so much that Ryan could see through it and beyond the *daemons* clinging like locusts to its surface. As far as the eye could see along the narrow highway, a handful of cars had been overturned, and *daemons* infiltrated passengers, transforming them into berserk animals. The temperature had plummeted until the breath of everything living fogged the air, mixed with a mind-numbing cacophony.

Beneath the fraying harmonic mesh, the pressure mounted. Markos wore a desperate expression, while Marta's face had gone blank. But Barts? The driver had a strange gleam in his eyes, the kind of light that didn't portend well for his sanity.

Ryan didn't have time to worry about that. He'd left his gun in the Rover's second-row seat when he'd gone to help Dianne with Germaine, but he needed it. And his backpack, which he'd filled with extra ammo. If he could get Dianne into a nearby vehicle, surely they could leave the others to deal with the few possessed, who'd be drawn to Germaine like flies to honey ...

"I've got to get my weapon," he said, setting Dianne on her feet. "Stay here."

And then Mihàil Kastrioti appeared in a white-hot blaze on the asphalt outside the shield and began ripping *daemons* off it. The *zoti* had near full-angel blood, and since marrying Olivia had become the next best thing to a Watcher Angel walking on earth. The *daemons* shrieked in agony as his hands disrupted what little control they had over the created world, turning them into what he'd described to Ryan as harmonic goo that he could disperse on superheated winds.

Dianne gasped. "Mihàil?"

Ryan ignored her to sprint around the Rover. He yanked open the rear door and reached in to grab the backpack from the far seat and the handgun in its holster from the seatback.

Unfortunately, Barts fell apart at the same time. Pivoting, he ran toward Marta with clawed hands. She, however, still carried the Defender combat rifle she held to ward off any possessed humans who made it into their haven. Turning, she managed a shot before the driver rushed her and grabbed the barrel. And then she engaged him in fierce hand-to-hand combat, her hands wielding the rifle like a club and her elbows striking in a syncopated rhythm.

Beyond them, Markos pulled his own pistol and began firing at *daemons*, a futile act that would leave him without bullets once the shield collapsed.

They didn't have much time.

Mihàil cleared all the evil spirits attacking their joined harmonics as they disintegrated into discord. His preternatural gaze took in the entire scene. Something sparked between him and Willem, who stood panting with his hands on his thighs.

Then the *zoti*'s unsettling gaze landed on Ryan, who'd returned to Dianne's side.

"Get her out of here now, Helsing." *Elioud* authority rang in Mihàil's voice, sending it echoing along the highway, where a small number of possessed humans momentarily milled in the disorienting heatwaves from the *zoti*'s assault. The disordered creatures shrieked as one, their hands going to their ears in a futile attempt to block the sound of their adversary's voice.

Ryan didn't need to be told twice. Grabbing Dianne's hand, he tugged her after him beyond the prototype helo to the sole car, its driver's door open and the engine still running.

Dianne looked behind them and screamed.

Ryan shot a glance over his shoulder, his stride lengthening into an all-out run at the sight.

Mihàil stood, undaunted, as a grotesque, glimmering black ethereal locust towered over him on hind legs thick with hooked, razorlike spurs.

"Abaddon." Fury and disgust roughened the *zoti*'s refined baritone. Beneath his feet, the asphalt smoked. Faint luminous wings rose from his back. "Time to return to your abyss where you belong."

"You are outnumbered, *drangùe*," said the Dark creature in soft, clicking sibilance before jumping on Mihàil, who disappeared inside its rapacious jaws.

Dianne screamed again, but Ryan forced her inside the car and shoved her into the passenger seat before dropping into the driver's side. He slammed the door shut, pulled the gearshift into drive, and then stomped on the accelerator. The little sedan fishtailed, burning rubber as two *daemoniacs* jumped on the hood and trunk, trying to stop them. Ryan, one hand on the wheel, leaned out the window and shot the one on the trunk before grappling with the other, who was only dislodged when he hit the brakes.

Ryan swerved to miss the possessed man, who'd tumbled onto the highway, pressed the gas pedal to the floor, and sped south toward Bosnia-Herzegovina.

The last thing he saw in the rearview mirror was Willem climbing into the back of the Range Rover while Marta unloaded the Defender against *daemoniacs*.

Eleven

As Ryan had anticipated, he and Dianne escaped the ambush on the highway while the diabolical spirits fixated on the others. He refused to think about what had happened to the *zoti*, one of the most powerful demi-angels walking on Earth. And there weren't many. Not nearly enough to protect humanity from the insatiable gluttony of *daemons*.

Dianne said nothing until they'd left the scene far behind.

"Is Mihàil an angel?" she asked, wonder and uncertainty making her sound young.

Ryan dared a glance at her. She looked forward through the windshield with unfocused eyes, her arms crossed as she rubbed them. The gossamer material of her tunic no longer glowed. It seemed too fragile to protect its wearer against the vicious claws and spurs of the *daemons*, who looked like nothing so much as obsidian locusts, gleaming and translucent and exuding a foul miasma of decay and death.

He shoved the memory into the back of his thoughts and looked back at the highway, which remained clear ahead of them. They hadn't even reached Trnbusi when the *daemons* attacked. Should he still head to the extraction point? What had happened to the *zoti*'s helicopter, the one with the QRF team he'd personally trained?

"No, your brother-in-law isn't an angel," he said to Dianne as he tapped his ear to re-engage his comm, but no chirp answered him to signal an active system.

"But I saw wings. And he just *appeared*."

There was *that*. In all of their training, Mihàil had only ever jumped harmonics a maximum of five klicks. The helo couldn't be far. He looked out the windshield, scanning the eastern horizon for the telltale rotors and gleaming glass before answering Dianne.

"His 'wings' are vestigial, more a suggestion than a reality." He glanced over at her again. The wound in his side hurt like a mother. But if he looked at Dianne every now and again, he could keep his vision from swimming. Maybe not remember to breathe, but that was a different issue. "Mihàil is an *Elioud*, a demi-angel. So is your sister."

Ryan wished he wasn't driving. He couldn't really evaluate Dianne's reaction to this news.

"I see." It was clear from her tone of voice that she did *not* see. But her next question caught him off guard. "They found us because of Germaine. She's possessed, isn't she?"

"Yes." He left it at that.

Dianne fell silent for a long while, long enough for Ryan to scan his senses for any connection with his harmonic tactical gear, which had been keyed to his fundamental frequency.

Nothing. It was completely offline.

At the time Miró fitted the custom full-body system onto Ryan, he'd understood the physics well enough, but even so, it was a mystery how his brainwaves interacted with the nanomachinery or how it converted environmental heat, sound, and light into energy to defend against *daemonic* power or communicate with the ops center.

And it was a mystery now whether the invisible network of tiny bots was temporarily drained or whether the *daemon* possessing Germaine had destroyed it.

Mihàil had called their Dark adversary *Abaddon*.

The name gave Ryan the willies. There were legions of *daemons*, lesser angels who'd followed the Dark *Irim* in their perfidy against Heaven. So many that the *Elioud* hadn't bothered to name them all for Ryan and their other human assets.

But everyone had been briefed on Abaddon, the Dark Angel of the Abyss, and his army of Locust *daemons*.

Dianne interrupted Ryan's thoughts. Apparently, she'd also been thinking about the terrifying abomination that had manifested just as they left the battle behind.

"What happened to Mihàil?"

"I don't know."

"What do you mean, you don't know?"

"Just what I said: *I don't know*. Abaddon doesn't normally visit humanity. In fact, he's only mentioned in Revelation as a sign of the End Times."

"Seriously?" She sounded both skeptical and worried.

Ryan shot Dianne another look. She still stared out the front window, but now her teeth worried her lower lip. It was getting harder to focus on both driving and talking—not a good sign. He clenched the steering wheel and sucked in a shallow breath, beating back the black velvet seeping into his vision before answering.

"Look, I know this is a lot to take in. When I met the *Elioud*, I at least had combat experience. And I'd seen a lot of truly evil things, not just watched fantasy versions in movies."

As he said this, Ryan thought of Arly. It had been a serious point of contention between them, this lack of understanding of the grim realities of warfare and man's inhumanity to man. Even if he'd wanted to share some of the nightmares he'd lived through—and he didn't—Arly had never shown an interest in sharing that burden with him. She hadn't seemed to want to share much of anything with him besides his bed and his paycheck, nor help him shoulder any of the burdens of fitting back into civilian life.

To his surprise, Dianne placed her hand on his forearm and gave it a gentle squeeze. "I'm sorry." She sounded sincere.

He glanced at her. Her pupils had returned to normal, revealing the mesmerizing blue of her irises. A sudden desire to protect her from the full knowledge of evil gripped him. But if he didn't deal with his gut wound soon, he'd be in no shape to do anything.

Dianne dropped her hand and turned to look out the side window. "If you don't know what happened to Mihàil, does that mean you haven't heard from anyone?" She looked back at him. "You seem to have some mysterious way to communicate with Olivia."

He shook his head and immediately regretted it. A wave of dizzy weakness washed over him. The car swerved abruptly. Thankfully, this stretch of highway seemed little traveled. Ryan pulled the car back into its lane.

Damn. He must have lost a lot of blood. He hadn't felt this weak since that Russian asshole had shot him last year. Come to think of it, this felt worse.

"Ryan!" said Dianne, her voice rising and sharp with concern. "Are you okay?"

He swallowed. He just needed to hold out until they got to Trnbusi. His sense of time had attenuated, and he couldn't focus on his watch, but surely they didn't have more than another fifteen minutes to reach the extraction point ...

"Just get me some chocolate," he said, shocked at how much effort it took to say that. "It'll be enough ... to keep me going ... until I can make sure you're safe."

The black velvet seeped farther into his vision. Rushing white noise muffled his hearing. Ryan gripped the steering wheel, struggling to keep the highway ahead of them in sight until Dianne pressed chocolate against his closed lips.

He couldn't open his mouth to eat it. Inhaling as much of the spicy-sweet scent as possible, Ryan jerked the steering wheel toward a field on the side of the road.

He managed to brake and stop the car before surrendering to the smothering dark.

Dianne realized that Ryan had lost consciousness in the same instant the car veered off the asphalt and down a slight incline before the car slowed and stopped at the edge of some low vegetation. Up ahead around a curve in the road, she could make out a small spire on a stone church behind a stone wall. Her heart, which had gotten tired of terror-filled shock, remained steady for the first time in the last hour.

Oh, God above, what should she do now?

First: turn the engine off she told herself.

Dianne reached over and turned the key in the ignition.

Second: put the car in Park.

Dianne lifted Ryan's surprisingly heavy hand from where it had slipped onto the gearshift in the center console before moving the lever into the topmost position.

She let out a breath. Taking it one, small step at a time was the trick. She could do this.

Third: check on Ryan.

Dianne forced herself to look at the large, unconscious male next to her. He was well over six feet tall and broader than any living male she'd ever been this close to save for her brother-in-law, whom she'd only a short while before learned was a demi-angel.

Ryan was clearly no demi-angel. The cut on his cheek and the ugly, oozing bite on his forearm attested to his humanity. And somewhere in his midsection was a hand-shaped puncture wound as deep as a woman's fingers.

Dianne studied Ryan, scanning for evidence that he still breathed, scarcely aware that she held her own breath. After an excruciating interval, she identified regular movement in his chest. Then she could resist touching him no longer.

She extended a tentative hand toward Ryan's relaxed face, her fingertips brushing his beard. She remembered how it had felt against her cheeks. She remembered how it had felt to kiss him. To be kissed by him. His hand had covered the entire back of her head as he drew her closer. She'd felt for the briefest moment as if he would consume her, and she wanted nothing else.

She allowed herself to trace his lips with a feather touch but then sat back, thinking.

They needed to get off this dangerous, if quiet, coastal highway before the *daemons* came looking for them. And she needed to do something about Ryan's injuries, which she now suspected required more than chocolate infused with unspecified healing properties.

Where was Mihàil's helicopter? His wings might not work, but he hadn't arrived in a helicopter either.

She frowned. Ryan had said that they'd meet Mihàil and his team along this highway forty klicks from the mall. A place called Trnbusi. How far was a klick? Surely not too far. And they'd already gone some distance since the plan was made. Maybe the helicopter waited for them a short distance ahead.

Dianne glanced at Ryan. He hadn't answered her question about how he stayed in touch with Olivia. Maybe he wore an invisible earbud tethered to a cellphone in his backpack or pants. She had to find it, but searching his pants' pockets would have to wait.

Kneeling, she reached into the backseat and pulled Ryan's backpack into her lap to search for a phone. Besides half a dozen chocolate bars, a wicked black knife that she almost cut herself on when she unknowingly engaged its release, and a large stainless-steel water bottle heavy with water, the bag held only flat, black cartridges filled with bullets.

In the front pocket, she found a leather travel wallet. Inside, besides an American passport, a credit card, and some cash, there was a worn photo of a beautiful woman with long light-brown hair and the head tilt of someone used to taking selfies. She wore a bikini and shiny lip gloss over a wide smile of bright teeth.

A surge of jealousy clutched Dianne's chest. Who was she? Ryan's girlfriend?

Just then Ryan muttered. Dianne shot a look at him. She needed to get her head in the game, *now*. Shoving the photo back into his wallet, she slid it into the backpack. There was no cellphone or anything that looked like a communication device in the pocket. She'd just have to get Ryan into the passenger seat somehow and drive farther on the highway, hoping that she'd stumble on Mihàil's helicopter or at least find a place to stop and get help. She had to trust that the *daemons* had targeted Germaine and that she and Ryan had been collateral damage.

Dianne got out and ran around the front of the car. She tugged and shoved at the unconscious Ryan for a good ten minutes before two preternaturally handsome men in T-shirts and jeans coming from the direction of the church approached their borrowed Volkswagen. Dianne didn't know whether to be thankful or terrified. She decided to be thankful when they asked her something in what she took to be Croatian, motioning to Ryan.

She tried to tell them what she needed in English in case they understood her. Miraculously, they did. They smiled and motioned to Ryan, signaling that they would move him. Dianne shot a nervous glance around the highway but saw no other cars or any sign in the clear-blue sky that a legion of *daemons* amassed above. She nodded and watched as the two men, one on each side of the Volkswagen, moved Ryan into the passenger seat. Dianne, who'd stood with her arms crossed scanning the environment for danger, realized with shock that it hadn't taken them more than a few seconds.

When they'd finished, she asked them about Trnbusi, though she wasn't sure what answer she expected to hear if they didn't speak English. To her surprise, one of the men smiled and gestured back toward the church. Was that Trnbusi? Relief flooded her.

She tried to warn her saviors not to head north, sure that the scene of the earlier attack would still be a mess, but they only smiled again.

One said, "We go to battle evil." And then the other said in a voice that Dianne felt inside her chest, "Dianne, May God bless you many times today."

Dianne's jaw dropped. How did he know her name? She wanted to ask, but her throat closed against the question.

The men smiled again, waved, got into their car and headed north against Dianne's advice.

In the time it took her to get into the driver's seat and look in the rearview mirror, the car carrying the two men had vanished. That's when she noticed that the tunic that Ryan had insisted that she wear glowed softly. Premonition moved through her, but of what, she couldn't say.

Closing her eyes, she inhaled and said aloud, "Please God, help me. I can't do this alone."

She didn't know what else to say or ask, so she put the car in drive, checked over her shoulder, and then backed up until she could pull out onto the highway.

Trnbusi turned out to be a small collection of white-stone houses with red-brick roofs two minutes' drive south of the church. Even though Dianne drove slowly through the village, she saw no helicopter. She had no idea where one would put down anyway.

Ryan did, however, stir enough to groan and open his eyes halfway as they drove through a deserted intersection. Dianne glanced at him, fear spiking at how pale he looked. He'd seemed so strong, so vital on the ship and later during their running battle against *daemons*. Now he seemed smaller and less intimidating somehow, even though the seat barely contained his massive bulk. She wanted more than anything to take care of him, to make sure he was safe and could heal.

"Hey," she said. "How're you feeling?"

"Like I've been hit by a truck. A tractor-trailer," he said, the humor in his voice undercut by its weakness.

He lifted his head to look around. She could see the strain it caused him to do that, something so simple as hold his head upright. He let it relax after only a few seconds and closed his eyes. "Where are we?"

"Trnbusi, but I don't see a helicopter anywhere."

"Guess we'll have to keep going then. How are you to drive? I need a little more time."

"I can drive," she said, studying him. "For as long as necessary. But we have to stop somewhere. You need medical attention, and I don't think it can wait until we get to Fushë-Arrëz. I doubt there's a hospital there anyway."

"Negative. We can't draw attention to ourselves. The *daemons* targeted Germaine and Mihàil, but they would have taken us if they could have. They just didn't have enough human foot soldiers there to throw at us." He paused, inhaling and holding his breath as if he held pain back with it. "You'd be surprised at the state-of-the-art private clinic your sister and brother-in-law funded."

"Do you have a cellphone to call my sister?" she asked, looking back at the empty road, her terror for Ryan warring with her terror about the *daemons* hunting them. "I looked in your backpack but didn't see one."

"In my pants' pocket." His voice sounded weaker. "Just get me some chocolate. I'll contact Olivia once I've eaten it. If we have to drive all the way, we can stop at the Shkodër safehouse for medical supplies. How do you feel about learning how to suture a wound?"

His question ended on a groan.

Panic gripped Dianne. She squelched it. She'd left the chocolate she'd tried to feed him in the center console. Even if it had made her feel better after being battered by vicious *daemoniacs*, she doubted it would dull the pain she'd cause by her clumsy stitching of his torn flesh. But it would certainly calm *her* nerves to give it to him.

In answer to his question about suturing his wound, she said, "About as happy as you sound," as lightly as she could.

Reaching down, she picked up the loose square from the chocolate-paprika bar and held it out to him. He leaned over on another, deeper, groan and held her wrist with shaking fingers while he guided her hand to his mouth.

He stopped midway to look at the ring on her middle finger. "That's an interesting design," he said. "I've never seen a ring with a skeleton key on the bezel of a ring before. It almost looks like it can be used to unlock something."

After he'd managed to get the chocolate square with his lips, Ryan sighed as he chewed.

Dianne brought her hand back to the steering wheel and gazed ahead, though she kept darting glances at him as much as she dared while driving.

They'd driven in silence for several minutes before she finally found the courage to confide in Ryan. "It does unlock something. The key, that is. It unlocks my cousin Emily's diary. I had it made into a ring to remember her. She died when I was sixteen."

"I'm sorry." He sounded sincere.

She looked at him. He also looked less tense and pale. "Thank you."

Before Ryan pulled out his cellphone, they came to a three-way intersection and had to choose whether to go left over a bridge or right around an outcropping of rock. No sign indicated where the latter headed, but Ryan seemed to know where they were.

"Take a right," he said, his voice sounding more normal. "We'll get on the A1/E65 toward Trebinje in Bosnia-Herze-govina. It's a bigger highway, which may be a problem if the *daemons* find us. But now that we've left the others behind, I think it's a better option."

"Copy that," said Dianne, echoing his earlier response to Olivia as she turned.

Ryan looked over at her, a smile quirking his mouth. "Thanks for helping with the Molotov cocktails back there in Split. We make a good team."

Dianne couldn't believe how good it felt to hear that. "I knew those long hours bartending in college would pay off eventually," she said, grinning at him.

"I guess facing a bar lined with drunken frat boys isn't too different from facing a line of *jihadis*," he said, humor clear in his tone. "They come in hot and take shots at a beautiful woman who's captive behind the bar. You probably got pretty good at defending yourself."

Beautiful woman. He thought she was beautiful. Now she felt downright giddy.

"More like drunken dads and husbands on vacation with their families," she said. "But yeah, I learned a few moves, starting with befriending the bouncer."

"Bet he expected a little quid pro quo for his services," said Ryan, his voice rough with something more than annoyance. Jealousy, Dianne realized, and she latched onto it.

She shot a glance at him, trying to see if her read of him was right. He was staring out the windshield, his jaw clamped, and his eyes narrowed. His clenched hand on his thigh told its own story. He didn't look like he was going to pass out again any time soon.

"What if he had?" she asked.

He looked at her, his eyes still narrowed. "That's not part of the job," he said, his jaw muscles working. "It makes him worse than the guys hitting on you. It makes him a bully and a manipulative asshole who uses women for sex."

"I never said the bouncer propositioned me or that I took him up on it," she said, holding his gaze, but her heart was pounding. His observation came way too close to describing her cousin Emily's ex-boyfriend. "He didn't, by the way."

"Not my business." Ryan looked away, but Dianne noticed that his hand unclenched and his battlefield glare disappeared. But then he looked back at her and said, "If he had, I'd beat the shit out of him if I ever met him."

"Good to know," she said, secretly pleased. She was also convinced that Ryan would be more than a match for the bouncer, who'd been large but soft and pudgy.

No guy had ever threatened physical violence on her behalf, but she realized she liked the idea of having her own personal defender. Too bad it had to end once they reached her sister's house in Fushë-Arrëz.

Or did it? She decided to see how he'd react to her next words. It wasn't the kind of thing you told someone over cocktails. But something about the way he looked at her—quiet, steady, no trace of amusement—made her want to try. Just to see if he'd flinch ... or lean closer.

She took a breath before saying, "Better than you beating the shit out of me." She used his words on purpose—not as an accusation, but to signal something raw, something she wasn't ready to name out loud.

The change that came over Ryan's features took her breath away. She imagined the lightning in his gaze could strike someone dead. It was in sharp contrast to the granite of his jaw.

When he spoke, his cold voice sent chills down her spine. "Any man who lays hands on a woman is less than a man. A beating is too good for him."

"You'd just love Jai then. He strangled my cousin Emily to death six weeks after she graduated high school."

Silence descended like a thunderclap. Dianne had no idea why she'd dropped that conversation bomb. Maybe it was to quell whatever crazy feelings had started to brew inside of her the longer she was in Ryan's presence.

Finally, Ryan said in a quiet voice, "That explains a lot."

Dianne glanced at him before staring straight ahead, her heart beating so fast she thought it would break out of her chest. She felt vulnerable, exposed in a way she couldn't explain. Somehow Ryan understood her. She said nothing else, and Ryan didn't press her for more.

After several moments, he continued as if she hadn't just unloaded too much information on him—TMI as her friends would say, laughing. "By the way, how did you get me into this seat?"

She glanced again at Ryan, now studying his cellphone. "A couple of guys came along, from the local church, I think, and moved you."

"Lucky for us," he said, giving her a critical look. But he didn't say anything else. Instead, he held the phone up and squinted at the black screen while squeezing his thumb on the power button on the side. The screen remained blank.

"Damn."

"What? Forgot to charge your phone on the ship?"

Ryan shook his head. "No, I never forget that."

He reached back for his backpack, dragging it into his lap before pulling out a black cord from the front pocket. He plugged it into the USB port on the console.

Dianne waited, dread crawling down her back.

Finally, Ryan sat upright. "The battery's not empty. The phone has been fried by the massive harmonic disruption this morning. Looks like we're incommunicado until we get to Shkodër. Better hope we don't cross paths with any *daemons* on the way."

His hard gaze caught and held hers. "Because I'm not exactly up for a firefight."

And saying this, he held up his hand to show her his side where blood had soaked his black T-shirt and pants all the way down to his ankles.

Twelve

Dianne gasped. "Oh, my God!"

"We may need to stop before we get to the safehouse," said Ryan, as though bleeding from deep puncture wounds was an everyday, ordinary occurrence.

"How far is it?" she asked, trying to still the fluttering of her heart before it made her feel sicker than she already did.

He closed his eyes as if thinking took all of his concentration. "Seven hours, give or take."

"You'll bleed to death long before then."

His eyes didn't open. "No, I won't. I trust you. You won't let that happen."

"What do you think I can do?"

"Give me more chocolate, for one thing."

"Chocolate! You've got to be kidding me. You need a hospital, Helsing," she said again.

This time he didn't warn of dire consequences. Instead, he said, "I don't exactly have access to Google maps." He paused, as if speaking took effort. "Might waste a lot of time we don't have trying to locate one."

He paused again. Now he when he spoke, he sounded tired. "And the chocolate *will* help, just maybe not enough to heal me on its own."

"But we have to stop the bleeding. I know that much."

"Of course." He paused, groaning and inhaling before asking, "Got any ideas about how to do that? And call me Ryan. Sounds better from your lips than Helsing."

Dianne wasn't going to honor that, not when she was so scared for him. She shot him a hard look, but he didn't open his eyes to look at her. "Well, *Helsing*, I can give you this magical tunic until we can find a better option. It would at least be something."

She paused to think, which was really hard through her fluttering heartbeat. Ryan started to say something, but she cut him off. "I know you don't want to get off this highway, but there has to be more along the coast. Stores. Pharmacies with bandages."

"How about a kiss?" he asked when she finally finished. "That would make me feel better."

"Not me," said Dianne, but she sounded unconvincing even to herself. She glanced at him. "Don't think your girlfriend would like it, either."

"No girlfriend. No fiancée. No wife."

"Oh." Dianne hoped he didn't hear the spark of joy she couldn't help giving off.

"Or I can do it the Ranger way: strip off my T-shirt, slap it on the wound, and hope you're not too distracted to drive." Now a hint of amusement colored his voice.

That pissed Dianne off. She shot him another glare. This time Ryan watched her. "Is this some kind of joke to you? Are you mocking me?"

A ghost of a smile flitted across his lips. "No. Distracting you. Did it work?"

"No." She clutched the steering wheel and stared out at the large, four-lane highway that they'd just merged onto. But it had, damn him. Now the thought of kissing him and running her fingers over his heavily muscled chest crowded out her worry. "Crap! We've got to pay a toll."

Ryan grunted as he reached into the center console. "Gotta be some change in here. Everyone leaves change in their car for just this reason."

He searched around and brought out some and handed it to her. "There. That should cover it."

She took it. "What about a passport for me? Got one of those in there, too?"

"We'll figure something out by the time we get to border control. That's not for another hour."

"Hm-mh." Dianne let him hear the skepticism in her voice.

They made it through the toll, where a bored-looking worker barely noticed their passing. Something about the mundane interaction made Dianne want to scream. Hadn't this woman heard about the violence in Split at least? Or was it just too far away to matter?

Not to *her*. She'd had the unsettling feeling that someone watched her ever since they'd driven from the ambush. Well, who wouldn't be a little paranoid? What was the saying? *You're not paranoid if they really are out to get you.*

Sighing, she punched the gas pedal until the car jumped forward and began racing down the highway. She wouldn't feel safe until they'd put several hundred miles between them and the port. Maybe not until they'd arrived at her sister's house, which now that she thought about it, had looked like a modern fortress surrounded by mountains.

"That was easy. Now let's look for a rest stop or a place with a parking lot."

Ryan didn't respond, not even a groan or a ridiculous question about taking off his T-shirt.

Dianne looked over at him. He'd slumped against the car door, completely unconscious.

What should she do?

Not panic for starters said a voice in her mind that sounded like her, but a much more confident version. *A guy his size has a lot of blood. He hasn't lost enough yet to die.*

I hope said the other, smaller, terrified part of her cowering in a corner of her mind.

She had to get off the tollway and find aid somewhere.

Ten minutes passed without an exit, and Dianne's palms began to sweat.

Steady, steady said the confident voice, urging her to stay calm. *You know panic never solves anything. It only makes it worse. Ryan's counting on you.*

Up ahead, a large green sign signaled an exit.

Šestanovac.

Please let there be help there said the smaller, normal Dianne voice as she took the off-ramp.

The highway curved all the way around and through a toll station before heading toward a traffic circle. She took the exit across from where she'd entered the circle. After a short distance, the road intersected another, tree-lined street. Although she could see nothing helpful in any direction, her gut told her that taking the right would prove more fruitful.

Her gut was right. Three minutes down the road she saw a small pharmacy. Ryan hadn't moved or made any sounds since losing consciousness, but he still breathed when she checked.

"Be right back," she said as confidently as she could in case he could hear her.

She grabbed his travel wallet with the credit card and cash, which included some euros. Once inside the small, immaculate store, she purchased antiseptic spray, antibiotic cream, cotton swabs and pads, and a plethora of gauze pads and medical tape along with the strongest pain reliever that the pharmacist recommended. Unlike American pharmacies, which had become convenience stores crossed with department stores, the Croatian pharmacy didn't offer any clothing or Dianne would have grabbed some underwear or socks or white T-shirts to stanch the bleeding. No cheap mobile phones with cards, either.

Back outside, she knelt in the driver's seat and pulled Ryan's wet T-shirt from his side. What she saw stopped her cold and made her stomach wrench.

Five deep puncture wounds oozed blood and fluid with every breath Ryan took. Swallowing against queasiness, Dianne forced herself to open the cotton pads before spraying the antiseptic spray over the taut skin of his stomach. She cleaned around the wounds, worried that she would hurt Ryan with her ministrations. But if she hurt him, he didn't show it. Worse, no matter how much she pressed gauze pads against the holes, they continued to bleed.

Dianne didn't know as much about emergency medical treatment as Olivia, who'd trained as an EMT during college. But even she knew that if Ryan continued to bleed, he'd go into shock long before they reached the border. In fact, he could be in shock right now.

She needed something to coagulate the blood. When she'd had her wisdom teeth out as a teen, the dentist had told her mom to give her cool, moistened black teabags because the tea's tannins would help the extraction site to clot.

The pharmacy had a tea section.

Dianne ran back into the pharmacy and grabbed several boxes of black teabags and a few bottles of different juices. Ryan was going to be weak. He'd had nothing to eat except a square of chocolate in the past twelve hours. Juice would be a quick way to get him some sugar.

Dianne had turned and almost left the store when she realized that she could ask an employee the location of the nearest hospital. A young clerk confirmed that it was fifteen minutes away on their route. She took the items and raced back to Ryan. She had no idea what the hospital would think of her improvised first aid, but she had to do everything she could think of to stop the hemorrhaging.

Back at the car, Dianne ripped open a box of black teabags and coated them with antiseptic spray before pressing them into each puncture hole.

Injuries delivered by her best friend.

That's when, she admitted to herself now, she'd known that Germaine was possessed. How else to explain the ability of a hundred-and-twenty-five-pound woman to punch her fingers into a muscular male abdomen?

Not sure she was doing the right thing but reckoning that it wasn't too different from the way the oral surgeon had packed the extraction site of her molars, Dianne pressed another teabag on top of each wound, taping them down with medical tape. When she'd finished, she covered the whole group with a large gauze pad and taped that down, too. The last thing that occurred to her was to pull the seatbelt across his waist to keep pressure on the bandage.

That turned out to be a fiasco, clever though it was.

She had to lean across Ryan's lap and dig around for the buckle, which meant pressing herself into his broad chest. Despite the inappropriate timing for noticing how hard and defined it was, she found her nipples tingling, and as soon as she noticed, she remembered his teasing about removing his shirt. She also had to feel his manhood under her hip, which wasn't something she wanted to be reminded about right now. If he came around with her practically grinding on him, it would be more than a little awkward.

However, while she worked, Ryan didn't flinch or move. This terrified Dianne. She hadn't met a man yet who wouldn't respond to breasts rubbing up against him.

At last, she sat back in the driver's seat and studied the injured warrior slumped in the seat next to hers, the one who'd saved her life more than once. The man who'd declared that he'd die to protect her.

She couldn't—she *wouldn't*—let this larger-than-life man who'd made her believe in heroes and love again bleed to death. Not now. Not now that she'd finally found him.

At that thought, Dianne snapped the seatbelt across her lap, turned on the car's engine, and headed back to the highway going south.

Ryan's awareness slowly returned to Dianne's muttering and an almost-imperceptible motion of the speeding car. His side burned and ached, the pain radiating throughout his entire torso and sending red-hot tendrils along the nerves of his arms and legs. Despite this, everything felt leaden, even his eyelids. He couldn't open them. He'd never felt this weak before, and that alone should have scared him, but he didn't have the energy for it. His head swam. He couldn't even form a rational thought.

Instead, he focused on Dianne's mellifluous voice. At first, he couldn't make out the words, but the sound soothed the fiery pain in his gut like a cool balm. After some vague amount of time, Ryan found himself exploring the connection between his harmonic system and the nanotracker that he'd put on Dianne, the one keyed to her fundamental frequency.

In his mind's eye, it took on a soft, glowing purple hue that revealed a twisted cord of many strands. When he traced it back to his own harmonics, he found to his shock that the threads had started to interweave with his own system in a complex pattern that made it impossible to tell where his frequency ended and Dianne's began. He hadn't experienced this during his short stint as the Kastriotis' chief of security, and he didn't know what it meant. But, right now, when his body hurt almost to his soul, he clutched at the connection as if it were a lifeline.

And slowly, painfully, he beat back the enervation keeping his eyes closed as he imagined pulling himself, hand-over-hand, along the braided cord between them.

"Hey," she said when he looked over at her. "We're almost at the hospital. I found a pharmacy and got directions. It's not far from the highway."

For a moment, Ryan couldn't comprehend the meaning of Dianne's words. All he knew was that he could listen to her voice for hours.

And then he took in the word *hospital*. "No," he said. Or rather croaked. He blinked several times trying to clear the lassitude still fogging his brain. "Not while my system is offline. I won't be able to sense *daemons*."

Even as he said this, he remembered the feeling of being connected to Dianne. That was a good sign. It meant that the *daemonic* attack hadn't blown out the receptors on his harmonics. They were recharging. He'd be able to contact the ops center once they got to the threshold necessary for long-distance communications.

"'Sense *daemons*'? What do you mean? What system?" She glanced over at him, an endearing little line between her brows. "Is that how you talked to my sister before?"

Ryan still felt woozy, but his thoughts had cleared even more as Dianne talked.

"Keep speaking," he said.

"What?"

"Say something else. Anything. Just keep speaking. How long have I been out?"

"Not long," she said. "Just a few minutes, if that's what you're worried about. Long enough for me to buy some supplies and bandage you."

Yup. Her voice sent a little jolt through him, and it wasn't entirely due to their sexual chemistry. That was just physical. This was on the harmonic plane.

Sighing, he shifted in his seat and felt at his side while he answered her. "To answer your questions: I've been equipped with *Elioud* tech that allows ordinary humans to use harmonics—sound and light waves, heat, motion, basically any physical properties that underpin Creation. It's what gives angels their unique powers."

"Okay," said Dianne, clearly trying to understand. "That's what lets you talk to Olivia without a cellphone?"

"Yes, and it's what protects you in that tunic. And gives the chocolate its healing powers." His fingers felt a bulky padded outline beneath a damp section of his T-shirt. "Good work, Markham. You'd make a fine medic."

"Thanks." She didn't sound grateful for the recognition, however. "The rest of the chocolate bar is in the center console along with some juice."

"Copy that."

As Ryan reached for both items, Dianne went on. "You said your system is offline. Does that mean that it's fried like your cellphone?"

Ryan took a large bite of the chocolate before answering. "I thought so, but I've started to get some minor feedback. Normally it's self-charging, but it got so depleted it just didn't have a chance to recharge."

Ryan didn't want to tell her that he thought his system had somehow managed to draw a charge from her tunic. That would be a little too complicated to try to explain, especially as he didn't know why that would be himself, though he suspected it had to do with the nanotracker he'd put on her back on the ship. It might be acting as an amplifier for another harmonic source, namely Dianne. They should have both been overwhelmed in the last attack, but maybe she had a little angel blood like her sister.

He took another bite of the savory-sweet paprika-infused dark cocoa, letting it melt on his tongue and fill his nostrils. It really was deeply, deeply invigorating beyond the expected effects. And it crowded out any lingering desire for Dianne.

"So we just need to keep driving until you can contact Olivia?" said Dianne, interrupting his thoughts. "What happens if we get to the border first?"

"We do what your parents told you." Ryan shoved the remainder of the chocolate into his mouth, feeling energy surging through him as he chewed and swallowed.

"What?" she asked, sounding startled. She looked at him, those mesmerizing eyes of hers making him lose his train of thought for a moment. "Don't accept candy from strangers?"

Reluctantly, Ryan pulled his gaze to the highway visible through the windshield and nodded at the vehicle in front of them. "Look for the helpers, Markham. Look for the helpers."

Dianne hadn't expected the 'helpers' that Ryan mentioned to be a tour bus. She did as Ryan instructed and kept the bus in sight, although it chapped her ass to drive past the exit leading to the hospital. Then again, Ryan seemed better after the chocolate and juice, at least as far as she could tell because he'd apparently used all of his conversation reserve and quit talking to stare, narrow-eyed and clenched jaw, around them.

After half an hour, the tour bus left the highway unaware of its tail and headed toward the small town of Vrgorac. Dianne, who'd stewed in curiosity the entire drive, wondered why Ryan thought that the coach bus would be of any use to them, especially when it turned into a parking lot behind a picturesque white-stone church dominated by a belltower. Another tour bus already sat in the lot, and dozens of people milled around. She parked next to a small gray car filled with four middle-aged women.

"'Meduhgorge'?" she asked, struggling to pronounce the word *Medugorje* written in black letters on the bus's side.

"Medyougoria," he said, correcting her. "It's a pilgrimage site in Bosnia-Hercegovina where the Virgin Mary appeared a few decades ago." He gestured toward the buses. "These faithful tourists are our ticket across the border."

Before Dianne could question him, Ryan opened his door and got out. After grabbing his backpack from the backseat, he bent over with a wince and said, "You coming, Markham?"

Markham. He wanted her to call him Ryan, but he kept calling her by her last name. She wasn't one of his damn soldiers. She wanted something more.

She got out of the car and followed him as he joined a knot of tourists chatting next to a coach bus. By the sounds of their accents, they were American.

Well, that was a good sign. But Dianne still didn't understand how they would infiltrate this group, especially when a tall, middle-aged man approached. But he seemed to think that they were a couple he had on his list and greeted them warmly. Dianne said nothing as Ryan drew her into his injured side, presumably to hide it, and spoke to the guide. Despite her tension, the warmth and strength of his arm around her made her feel safe. Cherished even.

She never wanted that feeling to end.

Twenty minutes later, they boarded the second coach bus with the others and found a seat in the back where they listened to the tour guide describe how the Virgin Mary originally appeared in these mountains to six young believers in 1981. It was only after they'd crossed the border into Bosnia-Herzegovina that Dianne remembered the two men near the church in Trnbusi. Making it past the border without incident sure counted as a blessing in her book.

"Here," said Ryan, who sat next to the aisle. He held out a wrapped bar. "I can hear your stomach. It's been a while since you had anything to eat."

Dianne realized she was hungry as he said this. When had she eaten anything? Right. The mall outside of Split. She accepted the candy, suddenly heartily sick of sweetened cocoa. What she wouldn't give for a hamburger. Maybe once they'd found another car, they could stop somewhere and eat.

Acutely aware of Ryan's thigh pressed against hers, she watched the scenery outside her window as the bus, now in a long line of buses, climbed the mountains to Međugorje.

In the small Balkan city, buses lined the traffic circle next to St. James Church, where countless pilgrims streamed toward an outside space capable of seating five thousand faithful during worship services. Today, the exterior overflowed, even in the sweltering heat of midsummer. More people appeared in the distance like ants, climbing the site of the first Marian visions, known as Apparition Hill, as well as a nearby hill known as Cross Hill.

Perhaps it was the earlier events as well as Ryan's shocking claims that Mihàil and Olivia had angel blood, but something washed over Dianne as they joined the masses of people behind the church. Something that touched her heart as the voice of the second man outside Trnbusi had.

Uneasiness brought her to a halt on a broad paved walk leading away from the church. Ryan, looking down at her, had a wide-eyed expression that looked totally foreign to him. He appeared decades younger under the rough stubble and scattered lacerations. Softer. More innocent.

Dianne reached up and touched his jaw. He placed one large palm over her fingers as their gazes locked. She caught her breath and waited.

Humming so low that she felt it in her bones filled the air around them as people stilled, expectant, gazing toward Apparition Hill. Static electricity danced over her skin and sent her hair fluttering in an invisible current. A palpable sense of raw power permeated everything—an exhilarating yet slightly unsettling sensation, as if every molecule around her vibrated with potential, ready to discharge at any moment.

A sound—not just a sound, but a melody woven into the very fabric of the air—rose, ghost-like, between the stillness and the coming shift. It wasn't music in the ordinary sense, but something older, deeper, rawer, reverberating beneath her skin, threading through her bones. A harmony just outside perception, one that had always been there but never recognized until now.

As the luminous hum swelled, the world *seemed to align around it*, each breath falling into the unspoken cadence. It was his frequency, his essence, wrapping around hers in invisible strands, pulling her toward a truth she hadn't dared to speak aloud.

Ryan's gaze dipped to her mouth. A moment later, he gripped the back of her head and brought his lips to hers. The pressure of his kiss, the warmth of his breath, the tremor of his touch—all of it resonated in sync with that song, a symphony only they could hear. A current rippled through them, electric, harmonic, inevitable.

And then, silence descended as everything using electricity quit working.

Thirteen

For a moment, Ryan couldn't speak. The reserves of his harmonic tactical gear filled to max capacity and spilled over into his very being. The lingering pain from his gut wound evaporated. Wordless, complex music swelled inside his head as he kissed Dianne.

It took all of his willpower to pull away from Dianne. When he did, it felt like he'd ripped his own arm off—with a rusty claw. In fact, ghostly ligaments trailed like ethereal contrails and broken glass tinkled. A faint aura limned his skin and energy crackled around them.

Across from him, Dianne's sheer robe radiated a soft, white glow that bathed her in an otherworldly light. She looked like an angel, too ethereal for this unforgiving and harsh world.

Ryan swallowed, hard.

"We've got to get out of here," he said, his voice rusty.

Confusion tumbled over Dianne's features, mixed with all of the other feelings that Ryan felt himself: longing, desire, hurt, hope, need.

"What?" Her voice sounded husky, vulnerable. She blinked as if half asleep.

A vision of Dianne lying against white sheets, her blond hair mussed and her cheeks pink just like they were now, knocked the breath from him. He wanted nothing more than to take her someplace secluded and make love to her before the world exploded. To anchor this fledgling bond, this perfect and pure bond, between them in the corporeal.

It would be the wrong thing to do. Hadn't he already learned that lesson with Arly? Put a relationship above his duty? In this case, it wouldn't even be that. It would be sex with a stranger. With his commander's sister. He wouldn't do that. He *couldn't* do that. In consummating his desire, he would be seeding its destruction.

He was a Ranger. He would finish this mission or die trying.

That's when he noticed fine, black filaments weaving into the gauzy fabric of the garment, ominous threads that he knew hadn't been there when Miró manufactured it. They didn't seem like added harmonics. In fact, from his untrained eye, it looked like the filmy garment had narrow bands missing ...

He growled to wake them both the hell up and put some distance between them.

Taking a step from Dianne, he said, "We've got to keep going, Markham. I don't know what happened here. My neck's itching. It's like there was a *daemonic* attack without the *dae-*

mons." He scanned the area around them. "These people will be fine. My guess is that it's too much work here for *daemons* when there's low-hanging fruit elsewhere."

"Then shouldn't we stay here?" she asked, her gaze also taking in the crowded plaza where hushed whispers had broken out among the people gathered there. "At least until we find a way to contact Olivia."

She made a good point. Ryan raised a hand to massage the back of his neck. Despite his gut urging him to keep moving, to get Dianne to safety in Fushë-Arrëz, it would pay to learn more about whatever had fully charged his system but knocked out the power at the church. Rudimentary diagnostics embedded in the nanotech had sent him an audio alert that a powerful electromagnetic wave had moved through the area, that in fact everything for at least the surrounding five kilometers—the limit of his system's range—retained an electric charge.

Dianne saw his hesitation. "Just try whatever way you have to communicate with her."

Before Ryan could act on that suggestion, Olivia's voice sounded in his ear. "Demon Slayer, this is Aerie Actual. Come in, over."

Ryan, tugging Dianne by the hand to follow him, tapped his earlobe, initiating his mic. "Go for Demon Slayer."

"Thank God," said Olivia, breaking comms protocol. "Tell me Dianne's safe."

He stopped twenty meters from the outdoor church and any potential listeners. "Dianne's safe. We're in Međugorje. Tell me you registered whatever harmonic event just blew through here, Aerie Actual. It's like we're standing right under the rotors of a Blackhawk."

As he spoke, he watched Dianne, who'd turned away from him while rubbing her palms over her upper arms, as if she were cold. He stepped closer and wrapped an arm around her. He could see gooseflesh on the back of her graceful neck. She shivered and leaned into him. It was like holding a live wire. His heartrate kicked up a notch.

"We registered a geomagnetic flare more intense than ever recorded in human history, Demon Slayer. Blackbird has been trying to identify the precise cause. We're still assessing the scope of the impact, but, so far, our network reports widespread power outages and everything that comes with that."

Ryan swore under his breath. "What about the rest of the extraction team?" he asked, bracing himself for the worst. "It didn't look good, Aerie Actual, but the *zoti* ordered me to get your sister out of there."

"Understood, Demon Slayer. It's why I ordered the helo to evacuate him and Marta from the ambush site. I knew you would keep Dianne safe."

Ryan squeezed his eyes shut and inhaled. He hadn't known until just this moment that the *zoti*'s fate had weighed on him like a ton of bricks. Even so, he'd do it exactly the same way if he had to do it over again.

"Thank you, ma'am, for your faith in me." He paused, afraid to ask the next question. He just prayed that Olivia knew what he really asked. "Casualties?"

"Barts and Markos didn't make it." She said this without inflection or explanation. It didn't matter that they probably killed each other. "Dutchman managed to extract Germaine using the proto-Eaglet, but she's in an induced harmonic coma to stem the damage from her possession. Marta has a dislocated collarbone and various bumps and bruises, but she'll be back for light duty in a few days."

When Olivia didn't say more, Ryan forced himself to ask, "And the *zoti*?"

Olivia cleared her throat. "Mihàil suffered burns over three quarters of his body." Her voice, normally so cool and confident, broke on the final three words. She paused before continuing in a near whisper. "He also lost an eye. We don't know yet if he'll be able to see from the other one."

"Shit." Ryan pulled away from Dianne and started pacing.

A waver moved through the comms' harmonics that he imagined came from Olivia's struggle with her emotions. Yet when she spoke, her voice had returned to its no-nonsense confidence.

"The flare grounded the AW139 and the vehicles we have on site. That's why I need you to get my sister to the safehouse in Shkodër, Demon Slayer. I'm working on getting assets in the area to assist you, but for now, you're on your own. Can you do it, soldier?"

Ryan answered without hesitation. "Hooah!"

"Tell her you're injured!" said Dianne across from him. Ryan looked up, irritation washing through him as he took in her flashing gaze and raised chin. She only folded her arms and glared back at him. "Tell her, *Demon Slayer*. Or you'll have to carry me out of this place. How's that going to work for you?"

"Stand by," said Olivia, who'd clearly heard Dianne's interjection, "while I review your vitals." Ryan didn't have to detail what the *daemon* had done to him through Germaine. It was all there in his gear's onboard diagnostics.

He continued glowering at Dianne and mouthed *Thanks for nothing*.

Olivia returned a minute later.

"*Helsing.*" Now her voice sounded anguished. "Your system shows you received a physical and harmonic injury just before Willem got to you. You've lost a lot of blood, and your diagnostics show significant trauma to the peritoneum and internal bleeding. You won't be able to make it to Shkodër without medical attention. In fact, I don't know how you're still conscious."

"It's nothing that your chocolate and some bandages can't handle until we get to the safehouse," he said, practically growling it. "In fact, the flare recharged me. Kicked me right back into the fight."

"He's in bad shape, Olivia," said Dianne, riding over his last words. She'd moved up next to him while Olivia spoke and now aimed her voice at his ear. "He could hardly stand up twenty minutes ago."

It seemed her efforts to speak to her sister directly worked. Another surprising ability conferred through their connected harmonics that he'd noted previously.

"Dianne?" Olivia asked in surprise. She sounded taken aback. "Can you hear me?"

"Yes." Dianne shot Ryan a narrowed look. "I've been picking up on words here and there, but after that 'flare' you mentioned, I hear you loud and clear."

Olivia was silent.

Tilting her head, Dianne continued. "Actually, now that I think about it, I hear you in my ear, like we're on the phone. Is that how it sounds to you?"

"Yes," said Olivia again. "What's a mystery is *why* you seem to be connected to our comms. That garment you wear was only calibrated as a local bodily defense against *daemons*, not as a means to receive and transmit audio data. But now that you have that capability, it's clear it should have been included in the tactical design given the current circumstances."

"What should we do?" asked Dianne. She looked over at Ryan, but she didn't seem to see him.

Ryan crossed his arms, listening to this conversation between his commander and his principal. As he did, he scanned their environment. Despite no alarms sounding in his sensors, he couldn't shake the feeling that they were being watched.

Olivia sighed. "As much as I hate to say it, Di, my orders to Ryan are the same. He needs to get you on the road to Shkodër. You two can't stay in one place too long. The flare might have disrupted the *daemons* in its in path, but until we know more, we can't take that risk."

"But—" said Dianne.

"No buts," said Olivia, injecting authority into her voice that Ryan had come to recognize as that of the *zonjë*, the lady wife of a powerful *zoti*. While not impossible to resist, it warned of dire consequences if the target did. "Helsing is a former Army Ranger, little sis. That means he's trained extensively for this kind of mission. If any human can do it, he can."

Dianne started to object anyway. "Olivia, please," she said, anguish twisting her voice. "You didn't see what Germaine did to him." She threw Ryan a tormented look that punched him in the gut. "I managed to get the bleeding to stop, but what happens when—not if—it starts again?"

Olivia relented at Dianne's impassioned plea, softening her tone. "Then all the more reason to get him to the safehouse, Di. There's a triage center, and the housekeeper has emergency medical training. If you care about what happens to Ryan, then make his job easier." She paused before adding, "I'm counting on you."

Ryan watched Dianne, whose open mouth showed how nonplussed her sister's counterplea had left her.

Then he watched her straighten her spine, square her shoulders, and lift her chin.

He recognized the behavior. There always came a moment when an Army Ranger candidate had to step up and accept the call to duty. Only those who did merited the name of Ranger.

"Rangers lead the way," he murmured to himself.

Dianne threw him a glance that told him she'd heard and understood the reference.

She shocked the hell out of him with her answer. "Hooah!" she said, not looking at him.

Ryan smiled to himself.

"That's my soldier," said Olivia, clear approval in her voice. "Find any vehicle still running. I assume you don't have a working phone. Now that your GPS and comms are back online, I'll be your eyes, ears, and all-round den leader. Demon Slayer, how copy?"

"Solid copy, Aerie Actual."

"Good. It's approximately five hours to the safehouse by car from your location. Be advised that you'll have to slip through border control on your own."

Ryan watched the surrounding pilgrims as they began to show signs of growing confusion and panic. Not a time to be armed with only a handgun and a combat knife wearing what amounted to a T-shirt and cargo pants. "Copy that" was all he said, however.

"Let me know when you've acquired a working vehicle, Demon Slayer. If nothing viable presents itself in the next hour, check in anyway. I should have an update for you on the safehouse and available assets in your area. Otherwise, conserve your comms battery."

"Wilco." Ryan stepped closer to Dianne, closing the gap between them.

"And Ryan? Stay frosty." Olivia paused. When she spoke again, she addressed her new recruit: her sister. "Dianne, remember your mission, and try to stay off comms until we understand how they work better. See you both on the other side. Aerie Actual out."

Ryan returned his gaze to Dianne, who watched him surveying the crowd. "Well, then, *soldier*, let's acquire a vehicle before this peaceful gathering turns into a desperate mob."

They moved away from the outside worship space toward the traffic circle in front of the church where buses and cars sat, the occupants standing next to open doors and talking amongst themselves. Multiple people had cellphones to their ears, while others tried to start their vehicles and became increasingly frustrated. Although the emotional temperature among the visitors remained low, it wasn't stable and would degrade if the power didn't return soon. Olivia's report made that seem very unlikely. They needed to get out of here before the nice people got ugly.

Ryan took Dianne's hand. Ignoring her protest, he led her to the street where he scanned the abandoned and unoccupied cars for an older one unlikely to have an electronic ignition.

There! An older model Opel sat a hundred meters down the two-lane highway that led into the center of Međugorje.

"With me," he said.

"Yes*sir*," said Dianne, breathless from the quick strides he forced her to take.

Ryan ignored her sarcasm. He needed to push forward while the flare's effects lasted. He wanted to be in Shkodër before the pain returned.

It was only after it had dissipated that he'd realized just how strong it had been.

The Opel sat unattended, parked against the curb as though the driver worked nearby. Ryan glanced around as he tested the driver-side door handle, on alert. No one appeared, angry and ready to assault him. The car was locked.

Ryan pulled his pack from his back and fished around for his stainless-steel water bottle, still heavy with water. Gripping it tightly, he looked at Dianne.

"You might want to stand back. There by the trunk is fine."

Dianne didn't pester him with any questions, simply nodded and moved to a safe distance.

Hefting the full metal container, Ryan aimed his blow at the corner of the driver's side window above the handle, where the glass would be the weakest. It cracked, sending small pieces onto the pavement. He smashed the bottle a second time, widening the hole.

Ryan stuck the bottle into the backpack before using the bag itself to clear the jagged edges of the glass enough that he could reach in without cutting his hand. He groped around until he found the lock button on the inside of the door. Twenty seconds later, he'd unlocked and opened the door. Thirty seconds after that, he'd popped the hood.

He shot a pointed glance at Dianne, who stood on the sidewalk watching his every move with a predatory focus. Good. He needed her fully present to help.

"Keep a lookout. Copy?"

She nodded. "Copy."

Ryan grinned to himself. He'd take his wins where he could get them.

Pulling his combat knife from his pack, he slid into the Opel. He used the knife to pry the cover from the wiring harness under the steering column. Quickly he stripped the insulation from the power, ignition, and starter wires before twisting the power and ignition wires together.

"Hey," he said to grab Dianne's attention. She stood in the middle of the sidewalk, her gaze sweeping the area around them. At his call, she looked over. "I've hotwired the engine. I'll need you to start it once I've jumped the battery."

"Jumped the battery?" she asked, sounding confused. "How are you going to do that? There's no Triple A around here or any other running vehicles as far as I can tell."

"No need," he said, sliding out of the driver's seat. He felt the bandage loosen and whatever Dianne had pressed into the puncture wounds slip as he moved. "I'm fully charged at the moment. Here, get in."

Confusion washed over Dianne's face, but thankfully she didn't question him again and slid into the driver's seat after he stood up.

"See that stripped wire hanging down beneath the steering column? The yellow and black?"

"Affirmative."

Now Ryan openly grinned at her. "You're a natural, Markham. I'll have to give you a proper call sign. How about Beauty Queen?"

Dianne scowled. "What do you want me to do with this wire exactly, *Helsing*?"

Ryan's grin faded a little. "When I give the go sign, touch the starter wire to the other two wires I twisted together. Those are the ignition and the power, so the car will start."

"Aye, aye, captain," she said, saluting.

Shaking his head while still smiling, Ryan went to the front of the car and opened the hood. His invisible tactical gear, newly recharged by the geomagnetic flare, had the benefit of being electrified during hand-to-hand combat, making it painful for an opponent to hold onto him. When the situation called for it, he could also tase a subject with his bare hands.

A situation such as a dead car battery.

Gripping the battery's positive terminal, he directed a concentrated charge into the electrical reservoir. Then he closed the circuit by placing his other hand on the car's metal frame, which was grounded by its tires. The only trick was not overcharging the battery, or he'd damage it, and they'd have to start over. By the looks of the people around them, they couldn't afford that delay.

Which was another issue. If he used the harmonic energy needed to jump the car quickly, he'd drain his replenished reservoir dangerously.

He chose the exigency of getting out of Dodge over keeping his tactical gear charged. The fight you won was the one you never got into in the first place.

After five minutes of intense electricity coursing through his hand into the battery, Dianne said, "The radio's on!" She sounded excited. "And the dash lights."

"Now's the time to tap that starter wire to the power and ignition," he said.

"Copy that."

A minute later, they were driving down the street with Ryan negotiating a path between stalled vehicles that sometimes took their stolen car up onto the sidewalk. As they made their way out of the small mountain town, Ryan saw more and more unhappy, frustrated people, many of whom began to shout and run after them.

"Lock your door," he said to Dianne, whose wide-eyed stare was glued to the world around them. "And grab the Glock and an extra mag from my backpack."

Dianne darted him a shocked look, but she complied with his order without question.

He took the gun from her and placed it in his lap for easy access. He shot a glance at her but kept driving. "Keep the clip. I'll let you know when I need it."

He switched the radio off. Its scratchy white noise boded nothing good for what they'd find beyond this secluded mountain holy site.

Time to call for ops support. "Aerie Actual, this is Demon Slayer. Over."

Olivia responded so quickly it was clear she'd been waiting. "Go for Aerie Actual."

"Acquired an older model Opel sedan with almost three-quarters of a tank of gas. Got any directions for me?"

"Take the next right onto R425a. You'll be on that for seven klicks. After that I'll have to direct you through various turns. It's approximately a hundred-thirty klicks to the Montenegrin border. Still no local assets to give you an escort, I'm afraid. And I haven't been able to raise the housekeeper in Shkodër."

"Once-in-a-lifetime solar tantrum, and everyone's acting like it's a snow day," said Ryan. Dianne snorted next to him.

Ryan turned right onto the route heading south. Buses, trucks, and cars lined the highway as far as the eye could see. Sweaty people milled around them, some trudging along the edge of the road toward Međugorje. In the rearview, he caught a glimpse of a fight breaking out.

It's started.

"By the way, Demon Slayer," said Olivia, bringing him back to their situation. "Your system shows a rapid depletion of energy, almost like you atomized several *daemon* legions."

"Not quite. Just defibrillated the dead battery."

"Clever."

"I aim to please, Aerie Actual."

"Watch your power reserves, Helsing. We should be able to recharge you remotely once you reach the Albanian border, but until then, you'll have to survive on your wits and brawn."

"Good thing I have plenty of both," he quipped, looking out of the corner of his eye at Dianne, who rolled her eyes.

What Ryan didn't—and wouldn't—say was that a sharp ache had returned in his side.

And blood once again seeped into the waist of his pants.

Fourteen

They crawled toward the border with Montenegro.

What should have taken a couple of hours on a normal Saturday morning in July took closer to four. Not only was the Bosnian highway not well maintained, a myriad of stopped vehicles blocked its twisting lanes through the mountains. Even if Ryan had stolen an old Jeep or whatever passed for a sport-utility vehicle in this part of the world, it wouldn't have helped. At least the vehicles had all died at different points along the way. Dianne pretended as Ryan maneuvered the Opel between them that they played a giant game of Tetris.

She was so busy worrying that the few flushed people trudging along the side of the road among the dense vegetation would become aggressive that at first she didn't notice anything unusual in Ryan's demeanor. It was only as they drifted toward the end of a long line of vehicles signaling the upcoming border crossing that she recognized the white knuckles and in-drawn breath for what they were, pain and not the tension of the trip.

Her glance darted to Ryan's set jaw where a pulse flickered before glancing back to his midsection. It was hard to tell given that the black T-shirt he wore didn't show blood as readily as other colors would have. She couldn't be certain, but she thought that it looked darker and wetter than it had a couple of hours before.

Pressing her lips together, she closed her eyes briefly and prayed for patience. And divine help. Because she had a feeling that things were about to heat up again.

"There's a good chance the crossing isn't staffed," said Ryan without looking at her.

"Are you going to run it?" she asked.

He glanced at her and back out the windshield as he answered. "Yes. I need you to keep your head on a swivel. These people have been out here more than two hours. Those who could walk home already have. Anyone left is hot, thirsty, and ready to jack a moving car." He lifted his chin. "Those two guys outside the blue car up there? They're about to pull us out of ours. We're not gonna let them."

"Copy that," she said, no longer earnest or joking. It just seemed the appropriate response to the man whose leadership was going to keep them alive.

No sooner had she responded than Ryan revved the little European sedan and swerved off the passing lane into the empty northbound lane. Almost at the same time the two men

Ryan had identified turned and sprinted for them, their hands clenched and wild expressions on their faces. The man on the passenger side reached the Opel first.

Dianne's heart lurched, but she remembered at the last moment to flip the door lock even as he grabbed the handle. There was something feral in his eyes as he locked his gaze on her. He actually snarled as the car sped up, forcing him to let the handle go. A moment later, he'd stumbled and fallen, rolling hard on the asphalt.

Ryan, however, hadn't locked his door. The other man managed to get the driver's door open and intermittently hung by its handle, his feet flying over the pavement, and clung to the doorframe as they raced toward the first empty border-control booth. As they passed the small structure, Ryan opened the driver's door wide, smashing the would-be carjacker into it.

Dianne winced at the heavy *thunk* and pained yell that followed. Twisting in her seat, she looked back behind them as the Opel ate up the open highway, free of the line of cars forever waiting in a queue. People streamed across the highway, watching them.

"What will happen to them?" she asked as Ryan swerved the car back into the southbound lane, now clear for the foreseeable distance.

"Some will give up waiting for the power and the police to return and set off on foot for the nearest village or city," he said, looking into the rearview mirror as he spoke. "The rest will realize that something big is happening. Your guess is as good as mine what anyone would do in this situation. If it were me? I'd head to the nearest store, grab some staples, then head into the wilderness to take my chances. I can survive a lot of time hunting and fishing. Long enough to build a secure shelter from which I can reconnoiter the cities and wait for order to be restored."

Dianne settled back into the passenger seat. "You'd do that now except for me," she said, feeling a bit sick at the thought. And scared, for him. She was the one keeping him in danger.

She was also terrified that he'd leave her. She swallowed and gazed out the side window.

"Hey," he said, shooting her a hard glance, "look at me." When she did, he said, "I will never leave you, Dianne. Never. We're in this together. I'm gonna get you to Fushë-Arrëz. Your sister and Mihàil have their own little secure compound with its own renewable power supply and food stores. We can survive a years' long siege or geomagnetic disruption without much hardship."

Dianne, her throat too thick to let words out, nodded.

Had she really been sailing the Adriatic only twenty-four hours ago, drinking cocktails while worried about friendship drama and pining for love?

It was so surreal.

Even more surreal? Finding the man she wanted more than anything at the heart of this mind-blowing situation. Somehow, everything was larger-than-life, including her growing feelings for this remarkable warrior. Feelings that might be a product of proximity. Wasn't it a common trope? A shallow romance that couldn't go the distance growing in the heat of a crisis? She didn't think she could settle for that. It would be worse than any one-night stand, which never promised her heart so much. In fact, they'd never promised her anything.

She glanced at Ryan from the corner of her eye, afraid to look too long and reveal how she felt.

How did he feel? If that kiss was anything to go by, he was feeling the same adrenaline-laden desire she was. But did it mean anything to him? What about the model-pretty woman in the worn photo he carried?

They drove in silence for another hour. Apparently, the highway into Montenegro was little traveled, despite the long queue at the border crossing. Long stretches of empty asphalt opened up before them as the highway snaked through the mountains. Even when they came across cars, by now abandoned, Ryan easily bypassed them. Sometimes they passed individuals and small groups of people walking along the highway. Many waved and shouted, but Ryan drove a wide berth around them, his jaw clenched. Dianne reached over and squeezed his forearm but said nothing. She knew that they couldn't stop to help anyone. Even so, seeing a mother holding a toddler with a slightly older boy clutching at her bag shook Dianne's resolve.

Nothing impeded their progress, not even when the deserted vehicles blocked both lanes. No one seemed inclined to violence, and the *daemons* had receded into the stuff of urban legend and half-remembered nightmare.

Until the highway intersected a larger road at an angle.

Up ahead, several cars blocked the intersection, which didn't have lights or signs, just multiple lanes for merging. Two cars, in the left and right lanes turning onto this new route, had stopped a few dozen feet from the intersection. The car in the right lane had its hood up, obscuring the view of the highway in front of it. In the other lane coming north toward them sat a box truck.

It would be difficult, but not impossible, for Ryan to navigate between these three vehicles given the spacing of the merging lanes, but he would have to slow down. Dianne, even without any battlefield experience, could see that they could be attacked from all sides.

Ryan braked a few feet behind the vehicles on the right. His hand strayed to the Glock where it rested in his lap.

"The roadblock is a trap," said Dianne.

Ryan squinted as he studied the silent scene. "Some-one's watched a few too many military thrillers," he said, "either that, or we've stumbled across a former soldier. I'm betting that there are at least a handful of people in that box truck waiting to jump anyone lucky enough to drive through here. And there are probably people in front of the other two vehicles where we can't see them from here. They may all be armed in one way or another."

"What do we do?"

"Your door still locked?"

"Yes, sir."

Ryan reached down and locked his.

"We run the gauntlet, Beauty Queen."

Dianne pressed her lips together and said nothing to the nickname as Ryan backed the Opel to the edge of the thick stand of trees on their right, a few hundred feet if she had to guess.

"Ready?"

She nodded.

He stomped on the gas. The little sedan fishtailed before pushing off and accelerating toward the open space between the truck and the lefthand car.

They'd reached the trunk of the car when two men stepped out of the box truck in front of them, one wielding a crowbar, the other a wrench. Ryan raised his Glock with his left hand and began shooting without slowing. The man with the wrench dove for the side, hitting the car next to them and rolling over its hood. At the same time, the man with the crowbar swung it at the Opel's windshield, stepping sideways to avoid being run over. The windshield cracked but held.

Two more men materialized in front of their car, each with other tools that they swung with desperate power at the little German sedan. Ryan retained his cool, shooting and steering straight at the men. From nowhere, another man smashed the passenger window. Dianne screamed. He clung to the car using the tire iron as a makeshift climbing hook and began battering the window with his other fist.

Ryan swerved at the intersection, scattering attackers in the wake of their passage, except for the shockingly stubborn man on the right.

"Move," he commanded Dianne as he slowed to shift the Glock to his right hand and the steering wheel to his left.

She ducked an instant before he shot the man clinging to their car. Dianne heard the awful grunt and saw a spray of blood as the bullet pierced their attacker. He fell to the pavement like a sack of potatoes, leaving the tire iron behind. She pulled the impromptu weapon into the car. It could come in handy later ...

A moment later, she sucked in a deep breath as Ryan said, "Good instincts, Beauty Queen."

She scowled at him. "Can you stop saying that? I was never a Beauty Queen. That was Olivia, your commander, by the way. She was All. The. Things. All-State soprano, classical pianist, candidate for the Olympic archery team ... Homecoming Queen whom everyone loved."

Ryan looked at her. He looked pale, tired, and sweaty. "Sorry. Old habits die hard. Nicknames and call signs are just a way of life in the military. Take it as a compliment. I meant it that way. You're turning into a solid team member."

Dianne's heart clenched. She kept her gaze on Ryan's face, afraid to look at his side. "I'm getting hungry and thirsty. I could really go for a bacon cheeseburger right now."

"Cooked medium?" he asked, looking back out the windshield. "With steak-cut fries?"

She nodded. "And onions and pickles and hot sauce."

"And a beer? Sold." Though he played along, Dianne saw the white knuckles of his left hand where it gripped the wheel. "But we'll have to make do with enhanced chocolate and water for now."

Dianne didn't wait for more confirmation but grabbed Ryan's backpack and pulled out the stainless-steel water bottle and another of the chocolate bars, this time one designated the 'Harmony Healing Bar." That sounded perfect. She read the ingredients on the line under the name: cloves, cinnamon, turmeric, and dried Montmorency cherries.

Here's hoping it helps, she thought, handing Ryan the bar and grabbing the last one for her, this time a bar with ginger and dried apricot.

They ate their chocolate bars in silence and shared the water bottle. After she'd finished, Dianne felt a little queasy. It was no surprise. She'd hardly had anything to eat since dinner last night, and the rich cacao of the gourmet candy after all of the adrenaline and fear of the morning didn't sit as well as the white chocolate that she'd sampled before sharing a piece with Germaine.

Who'd gotten sick almost as soon as it she'd tasted it.

Could it have been spoiled?

Maybe you're the one who's spoiled, said a little voice inside her. *These bars have been made by demi-angels with healing properties. Germaine was possessed. Maybe the two don't mix.*

Dianne shivered and shot a glance at Ryan, whose glazed gaze showed how much energy he focused on driving.

"I can drive," she said.

He looked at her. "Might be a good idea," he said. "Give the chocolate some time to work."

He pulled the car over, grinding to a bumpy stop on the side of the road that made Dianne's heart pound. She jumped out and came around only to find Ryan still sitting, the driver's side door open.

"Just taking a moment to catch my breath," he said, sending terror sliding down her spine.

He had to weigh almost a hundred pounds more than her. She'd never be able to get him out of the driver's seat without help or a miracle.

Desperate, she decided to take a drill sergeant's tack, or at least what she imagined a drill sergeant would say.

She put her hands on her hips and, glaring at him, lowered her voice to growl like a drill sergeant. *"No time to rest! On your feet and move!"*

Ryan, whose eyes had started to flutter closed, grabbed the steering wheel and stared at her.

"You're unbelievably beautiful when you yell at me like that," he said, a weak smile turning the corners of his mouth up. It didn't reach the rest of his pale, sweating face.

"You gonna make a beauty queen carry your heavy ass?" she asked, ignoring his comment and her rising panic.

"No," he said, sighing and getting his feet outside of the car and onto the grass of the berm.

Dianne couldn't let up now. "Pain is just weakness leaving your body. Push through it," she said, feeling heartless. *"Rangers lead the way*, huh? Prove it."

Ryan grimaced and pulled himself upright before catching himself on the doorframe.

"You've got this, Ranger," she said, trying a little more encouragement. When he didn't move, she followed inspiration. She lied. "Oh, no! I think they're coming!"

Ryan lifted his head and scanned the area, his eyes narrowed and his posture alert. After a moment he began shuffling around the end of the car with Dianne at his side, her fingers hovering at his elbow but afraid to touch him.

"Clever," he said as he finally maneuvered clumsily into the car and dropped into the passenger seat, but not before hitting his head on the doorframe.

"I aim to please," she said as she shut the door, echoing his earlier response to Olivia. Her heart pounded at his unintentional head injury, but she stuffed it away. There was no time for her emotions.

Hurrying back to the driver's side, she saw the handgun, which had slipped from Ryan's lap to the seat. Throwing a look at the battle-hardened Ranger, now slumped against the side door, she sat on the weapon and slammed her door shut.

As she put the car in gear, Ryan said, "Aerie Actual, this is Demon Slayer."

"Demon Slayer, this is Aerie Actual." Dianne was surprised to hear a male voice on the other end. Who could have taken Olivia's place? "Slow going, huh, Ranger?"

Ryan sighed and shifted painfully in his seat. Dianne saw the strain around his eyes and tight lips before he answered. "You can say that again, Aerie Actual. We may not make it to Shkodër before sunset. Sitrep vis-à-vis the flare damage?"

"We've had scattered reports from assets via the harmonic network. It doesn't look good for most of Europe, though there are some signs that it reaches beyond the continent. We're still scouring the neighborhood for older model vehicles to conscript. And Miró has been assessing the damage to the AW139's starter-generators and electronic components."

"So no Quick Reaction Force extraction?"

"No, not for the present. Your vitals are holding steady, Demon Slayer. You'll have to push on to the safehouse but be warned. We haven't heard from the housekeeper in two hours, not since she went out to help a stranded teammate."

"Copy that," said Ryan.

"Stay off comms unless absolutely necessary to conserve harmonic energy in your system. Looks like you need it."

"Wilco."

"Aerie Actual out."

Silence descended between them, Dianne to her vigilance and Ryan to his injury.

An hour and a half later, they arrived in Podgorica. It was early evening. All of the vehicles they'd passed along the highway had been abandoned, and no more ambushes awaited them. The absolute stillness and silence were eerie, even if the mountain route was never well traveled. When Dianne twisted the power knob for the radio, nothing but static filled the car interior.

What would it look like in a city? Especially at night, without any power.

Ryan read her mind. "We must be prepared for what we're likely going to encounter."

He seemed better after the brief interlude, less pale, though she could smell the warmth of his sweat. It was clean and masculine and layered with a bitter-green herbal scent that she'd started to identify as uniquely Ryan.

"We have to get gas," she said. "We're running on fumes, but I didn't see a gas station before now." She looked around at the widely spaced buildings along their route, many of them single-story cinderblock of indeterminate purpose. "Doesn't look so promising here, either."

"Not a problem as long as we can find some tubing. Know how to siphon gas?" asked Ryan.

"What?" asked Dianne, startled. She looked at him.

He closed his eyes. "Well, we're not going to get gas from a station, not without power. We'll have to steal it from another vehicle." He sounded tired.

Dianne's heart squeezed. "No. I don't know how to siphon gas. I think I saw someone doing it in the movies once."

Ryan sat upright with a grunt. "Never mind. I know how." He gestured with his chin toward a low white commercial building set back from the road coming up on their right. "Should have what we need in there."

Dianne didn't question why they'd find what they needed at a veterinary hospital. She knew enough to know that it would have medical tubing that they could repurpose. She parked next to a dirty van, whose gas gauge showed half a tank through a side window. It didn't matter, though, how much they got in one attempt. Once they had the tubing, they had an endless supply from all of the deserted cars they came across.

When they got from their sedan, Ryan managed it without Dianne's ordering him around like a drill sergeant, but his unsteady gait belied his regained strength. Seeing this, Dianne tucked the gun in the back of her waistband and waited for Ryan, who never asked for the weapon.

Not a good sign.

Ten minutes later, they'd returned from scrounging through the unlit facility, and Ryan bent next to the van as the sunlight faded. Dianne, a sensation of evil creeping over the back of her neck and arms, scanned the empty lot.

After a moment, she slipped the gun into her hands, its warm polymer weight comforting against her palms. Nevertheless, she kept her finger from the trigger, terrified that she might shoot Ryan or herself.

Ryan had the tube in his mouth and had just begun sucking the toxic liquid when a couple dozen people emerged from several stands of trees on either side of the lot. Most carried items, but in the gloaming, Dianne couldn't be sure what those were except when the setting sun glinted on metal. Weapons of some sort, in all probability.

Swallowing hard, she stepped forward to block access to Ryan, raised her hands and said in a loud, confident voice, "Stay back or I'll shoot."

Whether they understood English or not little mattered. They apparently understood the muzzle of a handgun, at least long enough to pause.

And then several of the menacing strangers continued toward Dianne and Ryan.

Four hundred miles west in the Italian city of Prato, Liú Xiù eased from the lengthening shadows that hid her under the Porta Pistoiese and moved along the walls of the medieval monasteries lining the Via San Vincenzo. She touched a fingertip to the small, warm disc hidden under her blouse, praying to its patron to protect her from the lurking dangers.

The power had gone out earlier in the day in the industrial park of Macrolotto di Iolo, north of the Tuscan city's Chinatown, known locally as Santo Beijing. Xiù had felt the invisible energy that rushed through the garment workshop that she managed for her cover as an immigrant owner of a medium-sized clothing exporter.

She'd known right away what it was: an electromagnetic pulse, or EMP, and wondered if a foreign agent had triggered a device to shut down the Chinese clothing industry in Italy—and along with it her operation. Now a rainbow of lights danced overhead in the night sky, and her St. Michael medal burned the skin of her chest.

This was no short-lived, ordinary high-voltage surge initiated by human antagonists.

It was a new era in the far-reaching and consequential war between St. Michael's warriors on Earth and the *daemonic* forces that plagued humanity.

And she was being recalled by her handler, from deep cover as a Chinese spy. Somehow, she must survive this new dystopian situation and find Olivia Markham, the American CIA officer that she'd saved in Macau more than a decade ago.

Fifteen

Miles sat in the nearly empty Aerie, his chin in his hand, lost in worst-case scenarios that felt less hypothetical by the hour. Somehow over the last year since joining the Kastriotis and their merry band of demi-angels and an unbelievable bevy of devoted human assets, he'd started believing that the good guys could actually make a difference in the world without being corrupted first. Hell, he'd had to see more than a few miraculous things in order to believe in the ultimate good in the first place.

Yet Mihàil Kastrioti, the demi-angel commander of this group of *Elioud* defenders of humanity, had seemed indomitable. Now he laid in a hospital bed, a large white patch where his left eye had been and severe burns over most of his body, burns that were worse than those scorched on his epidermis by an enraged *kulshedër*, a legendary seven-headed Albanian dragon once imprisoned by the Archangel Gabriel.

Miles was confronted with the real possibility that what he'd thought was the epic war-ending battle between the forces of Heaven and Hell only six months ago was simply the opening skirmish.

A young subordinate brought him a cup of fresh coffee without being asked.

Miles looked up at her. "Thanks, Greta."

The young Danish woman had been rescued by Mihàil on a business trip and then recognized him as a former European playboy known for socializing with the Danish royal family. Obsessed with him, she'd read up as much as she could online about his life. It was during this self-imposed investigation that she realized that he matched a story that her grandfather had told her from when he was in secondary school and nearly drowned on a holiday in Greece. Her grandfather had believed he'd been saved by his guardian angel.

Greta, intrigued, had staked out Mihàil's hotel and then caught him and Olivia as they attempted to sneak back into their room after an evening of *Elioud* heroics. She'd asked for a job, and the *zoti* had hired her on the spot.

As he watched the self-composed woman return to her ops station where she monitored reports from their network, Miles couldn't help but be a bit envious. If only he'd been as prescient as a young man ... but he could regret nothing because, as the saying went, the Creator writes straight with crooked lines, and, boy, howdy, had his life been filled with some crooked chapters. Yet now he was here working on behalf of the innocent with a squad of demi-angels, trying to redeem himself by writing a whole new book.

For a moment, green eyes in a frightened yet resolute face wavered before his mind's eye. Tadeja had caught his attention while undercover for the Company. Nothing had ever felt as good as taking down the sex-trafficking operation that held her captive. He thought of the young Croatian woman often with a mix of regret and longing. He'd been aware that she'd returned his interest, but he also knew that it was better for her in the long run that he not pursue anything more with her. He'd checked on Tadeja every now and then, and she'd been happy and safe working as a general manager of a high-end resort on the island of Hvar. He hoped she was still safe, but there was no way for him to find out. Their asset network didn't include the island.

Miles pinched the bridge of his nose and took a long, deep sip of the potent brew.

Hot coffee. Sign that the apocalypse hadn't arrived after all.

For a start, it meant they had full power at the Kastrioti estate as well as in Fushë-Arrëz. At minimum, it meant that Mihàil not only got the medical care he needed, but Dr. Armand had been able to layer on additional harmonic therapy with Willem's help. Anywhere else in the world without power after the flare, all those patients in hospitals, in surgery or using life-saving equipment ...

"We will be fine, *bello*," said a husky female voice, its warm tones soothing the aching muscles at the back of his neck and rejuvenating him, despite the late hour and his unending shift. "We have been preparing for the worst ever since Asmodeus set Kôkabîêl free from his underground prison."

Miles looked toward the door of the TOC where Stasia Kos stood with her husband Miró. The diminutive Italian, whose swollen belly attested to how close she was to giving birth to her first child, radiated concern and understanding. On the other hand, her husband's almost-inhuman light-blue stare gave nothing away.

Miles sat upright, his back straight, and set the coffee cup onto his desk. "Ma'am," he said, nodding at her. He looked at Miró, who watched him much as a wolf watched its prey. Miles held the *Elioud's* stare without flinching. "Sir. I didn't expect either of you in the ops center this late."

Miró nodded. "Understood. Given the situation, however, we thought it best to talk to you about the command structure going forward. András and Beta will join us in the conference room in a few minutes for a sitrep and planning."

This wasn't entirely unexpected. Miró, despite running the burgeoning research and development of the new Kastrioti Security Group, remained Mihàil's most senior *Elioud* lieutenant after the *zonjë*. But the Croat needed to get the helicopter and other ground-based vehicles operational. With Helsing in the field on a recovery mission, he would likely be transferring general command of their human forces to András to relieve Olivia, who was exhausted and torn between her nursing infant and wounded husband.

Miles stood and followed the *Elioud* couple to the door of the operations center. As he passed Greta's desk, he said, "Greta, I'll be in the conference room. You're in charge here until I come back. Forward all of the incoming situation reports to the conference-room display so that I can review them with the *Elioud*. If you get time, ask Stefan to go to the kitchen and have something sent up for everyone to eat. I know you missed dinner."

Greta gave a single, sharp dip of her head. "Yes, sir."

As Miles caught up with Miró and Stasia, he caught a secretive smile on the former operative's face. Working around her always unsettled him a bit, as if she understood him better than he did himself.

Inside the room, the large Hungarian sat on one side of the polished mahogany table while his wife paced around the space next to him, an Indonesian fighting knife called a *karambit* flashing between her hands in a deadly display. Miles had long had the impression that she practiced opening and closing the hooked blade of the knife to keep from sinking her own claws into anyone who annoyed her.

When Miles started to head to a seat on the other side of the table, Miró stopped him. "It is your command, Baxter."

Miles halted, his gaze meeting first Miró's and then the other three *Elioud* warriors. Stasia gave him a particularly warm smile. Beta narrowed her eyes and dipped her chin.

When he came to András, the big man leaned forward over the conference table and held Miles's gaze with his hard blue one. "When do Beta and I get to annihilate some *daemons*?"

Miles nodded and moved toward the chair at one end, the seat that Mihàil normally occupied. Then he turned to the curved OLED monitor hanging on the wall behind him—one of several in the large room—where Greta had sent the livestream of the incoming sitreps from their forces and assets in the region. A summary pane presented Greta's analysis of the regional situation following the geomagnetic flare as well as a map highlighting critical incidents within five hundred kilometers. He checked to confirm that his first order wasn't contradicted by any other status before swiveling and pinning the *Elioud* warrior with an equally hard stare.

"Well, Giant, funny you should ask. You and Draka head out as soon as Blackbird can task an operational vehicle. We have two assets, one critically wounded, who need evacuation before that black cloud you see off the Montenegrin coast erupts into a tsunami of *daemons*."

Ryan heard Dianne shouting a warning as he knelt next to the van, one end of a medical-grade rubber hose in his mouth and the other in the van's gas tank. Startled, he inhaled a mouthful of gasoline, causing him to sputter and choke on the poisonous liquid without actually swallowing any.

An instant later, the sound of a Glock 19 firing cleared his momentary confusion. He pulled the tube away and spat the gas onto the pavement under the van before swiveling to see what happened behind him. The movement clawed at his wounded side, sending a wet gush of fresh blood through his sopping T-shirt and a wave of dizziness through him.

Rapid footsteps sounded, followed by another shot, then another. Grunts and the meaty slap of bullet hitting flesh punctuated the unseen action. Ryan gritted his teeth and shook his head vigorously to clear it. When he opened his eyes, he took in two crumpled bodies ten meters away. A third person held her folded arm against her stomach as she bent over one of the fallen figures. In the dim shadows under the trees at the edge of the lot, he caught movement from human-sized silhouettes, like wolves wary of a campfire.

Three bullets, three hits.

"Olivia never said you can shoot," he said, pressing a palm against the van's side to keep from passing out.

"That's because I've never shot a gun before," said Dianne, glancing back at him while keeping the gun raised in both hands, which remained steady. She'd adopted a wide stance and looked like a trained shooter despite her answer.

"Could've fooled me," he said, pulling the slide back and checking the clip. "Though maybe don't shoot near an open gas tank. Sparks, flammable liquids, and all that."

"Oh, yikes! Sorry!"

"Try not to shoot anyone while I finish up here."

"Then hurry. Something tells me I don't have enough bullets for everyone."

"That's when you use the combat knife," he deadpanned, bringing his attention back to the task at hand. "After that, your teeth, maybe some elbows and a headbutt or two."

Despite his attempt at levity, adrenaline hit Ryan's system at the thought that Dianne might be rushed, and he wouldn't be able to protect her. Nevertheless, he ignored his racing heart to return to siphoning gas.

Slow is smooth. Smooth is fast, he reminded himself as he sucked the liquid gas until it rose high enough that he could transfer the end of the hose to the Opel's open tank and then let gravity take over.

The entire time the people in the shadows increased in number, and their muttering grew.

Ryan finished filling their gas tank, spilling extra gasoline under the van as he pulled the tubing from its side. Almost at the same time, the growing crowd spread out along the far edge of the parking lot.

"Let's go," he said. As they slammed their doors shut, he looked at Dianne. "You got the hotwiring? I'll take the gun."

Dianne handed him the pistol using a thumb and a finger to hold the grip. "Please."

"I don't know why you're so skittish. You handled yourself like a pro." Ryan pulled the slide back and checked the chamber as she bent down to twist the ignition and power wires together again. Half a clip. It would do if they got out of here pronto. "I wouldn't have done better."

"Beginner's luck," she said, grabbing the loose wires hanging below the steering column.

"Better hurry," he said, scanning the crowd. His spidey senses as Olivia called them had started to tingle.

Something metallic clattered, and angry voices rose in sporadic shouts. Shoes scuffed the pavement as an uneasy ripple of movement shifted the onlookers.

"Crap!" said Dianne, dropping the wires as a brief spark jumped between them.

Ryan looked back at her. "Slow is smooth, smooth is fast," he said, injecting a calm he didn't feel into his voice.

He surveyed the van through the driver's side window, a thought occurring to him as he focused on the crowd, which had by now divided into two clear groups. Was it chaos? Or something more organized?

Dianne heaved a sigh and grabbed the two wires again, twisting the exposed ends together before tapping the end of the starter wire to the bundle. The engine coughed, the Opel shook, and then the car died.

Ryan caught sight of a tall figure directing the onlookers with two fingers. The first group shuffled toward them as the second one disappeared around the corner of the veterinary hospital. It took only a moment to process what was happening. The second group would continue on around the other side of the building and come out behind the van.

They're flanking us.

Not good. Not good at all.

"Anytime, Markham," said Ryan, aiming the muzzle of the Glock at the ringleader, who like any rat bastard, hung back while the others risked their lives.

"I'm trying, I'm trying." Dianne pressed the starter wire against the combined ignition-power bundle, not dropping it even though it sparked again. The ringleader yelled something at the same time that she said, "I got it!"

Ryan didn't respond. Instead, he shot the ringleader, followed by three other people at the forefront of the first group, which now charged at them. As these attackers fell, those nearest them tumbled over their bodies, throwing the impetuous charge into disarray.

Ryan turned toward the hospital just as the other group emerged from behind the far corner. Dianne threw the Opel into drive and sped away. Ryan waited as long as he dared before rising through the open passenger window and, twisting, firing toward the spilled gasoline under the van.

Three things happened almost simultaneously.

First, Dianne plowed into two of the still-standing attackers, sending one flying over the car's hood and the other into the rest, who'd started to scatter.

Second, the bullet striking asphalt ignited the spilled gas.

Third, the flames rode on the fumes leaking from the open tank, igniting what gas remained.

As they raced onto the nearby street, the van exploded behind them. Ryan watched as the resulting blast threw the fastest attackers a dozen meters and the boiling flames caught the rest. Screams followed them into the night as he sagged into the passenger seat.

He checked the clip in his gun. Empty.

Dianne gave a little whoop. "Holy hell, that was insane. I thought I'd panic, but I didn't. I actually *did* something. I didn't freeze. I didn't fail." She glanced over at him. "That cartridge you asked me to hold is in the door pocket."

"Thanks."

Ryan ejected the spent cartridge and inserted the new one with a concerted effort before looking at Dianne. She looked tired. Yet despite the shadows under her eyes, he didn't think he'd ever seen a more beautiful—or brave—woman, and that was saying something given the *Elioud* warriors he knew.

"Listen, Markham—"

"Dianne."

"Dianne." He swallowed. They'd run out of water an hour ago. His throat was thick, and his mouth burned from the gasoline. "I don't know if I'm gonna make it to the safehouse. I have enough energy left in my system to set an EMS beacon. Someone from the ops center will contact you, give you directions. You keep the Glock until you get there."

He tried to hand the gun to her, but the exertion from their last action had finally drained him as the adrenaline rush faded. The Glock dropped to the center console.

"Ryan!" Dianne's piercing shriek penetrated the descending fog. "You said you'd never leave me. I can't do this without you, soldier. We're a team, remember?"

Ryan closed his eyes. He was more tired than he'd ever been in his life. "You've got this, Beauty. I trust you. Don't stop until you reach the safehouse."

"Do you know why I made the key to Emily's diary into a ring?" she asked out of nowhere.

"Hmnh," he said, not able to formulate the word *no*.

"Because I read it. I read her personal, private thoughts. I saw that she planned to break up with him, that she didn't love him and wanted to date someone else in college, to travel, to major in international relations. I read what she said about their breakup, the fact that he got so obsessed, so mean, so clinging. She thought he was following her."

Ryan forced himself to listen, but it was like he'd taken a narcotic or depressant. He didn't know why Dianne sounded so frantic about something that might as well have been a whole other life ago.

"Why ... are you ... telling me ... this ... now?" he asked.

"Because it's *my* fault! It's my fault that no one knew Emily was scared. They just saw her smiles, her concern for Jai when his mother said he was depressed."

"That's ... not ... your ... fault," he said, taking shallow breaths between words.

"It is! And it's going to be my fault if you die!" She was sobbing. "You can't die. Not now. I need you."

He couldn't stand to hear her sob. He tried to lift his hand, but it was too heavy. It fell against the console with a thud.

Dianne's heart jumped to her throat after Ryan lost consciousness. As panic beat at her, she gripped the steering wheel so hard her fingers ached. Outside, the moonless night seemed all-encompassing. Without intending to, she pressed on the accelerator until the Opel's engine roared, and cool air sent her hair whipping around her face.

Suddenly the highway curved. She barely managed to turn the wheel in time to keep them from smashing head-on into the trees and other foliage that lined the road. Even so, the rough sound of branches scraping the car's side snapped her back to reality.

Ryan didn't stir, however.

"Slow is smooth, smooth is fast," she said, easing her foot up off the gas and forcing herself to breathe more slowly.

She glanced down and saw the Glock where it had landed between her and Ryan, whose large frame had sagged against the passenger door. She picked the weapon up and put it into her lap, as certain as she'd ever been about anything that she'd use it to protect Ryan.

He'd said he trusted her.

"Teamwork means I've got your back, too, Demon Slayer," she said aloud. She wrapped her hand around the gun's grip, the hard polymer too light for its power. It settled against her thigh like a vow.

Somberly, she gazed at Ryan. *No matter what.*

She refused to think about what would happen if she didn't make it to the safehouse soon. If Ryan didn't recover.

Not yet.

The drive to Shkodër in the black night took three times as long as the male voice in Dianne's ear—Aerie Actual—said that it would under normal circumstances. Whoever he was, his no-nonsense tone kept her anchored and determined to get Ryan to safety and help. And he checked in with her in fifteen-minute intervals, sending music through the comms when they weren't speaking that reminded her of the sound-track of an epic movie. It galvanized her.

Dianne drove slowly enough that she didn't outpace the illumination of the Opel's headlights on the winding moun-tain highway. Overhead, faint stars sprinkled against the mid-night-blue sky delineated the outline of the charcoal moun-tains crowding the horizon. Even though she drove with the windows down, she heard nothing beyond the sound of the car. When they passed unlit buildings, their walls briefly illu-minated by the headlights, nothing moved. They could have been driving on the moon for all the signs of life that she saw.

Eventually the tension and Ryan's still form got to Dianne, whose adrenaline waned into exhaustion as the night elapsed. She began to imagine that the sheer white tunic she wore took on a faint, ethereal gleam. Blinking her eyes several times, she succeeded only in seeing ominous ghostly figures on the landscape. Unnatural elongated figures that seemed to keep pace with the car.

"Aerie Actual," said Dianne. The music in her ear cut off.

"This is Aerie Actual, do you have a situation to report?"

"A 'sitrep'?" she asked, trying to inject humor into her ques-tion. Instead, she sounded tired and scared even to herself. "No, just needing to hear a human voice."

"Not a problem. I'm here with you every step of the way."

"What's your name?" asked Dianne, gripping the wheel. "I'm Dianne, Olivia's little sister."

"Yes, I know." The voice paused. "I'm Miles Baxter. I used to work with your sister at the CIA."

"*CIA?*" *That* woke Dianne right up. "Olivia was a spy?"

"She didn't tell you?" Miles chuckled dryly. "It's not exactly Christmas-dinner conversation, if you know what I mean."

Dianne shook her head, half laughing. "It explains a lot."

She went silent, mulling over the craziness of Olivia being a spy. After everything she'd learned and experienced in the past twenty-four hours, her sister working for the CIA seemed as normal as a day at the spa followed by cocktails for her.

"Hey," said Miles, bringing her back to the present. "You're a lot like her, you know?"

"How's that? Olivia hasn't been a damsel in distress waiting for a knight in shining armor to rescue her in her whole life."

"From where I sit, you're the one doing the heroic rescue."

Dianne scoffed but didn't deny his observation. She looked at the creepy ethereal forms that had thickened around the car, turning the night into an oppressive otherworld. Her tunic glowed brighter, almost in counterpoint. At the same time, her heart felt inexplicably heavy, as though an unseen weight pressed against her chest with each passing moment.

Up ahead, buildings clustered. She prayed that it was Shkodër, that the safehouse was just inside the city limits, and there was a medical team there, just waiting to save Ryan.

"Listen, Dianne, we have a team on its way to you. They'll be there in just a few minutes. You just have to keep your head on straight and keep driving, no matter what." Dianne heard a thread of tension in Miles's voice that hadn't been there a moment ago. "Ryan's counting on you. Your sister's counting on you. We're all counting on you."

She could no longer see beyond the car's windows. An impenetrable fog surrounded them now. *He knows about the ghostly figures.*

Dianne felt a chill enter the car. Disembodied fingers began to run over her skin. The charm bracelet Germaine had given her felt cool against her wrist, a sensation that crawled up her arm like a whisper she couldn't quite hear.

"Miles," she said, keeping her voice steady. "Can you teach me St. Benedict's Prayer? The one for exor—"

He cut her off. "Absolutely I will. There are three lines. It starts *crux sacra sit mihi lux.*"

"*Crux sacra sit mihi lux,*" said Dianne. When she opened her mouth to repeat the line, her throat constricted, the words catching as if something inside her resisted. Her voice shook a little, but each word resonated. She imagined eyes and maws pressed against the windshield.

An unholy chorus of whispers filled the car interior, pushing against the words of the prayer. The fog thickened, tightening an invisible noose around her throat. For an instant, the thought skittered through her mind: what if the prayer wasn't enough?

"*Non draco sit mihi dux,*" said Miles, his words clipped, his tone sharpening like steel.

As she repeated that line, her own voice strengthened. Light seemed to emanate around her and Ryan. An answering glow radiated from the pendant he wore, just as it had done last night when the *daemons* attacked on the ship. The beacon pushed the fog back, casting fleeting shadows over it.

The *daemonic* faces sneered in response. The whispers turned to growls and hisses, and the temperature in the car dropped further. Grotesque shadows flickered like smoke around the edges of the light enveloping them.

"*Vade retro Satana.*" Miles's voice hardened into command.

The glow from Ryan's pendant flared higher and brighter with each line of the exorcism prayer, its light weaving into the cocoon around them.

"*Vade retro Satana.*" As Dianne struggled to repeat the final line, the *daemons* writhed and twisted as they breached the barrier of the windshield, their forms rippling like molten shadows. In an instant they were on her, their claws and teeth burning where they touched her skin. A cold, sharp pain lanced through her chest as the *daemons* smothered her, a sensation she couldn't explain but knew wasn't entirely their doing. She jerked the steering wheel, a scream caught in her throat, forcing the Opel's tires to grate across the pavement.

As the unnatural night swallowed them, Dianne braced herself, one thought looping in her head: *Vade retro Satana.*

Without knowing why, she knew what the Latin said.

Get behind me, Satan.

In the silence that followed, the words of the prayer hung in the air like the glow of Ryan's pendant—fragile, yet unyielding, a thin thread of hope against the encroaching void.

Sixteen

B eta saw the flare an instant before András, but only because he'd focused his internal radar on their surroundings in order to identify human threats—necessary as they drove through the benighted city of Shkodër. They'd had to travel in a 1994 Land Rover Defender 110, which Mihàil had bought at an auction of decommissioned NATO vehicles and retrofitted for his personal security while he traversed the poor roads on Albania's mountains. While newer, sleeker luxury SUVs had replaced the faithful Defender, Mihàil's loyal steward and chauffeur, Pjetër, had kept it in pristine working condition. It had started readily with a jumpstart using a portable harmonic generator, but it lacked the modifications with which Miró had outfitted the *zoti*'s current vehicle.

"Five klicks ahead," said Beta, her voice steady as they neared the southern outskirts of the ancient Albanian city in the foothills of the Albanian mountains.

The flare was faint but undeniable—a pulsating burst of energy rippling across the horizon to the northwest. She narrowed her eyes, her *Elioud* sight, enhanced with harmonic googles, teasing out fragmented shapes: twisting shadows clashing against a cocoon of flickering light.

András, who sat in the front passenger seat next to Edvard, their driver, turned his head from scanning their eastern flank to stare into the distance in front of them. "It's them. I recognize Helsing's signature. But we've got to hurry. It's so weak I fear we might lose him. And the *daemons* have nearly gained control of the other signature."

Beta said nothing, just pressed her lips together and squinted out the front windshield, her arm clutching the Disrupter combat shotgun in its sling across her chest. Miró had released the prototype harmonic weapon to her only after he'd caught her liberating it from the armory lab where it had been stored for testing and evaluation. Then again, she'd held his icy gaze until he'd backed down.

But Edvard, her fellow Czech, said what was better left unsaid anyway. "The other signature? That's the *zonjë*'s sister, Dianne Markham, correct?"

András threw a look at his wife and then looked out again at the lightless mass of Shkodër in front of them. "Yes."

Edvard whistled. "We're too late then."

"No, we are *not*," said Beta, exuding smoky-hot air that quickly filled the confines of the Defender. She leaned forward and angled her voice into his ear, barbing her words with the heat of her ire. "And if we are, it will be because you cannot drive."

Edvard visibly shuddered. And then accelerated as if trying to outrun her approbation, the sound of the engine growling loud on the deserted highway.

András didn't look at either of them again, just studied the eerie glow whose dancing shadows resembled a fire that didn't burn. "I read only half a dozen *daemons*." Again, he looked at Beta. What he didn't say this time was for Edvard's benefit: the *daemons* had a signature unlike any he'd ever seen before.

Almost all of Beta and András's speech—or judicious lack thereof—was for Edvard's benefit. The *Elioud* couple communicated telepathically as all *Elioud*, descendants of the Watcher Angels who'd mated with human women in prehistory, could. At least those with more than a drop of angel blood, and usually only those with some self-awareness. Until five years ago, Beta, along with Olivia and Stasia, had had no idea that they owed some of their talents and skills as operatives to their angel blood.

Beta kept her thoughts about what they would find to herself. She knew that András burned with fury at what had happened to Mihàil, who'd been like a father to him, rescuing him as an orphaned twelve-year-old from the brutal attentions of a street gang. But beneath András's fury laid an unsettling and unfamiliar fear. He'd never seen Mihàil so badly wounded. And despite facing one of the condemned Watcher Angels in the form of a seven-headed dragon last December, András feared these unknown *daemons*, whose manifestation had already shut down the world's power.

Beta felt her giant husband's unease but didn't let it affect her. She and the other former Wild *Elioud* had pretty much had a crash course in the hidden war being waged between the forces of the Dark *Irim*, that is, the fallen Watcher Angels, and the *Angeli Fidelis* under the command of the Archangel Michael. András would adapt. And she'd be right at his side, making sure he knew that she was with him all the way.

No, she was worried about Helsing.

Strange to admit that, even if only to herself.

Helsing had stepped in to defend her a year ago, inserting himself into a situation whose complexity he couldn't possibly grasp. But he was not about to let a Russian thug brandishing a gun in a crowded nightclub pistol-whip a woman in front of him. And he'd taken a bullet for his chivalry. Even after that, the former American soldier had been game to join the *Elioud* in their growing engagement with the Dark forces, a fight his heart was more than large enough to handle, but to which his human nature was vulnerable. Over the past year, he'd become the brother she'd never had.

She would *not* let the *daemons* break or take him.

Beta kept her grip steady on the Disrupter, but the flare, an echo of something wicked and corrupt, gnawed at her mind as Edvard navigated through the historic city, its streets littered with dead vehicles and, shockingly, personal items like clothing, shoes, even a doll.

To their west, the leaden mass of Lake Shkodër sucked in the illumination from the night sky like a black hole, sending a prescient shiver down Beta's spine.

The infernal balefire hovering above Helsing's location abruptly extinguished as they left Shkodër.

"Village of Dobraç on our right," said Edvard, glancing at the glowing map on the tablet that one of Miró's techs had mounted onto the dash. "Target appears to be located on the north side of the roundabout for the Shkodër Bypass."

"We've got some unfriendlies converging on them," said András. His hard voice no longer carried the playful tones it had when she'd fallen in love with him. Beta regretted that above else, the curtailment of András's fun-loving spirit during their ongoing war with the Dark forces.

"Like wolves," she said.

Dianne and Ryan's battle with the *daemons* had served as a beacon for nearby humans, the desperate as well as the opportunistic. Both would be dangerous, but how dangerous remained to be seen. Beta's hand drifted from the Disrupter's weight against her chest to the Czech handgun in its rig on her thigh.

"ETA one minute to target," said Edvard, tension tightening his voice. His hands in their tactical gloves clutched the wheel as if he feared control of the sturdy British SUV would escape him.

Beta remembered that he hadn't yet been in the field against *daemons*, just their human proxies.

"The *daemons* are gone, lieutenant," she said, her voice uncharacteristically soft. "You are more than a match for any mangy curs we stumble upon."

Edvard shot her a wide-eyed look. She nodded at him.

András glanced at their young driver, whom Beta had recruited earlier in the year. "Remember your training. The only easy day was yesterday as the Americans say." He shifted in his seat, his large hand where it rested on the dashboard fisting, as if he reminded himself as much as Edvard.

The Defender's headlights penetrated the inky night up ahead as they approached the roundabout. Beta caught a flicker of movement—a human-shaped silhouette darting past the edge of the high-powered beams.

Wolves, indeed.

But when they reached the Opel sedan driven by Dianne, nothing stirred in the night.

Edvard maneuvered the Defender off the highway toward the medium-sized German sedan, which had come to rest in a field to the northeast. It was pitch-dark, a troubling sign after the radiance of Ryan's valiant effort to vanquish the *daemons*. Two signatures inside the vehicle, however, showed that the human occupants lived. One was faint, but the other held steady, if vibrating with minor chords and fraying at the edges from discord.

Beta realized in shock that the weaker signature had keyed itself to the stronger. She looked at András. *You see it, too, do you not?*

I do. His tone was grim.

Edvard parked the SUV twenty meters from the Opel, and the three of them dismounted, switching their helmet lights to covert redlight mode. András gestured with sharp fingers for Edvard to take up position a few meters in front of the vehicle where the young team member set up a tactical light on a tripod. As he did, Beta and András ran to the car's front doors, he to the driver's side and she to the passenger side where Helsing would be.

They waited while their young team member set the infrared sensor to detect any unfriendlies approaching. If anyone got within fifteen meters of their position, the tac light would emit a pulsing strobe of 5,000 lumens in a three-hundred-sixty-degree perimeter as both a warning and a deterrent. It was as much for Edvard as his role guarding their position. The *Elioud* would sense attackers before the much-less-sensitive IR sensor.

"On three, illuminate," András ordered over their comms.

"Copy that," said Beta while Edvard responded, "Wilco, sir."

András counted down, and then Edvard activated the spotlight on the tactical light. The *Elioud* couple also flared, something that occurred spontaneously and often without their control before a battle but that they also employed in certain situations to baffle or disorient.

This was one of those times.

András spoke to Beta alone. *Together, Gomba?*

How else, Spratek?

Since their harmonic signatures were keyed to one another, their timing naturally synced in moments such as these. They moved toward the car as one, each pulling open a door at the same moment. András, whose fists radiated a deadly heat, held no weapon. Beta raised the Disrupter as soon as she swung the door wide. Edvard brought his conventional Czech Scorpion EVO semi-automatic carbine up to his shoulder.

The response that met them shocked Beta. And she wasn't easily shocked.

Helsing's body sagged like a marionette with its strings cut, his breath ragged and shallow as the seatbelt held him roughly upright and inside the small car. Across from him, the blonde rose up with a hoarse cry, lifting a handgun in both hands and aiming at first Beta and then András. She kept the gun trained on András while looking back and forth between the two stunned *Elioud* warfighters.

"Stay back or I'll shoot!" Her eyes burned with a raw, unyielding determination, whether from rage or survival instinct, Beta couldn't tell. Given that her hands didn't shake, Beta suspected that this woman—Olivia's younger sister—had lost any nerves at the prospect of firing the weapon somewhere along the journey here. Either that or defending Ryan meant more to her than her own preservation.

That is very interesting, Beta thought to herself.

"I guess we should have gone to comms to alert them we'd arrived," said András aloud, letting his hands cool as they drifted to his side. His flare retreated until it only limned him.

"Where would the fun be in that?" asked Beta, lowering her Disrupter in its sling on her chest and dimming her own internal light. Ignoring Dianne, who'd shifted at the move, she reached out to touch Helsing's shoulder. "Wake up, Demon Slayer," she said softly, running gentle harmonics over him before slipping them into a support mesh around him. His tactical gear responded with a faint glow.

"What—What are you doing to him?" asked Dianne, a desperate thread now making her voice tremble. Her own gossamer robe also began to glow, further confirming the fact that she and Ryan were tethered harmonically. While Dianne's garment had been keyed for defense against *daemonic* attack, they'd already been surprised by her ability to communicate with the ops center. This—this was something much different, but now wasn't the time to untangle it.

Beta didn't respond. Instead, she focused on Ryan, feeding him some of her energy. She ran hot, like a banked harmonic furnace. Normally, her tactical gear just siphoned off her fiery energy and saved it in power banks, but now she willingly gave a massive boost to the unconscious former Ranger. It wasn't the same as medical intervention, but it would sustain him for the long road ahead.

"How did you hold off the *daemons*?" she asked as András came around to help her free Ryan from the seatbelt and pull him from the car. When Dianne, who'd dropped the Glock she held down to her waist and watched, her mouth opening and closing, didn't respond, Beta looked at her. "It is clear that Ryan did not have the strength to do it."

Dianne looked between Beta and András before settling on Beta, who held her gaze while András took over checking Ryan, now sitting disoriented and blinking under András's careful probing, on the ground next to the Opel.

Dianne inhaled, squared her shoulders, and lifted her trembling chin. "I kept saying the exorcism prayer along with Aerie Actual. It made them very, very angry. I thought I was going to be suffocated. But I just kept thinking it over and over. And then they were gone. You showed up not long afterwards."

Beta, eyes narrowing, nodded. Dianne reminded her so much of Olivia, the operative who'd been instrumental in leading her out of the shadows and into the light with her strong moral compass and compassion. Because of Olivia, she'd eventually confronted her own personal *daemons* and conquered them, leading to love, the kind that only *Elohim* could bestow. Beta considered Olivia more than a friend. She was a sister of the heart.

"Can you walk or would you prefer that Giant carry you?" she asked Dianne, lifting her chin toward her husband, who now pulled Ryan to his feet. She let her enhanced vision scan the pitch-black around them. Something waited just beyond IR range. "We must get moving ASAP."

Dianne shot a wide-eyed glance at András. "No, I can walk." A minute later she was following them back to the Defender, Beta walking behind her. Edvard remained on watch, constantly surveying the limited area revealed by his helmet light.

As they reached the Defender, the air shifted—stale, sour, heavy with intent. Beta's skin prickled as a faint rustle broke the silence, coming closer. Too close.

That's when the now-feral humans attacked.

The tac light's strobe popped up and begin pulsing 5000 lumens in a defensive circle around their perimeter, fifteen meters out. Beta's battle senses clarified, slowing down the sensory input until she'd counted the numbers of attackers.

Fifteen, all males. Two or three hesitated, but the rest seemed undeterred by the bright light.

"Incoming!" yelled Edvard, who to his credit didn't lose his focus at this encounter with desperate people maddened by the loss of light in their world.

As Beta ran to join him, leaving Dianne to mount the step into the SUV alone, the young lieutenant squared his stance toward the closest oncoming attackers and depressed the button on his tactical vest that activated the blinding mode on the tac light. Erratic bursts of 10,000-lumen light arced into their eyes, causing the men directly in front of him to stumble and fall, stunned.

Beta fully flared, her own radiance more diffuse but equally intense. She raised the Disrupter, set on the lowest setting ideal for convulsing the human nervous system, and tagged five more attackers in quick succession. A moment later, András joined the melee, having secured Ryan in the Defender's backseat with a med kit filled with bandages and morphine.

It was a short, fierce fight, but the humans never stood a chance. They were also armed only with fists, pipes, and crowbars. While Beta and Edvard engaged three of the remaining seven between them, András handled the final four, his massive hands steaming in the cool night air as he threw his opponents ten meters in every direction. The air reeked of sweat and desperation, mingling with the tang of ozone from the harmonic bolts. Shadows moved erratically within the strobe's pulsing light, their lunges wild and primal.

One of the men managed to launch himself onto Edvard's back as the young warfighter traded punches with a second man, having dropped the carbine in favor of hand-to-hand combat. The final attacker closed on Beta before she could aim the Disrupter. Instead, she smacked the stock into his jaw, drawing him up short. A moment later, she'd brought him to the ground, choking him out from the rear with the Disrupter's stock. Then she went to Edvard's aid, blasting the man from his back with a well-aimed harmonic bolt.

The whole event lasted less than three minutes.

"Time to bug out," said András, his face shiny within the reduced glow of his harmonics. His shoulders moved as he breathed in, but he was far from panting.

Edvard recovered the tac light and its tripod, which had been knocked over in the chaos while András kept watch for any further incursions. Beta jogged back to the Defender and got in only to see Dianne watching her, the whites of her eyes prominent in her pale face. Sixty seconds later, the male warriors had joined them in the vehicle, and then Edvard had them back on the highway heading south through Shkodër.

"Next time, give me a weapon," said Ryan. His voice sounded hoarse with pain. Beta felt it buzz through his signature like a frayed wire—sharp, stinging, and unstable. "If I'm conscious, I can shoot."

Dianne turned to him. "Like hell you can. You're as weak as a kitten. Stop trying to be a damn hero—no one's impressed when a corpse saves the day."

He looked at Olivia's sister, his principal, with a flat stare that belied his physical condition, which was stable but dire. Then he looked at Beta without responding to the other woman. "I'm good to go, Draka. Give me a carbine like Edvard's." He paused, coughed, then added, "And some water. I inhaled some gasoline in Podgorica. It's making me dizzy."

Beta wondered at this human's willpower. Even now, when his body radiated pain like a dying star, his resolve refused to crumble. She could see it in his eyes, the set of his shoulders—the stubborn defiance of an ass of a man who didn't know when to quit.

She slid a glance at Dianne but nodded. She felt Dianne's glare as she handed a water bottle back to Ryan, followed by Edvard's carbine, which András passed her with the mental comment, *This should be a fun ride back. Between the* dae-mons, *roving marauders, and these two clueless lovebirds, we won't lack for distraction.*

She has a point, Spratek.

Then let her keep the Glock.

I planned on it.

After passing Dianne a water bottle, she opened an insulated container on the seat next to her containing handheld food, in this case something Olivia referred to as a hot pocket filled with spiced ground meat and cheese, and gave the couple each one. Then Beta held out an extra clip for the Glock and a spare thigh rig to Dianne.

"To defend the kitten," she said. Ignoring Ryan's scoffing noise, she went on, "You have earned that right."

They drove in silence for twenty minutes before Beta asked András the question that had bothered her ever since she saw the faint flare with its flickering shadows.

How did the daemons *breach the border of Albania?*

I don't know, Gomba, said András, his voice somber in her thoughts. *I have never seen it done. I didn't think that it could be done. But perhaps Mihàil's injury has something to do with it.* He paused, his fist clenching on the dashboard in front of him as he looked out into the night, scanning for threats, before adding, *But there is something following us. Something malevolent and tenebrous ... no, like the absence of all light.*

I sense it, too. Beta gripped the Disrupter on her chest. It suddenly seemed much too puny and weak for whatever it was that stalked them.

As if sensing the tension, Ryan leaned forward. He seemed more himself, and if his harmonics were anything to go by, the morphine and food had done their job.

"They've followed us into Albania, haven't they?" he asked in a low voice.

Beta glanced at him. "Yes."

Ryan's gaze went to Dianne, who slouched in the seat next to him, as if to a lodestone. Beta could see the taut harmonic chord between them, its purple, green, and gold threads alive with both raw emotion and something deeper, something that vibrated against the edges of Beta's understanding and added to the mystery of their tethering.

Twisting inside of that nascent bond? Black, vitriolic threads of discord, mistrust, and anger.

Those were familiar to Beta. Would the other couple wrestle with their *daemons* and win? Would they get that chance?

She pressed her lips together, her eyes narrowed. They would if she had anything to say about it.

The Defender's frame seemed to groan under an invisible weight, the very air pressing against Beta's skin like a cold, suffocating blanket. Overhead, the stars disappeared. Ominous silence squeezed at Beta's chest, blotting out the familiar comforting hum of creation.

"Sir," said Edvard glancing at András. "I've lost comms with Aerie. The harmonics nav keeps cutting out, and our sensor sweep just blacked out for no reason."

Edvard was adapting, faster than Beta had expected, his movements crisp and deliberate despite the chaos. He'd gained the confidence of another battle won.

He was going to need it.

András didn't look at the young warfighter, but her husband's worry clouded the harmonic plane around him like invisible steel wool. "I'm aware." He paused. "I'm more concerned with the Defender's electrical system."

Behind her, Beta read a spike of fear in Dianne and grim determination in Ryan, whose gut wound throbbed and radiated heat. The core of his infrared signature showed a sickly, green-tinged black that seeped into the rest of him as the *daemonic* energy engulfed them.

And Dianne's signature thrummed with stygian power.

Seventeen

Miles ducked out of the ops center after Beta and András recovered Olivia's sister and Helsing, whose vitals showed low blood pressure from blood loss and the start of sepsis, though the antibiotics in the med kit should stamp that out before it became dangerous. It seemed like the best time to grab a hot meal and another coffee, which at this point he was practically mainlining, before reporting to his superior, who waited on news of her sister's rescue.

Though it was late, Miles knew where he'd find Olivia: the state-of-the-art clinic Mihàil had built in Fushë-Arrëz for the townspeople to have access to the same medical care he provided his staff and security personnel. The *zoti*, gently goaded by his young American wife, had also built a restaurant next to the clinic where fresh local produce, meats, and herbs could be traded by poorer community members for care. The restaurant supplied all of the meals, prepared by a trained chef to focus on nutrition and quality, to the patients and their families, free of charge.

Miles didn't partake of a made-to-order meal, though. Instead, he scooped a bowl of fragrant *supa me mish*, a hearty lamb soup, wishing that he could take the time to enjoy a second bowl of *supë krem pulë*, a creamy chicken soup came damn close to his mama's—the last bowl of that was years, back before MREs took over his life. He ate quickly, dipping pillowy roll-sized *pogača* into the broth, then grabbed another to eat as he cleared his dishes and decanted coffee into a disposable cup. Not a real break, but already he felt refueled and ready to dive back into the crisis.

He wiped his hands on his pants before taking the stairs two-at-a-time to the third-floor ICU, an internal clock urging him on despite no clear reason for worry.

When he entered the ward, the nurse on duty, a young Albanian named Mirjeta who'd returned home from studying in the U.S. on the promise of a job working for her beloved *zoti*, escorted him to Mihàil's private room. Knocking, she peered around the open door as a soft female voice answered from inside. After a few quick words, she looked back at Miles, nodding for him to go in.

Inside, Miles found Olivia slumped in a chair next to the head of the bed where Mihàil lay asleep, the face of the *Elioud* general bandaged to cover the empty socket of his left eye, the rest of his body swathed in sterile wraps. At first, Miles thought that Olivia slept, but then he noticed her toying with the small silver disc of her St. Michael's pendant, the only jewelry she typically wore besides her wedding rings and, rarely, simple earrings or a bracelet.

She looked worn and pale, not as vibrant and glowing with rose-hued life as he was used to, her long, fine blond hair trailing in disarray around her shoulders where it had escaped from a silver clip. Miles's heart squeezed in his chest. He hadn't realized until just this moment how much he relied on Olivia's unwavering, no-nonsense optimism and faith even when odds seemed stacked against the *Elioud* and their mission.

She looked up at him, and he could see faint traces of crying in her face.

"Hey," he said in a low voice, nodding. He folded his arms, uncomfortable and not sure how to start. "How's he doing?" He lifted his chin toward the silent figure in the bed, formerly larger-than-life and magnetic in a way Miles had never encountered in a commander before.

"As well as a man who's fighting for his life can," she said. Something must have passed over Miles's face because she blinked and focused on him, dropping the pendant and her hand into her lap. And he saw her take up her mantle as *zonjë* again. "Willem came in earlier and left that." She nodded toward a distinctive sculpture dominated by an intricate stained-glass center on a table next to the head of the hospital bed. "He calls it the Resonator Rose. He's using it to shore up Mihàil's harmonics so that his body can heal, which is beyond my own abilities right now.'"

Miles heard the self-reproach in Olivia's voice.

He recognized it for what it was. He'd felt it himself, often, when still with the Agency. The sinking guilt that said you hadn't done enough to prevent something catastrophic, that you couldn't make it right.

Unfortunately, now wasn't the time for a pep talk. At least, not the gentle kind.

"Maybe you can get him to make one for you, too," he said. "Because I don't need to read harmonics like an *Elioud* to see that you're tapped out. Don't beat yourself up over this. It's not your fault. You need to pull up your big-girl panties now and put on a brave face. We need you."

Olivia pursed her lips but didn't respond to his comment. Instead, she said, "I gather you came to give me a status update for Dianne and Helsing?"

Miles nodded. The clinic, still under construction, had fully functioning shielded harmonics to protect patients and enable guided healing resonance. That meant that Olivia hadn't been able to tap into their comms network while here. Besides the ops center at the estate, it was the one building in Fushë-Arrëz whose power supply hadn't been affected by the geomagnetic storm.

"Draka and Giant have recovered Demon Slayer and your sister. They had a little trouble with some locals, but they extinguished it quickly and got on the road. We don't expect any other problems at this time of night. They should make it back in another hour. I can send someone to get you, but if you'll take my advice, you'll go home to your baby and sleep."

Olivia sighed and stood. "That sounds good, though I think a shower and some *salep* also sounds good. I'll follow you to the TOC in a few moments for a more official status report."

Miles paused at the door, watching Olivia lean over Mihàil, her hand hovering before she kissed his peeling lips.

Ryan knew they were in trouble when the temperature dropped inside the Defender, his breath fogging the faint light of the console as frost began to creep along the edges of the windows. On the bench seat next to him, Dianne murmured and shifted, her arms going around her torso as she tried to stop the sudden shivering quaking her.

"Here," said Ryan gruffly, lifting the thermal blanket that András had pointed him to in a storage container built under the seat. "Scoot over."

She slid into his side, her shaking briefly making her teeth rattle. She sighed and relaxed against him, her head sinking against his upper chest. "You feel so good." Ryan only had enough time to frown at his reaction to that observation when she added, "But that probably means you've got a fever."

He ignored the uneasy truth in her words. Fever or not, he was with her until she was safe or until he couldn't breathe anymore. His body could fail, his eyes could blur. But if she was in his arms, he wasn't letting go.

Ryan gritted his teeth and looked out the obsidian window glass. They could see nothing outside. The GPS failed forty-five minutes ago, leaving them blind as they climbed the Accursed Mountains toward Fushë-Arrëz. They'd had to pull over so that Beta could drive using her *Elioud* radar to navigate. Then the electrical system started to misfire, and András laid both hands on the dashboard, closing his eyes as he channeled a steady flow of harmonic energy from his reserves into the vehicle to keep it running.

Ryan had never felt so helpless. Or so angry. It was almost as if the evil beings played with them. He sensed the real fun wouldn't start until they were in sight of the fortified Kastrioti estate.

"How much longer until we reach Mihàil and Olivia's?" asked Dianne, drawing him out of his introspection as her chin moved against his chest. She yawned. She'd stopped shivering and sounded sleepy. He was grateful that the fear he'd felt emanating from her through the quirky bond that had developed between his harmonic gear and her protective tunic, which even now glowed softly where it touched him, had subsided.

A gentle vibration, making him think of a cat's purr, rippled along her skin, soothing him. Without conscious decision, he squeezed her against him. It felt *right*. It unnerved him. How could he protect her when their fates felt stitched together in ways he didn't understand?

If he couldn't shield her from marauding humans or Hellspawn, he could at least hold fear at bay a little longer.

· "We still have an hour before we reach their house," he said, brushing a soft kiss on her forehead. He was so tired, he wasn't even sure where the impulse had come from. "Why don't you try to get some sleep?"

"Mmm," she said, "I think I will." She settled further against him and was quiet for a long time. He thought she'd fallen asleep, but she said in a low voice, "I want you to wear the ring with my cousin Emily's key on it."

"Why?" he asked, startled.

"Because you're my hero," she said, her shadowed face unreadable. "You almost died for me. I want you to have it. It's the only thing I have that means anything to me."

Ryan didn't know what to say to that. He had a vague memory of her chanting before the team arrived. If anything, she'd saved him.

"Please," she said, her voice thick with strong emotion now. "I want you to have it."

"Okay."

Dianne turned, and picking up his hand, slid the silver ring onto his small finger. Then she raised his hand and kissed it before sliding back down with a sigh. He sat in turmoil, his heart and his head so full of conflicting thoughts he had no idea where to start unraveling them.

Within moments, he heard Dianne's quiet breathing and knew she'd fallen asleep. It reassured him to know that he made her feel secure enough to do that, and some of his own tension at the tenebrous Sword of Damocles hanging over them drained from him.

It didn't last. It was almost as if letting down his guard with Dianne let the *daemons* in.

The change was almost imperceptible at first—a subtle shift in the hum of the Defender's engine. Ryan tensed, glancing toward the faintly glowing dashboard. András, sitting rigid in the front passenger seat, opened his eyes suddenly, his hands still pressed against the dashboard. The harmonic energy he'd been channeling flared briefly, casting eerie shadows around the cabin before dimming again. The young warfighter Edvard, new to the *Elioud* cause, glanced between his superior officers and the opaque windows, his gaze tight with worry but edged with calculation.

"What's wrong?" Ryan asked, keeping his voice low so as not to wake Dianne.

András didn't answer immediately. He tilted his head, as if listening to something far away. His jaw clenched, and he let out a slow, measured breath. "They're closer."

Ryan's stomach sank. He shifted slightly, pulling the thermal blanket higher over Dianne's sleeping form, and peered out the window again. Night pressed against the glass, thick and suffocating. It felt almost alive, a heavy presence that made the skin of his neck tighten all the way to his temples where it drilled into his brain.

"Define 'closer,'" he said, his voice tight.

András turned his head just enough for Ryan to catch the faint glow in his eyes, a sign of the *Elioud*'s heightened awareness. "Close enough to taste our fear."

The words hit like a punch to the gut. Before Ryan could respond, a sharp, grating noise pierced the night—metallic and shrill, like claws dragging across the Defender's roof. The vehicle shuddered violently, throwing Dianne against him. Her eyes flew open, wide with terror.

"What—what's happening?" she asked, clutching at him.

"Stay down," Ryan said, his tone brooking no argument. He pressed her closer, his own heart pounding as the noise intensified. It wasn't just claws now; it was a cacophony of scraping, hissing, and a low, harsh growl that seemed to come from everywhere and nowhere all at once.

András snarled back and struggled, as if wrestling with an invisible force, his face twisting in effort. The air hung heavy with the scent of ozone. Sparks emitted from his fingers and the tips of his hair, while acrid smoke drifted to obscure his face. The console lights and the headlights wavered erratically, dimming and brightening as if power surged and receded with the battle.

Next to him, Beta struggled to maintain control of the Defender, a shimmering dance of colored light linking her to her husband. The vehicle lurched forward, the engine groaning as if under immense pressure. Outside, faint, shadowy shapes flitted just beyond the range of the flickering headlights—twisted, insectile forms that moved too quickly to be clearly seen.

Ryan tightened his grip on Dianne. His mind raced, calculating options, but there was nowhere to go, no way to fight back. The Locusts were here, and he could feel the malevolent presence of their master, the Dark Angel of the Abyss, like a boulder crushing his chest.

Against reason, he said, "We have to—" But his words were cut off by a deafening crack as something heavy slammed onto the hood of the Defender.

András shouted, a visceral cry for victory against an overwhelming foe to keep the vehicle running. Ryan had never seen the giant *Elioud* so stretched to the limits, not even in the *Elioud's* epic battle against the *kulshedër* and a host of *daemonia* last December.

Beta swerved violently, narrowly avoiding the edge of a steep drop into the blackness below.

Ryan's world contracted to two thoughts: keep Dianne safe and survive long enough for the intervention he didn't know he was hoping for.

Outside the SUV's windows, dimly lit sky pulsed as if the black heart of an enormous monster beat in irregular contraction. Forks of sickly green and amber rent the air around the armored vehicle, which had once seemed so sturdy. In between flashes, Ryan glimpsed trees swaying in a mighty wind. The Defender itself slid sideways while Beta wrangled the steering wheel to keep it on the road.

And then a brutal rhythmic chant began unlike anything he'd ever heard before.

No, scratch that. It sounded like an Army march, a Gregorian chant, and a dark club-dance mix rolled into one stomach-churning choral assault. A low, unholy voice led a deep male choir in a call-and-response that raked down his spine and raised his hair.

He caught the words *libera tenebrae* and *tenebrae vincit*. He didn't know much Latin, but he knew *tenebrae* meant darkness and *vincit* meant conquers.

He had a *bad* feeling about this.

The turbulence abruptly halted. The night sky brightened into a surreal sepia-toned landscape to reveal a massive, obsidian creature with wicked spurs and spikes protruding from its head, thorax and abdomen.

That wasn't the disturbing thing about this locust.

It was the human head wearing a crown.

Abaddon, Dark Angel of the Abyss, stood on the mountain highway before them.

The Defender skidded to a halt, its headlights catching the gleaming obsidian of Abaddon's armor and the horrifying crown-topped human head. Behind him, the rhythmic chant reached a crescendo, fueling a surge of blackened locusts that spilled across the road in a writhing tide. They swarmed toward the SUV, their wings emitting sharp, metallic clicks that pierced the night like daggers.

András snarled, launching himself from the vehicle before Ryan could react, his harmonic energy igniting in a radiant arc as he slammed his palm into the ground. The force sent shockwaves through the writhing mass, scattering the Locusts momentarily, their screeches blending with the chant as if enraged. Beta followed without hesitation, the shimmering bond between her and András intensifying to a blinding brilliance as she joined the fray.

Edvard dropped to a knee behind an open door of the Defender, his tactical gear flaring in response to the harmonic threat. He launched a swarm of gnats, the nanodrones that Miró had created as a force multiplier against a larger number of enemy combatants. They locked onto the multi-modal harmonic frequencies of the Locusts, bombing them with stinging harmonic rain designed to disorient.

Ryan protected Dianne instinctively as the swarm closed in again, forcing him to scramble for something—anything—that might hold the *daemon* locusts at bay. His chainmail flared into brilliance, shielding both him and Dianne in dense protective harmonics. He scarcely had time to note that the chainmail's strength had far exceeded its designed limits before Abaddon took a single step forward, his voice booming over the din.

"Bring them to me!" Abaddon's funereal voice echoed around the windswept mountains. The Locusts shifted direction almost as one, their focus now locked onto the Defender. The chant transformed, turning throaty and violent, each word striking Ryan like a hammer to the chest.

The vehicle trembled as the swarm battered against its exterior, the windshield spiderwebbing under the relentless assault. Ryan braced himself, adrenaline surging as he prepared to fight—for Dianne, for the team, for survival—knowing full well that even Demon Slayer wasn't enough against the Angel of the Abyss but refusing to let that stop him.

The Defender's occupants braced for the worst as Abaddon's towering form loomed, his obsidian armor glinting in the flickering green and amber light. The rhythmic chant of the Locusts became unbearable, reverberating in the bones, each syllable heralding doom. The Locusts surged forward, their spiked forms like a relentless tide of oil.

And then, cutting through the chaos, came a new sound—a commanding chorus that rose like a beacon and echoed from the surrounding slopes. The deep, resonant power of Gregorian chants filled the air, piercing the oppressive gloom. It was not the soul-crushing chant of Abaddon's horde, but a harmony suffused with strength and light. At the sound, the Locusts abruptly halted, screeching in agony, their heads thrown back and their maws gaping.

From the ridge above the road, they appeared—twelve mounted *donats* in black tactical gear, their modern armor gleaming with harmonic sigils. At the center rode Elias Klum, his steely gaze fixed on the battle, the white cross of the Order emblazoned over his breastplate. The *donats* bore harmonic shields that glowed faintly, their chant gauntlets emitting bursts of pure light with every verse they uttered. Blade-like ribbons of radiant energy unfurled from their bracers, rippling and snapping like living strands of poly-chromatic lightning.

Behind Elias rode a mid-twenties male who bore a strong resemblance to Olivia and Dianne, Michael Markham, whom Dianne had called a 'tech-finance bro.' Olivia and Dianne's younger brother still wore the rumpled polo and khakis he'd traveled in, now overlaid with a shimmering tunic. He looked dazed but determined, gripping his mount's reins with one hand. At his hip hung a mysterious shining orb and tucked in his belt was a chant gauntlet, far too advanced for him to understand, but carried, nonetheless.

The *donats* charged, their harmonics amplifying, each note lashing the Locusts with devastating precision. Waves of light tore through the swarm, scattering the insectile forms into fragments that disintegrated into the air. Elias led the charge with unerring focus, his harmonic ribbons slicing through the Locusts like divine blades.

Abaddon roared, his wings unfurling to their full span, blocking the road entirely. A tempest of blackened energy erupted from him, sending *donats* reeling. One fell from his horse, injured but alive, and Michael, dismounting, instinctively scrambled to the knight's side.

Grabbing the injured *donat*'s blade-like ribbon, Michael flicked his wrist as he'd seen the knights do, and, to his surprise, the ribbon responded. It sparked to life, glowing faintly as Michael slashed at an approaching Locust, driving it back just long enough to help the *donat* to his feet.

Abaddon stepped forward, his crowned head tilting as he took stock of the unexpected resistance. His voice broke and reformed as he spoke, as if he couldn't contain it within a single rasping tone. "You delay the inevitable."

At his words, a wave of *daemon* locusts sprang forward.

But Elias and his knights formed a protective phalanx, their chants reaching a crescendo. With each verse, their harmonic shields grew brighter, forming a dome of light that the Locusts could not penetrate. Elias himself turned to face Abaddon, his chant amplifying, harmonics sparking from his gauntlets and ribbons as he focused all his energy.

András and Beta, seizing the moment, harmonized their own energy with the knights' chorus. Together, the combined harmonics created a blinding pulse of light that shot outward, engulfing the Locusts in a searing wave. Abaddon staggered, his form faltering, the crowned head flickering as though losing cohesion.

Edvard, not to be left out of the combat, sent his gnats repeatedly at the Dark Lord of the Abyss, their tiny forms blazing briefly as they expended their harmonic energy in bursts that tore through the shadowy aura surrounding Abaddon, disrupting his focus and forcing him to shift his attention toward the relentless swarm.

With a final cry of defiance, Elias brought his harmonic ribbons down in a sweeping arc, striking the Angel of the Abyss with a blow that shattered the remnants of his shadowy form. Abaddon let out a guttural howl before disintegrating into the void, his presence extinguished.

The battlefield fell silent, save for the sound of the horses' heavy breathing and the faint hum of residual harmonics. Michael looked down at the ribbon still glowing faintly in his hand, his face a mix of shock and exhilaration. Ryan stumbled out of the Defender, Dianne at his side, to meet their unlooked-for saviors.

They walked with Edvard toward the *Elioud*, who stood beside the gathered *donats*, András sharing handshakes and hugs with the human knights while Beta scanned the pre-dawn landscape with her enhanced *Elioud* vision.

Elias remained on horseback in the faint afterglow of the *donats'* harmonic weapons, his face half in shadow and gleaming with sweat. Ryan gave the knight a sharp nod of thanks as he and Dianne came nearer. The older warrior nodded once in return.

Ryan glanced from Elias to Michael. "Finance bro, huh? If Elias doesn't recruit you to the Order of Malta, I've got a place for you on my security team."

A sheepish grin washed over Michael's face. He handed the ribbon back to the *donat* to whom it belonged, the ribbon still twitching slightly. "Guess I'm more versatile than I thought."

As Michael spoke, Dianne watched him with such affection and joy that Ryan would have been jealous if the younger man hadn't been her brother. As it was, the transformation on her face made something raw and vulnerable open inside him.

"That makes two of us," she said to her brother. "I've had a few moments these past couple of days where I rose to the occasion, too."

Michael turned to his big sister, bending to catch her up into a tight hug. She squealed and gripped him around the neck. "Di, thank God you're safe."

Ryan, conscious of not belonging in their family reunion, stepped back and surveyed the landscape around them, his nerves still humming in the aftermath of battle. His side ached worse as the adrenaline from the attack receded. Whatever *Elioud* magic Beta had performed had faded. He too faded. He'd need Dr. Armand's brand of medicine soon.

Dianne came up next to him, slipping her hand into his. "There you are." She didn't say more, but he felt her worry. And her hurt. She'd taken his distance for what it was.

He didn't pull his hand from hers, but neither did he draw her closer into his side where she belonged, where her presence would soothe the fierce ache from the wound that Abaddon's vessel had given him.

They were nearly in Fushë-Arrëz. Whatever had happened between him and Dianne on the road from Split, it was time to return to his duty.

Elias dismounted, his movements deliberate, his gaze sweeping across the battlefield's remnants. Relief swelled among the group, their laughter and easy breaths replacing the tension of the fight. Victory. A hard-won triumph. But Elias did not celebrate.

His attention flickered toward András and Beta, meeting their unreadable stares. No words were exchanged, only the quiet understanding of warriors who had seen too many battles end like this, with enemies retreating but never truly defeated.

Then his gaze drifted beyond them, past the scorched ground and broken stone, to the distant mountains. Cool, shifting tones of deep blue and indigo, fading into pale silver at the edges, signaled dawn's approach but not full arrival.

In Elias's eyes, it might as well have been the gathering of storm clouds on the horizon.

Ryan watched him, watched the stillness in Elias's stance and the weight in his expression. The others rejoiced, oblivious to what lurked in those fleeting glances between the veterans. But Ryan saw it—felt it creeping into his bones.

This wasn't over.

Eighteen

Before visiting his patron in the ICU for the Angelus prayer, Father Bekim stopped in the large conference room at the unfinished clinic that Mihàil had designated as a temporary chapel until a larger, freestanding one could be built next door. It was a plain space, yet warm and welcoming. Mihàil hadn't wanted Father Bekim or any of his parishioners to wait on the separate building that Willem DeVries, the *Elioud* architect who'd joined their community last year, even now designed. In addition to a small altar, crucifix, and tabernacle for the Blessed Sacrament, the room had a holy-water font, a credence table with sacred vessels, and a sanctuary lamp. Around the room were small ceramic plaques depicting

the Stations of the Cross crafted by local artisans using tradi-
tional techniques passed down through generations.

He was here, kneeling before the Eucharist in adoration
and prayer, when the *zonjë* entered. Father Bekim felt her
settle on her knees at his side, and then she slowly lowered
herself to a prone position. Although he couldn't make out the
words she murmured, their low hum moved across his skin,
warm as the whisper of the Holy Spirit.

They were there, together, quiet and breathing in the Sacred Presence, when a soft tap at the conference-room door
warned them that someone entered.

Father Bekim looked up to see the American Miles Baxter
step into the room, his gaze going around the space before
settling on Olivia Kastrioti. Fatigue etched the man's face in
hollow lines, but the priest saw a look of concern, love, and
respect flit across his features before he schooled them into
his usual opacity. The man was a cipher, but Father Bekim
understood instantly that he cared for his superior.

That was a very good thing. The *zonjë* would need all of the
love, support, and faithfulness her community could give her
in the days ahead.

Baxter waited behind the short row of chairs arranged in
front of the marble altar, his hooded gaze revealing nothing as
he studied the ostensorium displayed there. It was a modern
piece designed by Olivia with Father Bekim's help, crafted
from sleek polished platinum statue of an angel holding the
luna and inlaid with mother-of-pearl and iridescent blue lapis.
A subtle harmonic glow embraced the luna and its holy contents. Even without an expression on his handsome face, the
American conveyed a feeling of deep unease and discomfort.

Interesting. Even with the supernatural evidence of the *Elioud*, their *daemonic* foes, and the specialized harmonic technology that had begun to transform their lives here in Fushë-Arrëz and beyond, the man still held himself apart. Father Bekim made a note to dedicate prayer for Baxter's full change of heart.

At last, Olivia stood, rolling up to her feet gracefully even though she appeared as worn as Father Bekim, who'd seen more than five decades as Mihàil's family priest. She held out her hand and helped him to his feet before turning back to Baxter.

"Have you gotten word from András or Ryan?"

He nodded. Olivia stilled, and Father Bekim heard her soft intake of breath before Baxter spoke.

"Better. Elias and Michael came across them on the road." He paused and looked swiftly at Father Bekim before returning his gaze to Olivia and continuing. "Abaddon and his Locusts ambushed them, my lady. Elias and his *donats* repelled them, but they had to abandon the Defender and bring Ryan and Dianne and the others on horseback. András just sent word via personal drone that they'll be in Fushë-Arrëz anytime."

Father Bekim chose to speak now before Olivia could say anything. "My lady, it is almost time for the Angelus. With your permission, I will bring the lectionary. God willing, we can all pray in thanksgiving for their safe return."

Olivia blinked, looking almost overwhelmed for a moment with unshed tears misting her gaze. She nodded and cleared her throat. "Let it be done. And, please, Father Bekim, ring the bells to gather everyone from town. I'll need to address them about what we're facing."

Father Bekim nodded. In all things, gratitude to God. It was his calling to lead that public expression for the *zoti* and *zonjë* and their people.

Twenty minutes later Father Bekim stood outside the clinic on the site of the future chapel while the invisible harmonic bells rang for five kilometers around them, calling the faithful and the not-so-faithful alike to witness the arrival of the triumphant knights and their wards. As he looked down the slope toward the highway that bisected his little village, Father Bekim's throat thickened, and his heart was full. The *zoti* and his lady envisioned so much for this little hamlet that the elderly Albanian priest prayed he lived to see even half of it accomplished. The clinic and chapel, when finished, would comprise conjoined healing centers, the spiritual and physical blended in harmonic restoration.

This dawn, there was only the flat space that he stood on with a roughly graded terrace to the clinic on a nearby plateau. Below him was a beaten path to the valley and the highway through Fushë-Arrëz. Across from them and on the other side of the highway stood the Kastriotis' new home, a relatively modest limestone construction that served as the centerpiece of a small compound of buildings, including guesthouses for family and friends. And beyond that, Mihàil's modern security center, the Aerie, and associated training and living quarters for his warriors, *Elioud* and human alike. Next to it, along the base of the sheltering mountain, stood the unfinished research and development center where the *Elioud* found incredible and myriad ways to turn their angelic gifts into real-world technology to benefit humanity, especially in its longstanding war against the Dark forces of the Fallen Watcher Angels, who sought power over Creation.

Beneath him villagers from Fushë-Arrëz clustered on the raw earthen terraces that would form a natural amphitheater for outdoor Mass and other events. Across the highway, security personnel and staff for the command center stood in tense expectation outside the entrance to the Kastrioti estate. They would be able to hear him given the enhanced acoustics of the external harmonic audio mesh system, whose nodes covered most of the landscape for a radius of ten kilometers. Olivia and the other *Elioud* stood a short distance away between him and the clinic, their expressions inscrutable in the early morning light. Just behind the *Elioud*, the *zonjë*'s parents stood, Olivia's mother holding baby Luljeta, next to a young nanny.

Father Bekim raised his leatherbound lectionary and began to read the first antiphon of the Angelus prayer. Next to him, the candle that he'd lit and set on a small table wavered in the slight breeze, its flickering flame a symbol of divine protection. The sound of his voice echoed against the mountain ridges—a profound invocation that stretched beyond mere words.

And then, hoofbeats. Elias and the *donats* crested the ridge above the road, Ryan and Dianne in their midst, weary but whole. András, Beta, and Edvard brought up the rear.

The golden light of dawn caught the knights' harmonic sigils, sending flashes of brilliance across their battle-worn tactical gear as their breath and that of their horses misted the cold morning air.

The harmonic audio system amplified the collective gasp of all those gathered, their relief, awe, and unspoken reverence filling the stillness as Father Bekim continued to pray.

With more effort than he liked or would admit, Ryan pulled his jacket over his shoulders, still adjusting to the lingering ache in his side, not quite healed, but functional enough. The moment he stepped outside the clinic after a week lying weak and helpless in a hospital bed, the mountain air hit him, crisp and thin—a reminder that time hadn't slowed to keep pace with his plodding recovery.

Miles Baxter had demanded a full after-action report, but Ryan already knew the outcome: he was done being sidelined, done with IVs, done with physical therapy in hospital scrubs at the side of an overly concerned female therapist, and done with harmonic healing at the hands of his *Elioud* teammates. He was upright, mobile, and mad as hell. And he wasn't waiting for someone to clear him.

Still, protocol mattered. If Miles wouldn't stand in his way, someone else might. He didn't want to have that fight, but if it came to it, he'd win.

Which is why he found himself standing outside Olivia Kastrioti's office, knocking once before stepping inside without waiting for acknowledgement.

The soft hum of harmonic energy reverberated through the space, subtle, like an unseen pulse, reminding Ryan that everything in Fushë-Arrëz bent to forces deeper than blood, bullets, or steel.

Olivia was already standing, palms pressed against her desktop, gaze focused on nothing and everything at once. The weariness in her posture was unmistakable, but when she looked at him, her spine straightened as if the burden had momentarily lifted.

"Ryan," she said, choosing his first name over his last. That in itself was telling. And no pleasantries, just the weight of unspoken truths between them.

"Miles said I needed your sign-off to return to duty," he said. He didn't add that he was going back into the field whether or not his superior agreed.

Olivia exhaled, rubbing her temple. She looked tired, pale and drawn. She sat down and held his gaze with her steady one. "You're not fully recovered."

"Doesn't matter." He leaned against the chair across from her, arms crossed. "Unless you plan to remove me from command and throw me in the guardhouse, I'm going back to work."

She stared at him for a long moment. Then she asked in a mild voice, "Would you sit down?"

Ryan hesitated, then did. Not because he wanted to, but because something in her tone told him this conversation wasn't just procedural.

"You knew the risks," said Olivia quietly. "But that's not what this is about, is it?"

Ryan let out a slow breath. She was right. He had known the risks of the mission to bring Dianne to Fushë-Arrëz even without knowing the fine details of tactical gear. The risks were the same that they'd always been: protect the principal with your life.

And then Olivia addressed the elephant in the room: the revelation from Willem just this morning that Ryan's chain-mail and Dianne's tunic were tethered with the unique harmonic signature of the *zonjë*. That after what they'd experienced in the field, it went beyond the tactical gear to their individual harmonic signatures. They were indelibly—and perhaps permanently—linked on a spiritual level.

That was the real reason he was angry. This particular mission risk had been life altering in a way he couldn't possibly begin to comprehend, not life ending. That outcome he understood well enough. He'd accepted it when he entered the Rangers and doubled down on it when he witnessed his first friend and comrade-in-arms die in Afghanistan.

"I didn't tell you about the harmonic tether between your gear and hers." Olivia's voice was even, but something flickered in her expression. Guilt, maybe. A recognition too late to fix anything. "Just like you didn't tell Dianne about the nanotracker. It wasn't necessary."

He felt his jaw tighten and his fingers clench on his thighs. "You didn't think I needed to know?"

"No. I thought I was just being overly paranoid about my little sister. I wanted a failsafe in case the nanotracker died. I was the one who didn't know the risks, not fully." Her hands curled slightly on the gleaming black walnut of her desk, knuckles pale. "You have every right to be angry." She inhaled deeply, and then, holding his gaze with her open, luminous one, said, "I *am* sorry. Sorrier than you will ever know."

Suddenly Ryan understood the guilt shadowing the *zon-jë*'s features. Keeping this tactical decision from her chief of security paled against keeping the whole mission from her husband, now unconscious in their barely functional ICU.

Olivia hadn't said it, but Ryan knew that they'd both accepted the unknown unknowns in this unpredictable and dangerous *Elioud* world in which they operated. Laying the blame on his commanding officer for using the harmonic tether was stupid and arrogant.

Ryan slumped against his chair. He wasn't angry anymore. He was exhausted. And maybe somewhere deep inside, he was grateful, because if he hadn't gone, Dianne wouldn't be alive. He wasn't sure he had the strength to name the feeling, let alone face what it meant.

But this wasn't just about surviving.

"I need to know how deep this goes," he said at last. "How much that tether affected her. And me. If it's permanent and what that means."

Olivia nodded. "Miró can help you find the answers." She hesitated. "Ryan ... just be careful. There's something we still don't understand about your tether with Dianne. Abaddon has touched it. And what the Angel of the Abyss touches doesn't just fade away."

He pushed to his feet. "I never expected it to." He left it unsaid that he'd seen the black threads in his harmonic signature. And in Dianne's.

But he had no intention of sitting still while it coiled deeper into his skin—and hers.

As he turned to leave, Olivia halted him. "Ryan, something else is at play." She sighed. "We don't understand the timing or magnitude of the solar flare. Or if it was a coincidence or caused by Abaddon's appearance. He's not prophesied to appear above ground before the Apocalypse." She stopped before stating what everyone in Fushë-Arrëz already whispered: that Creation had indeed been thrust into the End Times, and the forces of Hell now ruled.

Ryan squared his shoulders and met her gaze. He couldn't carry her burden, but he could damn well do the job.

"You can count on me, ma'am."

The confrontation with Olivia left Ryan feeling as weak as he had in Shkodër before Beta had stabilized and recharged his harmonics. Once outside the operations center, he stopped and breathed deeply, feeling the soreness deep in his side. He noticed some trainees on the quad outside the building looking at him and realized that he'd placed his hand against his abdomen. He dropped it. He'd have to be more disciplined from now on. He couldn't let anyone else see how his wound still troubled him. Not if he was going to resume his leadership role as head of security for the Kastriotis.

Pulling himself to his full height, he glared at the trio of young men and one woman. "Haven't you got someplace to be right now?" He made a show of looking at his watch, which ran better than he did on the *Elioud* recharge. "According to the schedule I set, all recruits have shooting practice at 1100."

Their eyes widened, but only one had the presence of mind to nod and respond with a loud "Sir, yes, sir" before hitting his nearest friend on the back of the head. The group pivoted and ran toward the indoor range, the woman trailing as she glanced over her shoulder at Ryan. He didn't know where they'd come from, but it didn't matter: young people were the same all over the world.

Ryan stood upright, his eyes narrowed as he followed their progress, until the four had disappeared inside the shoot house. Then he relaxed, dizziness sweeping over him. A hard thrumming juddered him, making his knees buckle. He maintained his standing position by some miracle of will. And then the quaking subsided, gentle vibrations soothing his body as his harmonic signature calmed. He recognized the feeling, and his gaze scanned the quad.

There. Across from him, coming on a paved path through some trees. Dianne and Beta, deep in conversation. He faded behind a nearby tree not a moment too soon because Dianne looked at the spot where he'd stood only a minute before. Ryan drank in the sight of her, sunlight turning her blond hair into a physical halo around her skin with its undertones of roses and cream.

He should have told Willem or Olivia that he could read Dianne's harmonic signature. It had started after Međugorje, after the geomagnetic flare and that soul-searing kiss. He hadn't wanted to say anything until he understood how he felt about it, this surprising *Elioud* ability that he'd never thought to have. He realized part of him had wanted it to mean something—like a signal from Heaven that he and Dianne were meant for each other. Now his hopes seemed ill-founded at best, dangerous at worst.

But what if the flare had powered their bond? A bond that had been primed by the simple harmonic tether that Olivia had created? It had certainly recharged his harmonic chain-mail system. What else had the flare ignited in them? If the flare had sparked changes, were they permanent?

A gift—or a curse?

Ryan had already feared that his bond with Dianne was permanent by the time the Dutch *Elioud* suggested the possibility with a somber sympathy that had sent Ryan's hackles quivering. The man had loved his fiancée and lost her to the Dark *Irim* Yeqon, the original Seducer. Long before Ryan could read harmonic signatures, he'd sensed the pain shadowing Willem's spirit.

In fact, Ryan could see a lot more than that: he could see Beta's harmonics, and a slight, wavery sheen on the world around him. It was both disconcerting and awe-inducing.

Dianne's harmonic signature was a royal purple and gold, and a soft golden aura limned her form. Yet there was something malign corrupting its purity. Something that Ryan very much feared he'd gifted her on their escape from Split.

Dianne's glance lingered for a moment as she and Beta continued walking, their trajectory taking them to the outdoor shooting range. And then both women disappeared around the corner of a building on the north side of the quad.

After a long moment, Ryan shook himself from his involuntary reverie and continued on to the research and development complex beyond the quad in a quiet recess enlarged from a natural cavity in the base of the bordering mountain. He needed to give Miró the small charm that he'd recovered in Split after battling the one-eyed *daemoniac*.

What if whatever was between them was an illusion activated by that evil charm?

He found the intense *Elioud* scientist in a lab at the back of the main R&D building, the room lined on three sides with workbenches where tools and raw materials lay in neat groupings. Though the bare walls were pristine white, the large windows and skylights filled the space with natural light, softening its sterility.

After Miró surprised him with a warm handshake and slap on the shoulder, Ryan drew the metallic hand from his pocket—the one with its disturbing blue-white-and-black crystal—and passed it over. He knew something was wrong even before Miró examined it. Not just when he picked it up, but in the way it resonated near Dianne.

Miró turned the charm in his palm, studying it with *Elioud* precision. The lab was silent except for the low hum of harmonic instruments, casting gentle light across the tablet he was already pulling data from.

"This is not simply a token," said Miró. "It is an Eye of Hamsa. More than that, it is a lure *and* a tether."

Ryan frowned. "What do you mean?"

Miró's piercing gaze met his. "It draws those who are susceptible to Abaddon's influence. Makes possession easier. Less energy required."

Ryan's stomach knotted. His worst fears were true. He'd been unwittingly giving the Dark Lord of the Abyss access to Dianne ever since they escaped from Split.

"It affects Dianne Markham," he said.

A statement, not a question.

Miró's expression darkened. "It also explains a lot about how Abaddon and his Locusts penetrated the Albanian border. Granted Mihàil is wounded, but we have significantly strengthened the harmonic defenses along the Albanian border, especially in the southwest quadrant." His eyes narrowed as he stared at the Eye. "Even so, the Eye's power is too limited on its own. The flare likely supercharged its harmonics—a theory I am testing now. If that is true, its increased influence may still be active. Perhaps even *amplified* by your proximity."

"Are you saying that Dianne doesn't stand a chance?"

Miró shook his head, his ice-blue gaze intensifying until it seemed to glow from within. "Dianne is strong, Ryan. He will not be able to possess her unless—"

Ryan stood up, cutting Miró short. He didn't need the rest. If she was vulnerable, it was because of him, because of what bound them, and what he'd unknowingly carried. And now he'd do whatever it took to keep her safe.

"She can't know," he said immediately. "Not yet."

Miró studied him, gaze sharp with understanding. "You will have to tell her eventually."

"I know."

But not now. Not when the distance between them was already growing. It was the only way to protect her.

And not before he figured out how to stop Abaddon from taking her completely.

Dianne adjusted her grip, exhaling slowly as Beta placed two fingers lightly against her wrists to correct the angle.

"Do not overcompensate," said Beta, her voice quiet in Dianne's ear. The tall *Elioud* female moved with a practiced ease, standing near without imposing, adjusting Dianne's grip as if her presence was a necessary fixture rather than a disruption. "You want control, not stiffness."

Dianne nodded, rolling her shoulders back as she refocused on the target. The range was empty except for them, a pocket of quiet in a world that was anything but. There was comfort in the precision of Beta's instructions. No emotional clutter, no sympathy, just direct guidance, rooted in unrivaled expertise.

Which was exactly what she needed.

Since arriving in Fushë-Arrëz, she had buried herself in physical training, in learning to fire a weapon with the accuracy to land every shot where she intended, in absorbing everything Beta had to offer.

She'd grabbed onto the intimidating *Elioud*'s suggestion that she learn to shoot as well as train in hand-to-hand combat—her sister had been distracted, Mihàil still slept in an induced coma as his burns took everything anyone knew how to do for him.

And Germaine, her best friend and only link to her past life, had disappeared in an ICU unit shielded by harmonics to contain the *daemon* possessing her. Unlike Mihàil's medical coma, Germaine's catatonic state arose solely from the pernicious influence that malevolent spirit held over her body, mind, and soul.

Meanwhile, her parents spent their waking hours watching her baby niece, and Michael ... well, her brother the finance bro had started hanging out with the mysterious Elias and his otherworldly knights. Dianne refused to sit idle, waiting for the world to make sense again. Training was structure. Training meant control.

And Beta, even with her keen edges, had extended a steadying hand where no one else had.

"Take the shot," said Beta.

Dianne tightened her grip, centered herself, and fired. The bullet hit slightly off-bullseye, clean, but not perfect.

Beta let out a quiet hum of approval. "Better. But you need to trust yourself."

Dianne looked at her, blinking against the afternoon glare. "I do trust myself."

Beta gave a finely honed smile, fleeting but sincere. "Then your aim should reflect that."

Dianne huffed, shaking her head, but there was something reassuring in Beta's crisp honesty. She didn't waste words, didn't cushion failure or dress it up as something else—and that clarity helped Dianne recalibrate.

Then, mid-adjustment, a shudder of awareness crept through her, threading into her senses like the hum of what she now knew were harmonics, the pervasive, underlying energy that charged her new world. A shift. A presence.

She turned her head slightly. And there he was, the man she'd fallen hopelessly in love with, approaching with that unreadable expression, his posture steady but his energy taut.

For the first time in weeks, Dianne felt herself falter, misgiving creeping into the foundation she had carefully laid down. When she turned to see Ryan approaching, her stance shifted slightly. Still strong, still composed, just uncertain.

Beside her, Beta muttered something and drifted away, far enough to give them space to talk.

"You finally emerged from the clinic," said Dianne lightly to Ryan, though her heart beat like a hummingbird at the base of her throat. "I thought you were avoiding me."

He didn't answer right away. "You checked in on me," he said instead, his gaze everywhere but her face.

Had he felt her presence then? Was that a good thing? Suddenly she felt breathless. "You were unconscious."

"Or pretending to be." His words and tone were clipped, cold. Impersonal.

A flicker of irritation crossed her face before she could stop it. "Ryan," she said, quieter now. She could already feel the hurt well deep inside her, somewhere behind her breastbone and jagged as shattered ice. "Don't do this."

"Do what?" He folded his arms, increasing his distance. She realized that Emily's ring, which had never left his finger while he recuperated in the hospital, was gone.

"Pretend you don't feel it." Her voice didn't waver, but there was something raw in it.

"You're imagining things," he said, his voice unbelievably colder still. His hazel eyes had turned glacial.

Something inside her fractured at that. And before she could stop herself, she asked, "Is it because of her? The woman whose picture you carry in your wallet?"

He flinched—just slightly—but she caught it. A quick tightening around his mouth, a blink that lasted a beat too long. And then, as if her question had given him permission, he sealed himself off behind that blank, impenetrable stare she was only beginning to recognize as his armor.

"Because once is enough. You give someone everything, and when it goes sideways—" He cut himself off. "You learn not to go there again."

Dianne sucked in a breath and took a step back, her free hand going up as if to ward off a blow. His words had been a punch to her gut and a stab to her heart.

"I was your principal," she said, voice barely above a whisper. "Was that all?"

Ryan exhaled. His gaze was distant now. In fact, he looked over her head at a point farther along the shooting gallery. He might have been sighting a target that looked like her. "Yes."

She'd sensed the wall rising between them, slow and silent, but now he'd built it high enough to shut her out completely, leaving her questioning everything.

Dianne barely noticed the crunch of gravel as Ryan turned from her, favoring his injured side with every stiff, pained step, as if walking away cost him more than he let on.

Beta, who'd waited nearby, ear protection slung around her neck, while they spoke now observed her, not with pity, but with something steadier.

"Do you still think it is only about aim?" asked the formidable *Elioud*, her dark eyes watching Dianne closely, as she returned to Dianne's side.

Dianne shook her head slowly.

Beta nodded, satisfied. "I did not think so."

She didn't wait for more. Turning, she walked down the line to another target, leaving Dianne alone with her questions—and the charged silence Ryan had left behind.

Nineteen

The dire wolves arrived in the early evening some weeks later in the valley where Fushë-Arrëz sheltered among the bordering mountains.

Great beasts, they towered over their lesser relatives, the Old-World grey wolves, who at their largest and most fearsome—legendary animals from history—reached a measly one-hundred-seventy-five pounds and less than three feet tall. And who had been hunted mercilessly since the Middle Ages until they only dared hunt among humans when their hunger drove them.

These unreal and untimely monsters stood five feet at the shoulders and two-hundred-fifty pounds. Larger than most men. Lean and sinewy with dark, hollow gazes filled with a void-like shimmer as if something else looked through them, harmonic distortions laced their growls, making the very air itself vibrate unnaturally. Hardened patches of chitin mottled their fur, and their limbs were slightly elongated, giving them an ungainly, insect-like gait.

As they loped through the forests and rocky slopes of the Accursed Mountains, tendrils of harmonic distortion flickered along their unstable bodies, shifting them in and out of physical form. They were a misshapen, ruined echo of what a wolf should be.

The first to see them were the villagers of Breg, south of Fushë-Arrëz nearly ten kilometers and just outside the harmonic mesh system that served as both a means of public address and intrusion detection for the Kastrioti estate. The creatures prowled back and forth along the very edge of the harmonic defenses, their growls especially grotesque as black wisps of discord rolled off of them only to be pushed away by the mesh system. And, at first, the terrified villagers believed that the animals feared crossing the *zoti*'s invisible barrier.

And they grew complacent, coming out in small groups to watch the beasts, studying them at first before daring to approach the harmonic perimeter, seeing how close they could get to the ugly animals. The creatures neither approached nor retreated, their hollow gazes unreadable. The villagers mistook this for indifference. A few rowdy teen boys even darted across the *Elioud* boundary, staying beyond it longer and longer during the daylight hours. The dire wolves only watched, unmoved by the boys' antics.

Until the evening that they howled in prolonged, discordant triumph and tore through the barrier surrounding the *zoti*'s demesne, bursting from a cloud of warped shadow and flickering in and out of the visible plane.

Their first casualty was a farmer tending his horses in early evening. His wife, who'd come to their front door, wiping her hands on her apron, stood in frozen horror as she saw the monsters creep from under the trees at the forest's edge, their approach eerily silent and focused, and her husband with his back turned to them as he rubbed his favorite horse's muzzle, unaware of his impending doom.

The horse caught their scent first, rearing, its front legs flashing and its hooves connecting with the farmer's face. He went down, hard, stunned. And then the dire wolves were on him, still silent, still focused. Still vicious and thorough.

In a final act of dominance, they stopped ravaging her poor dead husband to stare at her, to let her know that they chose not to maul her as well. The largest beast then growled and whipped his head around, taking off at a trot for the forest with the others at his heels.

That moment haunted her for the rest of her life. It was the moment the farmer's wife realized that these creatures don't just kill. They understand the spiritual loss that they inflict.

William DeVries finished his quick shower and change of clothes, the weight of his current duties pressing on him, each task layering itself over the rising discord of the world around him. His harmonic signature felt inflamed, an ache just below awareness, like a low-grade autoimmune reaction.

He stepped from the large walk-in shower, its unpolished stone tile floor warm and wet, into the damp chill of the bathroom, and shivered.

Perhaps it was autoimmune. He hadn't entirely shed the aberrant harmonies that marked him as human.

Fallen. Incomplete.

The thought hung there, dissonant and unwelcome, as if Willem's very being resisted the idea that his corporeal nature might still hold sway over him despite working side by side with the other *Elioud* and on the same redemptive mission. Yet he felt those splintered chords and unfinished melodies in his spirit, lingering in the background, faint but persistent—like a harmony waiting for its counterpoint, unresolved.

It made him see the world differently, feel it differently.

He found himself framing reality in strange new ways: harmonics and medicine, frequencies instead of structures.

It used to be different. Architecture had been his lens, his way of imposing form on chaos. Before Mihàil had offered him a greater purpose, he'd thought in steel and stone, shape and shadow sculpted in space. Raw materials provided by man and nature, neatly arranged under his direction.

Now? Now, it was all harmonic planes intersecting the real world—music shaping matter. Frequencies piercing heart and spirit, stitching the tangible and intangible together like an unseen thread. *That* had become his reality ever since he'd joined the *Elioud* four years ago.

After he'd lost Eva.

Eva. Just the sound of her name in his thoughts resonated a world of pain and loss, though it had grown softer, more muted as he immersed himself in this new world of harmonic healing, as he worked to craft methods and instruments to care for troubled individuals, the sick of body as well as spirit.

Grabbing a heated towel from the harmonic drying rack on the wall, he raised his temperature enough to dry his skin as he drew the towel over it, capturing any stray moisture. The plush material absorbed the droplets, its warmth radiating back into his skin like a second layer of heat. He paused, noticing that he now rubbed his neck with heated fingertips, unconsciously sending low-level harmonies into the taut muscles, relaxing them.

He was no fool. He knew that the admonition *physician heal thyself* held true for him more than most. But he also knew that to do it, he needed to accomplish it through service to those more gravely in need.

Like Mihàil, who remained in the ICU in his new clinic, the one he'd prioritized over the tactical operations center *and* the chapel. The one who'd prepared to sacrifice himself, despite his wife and baby daughter, for his sister-in-law and her friend, both virtual strangers to him.

And like that friend, a young woman named Germaine, who lay in a special harmonically shielded suite on the top floor of the clinic, possessed by the terrifying and unheard-of *daemonic* influence of Abaddon, Angel of the Abyss. Even Eva hadn't suffered in the way that Germaine suffered. Continued to suffer despite the best care that medicine and *Elioud* harmonics could provide.

Finishing his simple grooming routine with a quick shave and hair comb, Willem dressed in a black polo and tan chinos—not nearly as fashionable as he'd been as an architect at one of the most prestigious firms in Amsterdam. But he couldn't think of a better uniform for his new role developing and testing music therapy that sought to align the disordered harmonics those here in this world with the celestial realm.

The last item he donned was a pendant, simple in shape but intricate in meaning. Crafted from polished metal, its center bore the image of St. Michael standing resolute against the forces of darkness, his armor gleaming in detailed relief. Encircling the archangel was an engraving of Van Gogh's starry night sky, each swirl and star etched with care—a quiet tribute to Eva and their shared connection to the divine. Beneath its artistry, subtle harmonic resonances hummed, tailored to soothe and shield Willem, reminding him with every breath of his commitment to protect and heal, to honor both her memory and the *Elioud* mission.

When he arrived at the clinic, he nodded at the staff behind the main desk tucked in the corner of the lobby. He allowed himself only a cursory glimpse of the spacious first-floor entrance, its walls lined with floor-to-ceiling windows on two sides, allowing mountain vistas to enter the sightlines of anyone working or visiting.

On the main wall, a central mosaic blended Albanian motifs of suns, stars, and eagles with *Elioud* harmonic designs, symbolizing the clinic's purpose as a bridge between Heaven and Earth. The limestone walls, marble floors, and beechwood rafters and furniture, upholstered in cream, ivory, and soft rose, lent a soothing air, their cushions embroidered in faintly shimmering thread with subtle flowing patterns that evoked the music of the spheres. The patterns had also been etched in copper light fixtures, whose frosted glass filled the interior with a soft, diffuse light.

At the shielded suite, he paused to center himself, breathing carefully to align his own harmonics with the grounded ones here. Beneath his feet, the stone shifted subtly as if alive, something only an *Elioud* would sense, accommodating and embracing his weight. Then he touched a fingertip to the St. Michael pendant, feeling the grooves of its stars and swirls, before placing his palm on the harmonic signature scanner at the suite's entrance. The quiet thrum of the scanner resonated in the air, its tone a gentle invitation to step forward.

He stepped into the outer room, designed to look like a small apartment with a round chestnut dining table positioned in the far corner with a sitting area next to it. There, a loveseat and two comfortable easy chairs, all upholstered in brocaded sage, silver, and cream sigils infused with healing harmonics, a low coffee table in the same rich color between them, beckoned with access to bookshelves, art on the walls, and reading lamp. Behind him was a small kitchenette, ideal for one. Floor-to-ceiling windows—glass so clear as to be invisible—opened up the entire wall between dining area and kitchen, making the tiny space feel larger and welcoming.

Not like the prison it was.

Well, perhaps *prison* was too strong a word. *Asylum. Sanctuary. Refuge.* Those terms better suited the genteel restraint intended for the person lying inside the inner room, the one whose physical body now acted as a vessel to one of the most powerful *daemons* known to *Elioud* and humanity alike. Or more precisely, it waited to act as a vessel. A shell, a pale shadow of its former animated personality.

A slow shudder coursed down Willem's spine. For a moment, he couldn't move. He almost didn't breathe.

He pictured the once-vital young woman inside, her fine, light-brown curls now lank and plastered to her cheeks, red scratches and cuts vivid against their wan skin, her body wracked with fever that he struggled to keep down with a constant flow of harmonically cooled air.

And then he squared his shoulders, pressed his lips together, inhaled the harmony programmed into the very materials of the carefully constructed apartment, and stepped forward to the panel hidden in the wall next to the dining table. When he pressed his hand against it, it came alive under his palm like liquid silver, steadying his own sudden, discordant nerves.

It also illuminated the mirror-like sheen of the framed panel next to the table, revealing a two-way mirror into the bedroom where Germaine Grimes, a 29-year-old research scientist from the U.S., lay writhing continuously on her bed, held in place by invisible and silent harmonic bonds to keep her—and the rest of the world—safe.

For a moment, Willem stared at his reflection in the panel, his features ghosted over hers. He erased the image with a blink and shifted focus, scanning the diagnostics that translated her fractured spiritual state into an intricate tapestry of frequencies and metrics.

After he studied the patient's baseline harmonic signature, he didn't trust himself to listen to its corrupted melody un-aided. Instead, he cleaned up the distortion with controlled swipes over the sound-engineering submenu, aligning it with the angelic frequencies known to the *Elioud*.

He wasn't prepared for the result.

A pure, sweet sound washed over him like fresh rain in April, lifting his spirit. He briefly closed his eyes and let it fill him like a depleted reservoir.

When he opened them, he was shocked to see Germaine awake, her pale blue eyes gleaming intensely at him from her ravaged face as if she could see him through the opaque harmonic panel separating them.

Willem sucked in a breath, his own heartbeat erratic against its hard bone cage, pinned and displayed like a butterfly against dark-blue velvet.

He placed a fingertip on his St. Michael pendant. His harmonics steadied, and his breathing eased. He buttressed them from the well of higher frequencies stored in the suite's reserve, itself grounded in the very bedrock of the mountain from which the clinic emerged.

Then opened the door to the inner room and stepped through the metaphoric looking glass to approach the beautiful young woman for the first time since snatching her from the clutches of the Angel of the Abyss.

Germaine no longer nailed him with a preternatural gaze. Instead, she shifted on the double bed, her movements increasingly energetic and exaggerated. As Willem approached, she growled and barked as she thrashed, her head rolling against the gel-cooled pillows in rapid denial of his presence.

Pain lanced Willem through the pendant on his chest like a bolt of lightning.

Swallowing hard, he ignored it, his attention drawn to the faint dark iridescence rising from her skin like an inverted aura, its source intricately linked to her signature and something glinting on her forearm.

The burning pain intensified as he halted within reach of his patient. It pierced his skull now. With a strange breathless horror, he reached for the bracelet whose gleaming metal links clamped onto her delicate wrist.

An engraved metal charm dangled from the sly cuff, a charm that radiated malign energy like a black hole in the firmament. Willem grasped it between finger and thumb, its icy cold freezing the marrow of his bones.

He focused his wavering vision on the hand with two short fingers splayed to reveal three longer middle fingers. And in its palm, a baleful blue eye that echoed Germaine's.

Ryan stood, frozen, his gaze compelled to look down at the monstrous beast lying at his feet. He hadn't quite believed the streaming video his security team had provided him when they identified this straggler among the dire wolves. But, if anything, this dead creature radiated a grotesque menace the high-def image had been unable to convey.

Dire wolves.

That's what they'd taken to calling them over the past few weeks they'd plagued the boundaries of the Kastriotis' land, though no one knew exactly what they were. Actual dire wolves had roamed North America during the Ice Age. They were extinct. They shouldn't exist here, in modern Albania, even in the mountains.

Even among those peaks called Accursed.

"Reminds me of a Warg," said Miles, coming to stand next to him. The former CIA officer and current director of the Kastriotis' Tac Ops center, had been tapped to help lead the security forces. Ryan was grateful for the older man's extensive SERE training in the Marines. It had come in handy when taking their quarry down.

"'Warg'?" he said, his arms crossed as he studied the unnatural animal. "You mean the evil wolves the orcs rode in *Lord of the Rings?*"

Miles nodded. "Same. Though I never thought I'd use a fantasy-lit reference in a real conversation before." He toed the carcass with his combat boot. It didn't budge. "Somehow I doubt Tolkien imagined the smell."

Ryan said nothing, just scanned the field around them. His people stood in a perimeter around the narrow area between the slope and forest, each armed with the Disrupter combat shotgun that Miró had worked around the clock to manufacturer in enough quantities—and with enough harmonic juice—to take down a dire wolf. Or at least, to deliver a shock to the creature's unfamiliar nervous system that would incapacitate it long enough for a conventional weapon to kill it. Their taut mouths and narrowed eyes told their own story about their unspoken thoughts, but every single one of them stood proud and kept watch.

The locals were another story, however.

The farmers and shepherds, the beekeepers and herbalists had all been terrorized for days, starting with the unprovoked killing of a farmer south of Mihàil's estate. Most refused to be outside between dusk and dawn, and many had quietly found lodging in Fushë-Arrëz itself, even sleeping in the open along the stretch of highway running through the town, or on the excavated grounds of the future chapel.

Now they stood in tight, murmuring clumps, the whites of their eyes glistening in the clear light shed by the extensive network of drones illuminating the shadowy field north of the small Albanian town.

Despite the careful calibration of light so that no shadows lingered within eyesight, a pall hung over the edges of the gathering. Ryan, however, didn't want to fuel their speculation by having his second-in-command escort them to a safe distance. The faint hum of the drones, programmed to send out soothing sounds for the non-combatant humans, only underscored the unnatural silence of the trees edging the rocky open area.

András and Beta arrived next, having been on scouting and overwatch duty, respectively. The big *Elioud* strode toward the dire wolf, his hands steaming in the cool evening air and his eyes glowing, reminding Ryan of an ancient Viking berserker who knew no fear. A few paces behind him walked his wife, her keen gaze continuously traveling the high ground around them before scanning the forest, a sniper rifle carried across her chest.

They drew close and halted on the other side of the dire wolf, András's fingers clenching and unclenching as his hands visibly reddened. Ryan hadn't ever seen the actual heat the *Elioud* conjured from their very signatures before. He stood pinned to the ground, fascinated at the power the large demi-angel wielded. All at once he understood that András intended to incinerate the foul beast—and profoundly grateful that the stink and evening chill would be driven away.

Nevertheless, he said, "Elias and his second are on their way. Maybe wait until he gets a chance to take a look at the dire wolf before you turn it to ash."

András didn't respond for a moment, and Ryan feared the *Elioud* battle commander would ignore his suggestion. Then the big male shrugged, and his hands returned to normal human flesh and the steam dissipated.

"That's fair."

They didn't have to wait long. Elias arrived with his second, Antonio, and a surprising third: Willem, the somber Dutch architect who hadn't been out in the field since the December campaign against Asmodeus and his pet dragon, Kôkabîêl. Willem had lost his fiancée Eva after she'd fallen under the harmonic control of Yeqon—the Seducer, the original Watcher who'd lured the first woman and set the *Elioud* legacy in motion. Willem looked ashen now, as if haunted by more than memory.

A viscous thrill of dread rolled over Ryan. He shifted his feet wider as it landed in his still-healing gut, which ached deep inside, especially in the middle of the night.

And the middle of his nightmares.

He caught Elias's serious gaze and nodded. They'd been in the training center together multiple times over the past week, each taking the measure of the other man, his leadership, and the warriors under his command. Ryan didn't care that the knights weren't 'real' soldiers in the sense of a modern army. Elias, Antonio, and the rest? They were the real deal.

He glanced at András as the three newcomers settled on the other side of the dire-wolf carcass. The giant Hungarian dipped his chin at Ryan: it was his show.

Ryan cleared his throat and rolled his shoulders, setting his feet in a wider stance and clasping his hands at his waist. "The rest have disappeared. Apparently, they don't give a crap about this ugly bastard here." He nodded toward the dire wolf, ignoring its open maw and dagger-length fangs.

Elias squinted and looked back toward the woods. "Until now, they have always hunted as a pack. This one is smaller than the others, yes, but they did not try to defend him. That strikes me as suspicious."

Beta squatted next to the animal. An instant later, a small hooked knife, her karambit, appeared in her left hand. She struck at the creature's throat before Ryan could anticipate her moves. Thirty seconds later, she'd detached the head. She looked over her shoulder at her husband, whose dark glare sent a shiver down Ryan's spine.

"It is a wolf. A perverted wolf, corrupted by Abaddon's influence," she said, standing and turning back to the group with the dripping head at her side. Beta gestured at the landscape around them as she spoke. "This pack comes from these mountains."

Tightness gripped Ryan's chest. Heat flamed in his wound. For a moment, he struggled again with Germaine, who raked her claws into his gut.

He looked at András and Beta. "The lure?" he asked, not elaborating. Miró had briefed the senior command staff at the after-action conference they'd held in order to review the state of the world post-geomagnetic flare when Ryan had recovered enough to attend.

The couple exchanged glances with Elias, who looked grim. His hand tightened on the hilt of his harmonic ribbon, one of the weapons the Archangel Zophiel had gifted the mysterious Order after the war with Kôkabîêl, the Fallen Watcher Angel known as the Star of God. Antonio, who stood next to his order's commander, shifted but said nothing.

Before the two *Elioud* warriors could answer, Willem took a step forward. "Miró sequestered the charm you brought back from Split, Demon Slayer." He shook his head. "This is not from that one."

He paused, seeming to gather himself before plunging on. "It is from the bracelet that Germaine Grimes wears that I discovered not half an hour ago. I was unable to remove it before I came, not without risking her life. It is powerful enough to warp susceptible creatures within a sphere of influence, although I do not know yet how wide that is."

He pointed toward the head that Beta still gripped. "These animals are neither dumb nor acting on their own evil instincts. Abaddon watches us even now through its eyes."

"Sweet Saint Zophiel," said Elias in a low murmur.

The pitspawn prick, Abaddon, had a toehold inside Albania. It was only a matter of time before he and his Locusts appeared. The dire wolves had been more than a harbinger: they'd been advance shock troops.

Before Ryan could lead the next conversation to a tactical response, the humming drones overhead began to shriek a high-pitched, staccato warning.

"Intrusion! Intrusion! Intrusion! Sectors Six, Seven, and Eight. Tactical breach confirmed. Deploy to assigned rally points. Condition Umbra. This is not a drill."

Holy crap. The dire wolves had used the straggler as a distraction to slip past their perimeter. The Kastrioti Estate was under attack with half-trained recruits as defenders.

Dianne.

Dianne had no one there to save her from the dire wolves.

In that moment, Ryan knew that whatever wall he'd erected to protect her from him had detonated into a fine mist of urgency, protectiveness, and love.

Love.

The realization he'd tried to bury echoed around his heart.

He wasn't about to lose the woman he loved to the motherfarging Angel of the Abyss. Abaddon could go screw himself—with a flaming sword.

Twenty

Dianne felt restless. She didn't know why. She'd spent the past weeks pushing herself to exhausted oblivion, training during the day using the workout regimen that Beta had provided her, learning hand-to-hand combat with the laconic *Elioud* warrior (in baby steps, yes), and hours at the range where she'd shown remarkable ability with guns of all types. When she wasn't running, grappling, or shooting, she was trying to learn her new world in as much detail as she could, the people, places, and culture.

Beyond that, she kept watch over her silent brother-in-law deep at night while Olivia slept, passed out in a nearby chair, or spent time with her niece, who'd decided to pull up and take her first wobbling steps in the midst of an adult world that had no time or awareness to celebrate.

Not unlike her.

Tonight, something pulsed in the air. Expectation. Warning. Foreboding. Dread. Whatever made up this toxic brew, it gripped her by the shoulders and twisted in her gut. The air was unnaturally still, a pungent hint of rot lingering like a bad taste over the training compound.

She wished she knew where Ryan was. She'd tried, over and over, to put him out of her mind. Out of her heart. But he always returned to her during her sleep. Him in the library of the cruise ship, startled and speechless as she leaned in to kiss him. At dinner in the steakhouse, his hazel eyes drawing her in, his powerful body a lure that still made her breathless thinking about it. Fighting against *daemoniacs* on the dock in Split. At her side as they made Molotov cocktails together, his fingers brushing hers when she handed him a bottle.

In Međugorje where the geomagnetic flare seemed to bring Heaven and Earth together. Where she'd first realized that she was all in. Falling in love and seeing it through. Even with Ryan's rejection, she wouldn't change that decision if she could. Because now she'd experienced something real, something worthy and lifechanging. The pain only brought that truth home.

What was the saying the British had? Keep calm and carry on. She just needed to face her own fears without Ryan at her side. Her fingers drifted to the thigh rig she wore, drawn to the grip of the Glock—Ryan's weapon of choice—she now carried openly everywhere with her, much to her mother's consternation and her brother's amusement.

"Rangers lead the way," she said to herself, remembering his quiet comment when Olivia had ordered her to support his efforts to get them safely back to Fushë-Arrëz.

As she walked toward the guesthouse that Olivia had offered her not far from the main Kastrioti house, Dianne saw Olivia's nanny emerge into the twilight with Luljeta. The little girl had likely had a late afternoon nap and would be awake into the evening, eager for stimulation and distraction. Dianne hastened her steps toward them, longing for the same.

The deep rumble of wolves caught her up short.

The hairs on the back of Dianne's neck fluttered as the skin there tightened uncomfortably in the suddenly chill air. She surveyed the area around them as she'd seen Beta do, almost as a tic it was so second nature for the *Elioud* warrior.

And then she saw them: half a dozen wolves as tall as a pony skulking under the dwarf ornamental trees on the far side of the back garden, the evening sunlight glinting from their hollow eyes.

Dianne choked a gasp back, her hand going to her throat. *Dire wolves*. Harbingers of evil.

The wild animals had appeared not long after she and Ryan had arrived in Fushë-Arrëz, killing a farmer and terrifying everyone, including the tough security forces and knights.

No one had told Dianne anything about them, but she knew in her bones that it was her fault.

At her reaction, the largest wolf, clearly the leader, looked at her before deliberately turning toward the young woman bouncing her giggling charge in her arms.

Dianne's petrified state exploded into hot motion. "Lirika!" she yelled as she pulled the Glock from her thigh rig and ran.

The nanny, who turned at her name, gave a hoarse shout at the sight of the massive predators stalking her but kept her presence of mind. Pivoting, she began sprinting back toward the Kastrioti house.

The lead dire wolf began to run as well, his pack trailing a few paces behind.

Dianne planted her feet, raised the Glock, and sighted on the beast's head. She took a moment to control her breathing, the memory of Beta's warm whisper brushing her ear, and then squeezed the trigger.

Her bullet impacted the brute behind an ear, causing him to stumble and then catapult and roll in a tangle of lanky legs and clublike paws. The other wolves, unable to stop in time, either veered around their fallen leader or crashed into him, turning the entire pack into a snapping, snarling mess.

Dianne launched herself on a path to block the wolves from following Lirika, who'd reached the steps to the Kastriotis' front door and took them two at a time, her hand pressing Luljeta's head into her shoulder despite the baby's scared wailing and efforts to free herself.

Dianne planted her feet on the wide walkway paved in flat Albania slate and allowed herself a quick glance at Lirika at the top of the flight of steps.

When she looked back, to her shock and horror, the lead dire wolf growled, and, shaking off his packmates, rose to his feet. His malign gaze settled on her, a large black, bleeding hole over one eye attesting to her marksmanship.

Dianne swallowed, heart jumping to flutter at the base of her throat like a moth beating itself against an outside light. Still, she straightened her shoulders and kept her gaze focused on the animal. She would *not* acknowledge her fear, even if the monster smelled her sweat or saw her trembling or whatever way an animal sensed the terror of its prey.

No. *Not* prey. She would not be its prey. She would make it take her down fighting.

At that thought, the beast opened its mouth into a recognizable—if gruesome—smile. The other dire wolves, eerily silent, lined up on either side of their captain, studying her. Then all at once, from some signal Dianne didn't see, they all extended their forearms and then leaned back into the familiar down-dog yoga position.

A clear bow. To *her*.

The charm bracelet on her wrist burned her as if the wolves' incendiary regard called something from it. She ignored the fiery pain to lift the Glock and sight it on the lead wolf's intact eye.

After a long moment in which Dianne's heart failed to beat, the dire wolves returned to a normal stance. The majestic villain in their midst winked—he *winked* for the love of all that was holy—and then spun away, his tail flying as he ran down the walkway toward the main path that circled the estate. The claws of the pack rattled against the smooth slate, shivering the stone under her feet. A fresh breeze sent a rank odor of decay and animal musk to her.

Dianne turned, sprinted to some bushes edging the walkway, and vomited.

Shaking, she stood up and wiped the back of her hand over her mouth. It wasn't until she glimpsed the vile creatures running down the terraced slope from Olivia's house toward the pass-through under the highway that led to the clinic on the other side that she realized the attack wasn't over.

Mihàil. Her brother-in-law, the *zoti*, had awakened for the first time today. A vivid image of him, his cheeks covered in rough stubble under the white bandage disguising half his face, lying propped upright against pillows while Olivia, silent tears sheeting her cheeks, stood next to his bed filled Dianne's tumultuous thoughts.

She didn't know how or why, but somehow the dire wolves *knew*. There were security guards at the clinic, but it was minimally staffed, especially now as the *Elioud* and Ryan had pulled many of their people onto guard duty on the perimeter of the Kastriotis' defenses in the Albanian countryside.

How many would die protecting their lord?

And Mihàil ... would he be able to defend himself against the dire wolves?

She didn't want to find out.

Taking off at a run, Dianne gave thanks that she'd spent the previous six months at the gym instead of clubbing. Never much of an athlete, she at least had the gas to plunge down the slope toward the ingenious stone-lined tunnel that Willem had designed to allow foot traffic to cross to the road without danger. The dire wolves ignored the tunnel and sped across the empty highway, their long legs flying over the shadowy ground at the bottom of the valley.

Crap, crap, crap.

In the evening air around her, a harsh programmed voice wailed, "Intrusion! Intrusion! Intrusion! Sectors Six, Seven, and Eight. Tactical breach confirmed. Deploy to assigned rally points. Condition Umbra. This is not a drill."

Yes! The harmonic public announcement system. She wasn't out here all by herself against the vicious monsters.

Those sectors, if Dianne remembered the map of the system displayed in every hall, office, and conference room at the training center, included the Kastrioti estate, clinic, and chapel grounds. But the alarm wasn't specific enough. The system relied on physical markers in the environment for data, and that included pings from on-duty personnel gear. As far as she could tell, she was the only one close enough to the dire wolves to know exactly where they were, at least until the clinic's system picked them up.

She needed to warn everyone, to get Ryan and the others to return to defend the clinic.

Dianne remembered the connection she'd had to the harmonic comms system. Everyone had seemed surprised—and not in a good way—that she'd been able to listen in and respond. They'd suggested it was tied to the special tunic that Olivia had sent for her to wear, but Dianne had also gotten the distinct impression that her communication ability didn't rely solely on that miraculous garment.

What if she had some innate harmonic talent that had been awakened during the *daemonic* assault in Split? She was Olivia's sister after all ...

And she'd definitely felt a connection to Ryan in Međugorje. Maybe it was still there even though he'd shut her out.

"Beast, Beauty Queen. How copy?" she said as she ran through the pass-through, focusing on Ryan's beloved face in her memory. Her words echoed against the stone, making her feel ridiculous for speaking into thin air.

"Dianne?" asked Ryan, sounding stunned.

"Who else do you call 'Beauty Queen'?" she asked, her breath coming in pants as she climbed the raw ground of the terraced slope where a future outdoor worship area would be built. "You need to get to the clinic. The dire wolves are heading there."

"You've seen them?" he asked, alarm making his voice rough. But his voice in her ear steadied her. She could almost feel the heat from his skin, smell his clean scent. She closed her eyes for a brief moment, inhaling an easier breath as Ryan's presence filled her.

"Seen them, shot the leader in the head. Outside Olivia and Mihàil's house. The creepy bastard just got back up and led the others to the clinic," she said, ignoring the burning in her thighs as she pushed uphill toward the clinic where the dire wolves had halted outside the entrance. She didn't like the way the largest dire wolf seemed to study the wide glass doors.

She knew when Ryan had figured out her position when he swore, vigorously and colorfully. Still, the fury in his next words nearly took her breath away—and told her more than he'd intended about how he felt about her. "What the hell are you doing outside the clinic? Get out of there! Go to the training center or better yet the ops center. Miles will protect you. How copy, Beauty Queen?"

Dianne halted at the next terrace down from the level that the clinic and site of the future chapel sat on. She was totally exposed, but none of the dire wolves even looked in her direction. She pressed against the exposed wall of packed earth at the rear of the terraced landscape as she moved closer to the pack of dire wolves above.

"Beauty Queen, confirm last order. How copy?"

"They aren't interested in me, Beast," she said, moving backwards on the terrace to catch a glimpse of the wolves' hollow gazes reflected in the last rays of the setting sun on the glass doors and walls of the clinic. She saw herself there, the sun highlighting her blond hair like a halo. For a moment her gaze locked with that of the leader, the ragged black bullet hole a third eye on his motley head. "They're here for Mihàil."

Ryan was silent for a moment, and then the comms, which had continued blaring their warning about an intrusion, switched to a different message with Ryan's voice.

"Updated enemy position confirmed—dire wolves advancing on clinic grounds! Sector Seven compromised. Repeat—Sector Seven compromised. Immediate Response Teams: Redirect to clinic perimeter. Non-combat personnel: Evacuate via rear tunnel immediately—priority exit route engaged. Medical staff: Transport all ambulatory patients to evacuation route. Immobile patients and remaining personnel: Secure-room lockdown activated—reinforced barriers engaged. Combat personnel—defensive protocols active! Weapons free. Authority override—priority defense-directive initiated. Protect the *zoti*. Hold the perimeter."

As the system announced this new protocol, steel security screens dropped over the glass doors and walls of the clinic entrance. They'd scarcely slammed into the limestone pavers forming a wide patio next to the building with a metallic crash before retractable bollards erupted from the pavers, jolting the compacted earth against which Dianne leaned. Finally, reinforced grilles locked into place over the security screens. Then electromagnetic locks engaged, resonating through the steel frame like a tuning fork.

Above the clinic's first floor, armed security guards appeared in the tall windows lining the front of the building.

"Impressive, Beast," said Dianne, rubbing her wrist, now scalded by the charm bracelet. Its weight dragged at her arm, almost as if it didn't want her to raise the Glock. "But something tells me it's not going to be enough."

"What do you see?" asked Ryan, coiled urgency driving his words into her brain. He almost sounded as if he was standing next to her.

Dianne watched as the largest dire wolf, who'd waited in a seated position while the clinic's defensive system activated, stood and began picking its way through the bollards as if navigating a path among roses. She glanced up at the sky, where roiling black clouds sailed in to obliterate the last of the setting sun, throwing the clinic into deep shadow.

The Glock slipped against her sweaty palm forcing her to bring her other hand to its grip as she answered. "The zombie bastard that I shot has gone right up to the doors. He seems to be studying them ... *oh, sweet Lord* ..." Dianne's voice wavered as the vibrations trailing through the lead dire wolf hit her like heatwaves around a desert mirage. They rolled down her body until she trembled like leaves pelted by hail. Her eyes refused to blink. Everything around her shimmered, even the solid glass, steel, and stone clinic.

The alpha dire wolf tilted his head before lifting his paw and pressing it against the steel grille in front of him. His paw disappeared beneath its surface like a dog patting a pond. The shimmer deepened, sending ripples across the rest of the grille, spreading out into the other door and windows.

Dianne's vision flickered. The air suffocated her.

"Dianne!" Ryan's yell hit her mind like thunder, breaking the spell. "Stay put! I'm coming for you. You got that, soldier? I. Am. Coming. For. You."

Dizziness flooded Dianne, dragging her to her knees. She choked, gasping as if trying to breathe water. Her hand holding the Glock fell to the unfinished terrace, sending a brown puff of dirt swirling around her face. Involuntary tears coursed down her cheeks.

Through her blurry vision, she saw the lead dire wolf stick his head into the liquified steel covering the clinic door to the ruff on his neck. As he did, shifting light overhead brought Dianne's gaze up to the windows several floors above the entrance to see a visibly trembling Mihàil being held upright between two men in hospital scrubs, his sole eye trained on the sky as if he could call down lightning from its heavy cumulonimbus shroud.

The clouds responded with an unnatural low moaning that raked the air with electricity. Something inside the storm moved. Or so it seemed to Dianne, now pressed against the ground, shaking in the icy wind that sent her hair dancing among dirt dervishes.

The dire wolves reacted, stiffening as their attention shifted from the clinic to the sky. Snarling, the lead dire wolf stepped back onto the terrace, its ears flat against its skull. He watched the storm like a soldier assessing a battlefield shift.

Lightning flickered, sending flashes of white-hot brilliance across Mihàil's half-ruined visage now free of its bandage, lighting up the ground around the clinic in a phosphorescent blaze. The thick looming clouds contracted inward as if recoiling from his glare. For a breath, the air held itself still, stretched thin, as though the storm itself was deciding whether to yield or strike.

Until the first dark-winged figure descended, its presence cutting through the unnatural weight pressing on Dianne. Other dark-winged figures rained down, their elongated shadows seeking the dire wolves. They were silent save for the crackling energy that emanated from them, disturbing everything. Leaves, dirt, even small stones swirled in the air around their grim cohort.

The dire wolves hesitated.

And then the dark-winged figures were upon them, bringing the storm to the beasts.

In the midst of chaos and furious snarling, Ryan appeared in a dazzling burst of lightning, running up the unfinished amphitheater's terraced steps toward her, relentless and implacable. The howling winds and crackling energy seemed to part before his determined onslaught, opening up a channel of stillness in the tumult.

For a moment, Dianne thought he was the king of the black-winged beings.

As Ryan reached the level where she lay sprawled, the calmness stretched before him, bringing Dianne sweet, clean air she didn't know she needed. Her lungs inhaled, and the pressure on her chest and head eased. But the unnatural storm refused to relinquish its hold on her. For a split second, as she struggled to focus on his blurred face, icy terror washed through her core.

Ryan slid to his knees in front of her, gripping her arms with bruising force. Dianne winced, and he immediately softened his hold before dragging her upright and searching her face with an intensity that laid her bare, bringing everything into focus. He was here. He'd come for her.

The next moment his big hands felt their way down her arms. A painful electric jolt surged up her arm as his fingers brushed over the bracelet.

"Are you all right?" His gaze burned like a promise. Like losing her now wasn't an option.

At Dianne's mute nod, he put both his hands on either side of her face and dipped his mouth to claim hers. Everything chaotic, fearful and angry, stilled inside her. It was as if she'd come home at last. The most beautiful music sang inside her, just as it had at Međugorje.

Her hands came of their own accord to Ryan's massive shoulders, bracing her against his warmth. Then he groaned, deepening the kiss, and pulled her snug against his broad chest while his arms went around her. His strong fingers pressed into her back and waist, molding her against him as if he could merge them with the force of his will.

The storm intensified around them as the wind roared, its pitch rising as lightning lit the night directly overhead. Sounds of vicious fighting between the dire wolves—snapping, growling, striking—and the mysterious figures wove a clashing counterpoint to nature's onslaught. The cheap souvenir trinket that Germaine had given her branded Dianne, the scorching pain mixing with the love, hope, and longing in their kiss as if something not of this world tried to break their bond, to rip them apart and steal her away.

Dianne snuggled against Ryan, seeking to get closer. She was never letting this man go. She felt her knees weaken as the drugging effect of his kiss made her reel.

Ryan tightened his arms to keep her upright, his body wrapped protectively around her, shielding her from the storm's fury which combusted in a spectacular lightning burst in the sky over them.

Silence descended over them as the storm ended.

When Dianne opened her eyes, the lightning lingered on her retinas even though everything, including the clinic above them, was dark.

The dire wolves and the dark-winged figures had vanished.

And the bracelet had seared its way beneath her skin, fused to her very bone like metal smelted into flesh, its heat lingering like the storm's dying embers.

Twenty-One

Dianne shivered.

Ryan, who'd turned to scan the landscape around them, faced her again as fat, cold raindrops began to fall. They clung to her skin instead of sliding away, heavier than they should be.

"We've got to get to shelter," he said, his voice rough. "Can you walk?"

She nodded. "I'm fine. Those dire wolves seemed less than concerned about me. In fact, it felt like they wanted me to watch them."

Ryan's expression tightened, his gaze flicking toward the trees on the slope above them to the north.

Something was off. Not just the eerie silence or the pressure in the air, but the way the landscape itself seemed to wait, as though the world had exhaled and refused to breathe in again.

Dianne's instincts prickled. She swallowed. The storm had ended. The quiet had not. Even the wind refused to stir. Whatever force had sent the wolves wasn't finished. It was watching.

But maybe it wasn't just about the *Elioud* and their longstanding battle against the Dark angelic forces.

Maybe it was her.

The thought chilled her more than the rain.

She'd been around too much *daemonic* activity, starting with the cruise, then Podgorica, then the mountains. Was she drawing them, or was she just unlucky enough to always be at the center?

Did Abaddon, the Angel of the Abyss, want her?

The hideous image of an immense black locust with a human head wearing a glittering obsidian diadem invaded her thoughts. The creature who'd roasted her powerful brother-in-law, who'd come to extract them on the highway as they escaped from Split?

She shoved it away, knowing it would surface later in her all-too-vivid nightmares.

Ryan gripped Dianne's elbows and, rising to his feet, hefted her to hers.

Dianne winced as the bracelet burned her.

"What? What is it?" Ryan began running his hands over her midsection, turning her to check her back and waist.

"It's nothing," she said, waving her unencumbered arm. "Just not really in shape to race up a mountainside and then sprawl in the dirt." She glanced down. "Make that mud."

Ryan ignored her for a moment to run his big hands down her thighs and calves. The pleasure that gave Dianne brought a low moan from her. Ryan shot a narrowed gaze at her. Dianne looked up, blushing. Before she could explain, his gaze softened and traveled to her mouth.

She closed her eyes and leaned toward him ...

... only to stiffen and pull back at the sound of her sister's voice on the terrace above them.

Ryan pivoted, putting distance between them as he did. A sour taste filled Dianne's mouth. Was whatever happened between them only moments before gone, like the dire wolves?

Olivia took in both of them, assessing Ryan's proximity to her sister. Dianne recognized the subtle tightening at the other woman's temple, the controlled breath that Olivia took. She found herself straightening her shoulders and lifting her chin in response.

"Demon Slayer, sitrep," said Olivia after a deliberate pause, her demeanor as brisk and focused as Dianne had ever seen it. Commanding warriors was clearly a familiar—and comfortable—role for her.

Dianne had the unsettling feeling that Olivia had seen everything that had just transpired between her and Ryan, and in fact understood better than they did what was going on. Yet Olivia's inscrutable expression gave away nothing regarding her approval or disapproval.

As Ryan cleared his throat to answer, Olivia signed with a sharp hand movement for several of the men behind her to go on toward the silent, unlit clinic. Four burly men in black tactical clothing and combat boots, wearing glowing eyepieces and earpieces with attached curved microphones, took off at a run for the entrance.

Ryan's gaze remained on his commanding officer. His jaw tightened ever so slightly as the men passed, and Dianne sensed a shift in his stance. The team reached the security grille, moving in a coordinated, precise series of actions with few words. In that moment, Dianne realized that these were Ryan's men, men he'd personally trained and led.

Not a twitch. Not a glance of recognition from them.

His men.

It dawned on her that perhaps his first order of business should have been to secure Mihàil, the commander-in-chief of all the security forces.

"I'm waiting, Demon Slayer," said Olivia, her voice tinged with impatience. Despite the steady rain now falling, she remained dry as her harmonics turned the water into a misty rose-tinted aura.

Ryan's chin came up in a subtle angle of confidence as he prepared to speak. Dianne wanted to move closer to him and take his hand, but she refrained. There was no telling how anyone would react if she did that, and she didn't want to add to the already fraught situation.

"Clinic is secured, ma'am," said Ryan, holding Olivia's gaze without waver. "My team accessed it through the emergency lift while I continued to this location to provide Ms. Markham with backup. Elias and Antonio remained behind with the staff and patients while Draka, Giant, and DeVries entered through the elevator and secured the clinic. As I'm sure you're aware, ma'am, the *zoti* has been moved to the secure bunker and is now guarded by Draka and Giant. DeVries has secured the harmonic healing suite and will remain in that post until I give him the order to stand down."

Something in Ryan's voice alerted Dianne about this last detail. *Germaine*. She'd been in a special suite at the top of the clinic. A place where the *Elioud* attempted to break the hold that Abaddon had on her. They'd let Dianne visit her best friend a few times. Her friend looked awful, pale and restless with her broken leg in a cast. Invisible harmonic bands kept Germaine from moving the leg with its high-tech brace, but even so, whenever Dianne came anywhere near her, Germaine began to thrash and utter guttural sounds. Only the staid *Elioud* named Willem could calm her. Dianne had glimpsed him staring at Germaine, a look of pity and compassion on his features so profound that she prayed he would continue to fight for Germaine's life and soul.

Olivia nodded. Across from them, the security team had disengaged the security grille and now had the steel screens raised. "Good work, Demon Slayer. I and this team will remain here at the secure bunker with the *zoti* and Dr. Armand. Everyone else will be transported to the Aerie where you will lock down the compound after the last of the townspeople arrive. Everyone from the estate has already been sent there."

She inhaled, straightened. For the briefest moment, she seemed to burn brighter against the deepening night. "We're surrounded, Demon Slayer. The dire wolves are just the tip of the spear. Abaddon's Locusts wait at the head of an army of thousands of frothing *daemoniacs*, who muster in the mountains around us. And we don't yet know who the dire wolves fought here in front of the clinic. Their harmonic signatures weren't human, but neither were they angelic."

Dianne chose to speak up. "Mihàil knows who they are."

Olivia swiveled her haunting gaze on Dianne, who was astounded to see the glowing blue-gray of her irises. Her sister looked angelic herself in this moment. There was even a faint radiance limning her skin. "What makes you say this?"

Dianne swallowed and held her sister's gaze. She wished that Ryan stood at her side rather than a step ahead and away. "I saw him. Ryan can confirm it. He stood at that window"–she gestured to the third-floor window—"and glared at the storm until lightning flashed and dark-winged figures dropped from the sky. He didn't stop until they fought the dire wolves."

Olivia narrowed her eyes but didn't say anything. Instead, she dipped her chin. "Thank you for your report." When she went on, a husky note vibrated in her voice. "And thank you for saving Luljeta and Lirika. I hear that you're quite a shot." She looked at Ryan. "Make sure you use her wisely, Demon Slayer. I already know you'll protect her with your life." She paused a fraction of a breath. "See you both on the other side."

Olivia turned without a backward glance and entered into the now-open clinic entrance. The four security members fell in behind her, followed by the steel security screens descending again with a clang. This time, when the reinforced grilles descended, they hummed with a dangerous energy that sparked into the heavy stillness as if the *zonjë* had powered them with her very own indomitable spirit.

Ryan led Dianne down the terraced path where low-voltage landscape lighting lit the levels in a warm glow despite the heavy rain. The emergency generator, a microreactor, had kicked on, powering essential equipment for the entire valley, estate to clinic, village to operations center.

Relief flooded him. He hadn't known for sure that the microreactor would actually work if their harmonic-energy grid went offline. He'd been at the meetings where Miró introduced the design and operational specifications for this cutting-edge technology.

Small nuclear reactors weren't a new thing; the U.S. Navy powered their submarines with them. Yet they still weren't used widely on land as alternate energy sources, although they were safe, low-carbon options, because of public fear about failures at prominent nuclear power stations: Three-Mile Island, Chernobyl, and Fukushima.

But Mihàil had been prescient about the need for the reliable and secure energy afforded by nuclear power. Long before the escalation between the *Elioud* and the Dark angelic forces, the *zoti* had sought infrastructure and industrial development in his home country. In 2015, shortly after Mihàil and Olivia had married, Kastrioti Industries contracted with a private energy company to fabricate and deliver a microreactor as a test implementation in the Albanian mountains before scaling up in various industrial locations.

The terminal engagement against Asmodeus and the *kul-shedër* that destroyed the Kastrioti estate six months ago made Mihàil, Olivia, and their *Elioud* brethren rethink everything, including their energy resilience. Installing the microreactor became an immediate priority rather than an abstract business goal.

Miró's R&D team, made up of some of the most advanced minds that he'd cultivated among human researchers, had supercharged the development of the microreactor, making it both more advanced and ready for installation sooner. In fact, it had only been hooked up to their harmonic grid a week before the geomagnetic flare.

There hadn't been enough time to harden its operation.

He could feel Dianne behind him. Close, steady. And that should have been enough. But it wasn't, not anymore. Not after the way his world had shifted the second she was in danger. Not after what he'd risked to get her back. Nothing else mattered. Dianne was his mission now. And Olivia had accepted his choice. He'd seen it in the *zonjë*'s eyes, heard it in her voice, in what she didn't say.

The tether Olivia had rigged between his and Dianne's harmonic gear didn't explain this, not entirely. The tunic she'd worn during their escape from Split had been gone for weeks, its resonance long faded. And yet, he still felt her.

More than that, he *knew* her presence, as if something had anchored them together beneath the surface, deeper than harmonic frequency. A memory stirred—barely conscious, but now undeniable—of that moment near the bus station in the port of Split, when he'd fired a bolt of energy into her tunic to protect her.

He hadn't known what he was doing then, only that he'd needed to keep her safe. Now he saw it for what it was: the first expression of something older than the tether Olivia had laid between them. The tether hadn't created their bond. It had only amplified what was already forming, into something unspoken, unplanned—yet unmistakably real, even if only one of them had dared to want it.

Now he just had to ensure that they got back to the Aerie before the Locusts and dire wolves attacked. Before Abaddon tried to claim Dianne.

Overhead, nanodrones thrummed in heightened surveillance. He felt the warm vibration as they passed the hidden sensors on the path, the ones that checked his signature and identified him as a friendly. Nevertheless, after what had transpired here earlier, he gripped his Disrupter shotgun tighter, scanning the environment around them for any signs of the dire wolves or the ominous beings that had seemed to materialize from volcanic lightning and pregnant thundercloud.

"Are you even going to look at me after that kiss?" Dianne asked, startling him.

"What?" he snapped, turning on her. It came out harsher than he meant—but she'd caught him raw, wide open. Ryan whirled to face her, furious. "What? What do you want, Dianne? A declaration of love?" Dianne blanched at his forceful tone, her gaze widening as she took in his face.

Now that he'd started, Ryan couldn't stop. "You've got it: I love you. Now. Is. Not. The. Time. Did you not hear Olivia? We're surrounded by thousands of possessed tools of Abaddon. The most powerful *Elioud* alive almost died facing the Angel of the Abyss. We've been fighting a running retreat ever since we left Split, and we don't have any place left to go. I've got to get you to the Aerie for us to make a stand."

Dianne's face took on a mutinous look. She halted and crossed her arms. "Then no time like the present to clear the air, Helsing," she said crisply, channeling her sister. Ryan continued to scowl, but secretly he exulted in her courage in confronting him. Not many Rangers would have. "Good to know the sitrep about us," she continued, clearly having picked up more operational lingo while at the Aerie training like a recruit. "That's all I wanted to know."

She started to step around him. But Ryan was having none of it. She'd forced the issue—made him say the thing he hadn't been brave enough to say—and now, with the world crumbling, he couldn't face dying without knowing where she stood. If she wanted honesty, she was going to give it, too. Turnabout was fair play.

"Wait, soldier," he said, reaching out to grasp her wrist.

Dianne gasped in pain as his fingers wrapped around something hot and metallic—only to be repelled an instant later as if his fingers had the same polarity as the object. The force echoed up his arm, leaving his fingers numb to the bone and the rest of his arm aching. He took a reluctant step backward, a sharp twinge of answering pain in his side, and gripped the Disrupter one-handed to his chest.

"Ryan!" Fear sharpened Dianne's voice. She started to reach for him and stopped. In the dimness from the emergency lighting, a black iridescence sinuated around her wrist like a living snake. From its midst, a glowing blue eye winked in and out, its baleful stare holding Ryan's. Sizzling and popping sounded as cold rain hit the heated bracelet.

Dianne's gaze dropped to the object. Whatever it was, she'd seen it before. So had Ryan. In the silence broken only by faint hissing, Ryan studied the woman he loved. Black filaments writhed in an unstable penumbra around her form, leaking from her like shadowed harmonics unraveling at the edges.

He'd been so sure, just moments ago, that Dianne was his. But the metal beneath his fingers had whispered otherwise. He wasn't the only one who thought she belonged to him.

"How long have you worn an Eye of Hamsa charm?" he asked, his voice so hoarse he could have been shouting for hours in a tempest. He clamped down on his rising horror, clenching his jaw until it ached. "How long have you been linked to Abaddon?"

Next time he saw Miró he was going to personally beat the *Elioud* scientist into a bloody pulp for not figuring out that Dianne also wore a charm.

Dianne, who'd stared in horror at the Dark angelic shackle on her wrist, looked up at him, terror and panic widening her beautiful eyes.

"Germaine gave it to me before the attack on the highway," she whispered, her voice thick with tears. She began tugging at the snake with her fingers, ignoring its angry sibilance. "It won't come off, Ryan! It's burning me to the bone." She sobbed, the sound twisting the pain in Ryan's gut like nothing he'd ever experienced before. "Is this what happened to Germaine?" She swallowed. "Is that how Abaddon possessed her?" She dropped to her knees before Ryan could answer and buried her face in her hands. "Oh, God! Am I going to attack you too?"

Ryan dropped to a knee next to her. Ignoring his own pounding heart, he put his good hand on her shoulder and lifted her face to his. "Look at me, Beauty Queen," he said, infusing his voice with command.

He waited patiently although he'd already started to receive warning vibrations from the drones overhead as more of them assessed the discord from Dianne. It was only moments before she was identified as an intruder or, worse, an enemy. He'd tried to override his earlier priority defense-directive, but the dissonance emanating from Dianne had blocked his comms.

Dianne dropped her hands and lifted her face, covered in rain and tears, to look at him.

"I'm not going to let anything happen to you, do you hear me, soldier? *You're mine*. You got that? I don't let what's mine go." He held her gaze with his unwavering one, narrowing his eyes but tracing her cheeks with tender fingertips. "Now, get to your feet and get a move on. We've got to get across this valley and to the Aerie."

Before the defenses target you, he refrained from adding.

She nodded, surrendering to his authority, and stood. The Glock was once again in her hand.

But it was too late. The nanodrones had locked in on her corrupted harmonic signature. Ryan tilted his head to see a glowing mass of the microscopic aerial vehicles converging into an attack formation above them.

Ryan swore and let the Disrupter swing in its sling across his chest. Then he bent down and grabbed Dianne around the waist. She shrieked as he tossed her over his shoulder. Holding her against him with his aching arm, he gripped the

Disrupter one-handed and began to jog down the rest of the terraced steps now turning to mud.

He wasn't running to escape. He was running to buy time—to let his harmonic signature override hers, to throw off the drones, to keep them from recognizing what she'd become. But he wasn't sure it would work. No one had told him he had the ability and the authority to take control of Dianne's signature. And if it didn't—he'd be the shield between her and whatever energy those drones carried.

He felt the shift in the rain-clogged air before he saw them—the formation descending, their energy pulsing like an impending storm.

No way to outrun them. No way to fight them.

He tightened his grip on Dianne, bracing. She stilled, as if sensing the imminent danger.

Then the first harmonic pulse struck.

Twenty-Two

Miles watched the monitor in front of Greta, activated from its recessed cabinet in the mahogany table in the conference room, its screen flickering with an array of live data feeds. They'd both set up office here hours ago, ever since Helsing and the *Elioud* had taken down the dire wolf, when it became clear that their usual workstations wouldn't be enough to manage the chaos. It was easier here—easier to track multiple data streams, monitor tactical deployments, and keep a direct line open to Olivia and Mihàil.

Now, every display hummed with real-time updates—bio-signatures, drone formations, harmonic-grid fluctuations—and Miles could feel the weight of it all pressing against his ribs. It had been years since he'd been deployed as a Marine, first to Iraq and then to Afghanistan, but no soldier ever forgot the anxiety and adrenaline rush of battle. He'd had more than one firefight where he and his fellow warfighters were surrounded and outnumbered.

But never surrounded by a vast army that had far more firepower than they could bring to bear, and only once without hope of support or rescue. As then, the only way forward was through. And to never lose hope. They were, after all, the Archangel Michael's favored troops.

Are you? asked a skeptical mental voice that sounded a lot like his last CIA case officer, the one who'd loved to test Miles's ingenuity at retrieving targets more than she cared about planning and preparing for complex operations. It might have made him legendary among Special Operations Group operators, but it almost cost him his life more than once. It certainly drove him to the edge of despair, at least until Olivia gave him a way out.

She was the one who was favored—her, and the other *Elioud*. Would the Commander of the Heavenly Host or his sidekick, the quirky cherub Zophiel, deem Miles and the other humans worth rescuing?

"Sir," said Greta, bringing Miles back to the conference room in the TOC, "I'm getting a harmonic anomaly on the pilgrim's path from the clinic. Surveillance drones register a modulation we've never encountered before." She paused and looked at him, her eyes wide. "Sir, Dianne Markham's harmonic signature has been overwritten, not just suppressed or corrupted. She has the signature of a powerful *daemon*."

Miles leaned closer to study the graph depicting the harmonic signatures in that sector. Historical data showed that

Helsing and Dianne Markham as well as Olivia and a team of four had been at the top of the mountain near the clinic only ten minutes before.

And then, Dianne's signature had disappeared, only to be replaced by a chaotic, almost formless, frequency that reminded him of Kôkabîêl, the Star of God, imprisoned in the Accursed Mountains as a seven-headed dragon and freed by the Dark *Irim* Asmodeus. The dragon who'd rampaged in this very valley, nearly killing them all until Zophiel lopped off its final head with an angelic broadsword called *Caelistra.*

Zophiel and her sword were nowhere around.

Miles's pulse hammered him behind his left eye, presaging a killer headache.

What did this mean? Had a *daemon* taken on Dianne's avatar in order to infiltrate the Kastrioti stronghold? Miles was a little shaky on his *daemon* lore.

"Replay video at timestamp 20:38," he said, reassured that his voice sounded unmoved.

Greta nodded. Miles saw her fingers tremble as she typed.

In a large pane on the young specialist's monitor, Ryan and Dianne stopped on a terraced step where they appeared to argue as rain soaked them. What little protection their harmonic gear had offered against the elements had been depleted.

Dianne moved to go around Ryan, who reached for her.

Only to reel backwards, one arm hanging awkwardly. His system diagnostics showed that severe dissonance had reverberated through his hand and up his arm, temporarily limiting the big soldier's motor control in both.

"Zoom in on Dianne Markham's wrist," he ordered, though he already knew what they'd see.

"What is that, sir?" asked Greta, her voice barely above a whisper as the video image enlarged on an intricately engraved metal artifact that radiated a malign energy.

"A tether to Abaddon," he said. "The *zonjë*'s sister has been claimed by the Angel of the Abyss. Open a line to the secure bunker." When Greta just stared at him open mouthed, he said, "Now, lieutenant."

Miles watched as the surveillance drones assessed the disharmony originating from Dianne Markham. He read Helsing's command logs, saw when the former Army Ranger tried to disarm the priority defense-directive that he'd ordered when the dire wolves had reached the clinic.

Tried, but the *daemonic* noise had blocked the command.

Miles didn't wait to speak to Olivia. Even as he bent to type in a system override for Helsing's directive, the livestream showed in color-coded visuals the powerful electromagnetic pulses that the drone swarm concentrated on their target, now moving as Ryan ran with Dianne in a fireman's carry.

Dumb grunt must have it bad, thought Miles, both amused and slightly horrified that his friend took a bolt of electricity that would have stunned a bear or disrupted a *daemon*'s fundamental frequency, scattering the fractured *daemonic* energy far and wide.

Fortunately for Helsing, his clothing and boots had enough grounding to protect against a lightning strike, so the current drained into the churning mud of the unfinished terrace path. That didn't stop the big man from pitching forward, unable to break his fall with either his disabled hand or the other one he used to keep Dianne from flying from him on the disintegrating slope.

"Go for Harlequin" came Olivia's matter-of-fact answer to Greta's comms request.

"Harlequin, this is Aerie Actual," said Miles, who clung to protocol now to keep his cool. He gripped the back of Greta's chair until his knuckles whitened as he went on. "We have a situation with Demon Slayer and Dianne. You might want to take a look at the live feed that Greta has shared with you."

"Reviewing now," she said, stress evident in her voice. "You overrode the priority protocol?"

"Yes, ma'am. But, ma'am, it appears that Demon Slayer's signature has stabilized Dianne's. In fact, their fundamental frequencies overlap in the system, almost as if they're co-dependent. As long as that holds, sensors won't flag Dianne as an enemy target. What does that mean given that she wears Abaddon's charm?"

Olivia ignored his question. "Draka and Giant are en route to you. Divert them to the pass-through to pick up Demon Slayer and Dianne. Once they arrive at the Aerie, Helsing will take command of our forces, such as they are. What to do about Dianne will be his decision."

Miles's frustration grew. He shoved it aside. "Yes, ma'am."

Olivia sighed. Miles could almost see her run her fingers through her fine blond hair as she paced in the small tactical operations center in the bunker built deep inside the mountain behind the clinic. "Miles, I need you to focus on what I'm asking you to do now."

Miles, hearing the gravity in her tone, turned and walked away from Greta so the young officer wouldn't overhear. "Asking?" he said. "Not ordering?"

Olivia laughed. There was a slight catch in the sound. "You and I both know that we pretend to have a command hierarchy here because it suits us. But I rely on your experience and good judgment more than you know." She inhaled loudly enough that he heard it over the comms. "I count you as a friend. What I'm about to ask you is something I won't order you to do."

Miles stilled. He'd never heard Olivia so uncertain before. "Anything," he said without hearing her request.

"I won't hold you to that," she said before adding, "but I will ask. I need you to make your way to Trieste and recover an MSS operative named Liú Xiù. She saved my life more than a decade ago. Now I need you to save hers."

Dianne's arm burned and ached to the bone, making it nearly impossible for her to think about anything except for the warm muscle and hard shoulder under her abdomen as Ryan carried her down the mountain. Darkness ate at her vision like acid. Low voices muttered and shrieked inside her head while invisible insects crawled on her skin, stinging and biting. She felt simultaneously feverish and chilled as the rain continued, waves of pain wracking her until she realized that the vibration originated somewhere in the air above her. It became stronger and stronger, threatening to split her head like a ripe cantaloupe.

Then lightning struck. Or that's what it felt like.

Electricity connected to the bracelet, coursing along her arm in a mad race for her heart.

She was falling through the void, breathless. Yet still connected to that warm mass ...

... that gripped her and rolled a moment before they hit the ground with a jarring thud and grunt, Ryan's body shielding her from the impact. Somehow, she'd managed to keep her Glock in her hand without shooting him.

For a stunned moment, they lay there, entwined as the rain soaked them, Ryan's chest heaving and her heart racing.

"What was that?" she asked.

"Just a little kiss from our surveillance drones. They seem to think you're owned by a *daemon.* But they're wrong."

Dianne swallowed. "Are they coming back?"

"No." He shook his head, his gaze never leaving her face. "Baxter overrode the protocol. Besides, your harmonic signature no longer reads as *daemonic.*"

"Why is that?" she asked, just wanting to keep him talking as long as she could, even if their surreal conversation took place amidst pouring rain, mud, and a looming *daemonic* invasion.

"Apparently my base frequency is rewriting yours." He grinned. His grin didn't just carry amusement. It held certainty. Defiance. A reckless dare to whatever force thought it could take her from him. "I told you you were mine. Even a *daemon* can't claim you."

At his words, Dianne realized that the searing ache in her arm had dissipated. She blinked against the rain, willing her body to believe what her mind couldn't comprehend. The pain was gone. Just—gone. Like he'd erased it.

"Is it strange that I never want to let you go?" she asked, her words watery and blurred. She hoped he thought it was from the rain sheeting over her mouth.

"Not any stranger than me never wanting to let you go," he said. His eyes glinted in the light from the landscape lanterns scattered among the unfinished tiers of the future chapel amphitheater around them.

Dianne gripped her courage. "Do you really love me?"

"Let me show you how much," he said, his gaze predatory. A moment later, he'd crushed her against his chest and captured her mouth with his.

Dianne's head swam, this time from his intoxicating kiss, the sheer pleasure in feeling his lips against hers, the taste and scent of him, the feel of his pectoral muscles molding her suddenly sensitive breasts against their hardness. Her breathlessness increased. Desire shot through her, pooling in her core. Small desperate sounds escaped her, and she snuggled against Ryan, trying to get closer. The cold soaked into her, chilling her bones—but the warmth of Ryan's body? It was the only thing anchoring her to reality. To safety. To him.

He opened his thighs, pulling her hips into their cradle with one big hand. A hand that felt like he could break her, and yet she knew without a doubt would always handle her with the utmost care. As if she were precious and should be cherished.

Something, a feeling rather than a sound or visual cue, caused Dianne to pull away. Around the amphitheater, luminous figures watched over them with wise gazes, deep and understanding. They hovered over the landscape, moving with the rain and air currents, as if nature itself subtly responded to their presence. The rain fell but not on them. It moved through the air around the figures, bending like light through glass. Although they glowed softly, they pushed back the encroaching murk until the area that formed the amphitheater vanquished the shadows. The world felt safer, calmer, even if danger lurked beyond their cool silver radiance.

Dianne didn't just see the newcomers, she sensed them. A warmth spreading beneath her skin, pushing back the exhaustion, the ache, the chaos. The transformative serenity that had filled her in Međugorje returned, as if something greater than Ryan and her surrounded and blessed them. Blessed what was between them. Something raw, unfinished, but powerful—almost sacred—waiting to be built and filled, just like this place.

Against the hush of the rain and the beating of her heart, Dianne heard delicate music, aching with longing. After a moment, she recognized the melody she'd first heard in the mountains of Bosnia waiting on the Virgin to appear.

"What are they?" she asked in a reverential voice. "Angels?

He answered without taking his gaze from the ghostly figures. His voice was quiet, lower than usual. Almost awed. "I don't think so."

"They're *zana*," said a male voice from several tiers below them on the slope.

When Dianne shifted to look down at him, she recognized András, who'd been on the team that rescued Ryan and her in Shkodër. He continued speaking as he moved toward them, his long legs taking swift strides. "Powerful Albanian spirits who protect the land—guardians of warriors like Mihàil."

András exhaled, steam curling into the air like smoke. "And now, apparently, Ryan, though why, only the Archangel knows." His tone carried an edge of wry amusement—as if to soften his implied joke about Ryan.

The *Elioud* warrior stopped one level down from them, his steady gaze telling Dianne that, despite his joke, he considered Ryan his brother-in-arms. His entire body radiated heat, sending steam in a dense cloud on a current of cool air.

Dianne looked around. The *zana* had disappeared. As their luminescence faded, the shadows crept back, though softer now, less oppressive. The air felt heavier, the rain returning with full force. Behind the giant *Elioud* warrior came Beta, his wife, whom Dianne had grown quite fond of over the past weeks in Fushë-Arrëz. The hawk-eyed *Elioud* female nodded at Dianne, a tiny grin at the corner of her mouth as she took in Ryan and Dianne's intimate posture.

Beta's grin widened, sharp and knowing. "Wrestling?" she asked, tilting her head, looking between Dianne and Ryan, who shifted and ducked his chin.

Dianne noted Ryan's reaction. She'd seen how he'd reacted around Beta before. He might not care about the opinion of most people, but he definitely held Beta in high regard.

Beta shook her head. "I do *not* recommend it. Mud gets into the most uncomfortable places."

Ryan grinned at her before turning back to Dianne. "Put your arms around my neck," he said, sounding as lighthearted as she'd ever heard him.

Dianne hesitated. "Are you sure?" she asked, hiding her sudden self-consciousness in concern. "What about your arm? Or your side?"

Ryan shook his head, watching her. "Can't say I've ever felt better. Not since our frequencies have merged." His tone was so light, so matter of fact, that it threw her off. "I guess you're good for me." He grinned at her.

Still, Dianne hesitated.

Beta rolled her eyes, something that Dianne wouldn't have thought possible for the acerbic *Elioud* female.

András grinned, utterly unhelpful. "Need some assistance there with your woman, *Demon Slayer?*"

Dianne let out a mock-insulted huff and threw her arms around Ryan's neck. Ryan's grip tightened around her hips, urging her legs around his waist. Dianne, her face burning in the misty air, wrapped them around his midsection, felt his large hands cup her buttocks to stabilize her. And then he leveraged himself into a standing position as if she weighed nothing.

"Good to go, Helsing?" asked András. "Would you like your Disrupter, too? Or are your hands too full?"

"Well, if I must ...." Ryan caught the combat shotgun that András tossed to him, his other hand forming a firm sling under her derriere.

Beta picked up the Glock that Dianne had put down while Ryan kissed her. "I will keep this for you. This slope is steep, and Helsing might lose his footing. I would not want him to lose his head also." She flicked a glance at Ryan that spoke volumes. "Although, frankly, that may already be a lost cause."

Dianne felt a lightness settle over her—a quiet thrill of acceptance. She hadn't realized until now how much she'd feared rejection. Now she wondered what Olivia would say—about her chief of security falling for her sister, but especially about the tether to Abaddon.

They made it down to the highway without any further banter, András stalking through the night radiating heat and intensity. Beta followed behind Ryan and Dianne, illustrating the concept "head on a swivel" as she continuously scanned the landscape around them, her eyes narrowed and the scent of ash mixing with her exotic perfume. Dianne couldn't see Ryan's expression, but from his alert posture and the way his own head moved, she knew that he'd gone into Ranger mode.

Near the entrance to the pass-through beneath the road sat one of the few vehicles, a Toyota Land Cruiser 70 series, that the Kastriotis' people had gotten running. András got into the driver's side while Beta held the rear passenger door open for Ryan, who settled Dianne into the seat. She handed the Glock back to Dianne along with a fresh clip.

"Playtime is over," she said. "The wolves are at the gate."

Then she slammed the door and got in. Ryan dropped into the seat next to Dianne, barely acknowledging her before he turned to the window next to him, the Disrupter resting against his chest as he looked out at the moonless night.

Somewhere in the near distance, a wolf howled, long and low. Deliberate. The sound slithered through the night, twisting in the air, echoing eerily as if seeping into the fabric of the landscape. Then came the unholy chorus, answering from all directions, sending chills down Dianne's back.

She exhaled slowly and gripped the Glock, her fingers tightening around the smooth polymer. She resisted the urge to check the magazine even though she knew it was loaded. She should have killed him—the king of the dire wolves. That bullet in his brain should have been enough. And yet, the howls told a different story.

And then András, his jaw tight, put the Land Cruiser in drive and headed for the Aerie.

Playtime was over indeed.

Twenty-Three

Ryan clenched his jaw against the need to keep checking on Dianne, who sat next to him in the backseat of the Land Cruiser, looking for the world like one of his team members. Despite wet hair clinging to her face and soaking clothes, her alert posture and keen gaze took in the night outside her window. In her hand, she held the Glock in a practiced, comfortable grip. Something told him that she intended to fight. He wanted her safe, secure—in a bunker somewhere far from Abaddon and his insect-like goons. But he also wanted her at his side where he could protect her, with ammo and with harmonics. He wasn't sure that he'd get either.

"You need a Disrupter," he said, his voice gruff. "Or better yet, a long gun. I'd prefer to have you on overwatch because it sounds like the dire wolves brought friends."

She looked at him, blue eyes gleaming in the SUV's dim interior. Her expression gave nothing away. "Happy to oblige, though Draka didn't spend a lot of time teaching me more than the basics."

Beta glanced back at Ryan. "*My* basics" was all she said before turning back to the front.

Ryan made a decision. "You're with Draka then. She's your team leader for the time being." He kept his gaze on Dianne, but he saw Beta's nod from his peripheral vision. He released a breath he didn't know he held. He hadn't been sure the *Elioud* warrior would accept his command.

They rode on in silence, the dire wolves' howls having faded away after they passed through the gate to the Aerie compound, where overhead drones illuminated coordinated movement as Stasio Kos's mellifluous voice resonated through the space, guiding them. Besides the Kastrioti security personnel, most of Fushë-Arrëz's inhabitants sought shelter within the compound's defenses. The few that didn't had already sought shelter at the Kastrioti estate, also fortified.

Ryan didn't wait for András to bring the SUV to a full stop before he opened his door to jump out and sprint toward the ops center, resisting the almost-overwhelming urge to abandon his command—to make sure Dianne was safe himself. Beta had charge of her now, and she would do a far better job of keeping Dianne out of harm's way than he could afford to.

The last view he had of Dianne before he entered the ops center was of her walking at the taller Beta's side, the two women deep in discussion. As far as he could tell, Dianne respected Beta, but she didn't fear her. That was something both unexpected and encouraging. Beta scared many of the recruits with her intensity and ferocity.

"That's one brave woman," said András, holding the door to the ops center open for Ryan. The *Elioud* had shifted his harmonics, easily beating Ryan to the entrance. "She's terrified, but she trusts you implicitly."

Ryan didn't want to talk about Dianne. Now was neither the time, nor the place. And he had a job to do. But András gripped his shoulder before he could move past the other man and into the building. Ryan halted and aimed a flinty stare at András.

András lifted his hand, palm up. "Hear me out, Helsing. This isn't just about her. It's about you, too." His tone was quiet, measured—but the weight behind it pressed like iron. "You didn't just claim her. You threw down a gauntlet to one of the most powerful Dark angels in creation. Your integrated harmonic signature may have fooled our sensors, but you won't fool him. Now he has an added target: *you*." András exhaled, steam curling into the chill night air. "If you fall, she falls with you. If he takes you, he takes her. This isn't just love. It's *daemonic* war."

Terror gripped Ryan's heart in its stony fist. He could accept laying down his life for Dianne—but not losing her in the process.

"What are my options?" he asked, the strain evident in his voice. "Because I wouldn't break our bond if I could."

"Understood, brother," said András, as serious as Ryan had ever seen the giant *Elioud*. "Stay off the battlefield. Keep her inside the harmonic defenses."

Just then commotion drew their gazes to the broad, tree-lined quadrangle in the center of the compound. Elias and a contingent of *donats* rode on horseback toward Ryan and András, Michael Markham, garbed in black Order tactical attire, among them.

Before Ryan could react, battle klaxons reverberated around the expansive quad, jarring the already discordant atmosphere. His Harmonic Tactical Synchronization system pulsed with incoming data—infrared heat signatures, directional resonance shifts, and angelic sonar echoes mapping enemy movement in spectral outlines.

But layered beneath the tactical readout, something else stirred—an instinctive recognition of the harmonics threading through the space. He no longer simply received battlefield data; he sensed it, the resonance patterns a silent rhythm threading through the clamor.

At the same time, a flood of additional tactical data from the ops center streamed into his system—unit positions, drone feeds, security-perimeter analytics. He scanned for Miles's comm ID, expecting the steady presence of Aerie Actual, but the line was blank. He swore, low and virulently, recalibrating his priorities with brutal efficiency.

András, who had no need of the HTS that translated sensor data in Ryan's tactical gear, vibrated on the edge of flaring, an instinctual *Elioud* reaction to a threat.

"Go!" he said through clenched teeth, heat shimmering around him.

He didn't wait for Ryan's response. Instead, he pivoted and ran toward the next building where lurid green and black light pulsed above the roofline before a mass of Locusts surged over the edge. With a great leap, he collided with the foul beings, his angelic light exploding outward, illuminating the entire quad. Beneath him, the *donats* began chanting, their harmonious voices a solemn bulwark against the cacophony of war. The Gregorian tones, rich and unwavering, carved through the night like sacred thunder, threading through the tumult with an authority beyond the physical. The resonance did not merely fill the fortified quadrangle—it altered it, weaving a harmonic barrier that pulsed against the dissonance, anchoring those who fought within its grasp. Where shrieks and howls threatened to consume, the ancient cadence held firm, steady as a heartbeat in the storm.

Ryan wrenched around and ran through the spacious lobby of the ops center, cursing himself for ever seeing it as well-designed, and headed toward the corridor that took him to the main control room. A young lieutenant, who sat at the closest workstation, raised her gaze as he came to stand near her.

"Where's Baxter?" he asked, ashamed at the hint of accusation in his voice.

"The *zonjë* sent him on a mission," she said, her own voice remarkably calm, though Ryan's growing sensitivity to harmonics revealed agitation in hers. "She wouldn't do that unless it was for him to get help, right?"

Ryan almost barked at her, but his new insight told him that she was barely holding on. "Yes," he said in answer to her question, though he had no idea what Olivia's reasons were. "More knights and other *Elioud* travel here from Eastern and

Southern Europe. Likely the *zonjë* sent Baxter to tell them we need reinforcements now."

She nodded and turned back to the composite data feed on her monitor. Ryan leaned over her shoulder, staring at a pane in the upper right that tracked the surges of dissonant energy from the Locusts, who swarmed over all of the buildings in the Aerie. The wolves had broken off circling their defensive perimeter and had melted into the wooded slopes around the compound. Ryan's battlefield instincts screamed at him. He didn't doubt that the death-class canines were searching for another vulnerability while the defendants of the Aerie had their hands full.

And their hands were full.

András commanded the Kastrioti forces, directing them to hold specific zones against the Locusts. The *donats* fought in two groups, one under the command of Elias and the other under an unfamiliar knight, who acted as harmonic pincers to contain and neutralize Abaddon's Swarmtroopers. Despite this, the defenders faltered as the Black Swarm pushed past the perimeter in a matter of minutes. The commanders rallied them, but their efforts barely held the line as men and women fell under the onslaught.

Ryan's nerves tightened. What looked like mad chaos had a method to it—a method unlike the wild abandon typical of *daemons* and the possessed. Anticipating a feint by a trio of Battlebugs, he was just getting ready to direct András to the indoor shooting range when a panicked voice broke in over the system-wide All-Call.

"Aerie Actual, this is Eaglet 1. We're being assaulted by hundreds of *daemoniacs*, some of them armed. They keep pushing past our perimeter from the northeast quadrant. Dozens of winged beings dropped from the sky not long afterwards. Now strong winds send rain and hail against our sensors, making it impossible to see."

Those dark-winged spirits from the clinic earlier? What the hell were they doing there? Did Mihàil have anything to do with their appearance? Or were they simply attracted to the tumult? Were they friend or foe?

Ryan shoved those questions aside. "Copy that," he said, scanning the monitor for tactical data on the Kastrioti estate. What he saw sent him back in time to a moment in Afghanistan where his squad was trapped on a mountain ridge, taking fire from the Taliban on all sides. He gritted his teeth, the phantom wind of that Afghan ridge whispering at the edge of his mind. He shoved it into the lightless hole where it belonged. "Prepare for Aegis Pulse in 30 seconds."

"Copy that, Aerie Actual."

Ryan nodded at Greta to initiate the weapon after the defenders synchronized for the short-range harmonic burst targeting the Kastrioti estate grounds. He watched the *daemoniacs* scatter like roaches under a spotlight, giving his fighters time to regroup.

The reprieve ended too quickly.

The Pulse rippled over the possessed. Even before the energy dissipated, Ryan saw it. The biggest roaches barely flinched. Instead, they shook off the powerful jolt of electromagnetic energy as dogs shake off water. Then they were on the defenders with renewed violence. He clenched his fists against the almost-undeniable urge to grab weapons and a vehicle and haul ass to engage the enemy from behind.

Before Ryan could direct Greta to send another localized Aegis Pulse with a higher frequency, harsh warning sounds blared throughout the TOC.

"Sir, the clinic is under assault," said Greta, terror turning her voice into a thready whisper.

Ryan stood, transfixed for a horrible moment as crazed humans mercilessly whipped by a towering obsidian Battlebug threw themselves at the entrance door. His breath stuck in his chest as he observed them slamming against the security grille, each impact draining the system's charge. As bodies fell, newcomers clambered over them. Behind the attackers, more humans lifted a battering ram and maneuvered their way up the terraced slope like some Hell-spawned millipede. A wide chasm opened in front of the clinic, issuing endless numbers of Locusts from its black depth who swarmed the entrance, crawled up the walls, and smashed now barrier-free windows.

At this rate, they'd be conquered before sunrise.

Movement in a lower monitor panel caught his gaze: mounted *donats*, led by Elias's second-in-command, Antonio, rode toward the clinic.

As their resonant and commanding chant swelled up the mountain slope ahead of their charge, an iridescent rainbow of divine music lit up the night. One group flicked their harmonic ribbons at the *daemoniacs*, slicing through them. Meanwhile, a handful of knights, flanked by the other *donats*, synchronized harmonic bursts from their chant gauntlets in layered waves of energy against the six-legged freaks.

Thank God. Elias had read the battlefield the same way Ryan had—Abaddon hadn't sent his troops against them in a frenetic solo attack. He'd sent them in a coordinated, multi-pronged assault that would make any Army general green with envy. The Dark Angel of the Abyss clearly sought the Kastriotis in their fortified bunker.

The bad news? The clinic wasn't designed for a focused, protracted siege.

Ryan was at the nexus of their defense, but he didn't know how to counter something like this. He belonged on the battlefield. He belonged out there, face-to-face with the enemy. Not relegated to a control room, watching the battle unfold from behind glass and circuitry.

He belonged with Dianne. Not here, not trapped in this room, but with her.

At the thought of her, he closed his eyes for a moment so that he could focus on picking out Dianne's unique signature in the maelstrom of music and cacophony within the Aerie.

There! She'd taken up a position on a sniper's tower behind the training center. Even inside the TOC, Ryan could feel her resonance with his own heart, could hear her unique melody—a sweet, high sound reminiscent of the Bosnian mountains where he'd fallen in love with her. Their individual signatures had melded into a new, richer harmony, knit together with the strength of her faith and underscored by his pain and loss, threading through him like a wordless song he could never forget.

Turning from the valiant young officer, Ryan paced away before activating Dianne's private comm channel. "Beauty Queen, this is Beast. Sitrep."

He felt her respond before he heard her in his ear—a tightening along their braided harmonic tether that echoed in his heartrate. He took an involuntary step toward her.

"Beast, this is Beauty Queen," she said, her voice husky as if she too felt him across the distance. He detected anxiety and fear as well as determination in her harmonics. "Bullets don't work on the Locusts. I'm focusing on the assholes at Mihàil and Olivia's house and grounds. Bullets *do* work on them."

"Copy that," said Ryan, letting his pride in her strengthen his voice and flow along their spiritual bond.

Before she spoke again, the tether between them burned—fury sizzled along the threads. "Those friggin' *daemon dogs* are sneaking along the slopes next to the Aerie."

Ryan stiffened. He could feel her swinging her sniper rifle around, locking onto the monsters. "Stay on overwatch," he said, tension crackling in his command. "Don't call attention to your location."

"Don't worry," she said, her voice lowering to that of the focused sharpshooter, "they won't know what hit them."

A moment later, the recoil from her shot rippled through space, its impact true.

She'd hit one of the dire wolves.

"Whoo-hoo!" said Dianne in a low whisper, putting glass onto another target.

Ryan turned back to the tactical feed on Greta's monitor. He frowned as he scanned it, then his breath stalled. A single marker blinked on the grid, well outside the Aerie compound's secured perimeter.

An instant later, Dianne's sharp hiss confirmed it. "Oh, crap! That's Michael. What the hell is he doing outside the quad?"

At the sight of the dire wolves surrounding her brother, mounted on a horse and flinging a glowing harmonic ribbon to keep them at bay, Dianne's numb fingers slipped from the sniper rifle. For a moment, she lost all thought, staring until her dry eyes burned.

And then she gripped the rifle again, sighted through the scope, and squeezed the trigger on a controlled exhale. A dire wolf's head exploded a few seconds later, but by then she'd moved the sight onto another target.

And for a minute—no more—she actually entertained the idea that together she and her brother could annihilate these foul Hellpuppies.

Until the alpha dire wolf sprang onto the rear of Michael's mount. The horse screamed and reared, its front hooves flailing as two more dire wolves came in low for its exposed belly.

It was enough to dislodge an experienced horseman. For Michael, who'd only learned to ride a few weeks ago, it was more than enough to throw him to the ground.

Two of the remaining dire wolves were on him before Dianne could re-center her scope. One clamped onto a leg while the other did something far more disturbing: he placed two meaty paws on Michael's shoulders and lowered his bloody muzzle to within inches of her brother's face.

The world dimmed for a fraction of a second. Then, as if torn from thin air, the mercenary commander from the ambush at the bus station in Split appeared next to Michael and his monstrous attackers. The one whose men had battered and brutalized Ryan.

Something about his corrupt body scared her in a way that seeing *daemons* didn't.

Fear corroded Dianne's stomach. For the first time, a splinter of doubt cracked through her fear. Was it just her and Germaine that Abaddon wanted? Or ...

Then the mercenary's cruel voice reached her, resonating everywhere all at once—honeyed, mocking, insidious. "Come to me, Dianne Markham, and I will release him. Wait, and you will hear his screams and taste his fear."

As if on cue, Michael's faint, strangled cry echoed around the mountainside, weirdly resonant in the predawn air.

"Let's end this tug-of-war over Dianne, Your Lowly Abysshole. You want a fight? Leave the boy and face someone who knows how to finish one."

Dianne barely registered Ryan's voice—until she realized she was already crawling toward the hatch, her body moving on instinct. She had to get down there, had to do something to keep Abaddon from taking Michael. From hurting the man she loved, who'd come out to save them.

Dianne started to protest, to pull at the hatch, when Beta's warm hand dropped onto her shoulder, grounding her. Startled, she looked up at the *Elioud* female to see her finger on her lips. Beta gestured back toward the edge of the nest. Together, they crawled to the lookout point.

Beta pointed toward the quad and the buildings surrounding it where an immense rhythmic glow swallowed the inky night like the first breath of dawn.

András and Elias come. Her crisp voice resounded in Dianne's thoughts, leaving no room for doubt.

But that promised rescue was moot. They wouldn't get here in time to save Ryan.

Because the Angel of the Abyss stepped toward the man she loved, who stood tall and erect on the Aerie's perimeter. As the Dark Angel came closer, overhead drones illuminated the field of combat, capturing the surreal moment that reality twisted and buckled around Abaddon—as if the battlefield itself shrank before him, bending to his presence.

He grinned, the evil expression underscored by his empty eye socket. "I only delayed the inevitable, Paladin, but now you will bow before your lord."

Then Dianne watched in utter horror as Ryan, instead of pulling out his combat knife, simply nodded. "Ryan, don't—" But the words choked in her throat.

He stepped forward. He knelt.

Something rippled in the warp and weft of the world around them, as if the very fabric of existence shuddered at the significance.

When Ryan spoke, the overhead drones amplified his voice so that all present heard his surrender. "You win. I have nothing left to give."

Twenty-Four

Through the disorienting acoustics of the battlefield, Ryan heard Dianne's anguished cry as he nodded acquiescence to his fate. "Ryan, don't—"

He shoved it away, deliberately rejecting their bond, though the pain and loss fileted him to the bone. He would deny it, when it came down to it—deny it to save Dianne. If one of them must fall to the Angel of the Abyss, let it be him. He would fight and die to distract Abaddon until András, leading the Kastrioti security forces and flanked by the Order of Malta knights, arrived to rescue her and Michael. As he vowed this to himself, he rubbed the tiny silver key set into the ring that Dianne had given him before they'd arrived in Fushë-Arrëz—the ring that he'd carried with him for weeks.

It was the last and most important decision he would make as commander of the forces of Light.

As his knees hit the cold earth before the one-eyed mercenary, the air split apart. Something powerful detonated on the harmonic plane, exploding away from the two of them in an immense, world-shaking tsunami. The overhead mesh of lights provided by the nanodrones, swept away on the airburst, winked out, leaving a starless, moonless black void.

Abaddon laughed, a horrific grating sound that seemed to come from the depths of the Abyss, which had, in fact, opened up around them. He raised his hand, twisting the fingers as if twisting a knob.

Or Ryan's gut, which began to buckle and burn where Germaine had gouged him weeks ago.

Germaine, who'd been Abaddon's vessel.

Ryan groaned and gritted his teeth, one hand pressing against his side as if he could stop the soul-crushing pain. Stop his insides from being torn apart. His vision wavered on the verge of blacking out.

Above him, he heard Dianne's sharp gasp, carried to him on air currents manipulated by the Dark angel before him.

Abaddon laughed again.

"Submission is the first step. Soon, your will won't matter at all." The one-eyed mercenary stepped closer to Ryan, an unholy gleam lighting his avid features. "I will shed this puny vessel for your body. And then I will possess your woman, body and soul."

Fury like magma erupted inside Ryan's core.

Above him, Dianne's husky alto began singing, sweet and low, and shaking. "*Crux sacra sit mihi lux. Non draco sit mihi dux. Vade retro Satana.*" The words illuminated a golden dome above her, faint at first but growing more forceful as she continued, drawing all eyes to her.

An answering glow sprang from the St. Benedict's medal on Ryan's chest, pushing the suffocating black shadows around him and his enemy back.

He pulled his combat knife from his boot and rose from his knees in one swift motion as Abaddon turned to scowl at Dianne's exposed position. The *daemon* lord jerked his head toward waiting *daemoniacs*, who took off at a run toward the sniper tower.

Then several things happened at once.

Voices joined Dianne's—the knights of the Order of Malta strengthening and bolstering her solo with their rich, confident chant, the Kastrioti security forces, the *Elioud*, including Miró and Willem. And filling out the female parts? The *zana*, whose voices added a thrilling majesty to the chant. The chorus drove the enveloping darkness before it as the sun banishes the depths of night at the breaking of dawn.

The sniper rifle sounded twice in quick succession as Beta took out the two dire wolves guarding Michael Markham, who rolled away and sprang to his feet, before running toward his companions-in-arms, who threw him a harmonic shield and mace.

And Ryan rammed his combat knife with all his strength and willpower into the gut of the human vessel of the Angel of the Abyss, whose shocked look would have been comical if Ryan had any humor in him.

He did not.

Instead, he pulled the shorter man towards him. With one hand clamping his enemy's shoulder, he jerked the blade from side to side as he glared at the other man. "You will take nothing. Not my body, not my soul, and sure as hell not her."

Then he shoved the dying man into the rapidly disappearing chasm while all around him, the *Elioud* and the *donats* made swift work of the dire wolves and *daemoniacs*. Only the Locusts hung on until the last possible moment before being dragged into the depths of the Abyss, screeching and pulling dead *daemoniacs* with them.

As for the *zana*, they disappeared with the last of the Locusts, their radiant forms fading into the last of the night like dew. Ryan, his Harmonic Tac Sync abuzz with data from all of the sensors and people reporting on their engagement with the forces of the Abyss, recognized the harmonic signatures of the *zana* near the Kastrioti estate where the dark-winged figures of chaos and storm had contributed to the confusion at the peak of the attack. The *zana* had subsumed the frequencies of the other beings, quelling their turbulence.

Ryan didn't know what that meant, but he hoped it was a good sign. Either way, the primeval Albanian spirits no longer appeared in system logs.

He'd finished reviewing all of the relevant statuses with as much patience as he could muster when András sauntered up to his side. The big Hungarian stood, drenched, the rising sun outlining his wavy hair and broad shoulders. He pulled out a canteen, drank deeply, and then handed it to Ryan, who accepted it without a word.

After Ryan had his share of water, András took the nearly empty canteen back and poured the remnants over his head, before shaking it vigorously. He grinned at Ryan, who wiped away the water that landed on his cheeks with a thumb. Ryan smiled back. His muscles ached; his senses had overloaded. Relief threatened to take the form of collapse, but the weight of Dianne's gaze in the pale dawn kept him standing.

András clipped the canteen to his utility belt. "You have put to bed any question about your call sign," he said. "You're absolutely a Demon Slayer. A ballsy one at that. Abaddon will think twice before he shows his head above that glorified crack in the ground he calls home again."

"No, he's The Beast," said Dianne as she walked up with Beta, whose lively dark eyes shared a private joke with her husband. Dianne came to a halt in front of Ryan, where she looked up at him with open adoration. "*My* Beast."

Ryan looked down at her with a corresponding expression of love. "My Beauty Queen," he said, lifting her hand and kissing the palm.

At her intake of breath, he grabbed her and tugged her against his chest. Dianne threw her arms around his neck and wriggled until his arms tightened, keeping her secure in his embrace. She grabbed his jaw and pulled his face down, meeting his mouth with her own.

András whooped. Ryan sensed Beta punching her husband on the shoulder, only to be grabbed by the big man and pulled into his arms. She struggled for a moment before settling against him. And then, they too shared a kiss.

Then Dianne slipped from Ryan. He frowned, but she put a finger over his mouth to stop his complaint. "I need to get rid of this," she said, holding up the charm bracelet that Germaine had given her a lifetime ago.

Dianne ran to the last visible crevice of the vast chasm that the *daemon* lord had opened up as he faced Ryan and dropped the bracelet into it. The earth immediately swallowed it up, closing over it as though healing from the unnatural rupture by sending the offensive item to its bowels. Then she ran back to Ryan and kissed him again.

The joy and celebration died down a moment later as the four of them turned to face the remnants of battle. The rising sun threw the dead and dying into stark relief. Dr. Armand moved among them, along with Willem, who applied a Vitae Seal, a palm-sized graphene patch which he keyed to the individual's fundamental frequency, to those hanging on by a thread. For those less injured, Willem stabilized them with an Aurora Pulse Beacon, with precise bursts of energy before Dr. Armand and his medical staff reached them for triage.

Dianne put her fingers over her mouth as she surveyed the lower slope of the bordering mountain and the rocky ground before it that led to the Aerie. It was her first battlefield, and it was a devastating sight. Ryan knew that she'd spent much of the summer running obstacle courses and tactical drills over its uneven surface. More advanced team members had used the rough ground for reconnaissance and stealth training. Ryan had even begun training an alpha team composed of infantry and cavalry knights in guerrilla combat. He'd believed all of that unnecessary, lessons to sharpen unneeded skills.

Lessons that had turned out to be decisive against the *daemoniacs*, many of whom appeared to have military training, all of whom had a level of mental discipline not usually found in the possessed. Even the dire wolves found the defenders to be hard targets.

Despite this, Kastrioti defenders and *donats* numbered among the dead and injured. Noble, magnificent horses and twisted, ugly dire wolves lay among them.

András's visage resembled a thundercloud while Beta scowled, her karambit now in her hand as she manipulated the folding mechanism of the Indonesian fighting knife with one hand. Ryan knew from experience that the former Czech Army officer used the activity as a kind of pressure valve for her temper. He smelled smoke anyway. The acrid scent curled at the edges of the breeze, mixing with blood, earth, and the lingering charge of harmonics.

A harmonic bell sounded above them.

The mesh network had been reformed, and now Olivia Kastrioti cantered toward them on horseback, flanked on either side by Elias and Antonio and followed by a small contingent of mounted *donats* and her personal security team, also mounted. Shadows sculpted the planes and hollows of her face. Ryan thought the *zonjë*, always serenely beautiful and confident, had matured into an imposing presence as she'd taken on her lord's authority while he healed. Although Olivia hadn't been present in the tactical operations center for last night's battle, he'd felt her presence, especially during the final moment facing Abaddon.

She'd even whispered in his mind *well done, good and faithful servant* after he'd slain the Dark Angel of the Abyss's vessel. The words had ghosted through his thoughts, gentle, solemn, final—a gossamer kiss from a queen.

Now she looked both grim and relieved.

Olivia reined to a halt five meters in front of their small group. Elias, Antonio, and her personal bodyguard Jesse rode and stopped beside her. Elias, who had decades of experience fighting *daemonic* foes, looked much the same, if tired, dirty, and bloody. Antonio, younger and less experienced, nevertheless seemed to take his cues from Elias and watched them gravely. Jesse, a young Australian veteran that Ryan had recruited earlier in the year, looked shellshocked but remained upright and focused.

Olivia studied the four of them for a long moment, calm and contained. When she came to Ryan, she simply nodded. He'd never know what prompted him, but at that regal gesture, he slid to his knee and bowed.

"*Zonjë ime*," he said.

Next to him, he felt Dianne glancing between them before she, too, slid to a knee. Before she could say anything (Ryan suspected that she intended to repeat his words), Olivia had dropped from her horse and darted to her younger sister.

Pulling her to her feet, Olivia hugged her sister. "Thank God you're safe!" she said, strong emotion making her voice rough. "I couldn't bear to lose you too."

Ryan saw tears coursing down the face of the woman he loved. He couldn't believe what it did to him, seeing Dianne cry. Just as he'd seen her crying in the rain last night, when she'd asked him if he really loved her. He couldn't wait to show her just how much, with his body and with his vow of eternal fidelity, made before man, *Elioud*, and God.

Because that's what he was going to give her, as soon as she—and the *zoti* and *zonjë*—would let him.

Olivia turned to him, a smile radiating from her tear-stained face. "Well, Helsing, do you have something that you want to ask my sister? Because I can't say yes until she does."

Stunned, Ryan, still kneeling on one knee, blinked a moment. And then, before Dianne could ask what they were talking about, he pivoted and pulled the silver ring with its delicate filigree skeleton key from his pocket. He held it out to her. It was time to make their harmonic bond permanent.

Dianne looked down in bemusement at the ring. "You kept this with you?" she asked.

"Not only kept it with me, vowed on it to give my life for yours," he said. "Will you do me the honor of marrying me so that I can live out that vow for the rest of my life?"

Dianne blinked rapidly, tears escaping her efforts. She looked at Olivia, whose smile had only broadened.

Olivia nodded and said, "Go on, dunderhead! Say yes before his knee gives out and that old wound in his side causes him to topple over."

Dianne squealed and turned to Ryan. "Yes! Yes! Yes! A thousand times yes, my Beast!" She grabbed his face and kissed him as a large grin split his cheeks from ear to ear.

"Excellent," said Olivia dryly once Dianne let Ryan go several seconds later. "Then you have my blessing, Helsing. You will have to wait, however, for the chapel to be constructed. Willem and Father Bekim tell me the foundation will be laid this week. Its construction was only delayed due to the problem of the dire wolves."

"Fully constructed?" asked Ryan shrewdly. Everyone laughed, even the quiet Elias.

Olivia shook her head, still smiling. "Incorrigible! No, the Bishop consecrated the land already, so I'll leave it to Father Bekim to decide whether he wants more than a foundation in which to perform the sacrament."

"How about the clinic chapel?" asked Dianne. She sounded tentative. Ryan suspected that she didn't want to challenge her sister so soon after her blessing. "So Mihàil can attend."

Olivia said nothing for several long moments, blinking rapidly, while she clearly got her emotions under control. Ryan had never seen her so close to losing it. Everyone waited.

At last, she cleared her throat and said in a strong, confident voice. "Indeed, he will insist on attending, and I don't think Ryan will wait long enough for him to dress appropriately for church. I'll have Father Bekim read the banns and set the date for three weeks from now."

Everyone laughed at the look of disappointment on Ryan's face, but he only grinned sheepishly and pulled Dianne to her feet before kissing her again.

Then he bent and whispered to her, "You're my mission from now on, Dianne Markham."

Baxter: Warhound

Book Two of The Dragon's Paladins

S he ran out of rice ten days after leaving Prato, Italy.

Then she ran out of tea, her favorite *jinjunmei*, the beautiful golden eyebrows that always reminded her of the mountains of home. Its bright-red color and lingering sweetness allowed her to fool her gnawing stomach. Or so she told herself. But even though she could brew a handful of the fermented threads a dozen times in her portable kit, she could not produce more of the expensive tea once her airtight foil pouch was empty.

A journey pre-flare that would have taken four or five days of steady walking had taken twice as long. Given her pace, she was still weeks away from Trieste. She should have pilfered food from the empty farms she'd passed. The broad valleys and cultivated plains of the Emilia-Romagna countryside weren't home. But they were a welcome sight, nonetheless.

Liú Xiù felt tears spring to her eyes, but she ignored them.

She'd barely had time to choose a route and pack her rucksack—a combination of spy go-bag and basic survival pack—before setting out from the Italian city known as Little Shanghai. There had been no time to study the terrain or plan for contingencies. If she hadn't grown up in Nanping northwest of Fujian province, she would have never survived this hasty trek through the rugged landscape dominated by dense forests and steep mountains.

Since leaving Prato, she'd encountered very few people in the Mugello Valley, the northernmost region of Tuscany. She'd avoided main roads and cities and hiked mostly at night, more than once detouring long kilometers to find shelter or evade other travelers—or dangerous wildlife. In the woods north of Monte Morello—barely a day outside of Prato—she'd nearly stumbled into the midst of a boar hunt led by a pack of wolves. That had focused her attention on more than fleeing disintegrating human society and what that meant. Nature was far from benign to the unwary traveler.

As she'd made her way through the rolling Tuscan landscape, Xiù had seen little beyond olive groves, iconic cypress-lined ridges, and abandoned farmsteads. She had no idea where the farmers had gone. It would have been better for them to remain in their homes, far from the madness she knew must grip the urban areas by now.

Closer to the Apennines rising to the north, her route had taken her through wooded foothills where she gave the isolated villages wide berth, not sure what she would find there.

And then she'd entered the densely forested Apennines, where the chestnut and beech trees sheltered haunting remnants of World War II fortifications. The Nazis and their Italian fascist partisans had dug in along the scarped ridgelines late in the war, drilling machine-gun nests and digging trenches along the Gothic Line, the last barrier to Germany. Japanese Americans, known as the Nisei, had broken that line—and broken the Germans. Within days, the Nazis in Italy had surrendered to the Allies.

The ghosts of the dead, the heroes and the villains, watched among the deeply shadowed, remote forest. Xiù had climbed in silence, gooseflesh crawling over her skin. She touched the St. Michael medal she wore, saying a soft, devoutly sincere prayer. Peace descended upon her, and the spirits shrank back into forgotten history.

As she'd approached the Passo della Futa—nearly a thousand meters above the valley below—she'd discovered two couples camping in a bivouac along the ancient Roman Flaminia Militare, the road linking Bologna to Arrezo. From their half-naked bodies and empty wine and liquor bottles strewn around the small camp, it was unclear whether they knew that civilization had ended. Xiù hoped that they didn't. But she suspected they'd opted to have a drunken orgy in a desperate attempt to put off facing reality.

It had been her experience that it was better to confront whatever scared you.

Had been being the operative phrase.

In this new world, she was alone with little to motivate her save the last cryptic message from her handler, her *spiritual* handler. Not the cold man who gave her orders for the MSS, the Chinese intelligence apparatus that had sent her to Italy to further the state's goals through business deals. No, the gentle Bishop of Shanghai, her cousin and confessor, whom the government had hidden away on house arrest. Even so, she'd trained for intelligence gathering and social engineering, not hiking for weeks through wilderness and hostile territory.

Exhausted and uncertain after cresting Futa Pass, Xiù had stopped at the Monte Castel Guerrino, her heart beating heavily and her breath nearly gone. Around her, the forested slopes of the Apennines opened into a natural balcony, offering her the first sweeping views of the Romagnolo hills and the cultivated plains beyond.

For a moment she couldn't bring herself to step forward on the path to the deceptively peaceful plain below. She'd shifted her rucksack, which, despite the belts at chest and waist, had grown almost too heavy in her weakened state and threatened to topple her.

Then she'd seen the horses and their riders heading east, toward the unknown town. Something about the horses sparked hope in her soul. It had been enough to propel her down the mountains and across the plains, dotted with vineyards, canals, and quiet villages.

Now she stood in a vineyard, gorging herself on sour-sweet black grapes warmed by the sun, their juice staining her mouth and fingers as she spat the seeds into the dust. Every few moments she stilled, jaw tight, eyes flicking toward the vineyard's edge, listening for hoofbeats, footsteps—anything that hunted as she did.

The only movement was the slow drip of juice from her fingers. Silence pressed in, thick as the heat. Then came hoofbeats on packed earth, faint but deliberate, just beyond the far rows of neatly tended vines. Their rhythm was slow and even, a quiet reassurance—they weren't in a hurry. They didn't expect her to run. The St. Michael medal, lying under her shirt, warmed uncomfortably against her skin in warning.

She might not have instruction in combat operations or fieldwork outside of offices, but she knew enough to hide. Hauling her rucksack onto her back, she ran toward the stone storage house, without a door and partially overgrown, at the end of the row of grapevines. Inside was cool, musty, and thick with cobwebs, but the shadowed interior gave her a place from which to observe the newcomers.

And defend herself if need be.

She set the rucksack down next to a wall and knelt beside it before opening the flap that covered the weapon compartment. She removed the Italian Beretta pistol she'd purchased on the black market and a clip, which she slammed home in the grip before racking the slide and seating a bullet in the chamber. She might not have been taught to carry a firearm, but she'd prepared herself to do so. The 92x handgun held two fifteen-round clips, and she was proficient in its use, standing, lying, or on the move.

More than proficient, if truth be told. She was an uncannily accurate shot, a talent given her, the woman whose first name meant, among other things, *outstanding* in Mandarin.

And from the looks of the men who'd ridden into the very part of the vineyard where she'd only moments before been eating pilfered fruit, she'd need to be if they chose to surround her hiding place.

There were five of them, not a large party, but each and every one of them looked as if they'd sprung from the Emilia-Romagna soil itself, suntanned and muscled. She'd had no idea that Italian men grew so large. In fact, the obvious leader, the one riding a proud chestnut horse whose coat gleamed in the sun, had thickly corded forearms and heavy thighs. All wore rough work clothes, sturdy leather boots, and intent gazes. And they were all armed with handguns strapped on their thighs like American cowboys. Two carried shotguns across their laps, a Beretta 686 Silver Pigeon used for hunting and a Benelli M4, a tactical shotgun used by the military and law enforcement.

But it was the last weapon, a Beretta ARX160, and the upright posture of the man holding it, that gave Xiù pause. It was a modern military rifle, and, if her intuition was right, in the possession of a man skilled in using it.

The leader cantered by the place that she'd stood, his gaze angling toward the ground before coming up to arrow toward the stone storage house. He reined to a halt, his men moving on either side of him in a line. The marksman jumped down and went to a knee to study the packed earth where Xiù knew he'd see little more than vague impressions and grape seeds in the dust.

Yet they all waited in silence, looking toward the stone storage house. The marksman nodded up at the leader before mounting his horse and joining the group.

"Signora, we all know you're in the storage house," said the leader, his voice a pleasing timbre. "Why don't you save us some time and spare us from having to come in there." It wasn't a question.

Xiù's breath caught, but she eased it out before glancing around the rough wooden door jamb. Taking careful aim, she fired a shot a hair's breadth wide of the marksman, now sitting his horse at the end of the line.

The shot echoed around the unspoiled vineyard, suddenly pregnant with violence.

The marksman didn't flinch, but Xiù saw the wind of the bullet's passing as it ruffled his hair. Keeping his gaze fixed on the doorway as if he could see her, he dipped his chin in acknowledgement of her skill.

The horses stamped the ground and moved restlessly, but they didn't bolt—a testament to their familiarity with gunfire and their training.

The men looked toward where the shot had traveled, but the leader didn't flinch. Instead, his eyes narrowed, and his fingers tightened on the reins in front of him.

"Message received," he said. "But have you considered that we may be friends and not enemies? Or would you rather eat only half-ripe Trebbianera grapes under the July sun—" he gestured back toward the grapevines where she'd been stuffing the sweet-tart globes into her mouth as fast as she plucked them— "and pay for it later with stomach cramps and diarrhea when you could have real food and wine in comfort and safety inside?"

Almost as soon as the handsome stranger asked this question, Xiù's gut gurgled a warning, and nausea made her mouth water. She said nothing, however.

The leader must have taken that as a sign to continue. "You won't do well, Signora, without friends. If we'd wanted to harm you, Matteo could have killed you from a thousand meters away. And the rest of my men have established a perimeter at a hundred meters around your position."

Xiù heard the truth in his voice. And reason—buttressed by the presence of the Beretta ARX160—confirmed that he was telling the truth.

The leader raised his voice, projecting it with the practiced ease of a commander. The hair stood on the back of Xiù's neck. "Alessio, show yourselves." Then he waited for Xiù to see that she was surrounded.

She focused her gaze beyond the five men in front of her, sweeping it in a broad arc along the rows of vine-covered trellises and dusty paths beaten between them toward the embankment on the north. Male heads peered around and above the rustic lattices—some shaded by unadorned straw hats, others bare, sweat gleaming on sun-darkened foreheads. None of them moved fast or showed any revealing expression. They simply made themselves known: deliberate, quiet, unthreatening in posture but unmistakably there.

To anyone else, they might have seemed like field workers pausing in their toil. But to Xiù—hollow with hunger, coiled with tension, Beretta in hand—they were undeniable evidence. This wasn't a bluff. These men had training, discipline, and a clear command structure. Whatever they wanted from her, they'd come prepared.

"So, you see, Signora, you can't possibly kill all of these men, even if you shoot like a sharpshooter, before we overtake your position."

He fell silent. None of the men, either at his side or along the perimeter, moved. Xiù found herself grateful that he respected her ability to reason through her situation without impatience or posturing.

This man was a true leader: formidable, sure of himself, and capable of immense brutality and destruction, yet all the more restrained for it.

"Perhaps I will kill as many of you as I can before that time, Signor," she said at last, pitching her voice to reach him. "One shot, one kill as the Americans say. Do you wish to test the number of bullets I have?"

She saw his eyes widen in surprise, not solely at the British-accented Italian she used. Another one of her peculiar gifts, this ability to send her voice, whether soft or ringing, wherever she wished.

She continued when he said nothing. "And you will die first, Signor." She paused. "Recall those men advancing on the back of this building."

The leader's brow furrowed as he took in her words before he clipped out a command. He handed his Benelli M4 to the man on his right. The men on either side of him wheeled their horses around and trotted back toward the perimeter. Then he looked toward Xiù's hiding place, gesturing sharply with his two fingers in a familiar military sign. She heard the scrabble of feet outside followed by the receding thud of steps.

The leader, who'd kept his predatory gaze on the doorway, spoke once silence descended as his men settled into their positions. "We are at a standoff, Signora." He spoke conversationally, pausing to give his words their desired effect. "I've no doubt you are an excellent shot with that Beretta 92x, but you and I know that its range is limited to fifty meters. I, however, have a sniper qualified at a thousand meters."

After a long moment in which the only sounds were the soft whickering of his chestnut and the buzzing of winged insects among the clustered fruit, the leader dismounted. Then he unsnapped the cover of his holster and pulled out his weapon with two fingers, exaggerating each movement. He bent, his gaze still on the doorway around which she peered, and laid the weapon at his feet before kicking it beyond easy reach.

"You're an intelligent woman, Signora. I very much want to help you, though I will also be honest with you: I think you can help us as much as we can help you."

Xiù waited, letting the silence stretch taut. It was merely to underscore her self-determination. She would not be compelled into action, regardless of her choices. In the time that she took, she studied her interlocutor. Besides being muscular without an ounce of fat on his frame, he wore his medium-brown hair long. His faded clothing had a lived-in appearance that stemmed from more than the past ten days.

Not in current military service then.

Yet he stood with the precise bearing of one who'd carried himself that way for years. A former military officer now farming or making wine who'd taken up arms and organized a militia after the power and local authorities failed. She assessed how quickly someone so disciplined and fit could dive into the dust for his discarded handgun. *Fast enough.*

She didn't want to die today. Her aching stomach, cramping around unripe grapes, attested to that. She was dehydrated, dirty, and sweaty. She needed someplace safe to recover, get food and supplies, assess her situation.

She needed to get to Albania and Olivia Kastrioti.

For that, she'd need to leave this suffocating stone house and let this man and his men take her. She had to trust that he wanted her alive.

Alive was all that mattered.

He would not find her an easy captive, if that's what his ulterior motive was.

After another moment, she stepped into the shadowed doorway, allowing her eyesight to adjust to the daylight before coming outside. She halted half a meter in front of the opening, both hands on the Beretta, which she kept trained on the Italian.

"I keep my weapon," she said.

He stood, blinking and nonplussed. Then he said, "You're not Italian."

Xiù tilted her head, the weight of her long, black hair swaying across her upper back. Suddenly she was aware of how dirty it was. "Your sniper must have lost his scope."

He held her gaze a moment longer before he smiled, a wide, lazy grin. "He never had glass on you. If he had, he would have told me how beautiful you are."

Admiration threaded his voice, but Xiù ignored it. It sounded sincere, not suggestive.

She shrugged a shoulder. "You didn't consider me a threat."

"My mistake." He paused, watching her. "I won't make it again. But, Signora, I promise you that I—we—are here to keep the wolves at bay, not join them."

Xiù kept her gaze on him. "What do you propose?"

He seemed to sense her acceptance. "First, I am Lorenzo DeNova. And this is my vineyard." As he said this, he gave a little flourish to include the land around them. "Well, one of them. We can escort you to Bagnacavallo"—here he gestured east toward the town— "where you will find food, shelter, and likeminded people."

Xiù lowered the Beretta. "I will go with you," she said. She didn't tell him her name, however.

Lorenzo assessed her. "Can you ride?" He didn't ask her for her gun or for her to holster it.

"I've never ridden a horse before."

"Then you'll ride behind me." He whistled and the chestnut walked forward, its front hooves stepping gracefully and its proud dark eyes watching Xiù as if it too assessed her.

Lorenzo turned without waiting for her answer and without fear and thrust his boot into the stallion's stirrup before vaulting into the saddle. Then he held out his hand to Xiù.

"Wait." She returned to gather her rucksack from the cottage. She levered it onto her back and cinched the top and bottom straps before slipping the Beretta into a side pocket of her cargo pants where its outline was visible.

Lorenzo gripped Xiù's hand, easily hauling her up and behind him as she sprang from the ground to a seat behind his saddle. He never said a word, but the four men who'd accompanied him earlier joined them as they crossed their defensive perimeter. Xiù, holding herself upright though it was impossible not to press her breasts against Lorenzo's broad back, noted when the other men in his contingent fell in behind them.

By her count, there were thirty of them. Impressive, given that they were only ten days from a massive geomagnetic flare that had extinguished all known electrical systems—and disrupted the civilized world. Now was the moment for people to become unhinged. Unless she was wrong about the magnitude of the disaster ...

The horses' hooves clattered against the worn stones of Bagnacavallo's narrow medieval streets, the sound swallowed by the thick summer air. As they turned onto Via Cadorna, the Convent of San Francesco rose before them—its ochre walls sun-bleached and weathered, the arched portico casting long shadows across the courtyard. A Renaissance cloister peeked through the open gate, its columns cool and pale beneath the midday heat.

Xiù caught the scent of rosemary and incense as they rode toward the entrance, where time seemed to fold in on itself.

As they neared the gate, a faint shimmer caught the sun. Xiù's gaze swept upward. A figure lay motionless along the roofline, half-shadowed by the terracotta tiles. Not a twitch, not a blink. She didn't need to see the rifle aimed at her to know it was there.

Two armed men stood inside the gate in the shadow of the arch, one straight-backed, the other leaning against a column. Both alert, however, eyes scanning with practiced detachment, fingers brushing the stocks of their rifles. Behind them, a substantial stone planter, its vibrant geraniums incongruous with the stark presence of weapons, provided a natural barrier for the courtyard beyond.

Lorenzo rode past the two guards, who saluted. He nodded once in crisp acknowledgement. The other riders followed them into the courtyard, where a woman stood wiping her hands on a towel lying on her shoulder, her eyes narrowed as she took in Xiù.

She whirled to look up at Lorenzo. Gesturing with a stiff hand chopping the air at face level, her eyes flashing and her voice rising, she said, "Lorenzo, you magnificent idiot! Did you rescue her or recruit her for bottling?"

That's when Xiù realized that her lips and cheeks were stained as black as her fingers. As scalding mortification seeped up her face and down her neck, the woman turned back to her, the exasperation on her features softening.

"You poor thing! You've been out there this whole time, haven't you?" She shook her head, tutting softly. "You're safe now, even if my brother—Our Lady's Gift to Bagnacavallo—let you poison yourself on grapes not yet fit for eating."

She glared at Lorenzo, who only chuckled and dismounted. He put his hands on Xiù's waist and lifted her off his horse as if she weighed nothing.

Lorenzo looked at Xiù. With a mock sigh, he said, "This, this is my sharp-tongued sister Beatrice, who always smells of tomatoes and who makes the best *cappalletti in brodo* in all of Emilia-Romagna."

His sister stepped closer, inserting herself between Xiù and Lorenzo. She slipped her arm inside Xiù's and ignored her brother. "Come, I'll feed you. While you eat some lentil soup,

I'll put my surprise-bringing brother and his always-hungry men to good use."

She looked at Lorenzo. "Since you've brought me another mouth to feed, you can make yourselves useful. Go see if that old tractor outside Lugo is hiding any gifts. And the residents need help with the laundry."

Beatrice pulled Xiù along at her side, hastening into the building. Xiù, dazed at how quickly everything had happened, looked back at Lorenzo, already deep in conversation with a small group of armed men.

He looked at her, flashing a brief smile punctuated by a nod before he returned to the men.

Xiù let herself be led into the cool hush of the ancient convent, the scent of broth and stone wrapping around her like a promise she wasn't yet ready to believe.

About Liane Zane

Liane Zane is the cover identity of a novelist who is an expert at hiding in plain sight. She has spent time interrogating a former Army intelligence officer and engaging in Open-Source Intelligence (OSINT) activities related to Italian slang words for naughty body parts and the proclivities of Eastern European criminals. She spends her days drinking New England chocolate cappuccino coffee and gazing at the magical brook in her back yard as she plots her romantic thrillers or walking her dogs along mountain trails near her estate-like home.

HELSING: DEMON SLAYER is the first book in the new THE DRAGON'S PALADINS series, which narrates an alternative apocalyptic future where angelic warfare transforms human society.

THE ELIOUD LEGACY, her first series, comprises THE HARLEQUIN & THE DRANGÙE (Olivia & Mihàil's story), THE FLOWER & THE BLACKBIRD (Stasia & Miró's story), and THE DRAKA & THE GIANT (Beta and András's story). All three books tell the complex legacy of the Elioud descendants of the Fallen Watcher Angels and are therefore best read in order.

THE UNSANCTIONED GUARDIANS includes the three novellas THE COVERT GUARDIAN (Book One), THE HARLEQUIN PROTOCOL (Book 2), and THE GUARDIAN INITIATIVE (Book 3). Together, the three books narrate the genesis of the team of guardians comprising the female main characters of THE ELIOUD LEGACY, Olivia, Beta, and Stasia. While each book has a complete story, the overarching narrative begins in Book One, continues in Book Two, and finishes in Book Three. While readers don't have to need to read THE ELIOUD LEGACY first, these novellas are best read in order.

Visit www.lianezane.com for updates and to buy merchandise related to all three series.

Also by Liane Zane

The Elioud Legacy

The Harlequin & The Drangùe

The Flower & The Blackbird

The Draka & The Giant

The Unsanctioned Guardians

The Covert Guardian

The Harlequin Protocol

The Guardian Initiative

The Dragon's Paladins
HELSING: Demon Slayer
BAXTER: Warhound (Coming 2026)

Available in paperback, ebook, and audiobook online at w
ww.lianezane.com as well as all major retailers or through
your local library by request. Check the copyright page for the
ISBN numbers to expedite ordering.

www.ingramcontent.com/pod-product-compliance
Lightning Source LLC
Chambersburg PA
CBHW030742310726
48969CB00005B/1282